YEAR'S BEST FANTASY 8

Year's Best Fantasy 8

EDITED BY

DAVID G. HARTWELL

& KATHRYN CRAMER

TACHYON PUBLICATIONS · SAN FRANCISCO

Year's Best Fantasy 8

Interior design & composition by John D. Berry.
The text is typeset in FF Quadraat & FF Quadraat Sans,
with FF Quadraat Display & FF Quadraat Sans Display.

Tachyon Publications
1459 18th Street #139
San Francisco, CA 94107
(415) 285-5615
www.tachyonpublications.com

Series Editor: Jacob Weisman

ISBN 10: 1-892391-76-7
ISBN 13: 978-1-892391-76-6

Printed in the United States of America
by Worzalla

9 8 7 6 5 4 3 2 1

First Edition: 2008

CONTENTS

Introduction

WELCOME to the eighth volume in this annual series.

When we launched the series eight years ago, we said that in this anthology series we will use the broadest definition of genre fantasy (to include wonder stories, adventure fantasy, supernatural fantasy, satirical and humorous fantasy). And furthermore, that out of respect for the genre at its best we stand by genre fantasy and promote it in this book. We believe that the best-written genre fantasy can hold up in the long run by any useful literary standard to fiction published out of category or genre. Each year we set out to find these stories, and we look for them in the genre anthologies, magazines, and small press pamphlets, in print and online. But you will find a broader set of examples, even from the very fringes of genre, where some of the finest work is being done, in this new, larger trade paperback volume. The new format gives us a bit more latitude to represent the edges.

In these latter days when there are a plethora of bests to choose from (somewhere around fifteen of them a year), we still maintain that genre-bending fiction is not superior to, or more interesting than, or better written than, genre fiction – except when it is so well-done that it expands the genre itself.

We like to provide fairly extensive and informative story notes, rather than a lengthy introduction promoting, or attacking, new trends, and do so in this volume. The one 2007 trend we will note here is that original anthologies are growing in importance. And it looks to us as if the online magazines are not in general getting the top stories.

Like the earlier volumes in this series, this book provides some insight into the fantasy field now, who is writing some of the best short fiction published as fantasy, and where. We try to represent the varieties of tones and voices and attitudes that keep the genre vigorous and responsive to the changing realities out of which it emerges. This is a book about what's going on now in genre fantasy.

The center of the field is still occupied by the few biggest genre magazines, *Asimov's SF*, *The Magazine of Fantasy & Science Fiction*, and *Realms of Fantasy*, with *Interzone*, the *Strange Horizons* webzine, *Weird Tales*, *Fantasy Magazine*, and a few smaller fry attendant. The other principal repository of new fantasy fiction is genre anthologies and collections, of which there are many. A few exceptional ones from 2008 are: *Wizards*, edited by Gardner Dozois and Jack Dann – simply the best fantasy anthology of the year; *The Solaris Book of New Fantasy*, edited by George Mann; *Inferno*, edited by Ellen Datlow; *The Secret History of Vampires*, edited by Darrell Schweitzer and Martin H. Greenberg; *The Dog Said Bow-Wow* by Michael

Swanwick. There were also a large number of single author collections from the small press with one or two original stories included among many reprints. The other loci of quality were the zines, little magazines of literary ambition such as *Electric Velocipede*, most of them descended from, or in partial imitation of, Gavin Grant and Kelly Link's zine, *Lady Churchill's Rosebud Wristlet*, which is still a leader. There seem to have been fewer issues, though, in 2007 from that community.

So 2007 has ended. The stories that follow show, and the story notes point out, the strengths of the evolving genre in the year 2007. But it is fundamentally a collection of excellent stories for your reading pleasure. It is supposed to be fun.

David G. Hartwell & Kathryn Cramer
Pleasantville, NY

Paper Cuts Scissors

Holly Black

Holly Black (*blackholly.com*) lives in Massachusetts with her husband Theo and a large book collection. It is not surprising to discover in her website bio that she once pursued a Masters in Library Science. She writes fantasy novels for the young adult market that have made her a famous, bestselling writer. She is best known for the series *The Spiderwick Chronicles*, illustrated by Tony DiTerlizzi.

"Paper Cuts Scissors" was published in *Realms of Fantasy*. It takes place in a private library and is about a student librarian who gets a job there to rescue his girlfriend. It is a love story for the obsessive reader that literalizes the idea that one can retreat from reality into a book, a theme also found in the Don Webb story later in this volume. The C. S. Lewis line that the only ones opposed to escape are jailers might have made a good epigraph.

000 – Generalities

When Justin started graduate school in library science, he tried to sit next to the older women that now needed a degree as media specialists to keep the same job they'd done for years. He avoided the hipster girls, fresh from undergrad, wearing black turtlenecks with silver jewelry molded in menacing shapes and planning careers in public libraries. Those girls seemed as dangerous as books that unexpectedly killed their protagonists.

He wasn't used to being around people anymore. He fidgeted with his freshly cut hair and ran shaking fingers over the razor burn on his pale skin. He didn't meet anyone's eyes as he dutifully learned about new user interfaces and how to conduct a reference interview. He wrote papers with pages of citations. He read pile after pile of genre novels to understand what people saw in inspirational romance or forensic mysteries, but he was careful to read the ends before the beginnings. He told himself that he could hold it together.

At night, when all his reading was done and he'd printed all the papers he needed for the next day, he tried not to open Linda's book.

He'd read it so many times that he should know it by heart, but the words kept changing. She was always in danger. She'd nearly got run over by a train and frozen on a long march to Moscow while Justin had sat on his parent's pull-out couch in the den and forgotten to eat. While his hair had grown long and his fingernails, jagged. Until his friends had stopped coming over. Until he'd remembered the one thing he could do to get her out.

One afternoon, Justin checked the notice board and saw a sign: *Looking for library student to organize private collection: 555-2164. $10/hour.*

His heart sped. Finally. It had to be. He punched the number into his cell phone and a man answered.

"Please," Justin said. He had practiced a convincing speech, but he couldn't remember a word of it. His voice shook. "I need this job. I'm very dedicated, very conscientio – "

"You're hired," said the man.

Relief made him lightheaded. He sagged against the painted cinderblock wall of the hallway.

After, in Classification Theory, Sarah Peet turned half around in her chair. Her earrings swung like daggers. "Rock, paper, scissors for who buys coffee at the break."

"Coffee?" His voice came out louder than he'd intended.

"From the vending machine," she said and made a fist.

One. Two. Three. Rock breaks scissors. Justin lost.

"I take it black," said Sarah.

100 – PHILOSOPHY & PSYCHOLOGY

The private collection that Justin was supposed to organize was located in the basement of a large Victorian house outside New Brunswick. He drove there in his beat up Altima and parked in the driveway. He didn't see another car and wondered if Mr. Sandlin – the man he was sure he'd spoken with on the phone – had forgotten that he was coming. According to his watch, it was quarter to seven in the evening. He was fifteen minutes early.

When Justin knocked on the door, he was met by a gentleman in a waistcoat. He had a slight paunch and long hair tied back in a ponytail.

"Excellent," the man said. "Eager. I'm Sandlin."

"Justin," said Justin. He hoped his palms weren't sweating.

"Each year I hire a new library student – you'll pick up where the last one left off. Dewey decimal. No Library of Congress, got it?"

"I understand perfectly," Justin said.

Sandlin led Justin through a house shrouded in white sheeting, down a dusty staircase to a cavernous basement. Masses of bookshelves formed a maze beneath swaying chandeliers. Justin sucked in his breath.

"There's a desk somewhere that way," Sandlin said. "A computer. Some books still in boxes. I used to run a bookshop, but I found that I wasn't suited for it. I didn't like when people bought things. I like to have all my books with me."

It was a vast, amazing collection. Justin could feel his pulse speed and a smile creep onto his face.

"Best to get started," said Sandlin, turning and walking back up the stairs. "You have to leave before midnight. I have guests."

Justin couldn't imagine that there'd been many visitors entering through the front door, considering how thick the dust was upstairs. The wooden planks under his feet, however, were swept clean.

Sandlin stopped at the landing, gesturing grandly as he called down. "It is my belief that books are living things."

That sent a shiver up Justin's spine as he thought of Linda.

"And as living things, they need to be protected." Sandlin walked the rest of the way up the stairs.

Justin rubbed his arms and bit back what he wanted to say. It was readers that needed to be protected, he thought. Books were something that happened to readers. Readers were the victims of books.

He'd considered this a lot at the bookstore, once Linda was gone and before he'd lost the job altogether. Grim-faced women would come in, dressed sensibly, pleading for a sequel like they were pleading for a lover's life. Children would sit on the rug and cry inconsolably over picture books where rabbits lost their mothers.

The desk – when he found it – was ordinary, gray metal rusted at the corners and the PC sitting on top was old enough that it had a floppy drive. The keyboard felt sticky under his fingers. Justin opened his backpack and looked in at Linda's book; when packing the night before, he found that he couldn't bring himself to leave it behind.

200 – Religion

Justin had always opened new books with a sense of dread, but no dread could compare with opening Linda's book. Sometimes the *militsiya* were arresting a member of her new family, or she was swallowing priceless rubies so that she could smuggle them out of Russia. Occasionally she was in love. Or drinking strong tea out of a samovar. Or dancing.

He remembered her with ink-stained fingers and a messy apartment full of paperbacks. He'd lived there with her when they both worked in the bookstore. She was allergic to cats, but she couldn't resist petting the stray that the owner kept and her nose was always red from sneezing. She made spaghetti with olives when she was depressed.

He remembered the way they'd curled up together on the futon and read to one another. He remembered his laughing confession that he opened new books with a sense of dread akin to jumping off a cliff with a bungee on. He knew he probably wouldn't hit the rocks, but he was never really sure. Linda didn't understand. She read fearlessly, without care for how things turned out.

Things, she said, could always be changed.

She told him that she knew how to fold stuff up and put it in books. *In* the books, inside the stories themselves. She'd proven it to him. She put a single playing card into a paperback edition of *Robin Hood*. The Ace of Spades. Little John had found it. He'd become convinced it was a sign that they would be defeated by the Sheriff of Nottingham and hanged himself. The Merry Men were less merry after they found his body. Justin had looked at other editions of *Robin Hood*, but they were unchanged.

After that, he'd believed her. He'd wanted her to alter other books – like fix *Macbeth* so that no one died. She said that Macbeth was unlucky enough without her tampering.

They'd fought a lot in their third year together. Linda had heard that there was a man named Mr. Sandlin that could take things out of books as well as putting them in. She wanted them to give up the lease on their apartment and their jobs at the bookstore. She wanted them to enroll in library school. Early one morning, after fighting all night – a fight that had started out about moving and wound up about every hateful thing they'd ever thought about one another, she folded herself up and put herself into a fat Russian novel.

"Ohgodohgodohgod," Justin had said. "Please. No. Please. Oh God. Please." He'd opened the cover to see an illustration of her in pen and ink, sitting in a group of unsmiling characters.

After that, he couldn't tell her that he was sorry or that her bolshie-sympathizing uncle was going to expose her in the next chapter or that she was going to regret leaving him now that she was stuck in an ice storm with only a mink cloak and muff to protect her. He was just a reader and readers can't do anything to make the story stop – except close the book.

300 – Social Sciences

The next time that Sandlin opened the door, he was dressed less impressively, in pajamas with blue stripes. He greeted Justin with a huge yawn.

"Am I early?" Justin asked, although he knew he wasn't.

Sandlin shook his head and waved Justin in. "Time I got up anyway."

"Right. I'll be downstairs," said Justin as Sandlin dumped out the coffeepot and filled it with water from the tap.

The collection, which had looked so grand at first sight, was, on closer inspection, quite odd. None of the books seemed to be first editions. Many were not even hardcover. Tattered paperbacks nestled up against reprinted hardcover editions of classics with their spines cracked. Some books even appeared to be galleys from publishers, marked, "FOR REVIEW PURPOSES ONLY – NOT FOR RESALE."

Most of the books were easy to classify. They were almost all 800s, mostly 810s or 820s.He glanced at the backs of their covers and the copyright pages and then typed their titles into the database. On the spines of each, he taped a label printed in marker.

After he finished a dozen, Justin decided that he should start shelving. He lifted the stack, inhaling book dust, and headed into the aisles.

The problem with everything being in the 800s is that the markers on the ends of the shelves blurred together. Justin took a few turns and then wasn't sure he knew where he was going or where he could find the places for the books in his arms.

"Sandlin?" he called, but although his voice echoed in the vast room, he doubted it was loud enough to carry all the way upstairs.

He turned again. A plastic drink stirrer rested on the floor. Bending to pick it up, he felt panic rise. Where was he? He'd thought he was retracing his steps.

By the time he found his way back to the desk, he felt a faintly ridiculous but almost overwhelming sense of relief.

Sarah leaned back in her seat and sat a roll of twine in front of him.

"I heard you got the Sandlin job," Sarah said. "My friend used to work there, said it was like a maze. This is his Theseus trick."

"That's smart," Justin said, thinking of Theseus picking his way through the Minotaur's lair, unwinding Ariadne's string behind him. Thinking of how his heart had pounded when he was lost in the stacks. It wasn't just smart, it was *clever*, even classical. He wished he'd thought of it.

"Rock paper scissors to see if I can come with you."

"No way," Justin said. "I could lose my job."

"My friend said some other stuff– about what happens after midnight. Come on. If you win, I'll tell you everything I know. If I win, I get to come."

"Fine." Justin scowled, but Sarah didn't seem cowed. She raised a brow studded with tiny silver bars.

Rock. Paper. Scissors. Her rock smashed his scissors.

"Best two out of three," Justin said, but he knew he was already defeated.

"Tomorrow night," said Sarah, with a smile that he couldn't interpret. In fact, the more he thought about it, the less he knew about why she'd started talking to him at all.

400 – LANGUAGE

That night, Justin tucked the string and Linda's book into his backpack and drove to Sandlin's house. He worked his way through cataloging an entire box of books, when, on impulse, he flipped a thin volume open.

The spine of the book read *Pride and Prejudice* so Justin was surprised to find Indiana Jones in the text. Apparently, he'd been sleeping his way through all the Jane Austen books and had seduced both Kitty and Lydia Bennet. Justin discovered this fact when Eleanor Tilney from *Northanger Abbey* showed up to confront Indy with his illegitimate child.

He looked at the page and read it twice just to be sure:

To Catherine and Lydia, neither Miss Tilney nor her claims were in any degree interesting. It was next to impossible that Miss Tilney had told the truth, and although it was now some weeks since they had received pleasure from the society of Mr. Jones, they had every confidence in him. As for their mother, she was weathering the blow with a degree of composure which astonished her husband and daughters.

He closed the book, set it back on the shelf, and opened another. *Peter Pan*. In it, Sherlock Holmes deduced that Tinkerbell had poisoned Wendy while Watson complained to the mermaids that no one understood his torrid romance with one of the shepherdesses from a poem. Wendy's ghost flitted around quoting lines from *Macbeth*. Peter wasn't in the book at all. He'd left to be a valet to Lord Rochester in a play of which no one had ever heard.

Justin shut *Peter Pan* so quickly that one of the pages cut a thin line in his index finger. He stuck his bleeding finger in his mouth and tasted ink and sweat. It made him feel vaguely nauseous.

500 – NATURAL SCIENCES & MATHEMATICS

Scrambling over to his backpack, Justin started unrolling the string. It dragged across the floors, through the aisles as he wound his way through the maze of shelves. At first, it was just books, but as he moved deeper into the stacks, he discovered a statue of a black-haired man in a long blue robe and eyes that glittered like they were set with glass, a velvet fainting couch and a forgotten collection of champagne flutes containing the dregs of a greenish liquid beside a single jet button.

He glanced at the shelves, thinking of Sandlin's pajamas and Sarah's words: *My friend said some other stuff – about what happens after midnight*. A party happened here, a party with guests that never disturbed the dust upstairs, that never entered or exited through the front hall.

A party with guests that were already in the house. Guests that were *inside the books*.

He shuddered, then laughed a little at himself. This was what he'd been hoping for, after all. Now he had to just count on the fact that Sandlin wouldn't notice one more book.

That night Justin called out his usual farewell to Mr. Sandlin, before sneaking back down the library stairs. He climbed one of the old ladders along the far wall and cracked open a high, thin window. Then he rolled onto the very top of the bookshelf and flattened himself against the wood. Something banged against the glass.

"Wow. We're pretty high up," said Sarah as she slid inside. Her foot knocked a stack of papers and a bookend shaped like a nymph crashed to the floor. "Shit!"

"Careful," whispered Justin. He knew he sounded prissy as soon as it came out of his mouth, but Sarah didn't seem like a very careful person.

"So," she said. She wore a tattered black coat covered in paint stains and a new hoop gleamed in her eyebrow. The skin around it was puffy and red. "Here we are. This is it."

"What's it?"

"This is where Richard hid. My friend. Pretty genius, right? He could see everything from up here. And whoever looks up?" She answered her own question with a nod. "Nobody."

"Did he say what happens now?"

"*The books come to life.*" Her voice was filled with awe, like she was about to take a sacrament from the Holy Church of Literature.

Justin looked at his bag where Linda's Russian novel rested. He had a sudden urge to pitch it out the window. "How do you think that happens? There are so many..." He wasn't sure how to end that sentence. Characters? Settings? Books?

A footfall kept him from finding out.

"Shhh," said Sarah, completely unnecessarily.

Sandlin appeared, walking down the stairs with a crate. Justin crawled forward to see him begin to set up bottles and a cheese platter. He removed red grapes from their plastic-covered package and set them carefully on one end of the tray, then stepped back to look at his arrangement.

He appeared to be satisfied because when he turned around, he made a motion with his hands and a ripple went through the shelves. The books shuddered and then, one by one, the room began to fill with people.

They climbed out of the stacks, brushing themselves off, sometimes hopping from a high place, sometimes crawling out of what seemed like a very cramped low shelf.

Justin looked over at his backpack in time to see women in high-necked dresses and men in uniforms scamper down. He looked for Linda, but from the back, he wasn't sure which one she was. He started to follow but Sarah grabbed his arm.

"What are you doing?" she hissed. "You said to be careful – remember?"

He leaned over the side, scanning all the faces for Linda's. He tried to remember what she looked like, he kept thinking of lines of description instead. Her hair was "thick chestnut curls like the shining mane of a horse" in the book. He was pretty sure he'd read a passage about her eyes being "amber as the pin at her throat" but he remembered them as brown.

Women with powdered cones of hair and black masks on sticks swept past knights decked out for jousting and comic book heroes in slinky, rubbery suits. A wolf in a top hat and tails conversed with a wizard in a robe of moons and stars as faeries flew over their heads.

He thought he saw Linda near the grapes, whispering behind a fan. He strained to hear what she said, but all he heard were other conversations. Without quite meaning to, he realized what he was hearing.

"Sarah." Justin pointed to a large-shouldered man decked out in lace, with a slim sword at his hip and a small reddish flower in his hands. He was lazily chatting up a skinny, red-headed young woman in jeans and a T-shirt.

"Demmed smart you are," said the man. "Pretty too. I've been assured my taste is unerring so there's no need to protest."

"Sarah," said Justin. "That's the Scarlet Pimpernel!"

"Oh my god," Sarah whispered back, wriggling closer. "I think you're right. Percy Blakeney. I had such a crush on him."

"I think he's hitting on that girl."

"Isn't that?" She paused. "It can't be...but I think the girl is Anne of Green Gables."

Justin squinted. "I never read it."

"I heard her say something about there being no one like him in Avonlea," said Sarah. "What's she doing in jeans? Anne! Anne! Don't do it!"

Shhh!" Justin said.

"He's married! Marguerite will kick your ass!"

Justin tried to put his hand over her mouth. "You can't just – "

Sarah pulled away, but she seemed a little bit embarrassed. "Chill out. She couldn't hear me anyway. And I wasn't the one that almost climbed down there."

He looked back into the crowd, tamping down both rising panic and chaotic glee. Characters shouldn't be able to meet like this, to mix and converse anachronistically and anarchically in the basement of a house in Jersey. It seemed profane, perverse and yet it was the perversion itself that tempted him to dangerous joy.

"Okay. Jeesh," said Sarah, mistaking the reason for his silence. "I'm sorry I got carried away – hey, who's that in the gold armor? Standing near. Oh." She stopped. "Is that Wolverine talking to a wolverine? In a dress?"

"Which one's wearing the dress?" Justin asked, but the grin slid off his face when he saw Linda move away from the refreshments. She was talking to a man in a doublet.

Sarah put her hand on his arm. "Who are you staring at? You look really weird."

"That's my girlfriend," said Justin.

"A character in a book is your girlfriend?"

"She put herself there. We had an argument – it's not important. I'm just trying to get her out again."

Sarah stared at him, but her expression said: *I don't believe you. You did something bad to your girlfriend to make her put herself in a book.* Her earrings swung like pendulums, dowsing for guilty secrets. "You knew what was going on when you applied for this job, didn't you?"

"So?" Justin asked. "Oh, you wanted it too, didn't you? I just called first."

"Well, she's out from the book now. You don't look too happy."

Justin scowled and they said little to each other after that. They just rested on their stomachs on the dusty bookshelves and watched the crowd swirl and eddy beneath them, watched Little Lord Fauntleroy piss in a corner and an albino in armor mutter to the black sword in his hands as he headed for one of the more private and shadowed parts of the library.

And Justin watched as Linda flitted among them, laughing with pleasure.

"Oh, you doth teach the torches to burn bright," the man in the doublet told her.

What a line, Justin thought ruefully. *I hope she knows he's quoting Shakespeare.* Then an unpleasant thought occurred to him. Who was Linda talking to?

"Lo, John Galt hath eaten all the salsa," said another knight in green armor adorned with leaves.

"Oh, how awful," said Dolly Alexandrovna from *Anna Karenina*. She smoothed her gown, looking exactly like a painting of her Justin had seen. "I won't forgive him and I can't forgive him. He persists in doing this every night."

Justin wondered why none of them spoke in Russian or French or whatever, but then it occurred to him that all the books were in translation. The logic made him dizzy.

"Who's John Galt?" growled Wolverine around the cigar in his mouth.

Anne of Green Gables danced a waltz with a man that Justin failed to recognize and wasn't going to ask Sarah about. Stephen Dedalus got into a fistfight with Werther. Hamlet shouted at them to stop, yelling, "It is but foolery," but they didn't stop until Werther got hit hard enough that his nose bled.

Justin thought that after being punched, he looked weirdly like the guy on the cover of the Modern Library reprint edition of *Werther*, where his whole face is wet with tears.

"How can I, how can you, be annihilated?" Werther spat. "We exist. What is annihilation? A mere word, an unmeaning sound that fixes no impression on the mind."

Stephen's knuckles looked bruised. "Whatever," he said.

Linda sunk down beside Werther, silky skirts billowing around her, and dabbed at the blood on his face with a handkerchief. What was she doing? It made no sense! She didn't even like Goethe! She'd complained that Werther was a coward, and whiny, besides.

Justin started to climb down the bookshelf.

Sandlin shouted something at that moment and then a great gust of wind blew through the library and when it had gone, so had all the party guests.

Gone. Linda was gone. Justin looked out the small window and, sure enough, the sky was beginning to lighten outside. Reaching for his pack, he opened Linda's book and flipped frantically, scanning each page for her name.

Nothing.

Gone.

600 – TECHNOLOGY (APPLIED SCIENCES)

The next day at the break, Sarah brought a cup of coffee from the machine and set it on the desk in front of him without resorting to rock, paper, or scissors. He still wore the same clothes from the night before and when he looked down at his notebook, all he had written was "faceted classification" with several lines drawn under the words. He had no idea what that meant.

"I should be mad at you," she said, "but you're just too pathetic."

He picked up the coffee and took a sip. He was glad it was warm.

She sat on the edge of his desk. "Okay, so tell me about your girlfriend. What happened?"

"I don't know. We just started fighting. She wanted to meet Sandlin, but I wanted to stay at the bookstore. Then this."

"And by *this*, you mean that instead of locking herself in the bathroom or throwing a vase at you, she put herself in a book and didn't come out."

"Yeah," Justin said, looking at the desk.

"You might seriously consider that that translates to breaking up with you."

He scrubbed his hand over his face. His skin felt rougher than his stubble. "I don't think she knew how to get out." But, as he thought back on it, he couldn't recall reading that she wanted to; characters in Russian novels are big on bemoaning their personal tragedy. It seemed that wouldn't have been left out.

Sarah shrugged. "You said that she wanted to meet Sandlin. You brought her to him. You're done."

"I never got to say I was sorry."

"Are you?" Sarah took a sip from her cup and made a face.

Justin scowled. "What kind of question is that?"

"Well you don't even seem to know what you did, or if you did anything."

He looked down at the laces of his sneakers, the dirty knots that he hated untangling so much that he'd just pulled the things off and on. Now they were hopeless. The knots would never come out. He sighed.

"Do you even like books?" Sarah asked. She waved her hand around. "Was all of this for her?"

"Of course I like books!" Justin said, looking up. He didn't know how to explain. He'd started library school to get Linda to Sandlin, but he actually liked it. It felt good to carefully organize the books so that other people would know what they were getting themselves into. "I've always liked books. I just don't *trust* them."

"What about people?" Sarah asked.

He looked at her blankly.

"Do you trust people?"

"I guess. I mean, sure. Within reason. I don't think people usually have terrible secrets the way characters do, but people often aren't as amazing either. We're watered down."

"I have a secret," Sarah said. "I compete in rock, paper, scissors tournaments."

He laughed.

"I'm serious," Sarah said.

"Wait a minute. You mean you cheated me out of all that coffee?" For a moment, Justin just looked at her. She seemed different now that he knew she had secrets, even if they were kind of lame ones.

"Hey," she said. "I won fairly!"

"But you're like a pool shark or something. You have strategies."

Sarah shook her head. "Okay, you want my RPS secret? It's about understanding people. Rock's basically a weapon. Like something an ogre might hurl. It's an angry throw. Some people shy away from it because it seems crude, but they'll use it if they're desperate."

"Okay," Justin said.

"Now, scissors. Scissors are shiny and sharp. Still dangerous, but more elegant, like a rapier. Lots of people make their first throw scissors because it seems like the clever throw. The rakish throw. The hipster throw."

"Really?" Justin frowned.

"*You* threw it the first time. And the second."

He thought back, but he couldn't recall. He wondered which play Sarah usually opened up with. Was it always rock?

"Now, paper. Paper's interesting. Some people consider it a wimpy throw and they use it very infrequently. Others consider it the most subtle throw. Words can, they say, be more dangerous than rocks or scissors.

"Of course, scissors still cut paper," Sarah said.

"Oh," said Justin suddenly, getting up. "They do. You're right." He could cut Linda out like a paper doll.

700 – The Arts

Justin pulled book after book from the shelves, not caring about their spines, not caring about the mess he made, scanning each one for a mention of Linda. They piled up around him and the dust coated his hands, ink smearing his fingers as he ran them down countless pages.

Heavy metal scissors weighed down the pocket of his coat and sometimes his hand would drop inside to touch their cool surface before emptying another shelf.

"What are you doing?" Sandlin asked.

Justin jumped up, hand still in his pocket.

Sandlin was dressed in another waistcoat. A single silver pin held a cravat in place at his neck. He sneezed.

"I'm looking for my girlfriend. She got out of her book but I don't know which book she got into."

"The girl with all the piercings I saw you hiding with last night?"

"No," said Justin, trying not to seem as rattled as he felt. *If Sandlin knew...* No, he couldn't dwell on that. "That's Sarah. Linda's my girlfriend, or she was, and she knew how to put things into books. She put herself in a Russian novel, but last night you took her out and I don't know what book she's in now."

Sandlin ran his hand over his short beard.

"You see," Justin said, his voice rising. "She could be anywhere, in danger. Novels are always putting characters in peril because it's exciting. Characters die."

"Your problem isn't with books, it's with girls," Sandlin said.

"What?" Justin demanded.

"Girls," said Sandlin. "You don't know why they do the things they do. Who does? I'm sure they feel the same about us. Hell, I'm sure they feel the same way about each other."

"But the books," said Justin.

"Fiction. I used to own a bookstore before I inherited a lot of money from my great aunt. The money went to a cat first, but when the cat died, I was loaded. Decided I'd shut my store down, sleep all day and do whatever I wanted. This is it."

"But...but what about what you said about books being alive? Needing our protection?"

Sandlin waved his hand vaguely. "Look, I love spending time with characters from books. I love the strange friendships that spring up, the romances. I don't want to lose any of them. Did you know that Naruto has become close to Edmond Dantès and a floating skull with glowing red eyes? I couldn't make that up if I tried! But it's still *fiction*. Even if it's happening in my basement. It's not real."

Justin looked at him in disbelief. "But books *feel* real. Surely they must seem more real to you than anyone. They can hurt you. They can break your heart."

"It wasn't a book," said Sandlin, "that broke your heart."

800 – Literature & Rhetoric

Justin went home and slept for the rest of the day and night. When he woke up too early to do much else, he opened a familiar paperback and re-read it. Then he went to a café and bought two cups of coffee to bring to class.

"Oh wow," said Sarah. "Double Latte with a sprinkle of cinnamon. I think I just drooled on myself."

"You still have to win it," he said. "You made up the rules. Now be made miserable by them."

She made a fist. "You sure you don't want to pick some game you're good at?"

Her earrings swung and glittered. Justin wondered if she wore them to tournaments to distract her opponents. He wondered if it worked.

He wished he could raise an eyebrow, but he tried to give her the look that might accompany one.

"Your funeral," said Sarah.

Rock. Paper. Scissors. Scissors cut paper. Justin won. He gave her the coffee anyway.

"I didn't think you'd throw scissors again," she said. "Since I pointed out that you threw it the first two times."

"Exactly." *See,* he thought, *I don't have a problem figuring out girls.*

Just one girl.

And possibly himself.

900 – Geography & History

Later that week, Justin attended the midnight party at Sandlin's house. He walked through the front door, disturbing as much dust as he could, before heading down the stairs. He arrived fashionably late. Characters were making toasts.

"Salut!" a group shouted together.

"To absent friends, lost loves, old gods, and the – " started another before Justin walked out of earshot.

He touched the heavy scissors in his pocket. His plan had changed.

Linda sat on a stool in black robes embroidered with the Hogwarts emblem and talked earnestly to a frog in a crown. Imps, nearby, appeared to be sticking a lit match between the stitches on the sole of a boot belonging to a chain smoking blond man with a thick British accent.

"Linda," said Justin, "I have to talk to you."

Linda turned and something like panic crossed her face. She stood. "Justin?"

"Don't bother thanking me for bringing you to Sandlin," he said. "I won't bother saying I'm sorry. You were right. I'm glad I moved, glad I started library school. But what you did – "

"I'd always wanted to," she said. "Put myself in a book. It wasn't you. It would have happened eventually."

"Look, what I came to say was that you have responsibilities in the real world. Your parents haven't heard from you in forever. What you're doing isn't safe. You have to come back."

"No," she said firmly. "I'm not ready yet. Not now, when I can visit any book I want. I'll come out when I'm ready."

"You should have stayed and fought with me," said Justin. "It wasn't fair."

"I could have put *you* in a book." She tilted her head. "I still could."

He took an involuntary step back and she laughed.

"You don't deserve it, though," she said. "You don't love books the way that I do."

He opened his mouth to protest and then closed it. It was true. He didn't know how she loved books, only that he loved them differently.

She turned away from him and he let her go. He stayed for the rest of the party and after all the characters were back in their books, he took *Harry Potter* off the shelf.

"Found the girl?" Sandlin asked.

Justin nodded and took the scissors out of his pocket.

"What are you going to do?" Sandlin sounded nervous.

Justin turned on the old computer. "I'm going to change the story. Just a little. No one will notice." He flipped to a page where Linda's name appeared and carefully cut her out. Sandlin winced.

"Don't worry," Justin said. "It's just fiction."

He typed a few words and printed out the page. Then he carefully taped Linda's name in place so that the sentence read:

"Linda doesn't just know how to put things in books. She knows how to get things out again, including herself. Hopefully someday she will."

Folding the paper in half, he tucked it between the pages. When he left, he didn't take the book with him.

A Portrait in Ivory

Michael Moorcock

Michael Moorcock (*multiverse.org*) lives near Austin, Texas, and in France. He is a paradoxical figure in SF, both a champion of the literary avant-garde and an icon of extreme production. Few others in fantasy and science fiction have managed a foot in both those camps so successfully. He's in his late sixties now, and his production has slowed a bit, but he is still writing fine fiction. He is now a recognized literary figure in the UK, a significant contemporary writer. But his fantasy adventures in the cycle of the Eternal Champion are still the basis of his popularity in the USA. To most genre readers, Moorcock still means the creator of Elric.

"A Portrait in Ivory" appeared in *Logorrhea*, a clever original anthology in which the stories are linked by the use of specific words, created and edited by John Klima. It is an Elric story in which Elric allows his portrait to be carved in dragon ivory. Moorcock explores the sometimes corrupt, sometimes tainted nature of art, and specifically of portraiture, and also art's purposes.

I. AN ENCOUNTER WITH A LADY

Elric, who had slept well and revived himself with fresh-brewed herbs, was in improved humour as he mixed honey and water into his glass of green breakfast wine. Typically, his night had been filled with distressing dreams, but any observer would see only a tall, insouciant "silverskin" with high cheekbones, slightly sloping eyes and tapering ears, revealing nothing of his inner thoughts.

He had found a quiet hostelry away from the noisy centre of Sered-Öma, this city of tall palms. Here, merchants from all over the Young Kingdoms gathered to trade their goods in return for the region's most valuable produce. This was not the dates or livestock, on which Sered-Öma's original wealth had been founded, but the extraordinary creations of artists famed everywhere in the lands bordering the Sighing Desert. Their carvings, especially of animals and human portraits, were coveted by kings and princes. It was the reputation of these works of art which brought the crimson-eyed albino out of his way to see them for himself. Even in Melniboné, where barbarian art for the most part was regarded with distaste, the sculptors of Sered-Öma had been admired.

Though Elric had left the scabbarded runesword and black armour of his new calling in his chamber and wore the simple chequered clothing of a regional traveller, his fellow guests tended to keep a certain distance from him. Those who had heard little of Melniboné's fall had celebrated the Bright Empire's destruction with great glee until the implications of that sudden defeat were understood. These days, certainly, Melniboné no longer controlled the world's trade and could no longer demand ransom from the Young Kingdoms, but the world was these days in confusion as upstart nations vied to seize the power for themselves. And meanwhile, Melnibonéan mercenaries found employment in the armies of rival countries. Without being certain of his identity, they could tell at once that Elric was one of those misplaced unhuman warriors, infamous for their cold good manners and edgy pride.

Rather than find themselves in a quarrel with him, the customers of *The Rolling Pig* kept their distance. The haughty albino too seemed indisposed to open a conversation. Instead, he sat at his corner table staring into his morning wine, brooding on what could not be forgotten. His history was written on handsome features which would have been youthful were it not for his thoughts. He reflected on an unsettled past and an uneasy future. Even had someone dared approach him, however sympathetically, to ask what concerned him, he would have answered lightly and coldly, for, save in his nightmares, he refused to confront most of those concerns. Thus, he did not look up when a woman, wearing the conical russet hat and dark veil of her caste, approached him through the crowd of busy dealers.

"Sir?" Her voice was a dying melody. "Master Melnibonéan, could you tolerate my presence at your table?" Falling rose petals, sweet and brittle from the sun.

"Lady," said Elric, in the courteous tone his people reserved for their own high-born kin, "I am at my breakfast. But I will gladly order more wine..."

"Thank you, sir. I did not come here to share your hospitality. I came to ask a favour." Behind the veil her eyes were grey-green. Her skin had the golden bloom of the Na'äne, who had once ruled here and were said to be a race as ancient as Elric's own. "A favour you have every reason to refuse."

The albino seemed almost amused, perhaps because, as he looked into her eyes, he detected beauty behind the veil, an unexpected intelligence he had not encountered since he had left Imryrr's burning ruins behind him. How he had longed to hear the swift wit of his own people, the eloquent argument, the careless insults. All that and more had been denied him for too long. To himself he had become sluggish, almost as dull as the conniving princelings and self-important merchants to whom he sold his sword. Now, there was something in the music of her speech, something in the lilt of irony colouring each phrase she uttered, that spoke to his own sleeping intellect. "You know me too well, lady. Clearly, my fate is in your hands, for you're able to anticipate my every attitude and response. I have good reason not to grant you a favour, yet you still come to ask one, so either you are prescient or I am already your servant."

"I would serve you, sir," she said gently. Her half-hidden lips curved in a narrow smile. She shrugged. "And, in so doing, serve myself."

"I thought my curiosity atrophied," he answered. "My imagination a petrified knot. Here you pick at threads to bring it back to life. This loosening is unlikely to be pleasant. Should I fear you?" He lifted a dented pewter cup to his lips and tasted the remains of his wine. "You are a witch, perhaps? Do you seek to revive the dead? I am not sure..."

"I am not sure, either," she told him. "Will you trust me enough to come with me to my house?"

"I regret, madam, I am only lately bereaved..."

"I'm no sensation-seeker, sir, but an honest woman with an honest ambition. I do not tempt you with the pleasures of the flesh, but of the soul. Something which might engage you for a while, even ease your mind a little. I can more readily convince you of this if you come to my house. I live there alone, save for servants. You may bring your sword, if you wish. Indeed, if you have fellows, bring them also. Thus I offer you every advantage."

The albino rose slowly from his bench and placed the empty goblet carefully on the well-worn wood. His own smile reflected hers. He bowed. "Lead on, madam." And he followed her through a crowd which parted like corn before the reaper and he left a momentary silence behind him.

II. The Material

She had brought him to the depth of the city's oldest quarter, where artists of every skill, she told him, were licensed to work unhindered by landlord or, save in the gravest cases, the law. This ancient sanctuary was created by time-honoured tradition and the granting of certain guarantees by the clerics whose great university had once been the centre of the settlement. These guarantees had been strengthened during the reign of the great King Alo'ofd, an accomplished player of the nine-stringed *murmerlan*, who loved all the arts and struggled with a desire to throw off the burdens of his office and become a musician. King Alo'ofd's decrees had been law for the past millennium and his successors had never dared challenge them.

"Thus, this quarter harbours not only artists of great talent," she told him, "but many who have only the minimum of talent. Enough to allow them to live according to our ancient freedoms. Sadly, sir, there is as much forgery practised here, of every kind, as there is originality."

"Yours is not the only such quarter." He spoke absently, his eyes inspecting the colourful paintings, sculptures and manuscripts displayed on every side. They were of varied quality, but only a few showed genuine inspiration and beauty. Yet the accomplishment was generally higher than Elric had usually observed in the Young Kingdoms. "Even in Melniboné we had these districts. Two of my cousins, for instance, were calligraphers. Another composed for the flute."

"I have heard of Melnibonéan arts," she said. "But we are too distant from your island home to have seen many examples. There are stories, of course." She smiled. "Some of them are decidedly sinister..."

"Oh, they are doubtless true. We had no trouble if audiences, for instance, died for an artist's work. Many great composers would experiment, for instance, with the human voice." His eyes again clouded, remembering not a crime but his lost passion.

It seemed she misinterpreted him. "I feel for you, sir. I am not one of those who celebrated the fall of the Dreaming City."

"You could not know its influence, so far away," he murmured, picking up a remarkable little pot and studying its design. "But those who were our neighbours were glad to see us humiliated. I do not blame them. Our time was over." His expression was again one of cultivated insouciance. She turned her own gaze towards a house which leaned like an amiable drunkard on the buttressed walls of two neighbours, giving the impression that if it fell, then all would fall together. The house was of wood and sandy brick, of many floors, each at an angle to the rest, covered by a waved roof. "This is the residence," she told him, "where my forefathers and myself have lived and worked. It is the House of the Th'ee and I am Rai-u Th'ee, last of my line. It is my ambition to leave a single great work of art behind, carved in a material which has been in our possession for centuries, yet until now always considered too valuable to use. It is a rare material, at least to us, and possessed of a number of qualities, some of which our ancestors only hinted at."

"My curiosity grows," said Elric, though now he found himself wishing that he had accepted her offer and brought his sword. "What is this material?"

"It is a kind of ivory," she said, leading him into the ramshackle house which, for all its age and decrepitude, had clearly once been rich. Even the wall-hangings, now in rags, revealed traces of their former quality. There were paintings from floor to ceiling which, Elric knew, would have commanded magnificent prices at any market. The furniture was carved by genuine artists and showed the passing of a hundred fashions, from the plain, somewhat austere style of the city's secular period, to the ornate enrichments of her pagan age. Some were inset with jewels, as were the many mirrors, framed with exquisite and elaborate ornament. Elric was surprised, given what she had told him of the quarter, that the House of Th'ee had never been robbed.

Apparently reading his thoughts, she said: "This place has been afforded certain protections down the years." She led him into a tall studio, lit by a single, unpapered window through which a great deal of light entered, illuminating the scrolls and boxed books lining the walls. Crowded on tables and shelves stood sculptures in every conceivable material. They were in bone and granite and hardwood and limestone. They were in clay and bronze, in iron and sea-green basalt. Bright, glinting whites, deep, swirling blacks. Colours of every possible shade from darkest blue to the lightest pinks and yellows. There was gold, silver and delicate porphyry. There were heads and torsos and reclining figures, beasts of every kind, some believed extinct. There were representations of the Lords and Ladies of Chaos and of Law, every supernatural aristocrat who had ever ruled in heaven, hell or limbo. Elementals. Animal-bodied men, birds in flight, leaping deer, men and women at rest, historical subjects, and group subjects and half-finished subjects which hinted at something still to be discovered in the stone. They were the work of genius, decided the albino, and his respect for this bold woman grew. "Yes." Again she anticipated a question, speaking with firm pride. "They are all mine. I love to work. Many of these are taken from life..."

He thought it impolitic to ask which.

"But you will note," she added, "that I have never had the pleasure of sculpting the head of a Melnibonéan. This could be my only opportunity."

"Ah," he began regretfully, but with great grace she silenced him, drawing him to a table on which sat a tall, shrouded object. She took away the cloth. "This is the material we have owned down the generations but for which we never yet found an appropriate subject."

He recognised the material. He reached to run his hand over its warm smoothness. He had seen more than one of these in the old caves of the Ph'oorn, to whom his folk were related. He had seen them in living creatures who even now slept in Melniboné, wearied by their work of destruction, their old master made an exile, with no one to care for them save a few mad old men who knew how to do nothing else.

"Yes," she whispered, "it is what you know it is. It cost my forefathers a great fortune for, as you can imagine, your folk were not readily forthcoming with such things. It was smuggled from Melniboné and traded through many nations before it reached us, some two and a half centuries ago."

Elric found himself almost singing to the thing as he caressed it. He felt back a mixture of nostalgia and deep sadness.

"It is dragon ivory, of course." Her hand joined his on the hard, brilliant surface of the great curved tusk. Few Ph'oorn had owned such fangs. Only the greatest of the patriarchs, legendary creatures of astonishing ferocity and wisdom, who had come from their old world to this, following their kin, the human-like folk of Melniboné. The Ph'oorn, too, had not been native to this world, but had fled another. They, too, had always been alien and cruel, impossibly beautiful, impossibly strange. Elric felt kinship even now for this piece of bone. It was perhaps all that remained of the first generation to settle on this plane.

"It is a holy thing." His voice was growing cold again. Inexplicable pain forced him to withdraw from her. "It is my own kin. Blood for blood, the Ph'oorn and the folk of Melniboné are one. It was our power. It was our strength. It was our continuity. This is ancestral bone. Stolen bone. It would be sacrilege..."

"No, Prince Elric, in my hands it would be a unification. A resolution. A completion. You know why I have brought you here."

"Yes." His hand fell to his side. He swayed, as if faint. He felt a need for the herbs he carried with him. "But it is still sacrilege..."

"Not if I am the one to give it life." Her veil was drawn back now and he saw how impossibly young she was, what beauty she had: a beauty mirrored in all the things she had carved and moulded. Her desire was, he was sure, an honest one. Two very different emotions warred within him. Part of him felt she was right, that she could unite the two kinsfolk in a single image and bring honour to all his ancestors, a kind of resolution to their mutual history. Part of him feared what she might create. In honouring his past, would she be destroying the future? Then some fundamental part of him made him gather himself up and turn to her. She gasped at what she saw burning in those terrible, ruby eyes.

"Life?"

"Yes," she said. "A new life honouring the old. Will you sit for me?" She too was caught up in his mood, for she too was endangering everything she valued, possibly her own soul, to make what might be her very last great work. "Will you allow me to create your memorial? Will you help me redeem that destruction whose burden is so heavy upon you? A symbol for everything that was Melniboné?"

He let go of his caution but felt no responsive glee. The fire dulled in his eyes. His mask returned. "I will need you to help me brew certain herbs, madam. They will sustain me while I sit for you."

Her step was light as she led him into a room where she had lit a stove and on which water already boiled, but his own face still resembled the stone of her carvings. His gaze was turned inward, his eyes alternately flared and faded like a dying candle. His chest moved with deep, almost dying breaths as he gave himself up to her art.

III. The Sitting

How many hours did he sit, still and silent in the chair? At one time she remarked on the fact that he scarcely moved. He said that he had developed the habit over several hundred years and, when she voiced surprise, permitted himself a smile. "You have not heard of Melniboné's dream couches? They are doubtless destroyed with the rest. It is how we learn so much when young. The couches let us dream for a year, even centuries, while the time passing for those awake was but minutes. I appear to you as a relatively young man, lady. But actually I have lived for centuries. It took me that time to pursue my dream quests, which in turn taught me my craft, and prepare myself for..." And then he stopped speaking, his pale lids falling over his troubled, unlikely eyes.

She drew breath, as if to ask a further question, then thought better of it. She brewed him cup after cup of invigorating herbs and she continued to work, her delicate chisels fashioning an extraordinary likeness. She had genius in her hands. Every line of the albino's head was rapidly reproduced. And Elric, almost dreaming again, stared into the middle-distance. His thoughts were far away and in the past, where he had left the corpse of his beloved Cymoril to burn on the pyre he had made of his own ancient home, the great and beautiful Imrryr, the Dreaming City, the dreamer's city, which many had considered indestructible, had believed to be more conjuring than reality, created by the Melnibonéan sorcerer kings into a delicate reality, whose towers, so tall they disappeared amongst clouds, were actually the result of supernatural will rather than the creation of architects and masons.

Yet Elric had proven such theories false when Melniboné burned. Now all knew him for a traitor and none trusted him, even those whose ambition he had served. They said he was twice a traitor, once to his own folk, second to those he had led on the raid which had razed Imrryr and upon whom he had turned. But in his own mind he was thrice a traitor, for he had slain his beloved Cymoril, beautiful sister of cousin Yyrkoon, who had tricked Elric into killing her with that terrible black blade whose energy both sustained and drained him.

It was for Cymoril, more than Imrryr, that Elric mourned. But he showed none of this to the world and never spoke of it. Only in his dreams, those terrible, troubled dreams, did he see her again, which is why he almost always slept alone and presented a carefully cultivated air of insouciance to the world at large.

Had he agreed to the sculptress's request because she reminded him of his cousin?

Hour upon tireless hour she worked with her exquisitely made instruments until at last she had finished. She sighed and it seemed her breath was a gentle witch-wind, filling the head with vitality. She turned the portrait for his inspection.

It was as if he stared into a mirror. For a moment he thought he saw movement in the bust, as if his own essence had been absorbed by it. Save for the blank eyes, the carving might have been himself. Even the hair had been carved to add to the portrait's lifelike qualities.

She looked to him for his approval and received the faintest of smiles. "You have made the likeness of a monster," he murmured. "I congratulate you. Now history will know the face of the man they call Elric Kinslayer."

"Ah," she said, "you curse yourself too much, my lord. Do you look into the face of one who bears a guilt-weighted conscience?"

And of course, he did. She had captured exactly that quality of melancholy and self-hatred behind the mask of insouciance which characterised the albino in repose.

"Whoever looks on this will not say you were careless of your crimes." Her voice was so soft it was almost a whisper now.

At this he rose suddenly, putting down his cup. "I need no sentimental forgiveness," he said coldly. "There is no forgiveness, no understanding, of that crime. History will be right to curse me for a coward, a traitor, a killer of women and of his own blood. You have done well, madam, to brew me those herbs, for I now feel strong enough to put all this and your city behind me!"

She watched him leave, walking a little unsteadily like a man carrying a heavy burden, through the busy night, back to the inn where he had left his sword and armour. She knew that by morning he would be gone, riding out of Sered-Öma, never to return. Her hands caressed the likeness she had made, the blind, staring eyes, the mouth which was set in a grimace of self-mocking carelessness.

And she knew he would always wonder, even as he put a thousand leagues between them, if he had not left at least a little of his yearning, desperate soul behind him.

The Witch's Headstone

Neil Gaiman

Neil Gaiman (*neilgaiman.com*) lives near Minneapolis. He rose to prominence as a popular writer of intellectually and aesthetically satisfying comics, a writer whom champions of the form pointed to when challenged on whether comics could be really literate and good art. Since crossing over to writing novels and short stories, he has been greeted by similarly hospitable audiences which have showered him with awards and honors. Nonetheless, he always wears black and remains cool.

"The Witch's Headstone" appeared in *Wizards*, edited by Gardner Dozois and Jack Dann, this year's strongest fantasy anthology, and from which several stories in this book are selected. It is about a nice little boy, who speaks only to ghosts, Nobody Owens, growing up in strange circumstances, and features some very memorable literary architecture. This is a story in Ray Bradbury's literary tradition, and is perhaps part of a novel in progress.

THERE WAS a witch buried at the edge of the graveyard, it was common knowledge. Bod had been told to keep away from that corner of the world by Mrs. Owens as far back as he could remember.

"Why?" he asked.

"T'aint healthy for a living body," said Mrs. Owens. "There's damp down that end of things. It's practically a marsh. You'll catch your death."

Mr Owens himself was more evasive and less imaginative. "It's not a good place," was all he said.

The graveyard proper ended at the edge of the hill, beneath the old apple tree, with a fence of rust-brown iron railings, each topped with a small, rusting spear-head, but there was a wasteland beyond that, a mass of nettles and weeds, of brambles and autumnal rubbish, and Bod, who was a good boy, on the whole, and obedient, did not push between the railings, but he went down there and looked through. He knew he wasn't being told the whole story, and it irritated him.

Bod went back up the hill, to the abandoned church in the middle of the graveyard, and he waited until it got dark. As twilight edged from grey to purple there was a noise in the spire, like a fluttering of heavy velvet, and Silas left his resting place in the belfry and clambered headfirst down the spire.

"What's in the far corner of the graveyard," asked Bod. "Past Harrison Westwood, Baker of this Parish, and his wives Marion and Joan?"

"Why do you ask?" said his guardian, brushing the dust from his black suit with ivory fingers.

Bod shrugged. "Just wondered."

"It's unconsecrated ground," said Silas. "Do you know what that means?"

"Not really," said Bod.

Silas walked across the path without disturbing a fallen leaf, and sat down on the stone bench, beside Bod. "There are those," he said, in his silken voice, "who believe that all land is sacred. That it is sacred before we come to it, and sacred after. But here, in your land, they bless the churches and the ground they set aside to bury people in, to make it holy. But they leave land unconsecrated beside the sacred ground, Potter's Fields to bury the criminals and the suicides or those who were not of the faith."

"So the people buried in the ground on the other side of the fence are bad people?"

Silas raised one perfect eyebrow. "Mm? Oh, not at all. Let's see, it's been a while since I've been down that way. But I don't remember anyone particularly evil. Remember, in days gone by you could be hanged for stealing a shilling. And there are always people who find their lives have become so unsupportable they believe the best thing they could do would be to hasten their transition to another plane of existence."

"They kill themselves, you mean?" said Bod. He was about eight years old, wide-eyed and inquisitive, and he was not stupid.

"Indeed."

"Does it work? Are they happier dead?"

Silas grinned so wide and sudden that he showed his fangs. "Sometimes. Mostly, no. It's like the people who believe they'll be happy if they go and live somewhere else, but who learn it doesn't work that way. Wherever you go, you take yourself with you. If you see what I mean."

"Sort of," said Bod.

Silas reached down and ruffled the boy's hair.

Bod said, "What about the witch?"

"Yes. Exactly," said Silas. "Suicides, criminals, and witches. Those who died unshriven." He stood up, a midnight shadow in the twilight. "All this talking," he said, "and I have not even had my breakfast. While you will be late for lessons." In the twilight of the graveyard there was a silent implosion, a flutter of velvet darkness, and Silas was gone.

The moon had begun to rise by the time Bod reached Mr Pennyworth's mausoleum, and Thomes Pennyworth (*here he lyes in the certainty of the moft glorious refurrection*) was already waiting, and was not in the best of moods.

"You are late," he said.

"Sorry, Mr Pennyworth."

Pennyworth tutted. The previous week Mr Pennyworth had been teaching Bod about Elements and Humours, and Bod had kept forgetting which was which. He was expecting a test but instead Mr Pennyworth said, "I think it is time to spend a few days on practical matters. Time is passing, after all."

"Is it?" asked Bod.

"I am afraid so, young Master Owens. Now, how is your Fading?"

Bod had hoped he would not be asked that question.

"It's all right," he said. "I mean. You know."

"No, Master Owens. I do not know. Why do you not demonstrate for me?"

Bod's heart sank. He took a deep breath, and did his best, squinching up his eyes and trying to fade away.

Mr Pennyworth was not impressed.

"Pah. That' s not the kind of thing. Not the kind of thing at all. Slipping and fading, boy, the way of the dead. Slip through shadows. Fade from awareness. Try again."

Bod tried harder.

"You're as plain as the nose on your face," said Mr Pennyworth. "And your nose is remarkably obvious. As is the rest of your face, young man. As are you. For the sake of all that is holy, empty your mind. Now. You are an empty alleyway. You are a vacant doorway. You are nothing. Eyes will not see you. Minds will not hold you. Where you are is nothing and nobody."

Bod tried again. He closed his eyes and imagined himself fading into the stained stonework of the mausoleum wall, becoming a shadow on the night and nothing more. He sneezed.

"Dreadful," said Mr Pennyworth, with a sigh. "Quite dreadful. I believe I shall have a word with your guardian about this." He shook his head. "So. The Humours. List them."

"Um. Sanguine. Choleric. Phlegmatic. And the other one. Um, Melancholic, I think."

And so it went, until it was time for Grammar and Composition with Miss Letitia Borrows, Spinster of this Parish (*Who Did No Harm to No Man all the Dais of Her Life. Reader, Can You Say Lykewise?*). Bod liked Miss Borrows, and the cosiness of her little crypt, and could all-too-easily be led off the subject.

"They say there's a witch in uncons- unconsecrated ground," he said.

"Yes, dear. But you don't want to go over there."

"Why not?"

Miss Borrows smiled the guileless smile of the dead. "They aren't our sort of people," she said.

"But it is the graveyard, isn't it? I mean, I'm allowed to go there if I want to?"

"That," said Miss Borrows, "would not be advisable."

Bod was obedient, but curious, and so, when lessons were done for the night, he walked past Harrison Westwood, Baker, and family's memorial, a broken-headed angel, but did not climb down the hill to the Potter's Field. Instead he walked up the side of the hill to where a picnic some thirty years before had left its mark in the shape of a large apple tree.

There were some lessons that Bod had mastered. He had eaten a bellyful of unripe apples, sour and white-pipped, from the tree some years before, and had regretted it for days, his guts cramping and painful while Mistress Owens lectured him on what not to eat. Now he waited until the apples were ripe before eating them, and never ate more than two or three a night. He had finished the last of the apples the week before, but he liked the apple tree as a place to think.

He edged up the trunk, to his favourite place in the crook of two branches, and looked down at the Potter's Field below him, a brambly patch of weeds and unmown grass in the moonlight. He wondered whether the witch would be old and iron-toothed and travel in a house on chicken legs, or whether she would be thin and carry a broomstick.

And then he was hungry. He wished he had not devoured all the apples on the tree. That he had left just one...

He glanced up, and thought he saw something. He looked once, looked twice to be certain. An apple, red and ripe

Bod prided himself on his tree-climbing skills. He swung himself up, branch by branch, and imagined he was Silas, swarming smoothly up a sheer brick wall. The apple, the red of it almost black in the moonlight, hung just out of reach. Bod moved slowly forward along the branch, until he was just below the apple. Then he stretched up, and the tips of his fingers touched the perfect apple.

He was never to taste it.

A snap, loud as a hunter's gun, as the branch gave way beneath him.

A flash of pain woke him, sharp as ice, the colour of slow thunder, down in the weeds that summer's night.

The ground beneath him seemed relatively soft, and oddly warm. He pushed a hand down and felt something like warm fur. He had landed on the grass-pile, where the graveyard's gardener threw the cuttings from the mower, and it had broken his fall. Still, there was a pain in his chest, and his leg hurt as if he had landed on it first, and twisted it.

Bod moaned.

"Hush-a-you-hush-a-boy," said a voice from behind him. "Where did you come from? Dropping like a thunderstone. What way is that to carry on?"

"I was in the apple tree," said Bod.

"Ah. Let me see your leg. Broken like the tree's limb, I'll be bound." Cool fingers prodded his left leg. "Not broken. Twisted, yes, sprained perhaps. You have the Devil's own luck, boy, falling into the compost. 'Tain't the end of the world."

"Oh, good," said Bod. "Hurts, though."

He turned his head, looked up and behind him. She was older than him, but not a grown-up, and she looked neither friendly nor unfriendly. Wary, mostly. She had a face that was intelligent and not even a little bit beautiful.

"I'm Bod," he said.

"The live boy?" she asked.

Bod nodded.

"I thought you must be," she said. "We've heard of you, even over here, in the Potter's Field. What do they call you?"

"Owens," he said. "Nobody Owens. Bod, for short."

"How-de-do, young Master Bod."

Bod looked her up and down. She wore a plain white shift. Her hair was mousy and long, and there was something of the goblin in her face – a sideways hint of a smile that seemed to linger, no matter what the rest of her face was doing.

"Were you a suicide?" he asked. "Did you steal a shilling?"

"Never stole nuffink," she said, "not even a handkerchief. Anyway," she said, pertly, "the suicides is all over there, on the other side of that hawthorn, and the gallows-birds are in the blackberry-patch, both of them. One was a coiner, t'other a highwayman, or so he says, although if you ask me I doubt he was more than a common footpad and nightwalker."

"Ah," said Bod. Then, suspicion forming, tentatively, he said, "They say a witch is buried here."

She nodded. "Drownded and burnded and buried here without as much as a stone to mark the spot."

"You were drowned *and* burned?"

She settled down on the hill of grass-cuttings beside him, and held his throbbing leg with her chilly hands. "They come to my little cottage at dawn, before I'm proper awake, and drags me out onto the green. 'You're a witch!' they shouts, fat and fresh-scrubbed all pink in the morning, like so many pigwiggins fresh-scrubbed for market day. One by one they gets up beneath the sky and tells of milk gone sour and horses gone lame, and finally Mistress Jemima gets up, the fattest, pinkest, best-scrubbed of them all, and tells how as Solomon Porritt now cuts her dead and instead hangs around the washhouse like a wasp about a honeypot , and it's all my magic, says she, that made him so and the poor young man must be bespelled. So they strap me to the cucking-stool and forces it under the water of the duckpond, saying If I'm a witch I'll neither drown nor care, but if I am not a witch I'll feel it. And Mistress Jemima's father gives them each a silver groat to hold the stool down under the foul green water for a long time, to see if I'd choke on it."

"And did you?"

"Oh yes. Got a lungful of water. It done for me."

"Oh," said Bod. "Then you weren't a witch after all."

The girl fixed him with her beady ghost-eyes and smiled a lopsided smile. She still looked like a goblin, but now she looked like a pretty goblin, and Bod didn't think she would have needed magic to attract Solomon Porritt, not with a smile like that. "What nonsense. Of course I was a witch. They learned that when they untied me from the cucking-stool and stretched me on the green, nine-parts dead and all covered with duckweed and stinking pond-muck. I rolled my eyes back in my head, and I cursed each and every one of them there on the village green that morning, that none of them would ever rest easily in a grave. I was surprised at how easily it came, the cursing. Like dancing it was, when your feet pick up the steps of a new measure your ears have never heard and your head don't know, and they dance it till dawn." She stood, and twirled, and kicked, and her bare feet flashed in the moonlight. "That was how I cursed them, with my last gurgling pond-watery breath. And then I expired. They burned my body on the green until I was nothing but blackened charcoal, and they popped me in a hole in the Potter's Field without so much as a headstone to mark my name," and it was only then that she paused, and seemed, for a moment, wistful.

"Are any of them buried in the graveyard, then?" asked Bod.

"Not a one," said the girl, with a twinkle. "The Saturday after they drownded and toasted me, a carpet was delivered to Master Porringer, all the way from London Town, and it was a fine carpet. But it turned out there was more in that carpet than strong wool and good weaving, for it carried the plague in its pattern, and by Monday five of them were coughing blood, and their skins were gone as black as mine when they hauled me from the fire. A week later and it had taken most of the village, and they threw the bodies all promiscuous in a plague pit they dug outside of the town, that they filled in after."

"Was everyone in the village killed?"

She shrugged. "Everyone who watched me get drownded and burned. How's your leg now?"

"Better," he said. "Thanks."

Bod stood up, slowly, and limped down from the grass-pile. He leaned against the iron railings. "So were you always a witch?" he asked. "I mean, before you cursed them all?"

"As if it would take witchcraft," she said with a sniff, "to get Solomon Porritt mooning round my cottage."

Which, Bod thought, but did not say, was not actually an answer to the question, not at all.

"What's your name?" he asked.

"Got no headstone," she said, turning down the corners of her mouth. "Might be anybody. Mightn't I?"

"But you must have a name."

"Liza Hempstock, if you please," she said tartly. Then she said, "It's not that much to ask, is it? Something to mark my grave. I'm just down there, see? With nothing but nettles to mark where I rest." And she looked so sad, just for a moment, that Bod wanted to hug her. And then it came to him, and as he squeezed between the railings of the fence. He would find Liza Hempstock a headstone, with her name upon it. He would make her smile.

He turned to wave goodbye as he began to clamber up the hill, but she was already gone.

There were broken lumps of other people's stones and statues in the graveyard, but, Bod knew, that would have been entirely the wrong sort of thing to bring to the grey-eyed witch in the Potter's Field. It was going to take more than that. He decided not to tell anyone what he was planning, on the not entirely unreasonable basis that they would have told him not to do it.

Over the next few days his mind filled with plans, each more complicated and extravagant than the last. Mr. Pennyworth despaired.

"I do believe," he announced, scratching his dusty moustache, "that you are getting, if anything, worse. You are not Fading. You are *obvious*, boy. You are difficult to miss. If you came to me in company with a purple lion, a green elephant and a scarlet unicorn, astride which was the King of England in his Royal Robes, I do believe that it is you and you alone that people would stare at, dismissing the others as minor irrelevancies."

Bod simply stared at him, and said nothing. He was wondering whether there were special shops in the places where the living people gathered that sold only headstones, and if so how he could go about finding one, and Fading was the least of his problems.

He took advantage of Miss Borrows' willingness to be diverted from the subjects of Grammar and Composition to the subject of anything else at all to ask her about money – how exactly it worked, how one used it to get things one wanted. Bod had a number of coins he had found over the years (he had learned that the best place to find money was to go, afterwards, to wherever courting couples had used the grass of the graveyard as a place to cuddle and snuggle and kiss and roll about. He would often find metal coins on the ground, in the place where they had been) and he thought perhaps he could finally get some use from them.

"How much would a headstone be?" he asked Miss Borrows.

"In my time," she told him, "they were fifteen guineas. I do not know what they would be today. More, I imagine. Much, much more."

Bod had fifty-three pence. It would not be enough.

It had been four years, almost half a lifetime, since Bod had visited the Indigo Man's tomb. But he still remembered the way. He climbed to the top of the hill, until he was above the whole town, above even the top of the apple tree, above even the steeple of the ruined church, up where the Frobisher vault stood like a rotten tooth. He slipped down into it, and down and down and still further down, down to the tiny stone steps cut into the center of the hill, and those he descended until he reached the stone chamber at the base of the hill. It was dark in that tomb, dark as a deep mine, but Bod saw as the dead see and the room gave up its secrets to him.

The Sleer was coiled around the wall of the barrow. It was as he remembered it, all smoky tendrils and hate and greed. This time, however, he was not afraid of it.

FEAR ME, whispered the Sleer. FOR I GUARD THINGS PRECIOUS AND NEVER-LOST.

"I don't fear you," said Bod. " Remember? And I need to take something away from here."

NOTHING EVER LEAVES, came the reply from the coiled thing in the darkness. THE KNIFE, THE BROOCH, THE GOBLET. I GUARD THEM IN THE DARKNESS. I WAIT.

In the centre of the room was a slab of rock, and on it they lay: a stone knife, a brooch, and a goblet.

"Pardon me for asking," said Bod, "but was this your grave?"

MASTER SETS US HERE ON THE PLAIN TO GUARD, BURIES OUR SKULLS BENEATH THIS STONE, LEAVES US HERE KNOWING WHAT WE HAVE TO DO. WE GUARDS THE TREASURES UNTIL MASTER COMES BACK.

"I expect that he's forgotten all about you," pointed out Bod. "I'm sure he's been dead himself for ages."

WE ARE THE SLEER. WE GUARD.

Bod wondered just how long ago you had to go back before the deepest tomb inside the hill was on a plain, and he knew it must have been an extremely long time ago. He could feel the Sleer winding its waves of fear around him, like the tendrils of some carnivorous plant. He was beginning to feel cold, and slow, as if he had been bitten in the heart by some arctic viper and it was starting to pump its icy venom through his body.

He took a step forward, so he was standing against the stone slab, and he reached down and closed his fingers around the coldness of the brooch.

HISH! whispered the Sleer. WE GUARDS THAT FOR THE MASTER.

"He won't mind," said Bod. He took a step backward, walking toward the stone steps, avoiding the desiccated remains of people and animals on the floor.

The Sleer writhed angrily, twining around the tiny chamber like ghost-smoke. Then it slowed. IT COMES BACK, said the Sleer, in its tangled triple voice. ALWAYS COMES BACK.

Bod went up the stone steps inside the hill as fast as he could. At one point he imagined that there was something coming after him, but when he broke out of the top, into the Frobisher vault, and he could breathe the cool dawn air, nothing moved or followed.

Bod sat in the open air on the top of the hill and held the brooch. He thought it was all black, at first, but then the sun rose, and he could see that the stone in the centre of the black metal was a swirling red. It was the size of a robin's egg, and Bod stared into the stone wondering if there were things moving in its heart, his eyes and soul deep in the crimson world. If Bod had been smaller he would have wanted to put it into his mouth.

The stone was held in place by a black metal clasp, by something that looked like claws, with something else crawling around it. The something else looked almost snakelike, but it had too many heads. Bod wondered if that was what the Sleer looked like, in the daylight.

He wandered down the hill, taking all the short-cuts he knew, through the ivy tangle that covered the Bartleby's family vault (and inside, the sound of the Bartlebies grumbling and readying for sleep) and on and over and through the railings and into the Potter's Field.

He called, "Liza! Liza!" and looked around.

"Good morrow, young lummox," said Liza's voice. Bod could not see her, but there was an extra shadow beneath the hawthorn bush, and, as he approached it, the shadow resolved itself into something pearlescent and translucent in the early-morning light. Something girl-like. Something grey-eyed. "I should be decently sleeping," she said. "What kind of carrying on is this?"

"Your headstone," he said. "I wanted to know what you want on it."

"My name," she said. "It must have my name on it, with a big E, for Elizabeth, like the old queen that died when I was born, and a big Haitch for Hempstock. More than that I care not, for I did never master my letters."

"What about dates?" asked Bod.

"Willyum the Conker ten sixty-six," she sang, in the whisper of the dawn-wind in the hawthorn bush. "A big E if you please. And a big Haitch."

"Did you have a job?" asked Bod. "I mean, when you weren't being a witch?"

"I done laundry," said the dead girl, and then the morning sunlight flooded the wasteland, and Bod was alone.

It was nine in the morning, when all the world is sleeping. Bod was determined to stay awake. He was, after all, on a mission. He was eight years old, and the world beyond the graveyard held no terrors for him.

Clothes. He would need clothes. His usual dress, of a grey winding sheet, was, he knew, quite wrong. It was good in the graveyard, the same colour as stone and as shadows. But if he was going to dare the world beyond the graveyard walls, he would need to blend in there.

There were some clothes in the crypt beneath the ruined church, but Bod did not want to go there, even in daylight. While Bod was prepared to justify himself to Master and Mistress Owens, he was not about to explain himself to Silas; the very thought of those dark eyes angry, or worse still, disappointed, filled him with shame.

There was a gardener's hut at the far end of the graveyard, a small green building that smelled like motor oil, and in which the old mower sat and rusted, unused, along with an assortment of ancient garden tools. The hut had been abandoned when the last gardener had retired, before Bod was born, and the task of keeping the graveyard had been shared between the council (who sent in a man to cut the grass, once a month from April to September) and local volunteers.

A huge padlock on the door protected the contents of the hut, but Bod had long ago discovered the loose wooden board in the back. Sometimes he would go to the gardener's hut, and sit, and think, when he wanted to be by himself.

As long as he had been going to the hut there had been a brown working man's jacket hanging on the back of the door, forgotten or abandoned years before, along with a green-stained pair of gardening jeans. The jeans were much too big for him, but he rolled up the cuffs until his feet showed, then he made a belt out of brown garden-twine, and tied it around his waist. There were boots in one corner, and he tried putting them on, but they were so big and encrusted with mud and concrete that he could barely shuffle them, and if he took a step, the boots remained on the floor of the shed. He pushed the jacket out through the space in the loose board, squeezed himself out, then put it on. If he rolled up the sleeves, he decided, it worked quite well. It had big pockets, and he thrust his hands into them, and felt quite the dandy.

Bod walked down to the main gate of the graveyard, and looked out through the bars. A bus rattled past, in the street; there were cars there and noise and shops. Behind him, a cool green shade, overgrown with trees and ivy: home.

His heart pounding, Bod walked out into the world.

Abanazer Bolger had seen some odd types in his time; if you owned a shop like Abanazer's, you'd see them too. The shop, in the warren of streets in the Old Town – a little bit antique shop, a little bit junk shop, a little bit pawnbroker's (and not even Abanazer himself was entirely certain which bit was which) brought odd types and strange people, some of them wanting to buy, some of them needing to sell. Abanazer Bolger traded over the counter, buying and selling, and he did a better trade behind the counter and in the back room, accepting objects that may not have been acquired entirely honestly, and then quietly shifting them on. His business was an iceberg. Only the dusty little shop was visible on the surface. The rest of it was underneath, and that was just how Abanazer Bolger wanted it.

Abanazer Bolger had thick spectacles and a permanent expression of mild distaste, as if he had just realised that the milk in his tea had been on the turn, and he could not get the sour taste of it out of his mouth. The expression served him well when people tried to sell him things. "Honestly," he would tell them, sour-faced, "it's not really worth anything at all. I'll give you what I can, though, as it has sentimental value." You were lucky to get anything like what you thought you wanted from Abanazer Bolger.

A business like Abanazer Bolger's brought in strange people, but the boy who came in that morning was one of the strangest Abanazer could remember in a lifetime of cheating strange people out of their valuables. He looked to be about seven years old, and dressed in his grandfather's clothes. He smelled like a shed. His hair was long and shaggy, and he looked extremely grave. His hands were deep in the pockets of a dusty brown jacket, but even with the hands out of sight, Abanazer could see that something was clutched extremely tightly – protectively – in the boy's right hand.

"Excuse me," said the boy.

"Aye-aye Sonny-Jim," said Abanazer Bolger warily. *Kids,* he thought. *Either they've nicked something, or they're trying to sell their toys.* Either way, he usually said no. Buy stolen property from a kid, and next thing you knew you'd an enraged adult accusing you of having given little Johnnie or Matilda a tenner for their wedding ring. More trouble than they was worth, kids.

"I need something for a friend of mine," said the boy. "And I thought maybe you could buy something I've got."

"I don't buy stuff from kids," said Abanazer Bolger flatly.

Bod took his hand out of his pocket and put the brooch down on the grimy counter-top. Bolger glanced down at it, then he looked at it. He took an eyepiece from the counter-top and he screwed it into his eye. He removed his spectacles. He turned on a little light on the counter and examined the brooch through the eyeglass. "Snakestone?" he said, to himself, not to the boy. Then he took the eyepiece out, replaced his glasses, and fixed the boy with a sour and suspicious look.

"Where did you get this?" Abanazer Bolger asked.

Bod said, "Do you want to buy it?"

"You stole it. You've nicked this from a museum or somewhere, didn't you?"

"No," said Bod flatly. "Are you going to buy it, or shall I go and find somebody who will?"

Abanazer Bolger's sour mood changed then. Suddenly he was all affability. He smiled broadly. "I'm sorry," he said. "It's just you don't see many pieces like this. Not in a shop like this. Not outside of a museum. But I would certainly like it. Tell you what. Why don't we sit down over tea and biscuits – I've got a packet of chocolate chip cookies in the back room – and decide how much something like this is worth? Eh?"

Bod was relieved that the man was finally being friendly. "I need enough to buy a stone," he said. "A headstone for a friend of mine. Well, she's not really my friend. Just someone I know. I think she helped make my leg better, you see."

Abanazer Bolger, paying little attention to the boy's prattle, led him behind the counter, and opened the door to the storeroom, a windowless little space, every inch of which was crammed high with teetering cardboard boxes, each filled with junk. There was a safe in there, in the corner, a big old one. There was a box filled with violins, an accumulation of stuffed dead animals, chairs without seats, books and prints.

There was a small desk beside the door, and Abanazer Bolger pulled up the only chair, and sat down, letting Bod stand. Abanazer rummaged in a drawer, in which Bod could see a half-empty bottle of whisky, and pulled out an almost-finished packet of chocolate chip cookies, and he offered one to the boy; he turned on the desk light, looked at the brooch again, the swirls of red and orange in the stone, and he examined the black metal band that encircled it, suppressing a little shiver at the expression on the heads of the snake-things. "This is old," he said. "It's – " *priceless*, he thought, " – probably not really worth much, but you never know." Bod's face fell. Abanazer Bolger tried to look reassuring. "I just need to know that it's not stolen, though, before I can give you a penny. Did you take it from your mum's dresser? Nick it from a museum? You can tell me. I'll not get you into trouble. I just need to know."

Bod shook his head. He munched on his cookie.

"Then where did you get it?"

Bod said nothing.

Abanazer Bolger did not want to put down the brooch, but he pushed it across the desk to the boy. "If you can't tell me," he said, "you'd better take it back. There has to be trust on both sides, after all. Nice doing business with you. Sorry it couldn't go any further."

Bod looked worried. Then he said, "I found it in an old grave. But I can't say where." And then he stopped, because naked greed and excitement had replaced the friendliness on Abanazer Bolger's face.

"And there's more like this there?"

Bod said, "If you don't want to buy it, I'll find someone else. Thank you for the biscuit."

Bolger said, "You're in a hurry, eh? Mum and dad waiting for you, I expect?"

The boy shook his head, then wished he had nodded.

"Nobody waiting. Good." Abanazer Bolger closed his hands around the brooch. "Now, you tell me exactly where you found this. Eh?"

"I don't remember," said Bod.

"Too late for that," said Abanazer Bolger. "Suppose you have a little think for a bit about where it came from. Then, when you've thought, we'll have a little chat, and you'll tell me."

He got up, and walked out of the room, closing the door behind him. He locked it, with a large metal key.

He opened his hand, and looked at the brooch and smiled, hungrily.

There was a *ding* from the bell above the shop door, to let him know someone had entered, and he looked up, guiltily, but there was nobody there. The door was slightly ajar though, and Bolger pushed it shut, and then for good measure, he turned around the sign in the window, so it said *Closed.* He pushed the bolt closed. Didn't want any busybodies turning up today.

The autumn day had turned from sunny to grey, and a light patter of rain ran down the grubby shop window.

Abanazer Bolger picked up the telephone from the counter and pushed at the buttons with fingers that barely shook.

"Paydirt, Tom," he said. "Get over here, soon as you can."

Bod realised that he was trapped when he heard the lock turn in the door. He pulled on the door, but it held fast. He felt stupid for having been lured inside, foolish for not trusting his first impulses, to get as far away from the sour-faced man as possible. He had broken all the rules of the graveyard, and everything had gone wrong. What would Silas say? Or the Owenses? He could feel himself beginning to panic, and he suppressed it, pushing the worry back down inside him. It would all be good. He knew that. Of course, he needed to get out...

He examined the room he was trapped in. It was little more than a storeroom with a desk in it. The only entrance was the door.

He opened the desk drawer, finding nothing but small pots of paint (used for brightening up antiques) and a paintbrush. He wondered if he would be able to throw paint in the man's face, and blind him for long enough to escape. He opened the top of a pot of paint and dipped in his finger.

"What're you doin'?" asked a voice close to his ear.

"Nothing," said Bod, screwing the top on the paintpot, and dropping it into one of the jacket's enormous pockets.

Liza Hempstock looked at him, unimpressed. "Why are you in here?" she asked. "And who's old bag-of-lard out there?"

"It's his shop. I was trying to sell him something."

"Why?"

"None of your beeswax."

She sniffed. "Well," she said, "you should get on back to the graveyard."

"I can't. He's locked me in."

"'Course you can. Just slip through the wall – "

He shook his head. "I can't. I can only do it at home because they gave me the freedom of the graveyard when I was a baby." He looked up at her, under the electric light. It was hard to see her properly, but Bod had spent his life talking to dead people. "Anyway, what are you doing here? What are you doing out from the graveyard? It's daytime. And you're not like Silas. You're meant to stay in the graveyard."

She said, "There's rules for those in graveyards, but not for those as was buried in unhallowed ground. Nobody tells *me* what to do, or where to go." She glared at the door. "I don't like that man," she said. "I'm going to see what he's doing."

A flicker, and Bod was alone in the room once more. He heard a rumble of distant thunder.

In the cluttered darkness of Bolger's Antiquities, Abanazer Bolger looked up suspiciously, certain that someone was watching him, then realised he was being foolish. "The boy's locked in the room," he told himself. "The front door's locked." He was polishing the metal clasp surrounding the snakestone, as gently and as carefully as an archaeologist on a dig, taking off the black and revealing the glittering silver beneath it.

He was beginning to regret calling Tom Hustings over, although Hustings was big and good for scaring people. He was also beginning to regret that he was going to have to sell the brooch, when he was done. It was special. The more it glittered, under the tiny light on his counter, the more he wanted it to be his, and only his.

There was more where this came from, though. The boy would tell him. The boy would lead him to it...

A knocking on the outer door of the shop.

Bolger walked over to the door, peering out into the wet afternoon.

"Hurry up," called Tom Hustings, "it's miserable out here. Dismal. I'm getting soaked."

Bolger unlocked the door and Tom Hustings pushed his way in, his raincoat and hair dripping. "What's so important that you can't talk about it over the phone, then?"

"Our fortune," said Abanazer Bolger, with his sour face. "That's what."

Hustings took off his raincoat and hung it on the back of the shopdoor. "What is it? Something good fell off the back of a lorry?"

"Treasure," said Abanazer Bolger. He took his friend over to the counter, showed him the brooch, under the little light.

"It's old, isn't it?"

"From pagan times," said Abanazer. "Before. From Druid times. Before the Romans came. It's called a snakestone. Seen 'em in museums. I've never seen metalwork like that, or one so fine. Must have belonged to a king. The lad who found it says it come from a grave – think of a barrow filled with stuff like this."

"Might be worth doing it legit," said Hustings, thoughtfully. "Declare it as treasure trove. They have to pay us market value for it, and we could make them name it for us. The Hustings-Bolger Bequest."

"Bolger-Hustings," said Abanazer, automatically. Then he said, "There's a few people I know of, people with real money, would pay more than market value, if they could hold it as you are – " for Tom Hustings was fingering the brooch, gently, like a man stroking a kitten – "and there'd be no questions asked." He reached out his hand and, reluctantly, Tom Hustings passed him the brooch.

And the two men went back and forth on it, weighing the merits and disadvantages of declaring the brooch as a treasure trove or of forcing the boy to show them the treasure, which had grown in their minds to a huge underground cavern filled with precious things, and as they debated Abanazer pulled a bottle of sloe gin from beneath the counter and poured them both a generous tot, "to assist the cerebrations."

Liza was soon bored with their discussions, which went back and forth and around like a whirligig, getting nowhere, and so she went back into the storeroom, to find Bod standing in the middle of the room with his eyes tightly closed and his fists clenched and his face all screwed up as if he had a toothache, almost purple from holding his breath.

"What you a-doin' of now?" she asked, unimpressed.

He opened his eyes and relaxed. "Trying to Fade," he said.

Liza sniffed. "Try again," she said.

He did, holding his breath even longer this time.

"Stop that," she told him. "Or you'll pop."

Bod took a deep breath and then sighed. "It doesn't work," he said. "Maybe I could hit him with a rock, and just run for it." There wasn't a rock, so he picked up a coloured glass paperweight, hefted it in his hand, wondering if he could throw it hard enough to stop Abanazer Bolger in his tracks.

"There's two of them out there now," said Liza. "And if the one don't get you, t'other one will. They say they want to get you to show them where you got the brooch, and then dig up the grave and take the treasure." She shook her head. "Why did you do something as stupid as this anyway? You know the rules about leaving the graveyard. Just asking for trouble, it was."

Bod felt very insignificant, and very foolish. "I wanted to get you a headstone," he admitted, in a small voice. "And I thought it would cost more money. So I was going to sell him the brooch, to buy you one."

She didn't say anything.

"Are you angry?"

She shook her head. "It's the first nice thing anyone's done for me in five hundred years," she said, with a hint of a goblin smile. "Why would I be angry?" Then she said, "What do you do, when you try to Fade?"

"What Mr. Pennyworth told me. *I am an empty doorway, I am a vacant alley, I am nothing. Eyes will not see me, glances slip over me.* But it never works."

"It's because you're alive," said Liza, with a sniff. "There's stuff as works for us, the dead, who have to fight to be noticed at the best of times, that won't never work for you people."

She hugged herself tightly, moving her body back and forth, as if she was debating something. Then she said, "It's because of me you got into this.... Come here, Nobody Owens."

He took a step towards her, in that tiny room, and she put her cold hand on his forehead. It felt like a wet silk scarf against his skin.

"Now," she said. "Perhaps I can do a good turn for you."

And with that, she began to mutter to herself, mumbling words that Bod could not make out. Then she said, clear and loud,

"Be hole, be dust, be dream, be wind

Be night, be dark, be wish, be mind,

Now slip, now slide, now move unseen,

Above, beneath, betwixt, between."

Something huge touched him, brushed him from head to feet, and he shivered. His hair prickled, and his skin was all goose-flesh. Something had changed. "What did you do?" he asked.

"Just gived you a helping hand," she said. "I may be dead, but I'm a dead witch, remember. And we don't forget."

"But – "

"Hush up," she said. "They're coming back."

The key rattled in the storeroom lock. "Now then chummy," said a voice Bod had not heard clearly before, "I'm sure we're all going to be great friends," and with that Tom Hustings pushed open the door. Then he stood in the doorway looking around, looking puzzled. He was a big, big man, with foxy-red hair and a bottle-red nose. "Here. Abanazer? I thought you said he was in here?"

"I did," said Bolger, from behind him.

"Well, I can't see hide nor hair of him."

Bolger's face appeared behind the ruddy man's and he peered into the room. "Hiding," he said, staring straight at where Bod was standing. "No use hiding," he announced, loudly. "I can see you there. Come on out."

The two men walked into the little room, and Bod stood stock still between them and thought of Mr. Pennyworth's lessons. He did not react, he did not move. He let the men's glances slide from him without seeing him.

"You're going to wish you'd come out when I called," said Bolger, and he shut the door. "Right," he said to Tom Hustings. "You block the door, so he can't get past." And with that he walked around the room, peering behind things, and bending, awkwardly, to look beneath the desk. He walked straight past Bod and opened the cupboard. "Now I see you!" he shouted. "Come out!"

Liza giggled.

"What was that?" asked Tom Hustings, spinning round.

"I didn't hear nothing," said Abanazer Bolger.

Liza giggled again. Then she put her lips together and blew, making a noise that began as a whistling, and then sounded like a distant wind. The electric lights in the little room flickered and buzzed. Then they went out.

"Bloody fuses," said Abanazer Bolger. "Come on. This is a waste of time."

The key clicked in the lock, and Liza and Bod were left alone in the room.

"He's got away," said Abanazer Bolger. Bod could hear him now, through the door. "Room like that. There wasn't anywhere he could have been hiding. We'd've seen him if he was."

A pause.

"Here. Tom Hustings. Where's the brooch gone?"

"Mm? That? Here. I was keeping it safe."

"Keeping it safe? In your pocket? Funny place to be keeping it safe, if you ask me. More like you were planning to make off with it – like you was planning to keep my brooch for your own."

"Your brooch, Abanazer? Your brooch? Our brooch, you mean."

"Ours, indeed. I don't remember you being here, when I got it from that boy."

There was another long silence, then Abanazer Bolger said, "Well, look at that, we're almost out of sloe gin – how would you fancy a good Scotch? I've whisky in the back room. You just wait here a moment."

The storeroom door was unlocked, and Abanazer entered, holding a walking stick and an electric torch, looking even more sour of face than before.

"If you're still in here," he said, in a sour mutter, "don't even think of making a run for it. I've called the police on you, that's what I've done." A rummage in a drawer produced the half-filled bottle of whisky, and then a tiny black bottle. Abanazer poured several drops from the little bottle into the larger, then he pocketed the tiny bottle. "My brooch, and mine alone," he muttered, and followed it with a barked, "Just coming, Tom!"

He glared around the dark room, staring past Bod, then he left the storeroom, carrying the whisky in front of him. He locked the door behind him.

"Here you go," came Abanazer Bolger's voice through the door. "Give us your glass then, Tom. Nice drop of Scotch, put hairs on your chest. Say when."

Silence. "Cheap muck. Aren't you drinking?"

"That sloe gin's gone to my innards. Give it a minute for my stomach to settle..." Then, "Here – Tom! What have you done with my brooch?"

"*Your brooch* is it now? Whoa – what did you...you put something in my drink, you little grub!"

"What if I did? I could read on your face what you was planning, Tom Hustings. Thief."

And then there was shouting, and several crashes, and loud bangs, as if heavy items of furniture were being overturned...

...then silence.

Liza said, "Quickly now. Let's get you out of here."

"But the door's locked." He looked at her. "Is there something you can do?"

"Me? I don't have any magics will get you out of a locked room, boy."

Bod crouched, and peered out through the keyhole. It was blocked; the key sat in the keyhole. Bod thought, then he smiled, momentarily, and it lit his face like the flash of a lightbulb. He pulled a crumpled sheet of newspaper from a packing case, flattened it out as best he could, then pushed it underneath the door, leaving only a corner on his side of the doorway.

"What are you playing at?" asked Liza, impatiently.

"I need something like a pencil. Only thinner..." he said. "Here we go." And he took a thin paintbrush from the top of the desk, and pushed the brushless end into the lock, jiggled it and pushed some more.

There was a muffled clunk as the key was pushed out, as it dropped from the lock onto the newspaper. Bod pulled the paper back under the door, now with the key sitting on it.

Liza laughed, delighted. "That's wit, young man," she said. "That's wisdom."

Bod put the key in the lock, turned it, and pushed open the storeroom door.

There were two men on the floor, in the middle of the crowded antique shop. Furniture had indeed fallen; the place was a chaos of wrecked clocks and chairs, and in the midst of it the bulk of Tom Hustings lay, fallen on the smaller figure of Abanazer Bolger. Neither of them was moving.

"Are they dead?" asked Bod.

"No such luck," said Liza.

On the floor beside the men was a brooch of glittering silver; a crimson-orange-banded stone, held in place with claws and with snake-heads, and the expression on the snake-heads was one of triumph and avarice and satisfaction.

Bod dropped the brooch into his pocket, where it sat beside the heavy glass paperweight, the paintbrush, and the little pot of paint.

Lightning illuminated the cobbled street.

Bod hurried through the rain through the old town, always heading up the hill toward the graveyard. The grey day had become an early night while he was inside the storeroom, and it came as no surprise to him when a familiar shadow swirled beneath the street lamps. Bod hesitated, and a flutter of night-black velvet resolved itself into a man-shape.

Silas stood in front of him, arms folded. He strode forward, impatiently.

"Well?" he said.

Bod said, "I'm sorry, Silas."

"I'm disappointed in you, Bod." Silas said, and he shook his head. "I've been looking for you since I woke. You have the smell of trouble all around you. And you know you're not allowed to go out here, into the living world."

"I know. I'm sorry." There was rain on the boy's face, running down like tears.

"First of all, we need to get you back to safety." Silas reached down, and enfolded the living child inside his cloak, and Bod felt the ground fall away beneath him.

"Silas," he said.

Silas did not answer.

"I was a bit scared," he said. "But I knew you'd come and get me if it got too bad. And Liza was there. She helped a lot."

"Liza?" Silas's voice was sharp.

"The witch. From the Potter's Field."

"And you say she helped you?"

"Yes. She especially helped me with my Fading. I think I can do it now."

Silas grunted. "You can tell me all about it when we're home." And Bod was quiet until they landed beside the church. They went inside, into the empty hall, as the rain redoubled, splashing up from the puddles that covered the ground.

"Tell me everything," he said.

Bod told him everything he could remember about the day. And at the end, Silas shook his head, slowly, thoughtfully.

"Am I in trouble?" asked Bod.

"Nobody Owens," said Silas. "You are indeed in trouble. However, I believe I shall leave it to your foster-parents to administer whatever discipline and reproach they believe to be needed."

And then, in the manner of his kind, Silas was gone.

Bod pulled the jacket up over his head, and clambered up the slippery paths to the top of the hill, to the Frobisher vault, and then he went down, and down, and still further down.

He dropped the brooch beside the goblet and the knife.

"Here you go," he said. "All polished up. Looking pretty."

IT COMES BACK, said the Sleer, with satisfaction in its smoke-tendril voice. IT ALWAYS COMES BACK.

The night had been long, but it was almost dawn.

Bod was walking, sleepily and a little gingerly, past the final resting place of Harrison Westwood, Baker of this Parish, and his wives Marion and Joan, to the Potter's Field. Mr. and Mrs. Owens had died several hundred years before it had been decided that beating children was wrong, and Mr. Owens had, regretfully, that night, done what he saw as his duty, and Bod's bottom stung like anything. Still, the look of worry on Mrs. Owens' face had hurt Bod worse than any beating could have done.

He reached the iron railings that bounded the Potter's Field, and slipped between them.

"Hullo?" he called. There was no answer. Not even an extra shadow in the hawthorn bush. "I hope I didn't get you into trouble, too," he said.

Nothing.

He had replaced the jeans in the gardener's hut – he was more comfortable in just his grey winding sheet – but he had kept the jacket. He liked having the pockets.

When he had gone to the shed to return the jeans, he had taken a small hand-scythe from the wall where it hung, and with it he attacked the nettle-patch in the Potter's Field, sending the nettles flying, slashing and gutting them till there was nothing but stinging stubble on the ground.

From his pocket he took the large glass paperweight, its insides a multitude of bright colours, along with the paintpot, and the paintbrush.

He dipped the brush into the paint and carefully painted, in brown paint, on the surface of the paperweight, the letters

E H

and beneath them he wrote

we don't forget

It was almost daylight. Bedtime, soon, and it would not be wise for him to be late to bed for some time to come.

He put the paperweight down on the ground that had once been a nettle patch, placed it in the place that he estimated her head would have been, and, pausing only to look at his handiwork for a moment, he went through the railings and made his way, rather less gingerly, back up the hill.

"Not bad," said a pert voice from the Potter's Field, behind him. "Not bad at all."

But when he turned to look, there was nobody there.

The Ruby Incomparable

Kage Baker

Kage Baker (*kagebaker.com*) lives in Pismo Beach, California, in what she describes as "a charming seaside cottage." She grew up in Hollywood, California, as one of six children, and attended parochial school, which she says left her with a good education and "numerous emotional scars." She is best known for her very dark and romantic Company stories and novels about a CIA-like organization staffed by immortals who travel in time, preserving (or stealing) lost treasures and organizing things to its liking and benefit. The main story arc was completed in 2007 in *The Sons of Heaven*. In addition to publishing thirteen or so books and many short stories, she has held the usual writerly assortment of odd, creatively oriented jobs.

"The Ruby Incomparable," another story from *Wizards*, is a *Bildungsroman* about a promising young female wizard with a formidable mother. Her fantasy novel, *The Anvil of the World*, and another set in the same fantasy world, *The House of the Stag*, forthcoming in 2008, follow the lives and exploits of some of the family members, the brother and father of the central character of this story.

THE GIRL surprised everyone.

To begin with, no one in the world below had thought her parents would have more children. Her parents' marriage had created quite a scandal, a profound clash of philosophical extremes; for her father was the Master of the Mountain, a brigand and sorcerer, who had carried the Saint of the World off to his high fortress. It's bad enough when a living goddess, who can heal the sick and raise the dead, takes up with a professional dark lord (black armor, monstrous armies and all). But when they settle down together with every intention of raising a family, what are respectable people to think?

The Yendri in their forest villages groaned when they learned of the first boy. Even in his cradle, his fiendish tendencies were evident. He was beautiful as a little angel except in his screaming tempers, when he would morph himself into giant larvae, wolf cubs, or pools of bubbling slime.

The Yendri in their villages and the Children of the Sun in their stone cities all rejoiced when they heard of the second boy. He too was beautiful, but clearly good. A star was seen to shine from his brow on occasion. He was reported to have cured a nurse's toothache with a mere touch, and he never so much as cried while teething.

And the shamans of the Yendri, and the priests in the temples of the Children of the Sun, all nodded their heads and said: "Well, at least we have balance now. The two boys will obviously grow up, oppose each other, and fight to the death, because that's what generally happens."

Having decided all this, and settled down confidently to wait, imagine how shocked they were to hear that the Saint of the World had borne a third child! And a girl, at that. It threw all their calculations off and annoyed them a great deal.

The Master and his Lady were surprised, too, because their baby daughter popped into the world homely as a little potato, by contrast with the elfin beauty of her brothers. They did agree that she had lovely eyes, at least, dark as her father's, and she seemed to be sweet-tempered. They named her Svnae.

So the Master of the Mountain swaddled her in purple silk, and took her out on a high balcony and held her up before his assembled troops, who roared, grunted, and howled their polite approval. And that night in the barracks and servants' hall, around the barrels of black wine that had been served out in celebration, the minions of the proud father agreed amongst themselves that the little maid might not turn out so ugly as all that, if the rest of her face grew to fit that nose and she didn't stay quite so bald.

And they at least were proved correct, for within a year Svnae had become a lovely child.

On the morning of her fifth birthday, the Master went to the nursery and fetched his little daughter. He took her out with him on his tour of the battlements, where all the world stretched away below. The guards, tusked and fanged, great and horrible in their armor, stood to attention and saluted him. Solemnly, he pulled a great red rose from thin air and presented it to Svnae.

"Today," he said, "my Dark-Eyed is five years old. What do you want most in all the world, daughter?"

Svnae looked up at him with her shining eyes. Very clearly she said:

"Power."

He looked down at her, astounded; but she stood there looking patiently back at him, clutching her red rose. He knelt beside her. "Do you know what Power is?" he asked.

"Yes," she said. "Power is when you stand up here and make all the clouds come to you across the sky, and shoot lightning and make thunder crash. That's what I want."

"I can make magic for you," he said, and with a wave of his gauntleted hand produced three tiny fire elementals dressed in scarlet, blue, and yellow, who danced enchantingly for Svnae before vanishing in a puff of smoke.

"Thank you, Daddy," she said, "but no. I want *me* to be able to do it."

Slowly he nodded his head. "Power you were born with; you're my child. But you must learn to use it, and that doesn't come easily, or quickly. Are you sure this is what you really want?"

"Yes," she said without hesitation.

"Not eldritch toys to play with? Not beautiful clothes? Not sweets?"

"If I learn Power, I can have all those things anyway," Svnae observed.

The Master was pleased with her answer. "Then you will learn to use your Power," he said. "What would you like to do first?"

"I want to learn to fly," she said. "Not like my brother Eyrdway. He just turns into birds. I want to stay me and fly."

"Watch my hands," her father said. In his right hand, he held out a stone; in his left, a paper dart. He put them both over the parapet and let go. The stone dropped; the paper dart drifted lazily down.

"Now, tell me," he said. "Why did the stone drop and the paper fly?"

"Because the stone is heavy and the paper isn't," she said.

"Nearly so; and not so. Look." And he pulled from the air an egg. He held it out in his palm, and the egg cracked. A tiny thing crawled from it, and lay shivering there a moment; white down covered it like dandelion fluff, and it drew itself upright and shook tiny stubby wings. The down transformed to shining feathers, and the young bird beat its wide wings and flew off rejoicing.

"Now, tell me," said the Master, "was that magic?"

"No," said Svnae. "That's just what happens with birds."

"Nearly so; and not so. Look." And he took out another stone. He held it up and uttered a Word of Power; the stone sprouted bright wings, and improbably flew away into the morning.

"How did you make it do that?" Svnae cried. Her father smiled at her.

"With Power; but Power is not enough. I was able to transform the stone because I understand that the bird and the stone, and even the paper dart, are all the same thing."

"But they're not," said Svnae.

"Aren't they?" said her father. "When you understand that the stone and the bird are one, the next step is convincing the *stone* that the bird and the stone are one. And then the stone can fly."

Svnae bit her lip. "This is hard, isn't it?" she said.

"Very," said the Master of the Mountain. "Are you sure you wouldn't like a set of paints instead?"

"Yes," said Svnae stubbornly. "I *will* understand."

"Then I'll give you books to study," he promised. He picked her up and folded her close, in his dark cloak. He carried her to the bower of her lady mother, the Saint of the World.

Now when the Lady had agreed to marry her dread Lord, she had won from him the concession of making a garden on his black basalt mountaintop, high and secret in the sunlit air. Ten years into their marriage, her orchards were a mass of white blossom, and her white-robed disciples tended green beds of herbs there. They bowed gracefully as Svnae ran to her mother, who embraced her child and gave her a white rose. And Svnae said proudly:

"I'm going to learn Power, Mama!"

The Lady looked questions at her Lord.

"It's what she wants," he said, no less proudly. "And if she has the talent, why shouldn't she learn?"

"But Power is not an end in itself, my child," the Lady said to her daughter. "To what purpose will you use it? Will you help others?"

"Ye-es," said Svnae, looking down at her feet. "But I have to learn first."

"Wouldn't you like to be a healer, like me?"

"I can heal people when I have Power," said Svnae confidently. Her mother looked a little sadly into her dark eyes, but saw no shadow there. So she blessed her daughter, and sent her off to play.

The Master of the Mountain kept his promise and gave his daughter books to study, to help her decipher the Three Riddles of Flight. She had to learn to read first; with fiery determination she hurled herself on her letters and mastered them, and charged into the first of the Arcane texts.

So well she studied that by her sixth birthday she had solved all three riddles, and was able at will to sprout little butterfly wings from her shoulders, wings as red as a rose. She couldn't fly much with them, only fluttering a few inches above the ground like a baby bird; but she was only six. One day she would soar.

Then it was the Speech of Animals she wanted to learn. Then it was how to move objects without touching them. Then she desired to know the names of all the stars in the sky: not only what men call them, but what they call themselves. And one interest led to another, as endlessly she found new things by which to be intrigued, new arts and sciences she wanted to learn. She spent whole days together in her father's library, and carried books back to her room, and sat up reading far into the night.

In this manner she learned to fly up to the clouds with her rose-red wings, there to ask an eagle what it had for breakfast, or gather pearls with her own hands from the bottom of the sea.

And so the years flowed by, as the Master throve on his mountain, and the Saint of the World brought more children into it to confound the expectations of priests and philosophers, who debated endlessly the question of whether these children were Good or Evil.

The Saint held privately that all her children were, at heart, Good. The Master of the Mountain held, privately and out loud too, that the priests and philosophers were all a bunch of idiots.

Svnae grew tall, with proud dark good looks she had from her father. But there were no black lightnings in her eyes, as there were in his. Neither were her eyes crystal and serene, like her mother's, but all afire with interest, eager to see how everything worked.

And then she grew taller still, until she overtopped her mother; and still taller than that, until she overtopped her brother Eyrdway. He was rather peevish about it and took to calling her The Giantess, until she punched him hard enough to knock out one of his teeth. He merely morphed into a version of himself without the missing tooth, but he stopped teasing her after that.

Now you might suppose that many a young guard might begin pining for Svnae, and saluting smartly as she passed by, and mourning under her window at night. You would be right. But she never noticed; she was too engrossed in her studies to hear serenades sung under her window. Still, they did not go to waste; her younger sisters could hear them perfectly well, and they noticed things like snappy salutes.

This was not to say that Svnae did not glory in being a woman. As soon as she was old enough, she chose her own gowns and jewelry. Her mother presented her with gauzes delicate as cobweb, in exquisite shades of lavender, sea mist, and bird-egg-blue; fine-worked silver ornaments as well, set with white diamonds that glinted like starlight.

Alas, Svnae's tastes ran to crimson and purple and cloth of gold, even though the Saint of the World explained how well white set off her dusk skin. And though she thanked her mother for the fragile silver bangles, and dutifully wore them at family parties, she cherished massy gold set with emeralds and rubies. The more finery the better, in fact, though her mother gently indicated that perhaps it wasn't quite in the best of taste to wear the serpent bracelets with eyes of topaz and the peacock necklace of turquoise, jade, and lapis lazuli.

And though Svnae read voraciously and mastered the arts of Transmutation of Metals, Divination by Bones, and Summoning Rivers by their Secret Names, she did not learn to weave nor to sew; nor did she learn the healing properties of herbs. Her mother waited patiently for Svnae to become interested in these things, but somehow the flashing beam of her eye never turned to them.

One afternoon the Master of the Mountain looked up from the great black desk whereat he worked, hearing the guards announce the approach of his eldest daughter. A moment later she strode into his presence, resplendent in robes of scarlet and peacock blue, and slippers of vermilion with especially pointy toes that curled up at the ends.

"Daughter," he said, rising to his feet.

"Daddy," she replied, "I've just been reading in the Seventh Pomegranate Scroll about a distillation of violets that can be employed to lure dragons. Can you show me how to make it?"

"I've never done much distillation, my child," said the Master of the Mountain. "That's more in your mother's line of work. I'm certain she'd be delighted to teach you. Why don't you ask her?"

"Oh," said Svnae, and flushed, and bit her lip, and stared at the floor. "I think she's busy with some seminar with her disciples. Meditation Techniques or something."

And though the Master of the Mountain had never had any use for his Lady wife's disciples, he spoke sternly. "Child, you know your mother has never ignored her own children for her followers."

"It's not that," said Svnae a little sullenly, twisting a lock of her raven hair. "Not at all. It's just that – well – we're bound to have an argument about it. She'll want to know what I want it for, for one thing, and she won't approve of my catching dragons, and she'll let me know it even if she doesn't say a word, she'll just look at me – "

"I know," said her dread father.

"As though it was a frivolous waste of time, when what I really ought to be doing is learning all her cures for fevers, which is all very well but I have other things I want to be learning first, and in any case *I'm not Mother*, I'm my *own* person, and she has to understand that!"

"I'm certain she does, my child."

"Yes." Svnae tossed her head back. "So. Well. This brings up something else I'd wanted to ask you. I think I ought to go down into the world to study."

"But – " said the Master of the Mountain.

"I've always wanted to, and it turns out there's a sort of secret school in a place called Konen Feyy-in-the-Trees, where anybody can go to learn distillations. I need to learn more!"

"Mm. But – " said the Master of the Mountain.

She got her way. Not with temper, tears, or foot-stamping, but she got her way. No more than a week later she took a bag, and her bow and quiver, and, climbing up on the parapet, she summoned her rose-red wings, that now swept from a yard above her dark head to her ankles. Spreading them on the wind, she soared aloft. Away she went like a queen of the air, to explore the world.

Her father and mother watched her go.

"Do you think she'll be safe?" said the Saint of the World.

"She'd better be," said the Master of the Mountain, looking over the edge and far down his mountain at the pair of ogre bodyguards who coursed like armored greyhounds, crashing through the trees, following desperately their young mistress while doing their best not to draw attention to themselves.

Svnae sailed off on the wind and discovered that, though her extraordinary heritage had given her many gifts, a sense of direction was not one of them. She cast about a long while, looking for any place that might be a city in the trees; at last she spotted a temple in a wooded valley, far below.

On landing, she discovered that the temple was deserted long since, and a great gray monster guarded it. She slew the creature with her arrows, and went in to see what it might have been guarding. On the altar was a golden box that shone with protective spells. But she had the magic to unlock those spells, and found within a book that seemed to be a history of the lost race whose temple this was. She carried it outside and spent the next few hours seated on a block of stone in the ruins, intent with her chin on her fist, reading.

Within the book, she read of a certain crystal ring, the possession of which would enable the wearer to understand the Speech of Water. The book directed her to a certain fountain an hour's flight south of the temple, and fortunately the temple had a compass rose mosaic set in the floor; so she flew south at once, just as her bodyguards came panting up to the temple at last, and they watched her go with language that was dreadful even for ogres.

Exactly an hour's flight south, Svnae spotted the fountain, rising from a ruined courtyard of checkered tile. Here she landed, and approached the fountain with caution; for there lurked within its bowl a scaled serpent of remarkable beauty and deadliest venom. She considered the jeweled serpent, undulating round and round within the bowl in a lazy sort of way. She considered the ring, a circle of clear crystal, hard to spot as it bobbed at the top of the fountain's jet, well beyond her reach even were she to risk the serpent. Backing away several paces, she drew an arrow and took aim. *Clink!*

Her arrow shuddered in the trunk of an oak thirty paces distant, with the ring still spinning on its shaft. Speedily she claimed it and put it on, and straightway she could understand the Speech of Water.

Whereupon the fountain told her of a matter so interesting that she had to learn more about it. Details, however, were only to be had from a little blue man who lived in dubious hills far to the west. So away she flew, to find him…

She had several other adventures and it was only by chance that, soaring one morning above the world, deep in conversation with a sea-eagle, she spotted what was clearly a city down below amongst great trees. To her inquiry, the sea-eagle replied that the city was Konen Feyy. She thanked it and descended through the bright morning, to a secluded grove where she could cast a glamour on herself and approach without attracting undue notice. Following unseen a league distant, her wheezing bodyguards threw themselves down and gave thanks to anyone who might be listening.

The Children of the Sun dwelt generally in cities all of stone, where scarcely a blade of grass grew nor even so much as a potted geranium, preferring instead rock gardens with obelisks and statuary. But in all races there are those who defy the norm, and so it was in Konen Feyy. Here a colony of artists and craftsmen had founded a city in the green wilderness, without even building a comfortingly high wall around themselves. Accordingly, a lot of them had died from poisoned arrows and animal attacks in the early years, but this only seemed to make them more determined to stay there.

They painted the local landscapes, they made pots of the local clay, and wove textiles from the local plant fibers; and they even figured out that if they cut down the local trees to make charmingly rustic wooden furniture, sooner or later there wouldn't be any trees. For the Children of the Sun, who were ordinarily remarkably dense about ecological matters, this was a real breakthrough.

And so the other peoples of the world ventured up to Konen Feyy. The forest-dwelling Yendri, the Saint's own people, opened little shops where were sold herbs, or freshwater pearls, or willow baskets, or fresh produce. Other folk came, too: solitary survivors of lesser-known races, obscure revenants, searching for a quiet place to set up shop. This was how the Night School came to exist.

Svnae, wandering down Konen Feyy's high street and staring around her, found the place at once. Though it looked like an ordinary perfumer's shop, there were certain signs on the wall above the door, visible only to those who were familiar with the arcane sciences. An extravagant green cursive explained the School's hours, where and how she might enroll, and where to find appropriate lodgings with other students.

In this last she was lucky, for it happened that there were three other daughters of magi who'd taken a place above a dollmaker's shop, and hadn't quite enough money between them to make the monthly rent, so they were looking for a fourth roommate, someone to be Earth to their Air, Fire, and Water. They were pleasant girls, though Svnae was somewhat taken aback to discover that she towered over them all three, and somewhat irritated to discover that they all held her mother in reverent awe.

"You're the daughter of the Saint of the World?" exclaimed Seela, whose father was Principal Thaumaturge for Mount Flame City. "What are you doing here, then? *She's* totally the best at distillations and essences. Everyone knows that! I'd give anything to learn from her."

Svnae was to hear this statement repeated, with only slight variations, over the next four years of her higher education. She learned not to mind, however; for her studies occupied half her attention, and the other half was all spent on discovering the strange new world in which she lived, where there were no bodyguards (of which she was aware, anyway) and only her height distinguished her from all the other young ladies she met.

It was tremendous fun. She chipped in money with her roommates to buy a couch for their sitting room, and the four of them pushed it up the steep flight of stairs with giggles and screams, though Svnae could have tucked it under one arm and carried it up herself with no effort. She dined with her roommates at the little fried-fish shop on the corner, where they had their particular booth in which they always sat, though Svnae found it rather cramped.

She listened sympathetically as first one and then another of her roommates fell in love with various handsome young seers and sorcerers, and she swept up after a number of riotous parties, and on one occasion broke a vase over the head of a young shapeshifter who, while nice enough when sober, turned into something fairly unpleasant when he became unwisely intoxicated. She had to throw him over her shoulder and pitch him down the stairs, and her roommates wept their thanks and all agreed they didn't know what they'd do without her.

But somehow Svnae never fell in love.

It wasn't because she had no suitors for her hand. There were several young gallants at the Night School, glittering with jewelry and strange habits, who sought to romance Svnae. One was an elemental fire-lord with burning hair; one was a lord of air with vast violet wings. One was a mer-lord, who had servants following him around with perfumed misting bottles to keep his skin from drying out.

But all of them made it pretty clear they desired to marry Svnae in order to forge dynastic unions with the Master of the Mountain. And Svnae had long since decided that love, real Love, was the only reason for getting involved in all the mess and distraction of romance. So she declined, gracefully, and the young lords sulked and found other wealthy girls to entreat.

Her course of study ended. The roommates all bid one another fond farewells and went their separate ways. Svnae returned home with a train of attendant spirits carrying presents for all her little nieces and nephews. But she did not stay long, for she had heard of a distant island where was written, in immense letters on cliffs of silver, the formula for reversing Time in small and manageable fields, and she desired to learn it...

"Svnae's turned out rather well," said the Master of the Mountain, as he retired one night. "I could wish she spent a little more time at home, all the same. I'd have thought she'd have married and settled down by now, like the boys."

"She's restless," said the Saint of the World, as she combed out her hair.

"Well, why should she be? A first-rate sorceress with a double degree? The Ruby Incomparable, they call her. What more does she want?"

"She doesn't know, yet," said the Saint of the World, and blew out the light. "But she'll know when she finds it."

And Svnae had many adventures.

But one day, following up an obscure reference in an ancient grimoire, it chanced that she desired to watch a storm in its rage over the wide ocean, and listen to the wrath of all the waters. Out she flew upon a black night in the late year, when small craft huddled at their moorings, and found what she sought.

There had never in all the world been such a storm. The white foam was beaten into air, the white air was charged with water, the shrieking white gulls wheeled and screamed across the black sky, and the waves were as valleys and mountains.

Svnae floated in a bubble of her own devising, protected, watching it all with interest. Suddenly, far below in a trough of water, she saw a tiny figure clinging to a scrap of wood. The trough became a wall of water that rose up, towering high, until into her very eyes stared the drowning man. In his astonishment, he let go the shattered mast that supported him, and sank out of sight like a stone.

She cried out and dove from her bubble into the wave. Down she went, through water like dark glass, and caught him by the hand; up she went, towing him with her, and got him into the air and wrapped her strong arms about him. She could not fly, not with wet wings in the storm, but she summoned sea-beasts to bear them to the nearest land.

This was merely an empty rock, white cliffs thrusting from the sea. By magic she raised a palace from the stones to shelter them, and she brought the man within. Here there was a roaring fire; here there was hot food and wine. She put him to rest all unconscious in a deep bed, and tended him with her own hands.

Days she watched and cared for him, until he was well enough to speak to her. By that time, he had her heart.

Now, he was not as handsome as a mage-lord, nor learned in any magic, nor born of ancient blood: he was only a toymaker from the cities of the Children of the Sun, named Kendach. But so long and anxiously had she watched his sleeping face that she saw it when she closed her eyes.

And of course when Kendach opened his, the first thing he saw was her face: and after that, it was love. How could it be otherwise?

They nested together, utterly content, until it occurred to them that their families might wonder where they were. So she took him home to meet her parents ("A *toymaker?*" hooted her brothers) and he took her home to meet his ("Very nice girl. A little tall, but nice," said his unsuspecting father. They chose not to enlighten him as to their in-laws).

They were married in a modest ceremony in Konen Feyy.

"I hope he's not going to have trouble with her brothers," fretted Kendach's father, that night in the innroom. "Did you see the way they glared? Particularly that good-looking one. It quite froze my blood."

"It's clear she gets her height from her father," said Kendach's mother, pouring tea for him. "*Very* distinguished businessman, as I understand it. Runs some kind of insurance firm. I do wonder why her mother wears that veil, though, don't you?"

Kendach opened a toyshop in Konen Feyy, where he made kites in the forms of insects, warships, and meteors. Svnae raised a modest palace among the trees, and they lived there in wedded bliss. And life was full for Svnae, with nothing else to be asked for.

And then...

One day she awoke and there was a grey stain on the face of the sun. She blinked and rubbed her eyes. It did not go away. It came and sat on top of her morning tea. It blotted the pages of the books she tried to read, and it lay like grime on her lover's face. She couldn't get rid of it, nor did she know from whence it had come.

Svnae took steps to find out. She went to a cabinet and got down a great black globe of crystal that shone and swam with deep fires. She went to a quiet place and stroked the globe until it glowed with electric crackling fires. At last these words floated up out of the depths:

YOUR MOTHER DOES NOT UNDERSTAND YOU

They rippled on the surface of the globe, pulsing softly. She stared at them and they did not change.

So she pulled on her cloak that was made of peacock feathers, and yoked up a team of griffins to a sky chariot (useful when your lover has no wings, and flies only kites), and flew off to visit her mother.

The Saint of the World sat alone in her garden, by a quiet pool of reflecting water. She wore a plain white robe. White lilies glowed with light on the surface of the water; distantly a bird sang. She meditated, her crystal eyes serene.

There was a flash of color on the water. She looked up to see her eldest daughter charging across the sky. The griffin-chariot thundered to a landing nearby and Svnae dismounted, pulling her vivid cloak about her. She went straight to her mother and knelt.

"Mother, I need to talk to you," she said. "Is it true that you don't understand me?"

The Saint of the World thought it over.

"Yes, it's true," she said at last. "I don't understand you. I'm sorry, dearest. Does it make a difference?"

"Have I disappointed you, Mother?" asked Svnae in distress.

The Lady thought very carefully about that one.

"No," she said finally. "I would have liked a daughter to be interested in the healing arts. It just seems like the sort of thing a mother ought to pass on to her daughter. But your brother Demaledon has been all I could have asked for in a pupil, and there all my disciples. And why should your life be a reprise of mine?"

"None of the other girls became healers," said Svnae just a little petulantly.

"Quite true. They've followed their own paths: lovers and husbands and babies, gardens and dances."

"I have a husband too, you know," said Svnae.

"My child, my Dark-Eyed, I rejoice in your happiness. Isn't that enough?"

"But I want you to *understand* my life," cried Svnae.

"Do you understand mine?" asked the Saint of the World.

"Your life? Of course I do!"

Her mother looked at her, wryly amused.

"I have borne your father fourteen children. I have watched him march away to do terrible things, and I have bound up his wounds when he returned from doing them. I have managed the affairs of a household with over a thousand servants, most of them ogres. I have also kept up correspondence with my poor disciples, who are trying to carry on my work in my absence. What would you know of these things?"

Svnae was silent at that.

"You have always hunted for treasures, my dearest, and thrown open every door you saw, to know what lay beyond it," said the Saint of the World gently. "But there are still doors you have not opened. We can love each other, you and I, but how can we understand each other?"

"There must be a way," said Svnae.

"Now you look so much like your father you make me laugh and cry at once. Don't let it trouble you, my Dark-Eyed; you are strong and happy and good, and I rejoice."

But Svnae went home that night to the room where Kendach sat, painting bright and intricate birds on kites. She took a chair opposite and stared at him.

"I want to have a child," she said.

He looked up, blinking in surprise. As her words sank in on him, he smiled and held out his arms to her.

Did she have a child? How else, when she had accomplished everything else she wanted to do?

A little girl came into the world. She was strong and healthy. She looked like her father, she looked like her mother; but mostly she looked like herself, and she surprised everyone.

Her father had been one of many children, so there were fewer surprises for him. He knew how to bathe a baby, and could wrestle small squirming arms into sleeves like an expert.

Svnae, who had grown up in a nursery staffed by a dozen servants, proved to be rather inept at these things. She was shaken by her helplessness, and shaken by the helpless love she felt. Prior to this time she had found infants rather uninteresting, little blobs in swaddling to be briefly inspected and presented with silver cups that had their names and a good-fortune spell engraved on them.

But *her* infant – ! She could lie for hours watching her child do no more than sleep, marveling at the tiny toothless yawn, the slow close of a little hand.

When the baby was old enough to travel, they wrapped her in a robe trimmed with pearls and took her to visit her maternal grandparents, laden with the usual gifts. Her lover went off to demonstrate the workings of his marvelous kites to her nieces and nephews. And Svnae bore her daughter to the Saint of the World in triumph.

"*Now* I've done something you understand," she said. The Saint of the World took up her little granddaughter and kissed her between the eyes.

"I hope that wasn't the only reason you bore her," she said.

"Well – no, of course not," Svnae protested, blushing. "I wanted to find out what motherhood was like."

"And what do you think it is like, my child?"

"It's awesome. It's holy. My entire life has been redefined by her existence," said Svnae fervently.

"Ah, yes," said the Saint of the World.

"I mean, this is creation at its roots. This is Power! I have brought an entirely new being into the world. A little mind that thinks! I can't wait to see what she thinks *about*, how she feels about things, what she'll say and do. What's ordinary magic to this?"

The baby began to fuss and the Lady rose to walk with her through the garden. Svnae followed close, groping for words.

"There's so much I can teach her, so much I can give her, so much I can share with her. Her first simple spells. Her first flight. Her first transformation. I'll teach her everything I know. We've got that house in Konen Feyy, and it'll be so convenient for Night School! She won't even have to find room and board. She can use all my old textbooks..."

But the baby kept crying, stretching out her little hands.

"Something she wants already," said the Lady. She picked a white flower and offered it to the child; but no, the little girl pointed beyond it. Svnae held out a crystal pendant, glittering with power, throwing dancing lights; but the baby cried and reached upward. They looked up to see one of her father's kites, dancing merry and foolish on the wind.

The two women stood staring at it. They looked at the little girl. They looked at each other.

"Perhaps you shouldn't enroll her in Night School just yet," said the Saint of the World.

And Svnae realized, with dawning horror, that she might need to ask her mother for advice.

And Such Small Deer

Chris Roberson

Chris Roberson (*chrisroberson.net*) lives in Austin, Texas, and with his wife Allison Baker runs the small press MonkeyBrain Books. He is an up-and-coming writer of fantasy and science fiction and has so frequently been praised as a writer to watch that he remarks, "With all of these recommendations that people should watch me, I get the feeling I can't be trusted."

"And Such Small Deer" was published in George Mann's fine anthology *The Solaris Book of New Fantasy*. It features a character with the familiar name of Van Helsing, is set in nineteenth-century Sumatra, and seems to have been inspired by an intriguing passage in Sir Arthur Conan Doyle's "The Adventure of the Sussex Vampire."

"Matilda Briggs was not the name of a young woman, Watson," said Holmes in a reminiscent voice. "It was a ship which is associated with the giant rat of Sumatra, a story for which the world is not yet prepared. But what do we know about vampires?"

So here it is, the untold story for which the world was not prepared.

Letter to Frédéric Lerne, student, c/o University of Paris, Sorbonne, July 15, 1860
Monsieur Lerne, I am writing in regards to your recent correspondence on the inheritance of characteristics from one generation to another. I would like to thank you for your kind and insightful words, and I only wish that my recently published paper had been as well received here at home in England. Sadly, it was not, and I am forced temporarily to look beyond the arena of pure research for employment. Luckily, I have received an offer to practice medicine in the Dutch East Indies, and have only this past week accepted. *Bidui luminosua praecursionis*, in my bad, schoolboy Latin. Brighter days ahead!

– F.A.M.

Abraham Van Helsing's Journal
(translated from the Dutch)

1 Mar., 1861. Belawan – After a journey of several days from the northern coast of Borneo, past Singapore and through the Strait of Malacca, I arrived at the newly built port of Belawan, in the North Sumatran province of Deli. The region has only recently come under the colonial jurisdiction of my countrymen, so I had hoped to find some relative comfort in my brief stay here. The ship that makes the regular circuit between the Dutch East Indies and India, though, is not due to arrive for another week, and I am finding conditions less hospitable than I might have expected. I wonder now whether I might have been better off waiting in Sarawak for the next ship to England, but to do so would have meant another week in the company of the mad Raja Brooke, and any deprivation is better than that.

Carrying my small amount of luggage with me, nothing more than a valise and a small case, I left the rough docks behind and tried to find an inn in the town. To my disappointment, I found very little of note in the whole of Belawan. The buildings all look as though they've been constructed in the last year; some of them bare wood without stain, paint or varnish, while the roads are newly made tracks of dirt running between. Besides a small port authority building and a warehouse for the storage of goods being sent and received by the dock, the only other structure of note in all of Belawan is a store of sorts. Not very imposing, but needs must when the devil drives.

I entered the store, hoping to find direction to accommodations, and perhaps a bite to eat. The store was ramshackle, bare wooden floors and walls, and roughly hewn shelves piled high with haphazard goods, alcohol, cigars, salt, sugar, some items of clothing, sweets, and the like. Behind the counter was an ancient native man, while in a back corner, a European man in shirtsleeves rolled to his elbows was knelt down, bandaging the foot of a native man beside a broken crate.

Before I'd had the chance to address the man behind the counter, my eyes fell on a package of Dutch chocolates perched on a high shelf. My mouth began immediately to salivate. I'd not seen any confections of that brand since I'd left Amsterdam early the year before, and the mere sight of them caught me in a brief wave of nostalgia. I remembered sharing them with my late wife early in our courtship, or seeing my young son eating them messily on a birthday outing. Whatever the price, I knew I would be willing to pay to recapture those moments, if only for a fleeting instant.

As this is a Dutch colony, I hoped that the few bits of coin from home still rattling in the far reaches of my valise might be considered legal tender in the local economy.

"What is the price?" I asked of the native man behind the counter, motioning to the chocolates on the shelf above his head.

"Fifteen," the man said simply, through tight lips, his face a perpetual scowl.

I scratched my chin.

"Fifteen what, if you don't mind?" I asked.

The ancient man didn't speak, just pointed a calloused finger at a sheet of paper lacquered to the countertop. On it was written, like some Rosetta stone in miniature, a block of text repeated in several languages, one of them my native Dutch. It was a simple statement, informing the reader that this store was only for employees of the Netherlands–Sumatra Company, and that the store didn't accept any currency besides company scrip.

My gaze lingering on the chocolates, I pressed on with business.

"In that case," I asked, "can you tell me if there is an inn in the near vicinity?"

The ancient man looked at me blankly.

"A place where one might hire a room?"

The ancient man took a deep breath through his wide nostrils and shook his head once, side to side.

"No," he said simply.

"Well," I went on, undeterred, "can you tell me if there is a carriage to the nearest town that *does* have an inn?"

Again the long pause, the deep intake of breath, and the single shake of the head.

"No."

I was growing exasperated, not sure whether the native man failed to understand my Dutch and was only shamming responses, or understood and just wished to be unhelpful, but before I could say another word a third party joined the stunted conversation.

The European man who'd been bandaging the native's foot at the rear of the store had looked up on first hearing the discussion between me and the man behind the counter, and finishing his ministrations came forward into the light. He was a powerfully built man in his mid-thirties, with a fine forehead and rather heavy features, with a full, heavy mouth turned down at the corners, giving him an expression of pugnacious resolution. He was well muscled, standing a good six feet in height, with an unkempt mess of dark hair sticking out above his ears, hanging down just below his collar at his neck.

"Van Helsing?" he said, looking at my face intently. Speaking English with a British accent, he added, "Is that you?"

I was startled to be recognized, to say the very least. I had no notion who the man might be. I found in the misty reaches of my memory a dim recollection of the man's face, but nothing else.

"Yes," I said warily. "And whom do I have the pleasure of addressing?"

The man brightened immediately, and came forward, arms outstretched. "Abraham, surely you remember your old friend! Have so many days passed since we haunted the halls of Oxford?"

The man seemed overjoyed at our unexpected reunion. For my part, I could barely remember ever having known the man, much less his name. I had vague memories of a lanky, obsessed creature, who was always at the rear of the surgical amphitheater, always asking the strangest questions.

What was his name again? I thought to myself. *Something with an "F" sound...*

I began to form the initial consonant in my mouth, the first hiss of air escaping between my teeth, and the tall man rushed to complete the work for me.

"Francis!" the man said, pounding his chest with a heavy fist and then taking me in his arms in an embrace not at all characteristic of the English. "I knew you'd not have forgotten your bosom chum Francis, even after the years and miles, old Abe."

"I sometimes think the past is different country," I said, trying to extract myself from his embrace as diplomatically as possible.

"And besides, the wench is dead," the man called Francis answered, leering. "Ah, Abe, remember our days together, studying anatomy and chemistry, dreaming our grand dreams of the future. I had hopes to add a new star to the firmament, my name included in the list of luminaries in the sciences." He breathed a sentimental sigh, but continued before I could respond. "Sadly, I've had to leave the field of pure research behind for the moment, and instead earn a crust of bread in the practice of medicine. I've come to the east to find work, but find that there is little intellectual stimulation to be had, so little, indeed, that I have had to make my own diversions. Still, I'm eager for a receptive audience for my discussions, since so often here my talks fall on deaf ears."

I explained that I, too, had come to the Orient for employment, but found it not to my liking, and am currently in the process of returning home to Europe.

Francis, which is all he is to me still, as I cannot recollect his surname, continued on, talking in an animated fashion, as though we were just rejoining a conversation left dangling the night before, rather than more than a decade since. I have only vague memories of Francis from school, and can't call to mind a single discussion or meal we shared. But as he went on and on, I came to realize that the moment had passed when I could admit to forgetting his name. He remembers me, and assumes I remember him. I have no choice but to continue under the pretense that we are old friends reunited and hope that someone utters his full name in my hearing before too long a span has passed.

"In any event," Francis said, "I'm employed at a nearby plantation, and you simply must come and be my guest."

"Oh, well," I said, playing for time and trying to devise a suitable alternative, "I am of course grateful for the offer, but I don't want to be any bother. If you can just direct me to the nearest inn, I'll be out of your hair."

Francis shook with a braying laughter and clapped me hard on the shoulder with one of his massive hands. He explained that the nearest inn is in Medan, the capital city, fourteen miles away, but that there is no regular carriage service along that route. My only real option was to come with Francis back to the plantation.

Having no choice, I accompanied Francis back to the rustic plantation house, and he showed me to the guest quarters. I've unpacked my valise, and settled in as best as I can. The accommodations are somewhat rough, little more than a rickety chair, a low desk, a hard and narrow bed covered in a thin sheet, and a jug and bowl for washing up. I've heard about the wealth of the Dutch plantations in Java, but these are early days for the expansion of such cultivation into the northern regions of Sumatra, and such successes appear not yet to have followed.

I am invited to dine this evening with the plantation's staff. I hope, at least, to hear at least one Dutch voice among them. I have been in the company of foreigners and mad Englishmen for too long, and could do with some familiar tones.

Letter to Frédéric Lerne, student, c/o University of Paris, Sorbonne, August 30, 1860

I've only just arrived in the Dutch East Indies, and have been installed as staff physician at the Netherlands–Sumatra Company's tobacco plantation in Northern Sumatra. The plantation was only started early this year, and is roughly halfway up the road to Medan, capital of the province of Deli. To call it a capital, though, is to slight capitals everywhere. It is a dusty village of a few hundred souls, and nothing more besides. The job is a meager one, but I suppose I am lucky to have it, as it was only family connections that brought me this far. I have a French cousin on my father's side of the family who is in the region working as an overseer for the plantation, which is owned by a Dutch consortium. My cousin is penniless, but styles himself the "Baron de Maupertuis," laying claim to a hereditary title that held no cachet even before the storming of the Bastille, much less after the rousing cries of "*liberté, egalité, et fraternité*" from the proletariat.

My cousin invited me to the plantation to act as physician on the staff. As I believe I mentioned in an earlier missive, I have had some difficulty in the London scientific community following the recent publication of my paper, with certain intractable elements of the medical establishment objecting to my arguments on the proper uses of science and medicine. As a result, I was grateful for the opportunity of gainful employment, and especially grateful that I will have the time and space here to continue my researches unmolested.

– F.A.M.

Abraham Van Helsing's Journal

1 Mar. Later – Since I hoped to hear at least one Dutch voice among the plantation staff, I suppose I should count myself lucky. But Dame Fortune is not overly generous, as there is only one of my countrymen among all those employed here, the balance of them being Frenchmen and more mad Englishmen.

In the drawing room, before the evening meal, Francis introduced me to his cousin, the supervisor of the plantation, the self-styled Baron de Maupertuis. With him was the sole Dutchman of the crew, the accountant, Kasper de Vries, and the accountant's clerk, an Englishman in his early twenties introduced to me only as Culverton, though whether this is his given or surname, I cannot say.

The baron is a large man with a barrel chest, and a somewhat smug, self-important look plastered to his crude features. De Vries is the perfect model of the accountant, thin, wan, with long and precise fingers that seem always to be in motion; behind thick glasses, his liquid eyes seem to take inventory of his surrounding at every moment, calculating values and risks. Culverton, the young man, is small and frail, his shoulders and back twisted like someone who had suffered from rickets in childhood, with an oversized head perched on his uneven shoulders, thin blond hair already beginning to thin.

They were a strange lot, the baron as loud and boisterous in his way as his cousin Francis was in his; de Vries quiet and calculating; Culverton timid and retiring. Dinner was served, a simple but passable fare, and the subject of the discussion turned to fortunes of the plantation, such as they were, and better days ahead. This entire region has only recently fallen to Dutch control, and as always the businessmen waste little time in exploiting the region's usefulness. That the Dutch foreign offices were so overtaxed as to hire a threadbare Frenchman with a valueless title as overseer only serves as evidence of the strain the rapid colonial expansion is having on the infrastructure.

During the dessert course, Culverton mentioned rumors he'd heard from one of the household servants. The plantation workers, so the rumor went, were nervous. In the fields by day and in their tarpaper shacks by night, they talk of a foul spirit that haunts the area, preying on the flesh of men. It is supposedly some ancient Sumatran spirit, servitor of the ancient Batak kings, that finds the presence of the Dutch colonial masters to be offensive. The baron joked that if that were true, then they'd have only to feed the spirit de Vries and me, and the rest could work in peace. The laughter, what little laughter followed, was thin and anemic.

Abraham Van Helsing's Journal

2 *Mar.* – This morning I dined again with the plantation staff, and Francis (whose surname no one last night had the courtesy to utter) invited me to come visit his facilities. He explained that the building had been intended for use as a surgery, but that he had devoted a small portion of the space to his researches, continuing the work begun back in England.

I wished I had some suitable excuse, some alternative to a day in this virtual stranger's company, but I could not help but feel gratitude to the man for taking me in off the streets, and so reluctantly I agreed.

On our exit, the baron called after me, his manner blustery.

"*Au revoir,*" he said with a raucous laugh. "Enjoy the House of Pain."

Once we were outside and on our way to the surgical facilities, I asked Francis what his cousin had meant. His expression distracted, he waved a hand as though to dismiss the matter entirely.

"Oh, it is just a name given by the plantation workers to my offices," he said. "They are a rude and unrefined segment of humanity, if ever there were."

We entered the rude building, little more than four walls and a sloped roof, with planks of wood laid directly on the hard-packed dirt for flooring. There was a long, narrow bench along one side, a desk and chair along the back, and an array of surgical equipment hanging from hooks on the walls. Oil lanterns hung from the rafters, which issued tongues of foul black smoke when Francis lit them one by one.

Francis made his way to the desk at the rear and returned holding a sheaf of papers under his arms.

"I've been doing some researches into the uses of blood transfusions, these past months," he explained, growing excited as a child on Christmas morning, "and on the inheritance of characteristics. As every educated man knows, Lamarck has been completely contravened, his notion that organisms pass attributes acquired in life to their offspring revealed for the unadulterated poppycock it patently is. But the rejection of a negative does not necessitate a positive, and we are left with the simple question: how *do* organisms pass inherited traits from one generation to the next?"

"So you're an adherent to Charles Darwin?" I asked, referring to the evolutionary theories published in England only two years ago, which caused some significant controversy among the scientific establishment.

"I agree in principle with Darwin, I suppose," Francis answered with a dismissive wave, "but he is only in essence restating the doctrine first put forth by my own famous forebear, Pierre Louis Moreau de Maupertuis, my grandsire several times removed, who anticipated the evolutionary theories of Darwin by more than a century. Why, in his *Système de la nature* he clearly stated – "

A commotion at the door saved me what promised to be a lengthy response to such a simple question, but my escape from the litany came at a heavy price.

A group of men were bustling through the door, carrying between them a wounded man, shrieking in agony. As they arranged their wounded comrade on the narrow bench along the wall, they explained to Francis what had happened in their broken English. The man had gone missing in the night, and when they went out to the tobacco fields in the morning, they found him, mauled by some enormous animal.

The man was in tremendous pain, and as Francis arranged his medical equipment, I stood at the man's head, his hand in mine, doing what I could to comfort him. Francis began to treat his wounds, deep gashes in his abdomen from which viscous, dark blood burbled.

"Relax," I told the man, in as comforting a tone as I could manage. Mustering my best bedside manner, I uttered soothing words, such as "You're in good hands" and "We'll put you to right," and further such imprecations of good will.

Francis, on hearing me, laughed.

"Oh, Abraham," you surprise me. "Surely you've come to realize that pain is needless, a residual instinct from man's more animalistic past, and should hold no sway over a rational man."

I was shocked.

"Have some pity, man," I said. "This poor devil is suffering."

"Ah," Francis answered, glancing up from his ministrations, "we are on different platforms. You are a materialist."

"I am not a materialist," I began hotly.

"In my view, in my view. For it is just this question of pain that parts us. So long as visible or audible pain turns you sick; so long as your own pains drive you; so long as pain underlies your propositions about sin – so long, I tell you, you are an animal, thinking a little less obscurely what an animal feels."

The man screamed, insensate in agony, but Francis remained obdurate, merely shrugging.

"You see," Francis said, "like the beasts of the field."

Without warning, the crying stopped. I laid a finger against the wounded man's wrist, felt the beating of his life fluttering away, and when it was still, tenderly lowered the man's arm onto the bench.

"You've one less beast to worry after, in that case," I told Francis, my face flushed red and my hands tightened into fists at my sides. "He is dead."

"Just like the others," Francis said, annoyed. He wiped his hands clean on a rag, and began to roll down his sleeves.

"Others?" I asked. "What others?"

"Oh," Francis answered, dismissively. "This is not the first, but the sixth to have died of similar wounds in the last week." He shook his head, his expression dark. "Damnably disruptive, I have to say. How I'm expected to get any work done under these conditions, I'm sure I don't know."

I had little patience for Francis at this stage, and while he returned to his notes and papers at his desk, I made my own postmortem examination of the man. My initial suspicions were that a tiger had gotten to him, based on the extent and savagery of the wounds, but on closer examination, I found that the bite marks were not consistent with a tiger attack. There were the impressions of incisors, but they were too closely spaced and shallow to be those of a cat; the majority of the injury resulted from incisors. The man looked more like he'd been gnawed.

Leaving Francis to his solitude, I made my slow way back to the main house and my guest room, rambling near the workers' quarters as I went. I've come to learn that the majority of the plantation's laborers are Chinese, with a mix of Javanese, coastal Malay, Tamils brought over from Ceylon, and native Bataks. They bring with them their religions and superstitions, their work huts by nature a latter-day Babel, but they all agree on one thing: something hunts the night, stalking them.

Letter to Frédéric Lerne, October 1, 1860

Frédéric, I was heartened to get your last letter. Your questions are very much in line with my own thinking of the moment. I have begun to suspect that there is in the blood or flesh of the body some element that governs the inheritance of characteristics from one generation to the next. If that be true, then it stands to reason that by transposing these miniscule elements from one body to another (supposing that we can overcome the problems attendant with the host body rejecting the introduction of the foreign material), then one might be able to introduce novel characteristics into the organism.

To be frank, I am lucky to find myself in Sumatra at this juncture, for one reason if no others, and that is down to the abundant variety of fauna ready to hand. There is an abundance of organisms for my experiments – birds, butterflies, buffaloes, deer, mouse deer, orang-utans, and rodents.

Yours, Francis

Abraham Van Helsing's Journal

2 Mar. Later – Tonight, in the drawing room after the evening meal, I asked whether the baron was going to intervene in the matter of the attacks, or else appeal to the colonial government for assistance.

"Well," the baron said, absently scratching his ample belly, thinking it through, "I have no desire to involve the Regent of Deli, squatting over in the capital city of Medan. He was only some months ago an independent sovereign, and still ill wears the yoke of the Dutch colonial government. You see? For that matter, I've no interest in attracting the attention of his 'advisor,' the Assistant Resident Max Havelaar."

The baron paused, taking a long draw on his cigar.

"Havelaar is entirely too soft on the natives," he went on, "and no doubt would arrive lobbying the Netherlands–Sumatra Company to reduce productivity by better treatment of the plantation workers, were we to invite him into our midst."

"Yes," de Vries offered, uncharacteristically forthcoming. "Havelaar is one of those who think that the plantations draw too heavily on the labor of their workers, such that their rice crops have materially diminished and famine has been the result. He was previously Assistant Resident in Java and was transferred after conflicts with the colonial authorities there."

"That said," the baron pointed out impatiently, interrupting de Vries as though he were a constant chatterbox, "a hunting party is not a bad idea. How about it?" He motioned to de Vries and Culverton, who sat by the side table. "Will you come along if I mount an expedition?"

"I cannot, sadly," de Vries answered without a hint of regret, "as I'm too busy with my tallies." He paused, and then added with some kindness, "However, Culverton, you may go along if you wish. Your duties this week are light enough that they won't suffer as a result of a few days' inattention."

"That's two, then," the baron said, thumping his chest and pointing his cigar at the young Englishman. "We'll need a doctor along, as well, in the event that someone is injured and needs medical attention. Francis, *ça va?*"

"Well, I suppose, but..." Francis began, then trailed off. His gaze shifted sheepishly around the room. "My researches are in a critical state at the moment, and I don't want to leave them unfinished."

The baron began to sit up straighter in his chair, his face flushing red.

"Francis," he said, his tone strained, "need I remind you that you are being paid to be our staff physician, and not a general researcher. Perhaps if I were to..."

"If I might," I said, holding up a hand apologetically and interrupting. "I'd be happy to take Francis' place on your hunting expedition, if you'd have me."

The baron looked from me, to his cousin, and back, his expression dark, but then relaxed by inches and settled back in his chair.

"Very well," he said. "So we'll be three. *Très bien.* We'll leave tomorrow."

And that, apparently, was an end to the discussion.

I am hardly excited about a few days' march through the jungle, much less with a timid Englishman and a blustering Frenchman, but in the face of another day spent in the company of this foul Francis, I will persevere.

Abraham Van Helsing's Journal

3 Mar. – This morning we set out, Baron de Maupertuis, Culverton, and myself, along with half a dozen plantation workers brought along as bearers. The jungle tracks and paths are too narrow for horses, and so we are traveling, as the baron puts it, *à pied*. I am reminded uncomfortably of my journey last month through the wilds of Borneo, lashed by wind and rain, stalked on all sides by fierce creatures. That this morning presented a truly Edenic scene, sunny and bright, the lush greens of the landscape brushed lightly with dew, did much to quell my nascent fears.

Previously, I had seen the tobacco fields only from a distance, but our course to the wilderness beyond took us right through them. As we passed through the rows of plants in their serried ranks, the baron explained that the tobacco grown here is used as cigar wrappers, rather than providing the meat of the cigar itself. The plants this week are in their first flush of growth for the season. The season will last for six months, and then after harvest the fields must be used to grow sugarcane for two and a half years, and then left fallow for two years beyond that. This, then, explains why so much of the land around the plantation is fallow.

At the borderland between the cultivated fields and the forests, we came upon strange tracks, the likes of which none of us had ever seen. They were as long as my foot, with phalanges that flared wider, so that the tracks were fanned out like a rake. The baron in the lead, we followed the tracks, on into the thick virgin forests and up among the low hills.

Near midday, we paused near a swift-moving river, just above a coruscating waterfall. Birds wheeled overhead, and a riot of butterflies drifted by like a kaleidoscopic cloud. On the far side of the river, a deer appeared, gently grazing, eying us with disinterested eyes black as midnight pits. I sat watching the deer in quiet contemplation, but Culverton jumped to his feet and raised his rifle, eager to shoot.

"*Un instant!*" the baron shouted, stepping forward and placing his hand on the barrel of the young man's rifle.

"Yes?" Culverton asked, confused and not a little startled.

"Do you want to be the one to swim to the far side and swim back against this current with the corpse of a deer on your back?"

Culverton shook his head, his expression sheepish.

"Besides," the baron went on, "the shot could frighten off better sport, the beast we are after. This is one instance, Englishman, where the proverbial birds in the bush may be worth more to us than that we have already in hand. *C'est vrai?*"

Culverton, cowed, agreed, shouldering his rifle.

We continued on, deeper into the woods, higher into the foothills. From all sides came slight noises, rustling in the forests underground around us. Remembering the forests of Sarawak, I grew increasingly nervous and clutched my rifle tighter, my eyes shifting warily from one side of the forest track to the other.

The baron, watching alongside, read the tension in my expression and attitude, and laughed.

"What is it, my friend?" he asked. "Do you fear the Wild Man of the forests?"

Culverton, following close behind, looked at the baron with eyes wide.

"What is that?" the young Englishman asked.

The baron puffed up, his manner grandiloquent.

"Well," he answered, his laughter barely restrained, "it is a primitive species of man from primeval times that haunts the woods hereabouts."

Culverton shuddered.

"Those are just stories, surely," he said, uneasy.

"No," I interjected, finding myself with little patience for jibes and games, "it is neither mythical, nor man, but rather a species of anthropoid ape called the orang-utan. They are herbivores, Culverton, and quite harmless."

This recitation of scientific fact worked on my nerves almost as a mantra is said to function for the fakirs of the east. To apply a taxonomy to the unknown, to bound the noises beyond the sphere of our senses in categorical boxes, went a great distance towards calming my nerves. It reminded me that, but for minor exceptions, we live in a comprehensible world.

"So it doesn't eat meat?" Culverton asked, not letting go of his own misgivings quite so easily.

"It eats nothing living that is larger than an insect, I shouldn't think," I answered.

"Then Culverton should suit its appetites just fine," the baron said, laughing.

Culverton shrank back, and we continued, keeping our silence.

Tonight, in a clearing, we rest our weary bones by a crackling fire. We've still had no sign of the strange beast that has attacked the men. Even so, the tracks have persisted, and it is clear that whatever our quarry is, it is large and makes frequent pilgrimages from the forest deep, high on the hills, down into the fields, and back again. There is disagreement among the men as to whether there is one or more of the creatures, with some saying there is variation in size of the tracks, and others insisting they are all of the same size. All we've learned is that the animal seems to favor the lowland forests and likes to stay close to rivers and streams.

We have brought bearers along on the trip, a half-dozen plantation workers impressed into service on the journey. Earlier tonight, after we ate our rough meal, Culverton and I sat near one another in quiet contemplation. Culverton, for his part, continually glanced nervously at the far side of the clearing, where the workers sat huddled around another fire. Seeing his suspicious glances, I asked why he was so nervous. After all, weren't these men in the company's employ?

What would it profit them to turn their hands against their supervisors?

"Oh," Culverton answered me, his voice low, "there's many a man among them would turn against us in a trice if they only had the sense to twig how bad off they are."

"But, they are paid, surely?" I asked.

Culverton explained that they are, but that few of them ever collect. Given unlimited credit at the company store, whether for liquor, what is euphemistically termed "female service," or tobacco, ironically enough, the workers to a man will spend faster than they earn. And if any do make it to the end of the harvest season with any money in hand, management licenses gambling during this brief intermission, to milk what little more blood they can from the stones. Any man left owing the company money at the end of his contract is obligated to renew for another three years until his debts are made good.

I listened while Culverton explained these practices, and then could contain my reaction no longer.

"It sounds monstrous!" I barked.

"That's as may be," Culverton said, brightening. "But from a management perspective, it's bloody brilliant!"

Excusing myself, I retired to my tent. I've had enough of these madmen, all of them, and wish I could be home in Holland tomorrow.

Abraham Van Helsing's Journal

6 Mar. – Several days now have passed since the Fourth of March, but the events of that day are still fresh in my thoughts. Were I not a rational man, I would think myself laboring under some sort of curse. First China, then Borneo, now Sumatra – in each instance I find myself hurled against my will into some sea of madness or another, adrift amongst the impossible. That I have survived all these trials so far, I sometimes fear, perhaps only suggests that I am being preserved for even greater tests to come.

On the morning of the fourth, the second day of our expedition, we continued on. The baron had sent one of the bearers ahead in the night to scout the way before us and he had not yet returned. The baron, always anticipating the worst from those in his employ, thought that the man had likely fled, trying to escape his debt to the company. The baron swore that when the bearer was recaptured, as such escapees always were, things would not go well for him.

Had the bearer, in truth, fled his employment and debts, things could have gone no worse for him than they did.

Midmorning, we found the body of the bearer, or rather his remains. A few limbs and most of the abdomen were missing, the rest left covered by the strange side-by-side gnaw marks seen on the other victims. There were tracks all around, the same we'd followed from the edge of the field. We followed them, deeper into the forest, now more cautious, our rifles always at the ready.

We came to a stand of trees ringing a clearing. The trees above, though, were bent over towards one another, creating a sort of naturally occurring arbor, a bower shaded by the domed lattice of trunks and branches overhead. There was a break in the tree line, and tracks leading up to it.

We all readied our weapons and, with the baron in the lead, entered the shady bower. While our eyes adjusted to the darkness, our senses were assaulted with an aroma like the smell of rotten onions, or ammonia.

The area within the arbor was large, with piles of branches and twigs scattered around. In the gloom, we could not see to the far side, with only large shadows lumped on the ground all around us. Which were piles of branches and which something more sinister, though, we couldn't say.

The baron called for a torch to be lit, and one of the bearers rushed in with one. We now stood in a semicircle around the entrance, our backs to the light, our faces to the darkness, with only the flickering light of the torch to guide us.

We didn't have long to wait. One of the dark piles erupted, and a massive figure lurched forward, baleful eyes glittering in the torchlight.

The creature was long and narrow, its head white, a uniform midnight black everywhere else. The long tail was scaly and hairless, and there were black spots on the long face above and below the eyes. On the long, mobile nose was a groove along the underside that ran from the nose's tip to a point between the upper incisors. Its canines were most prominent, two of them pointing downwards, like drawn sabers flashing dully in the dim light.

We fired into the enormous figure, the baron, Culverton, and I all together, which seemed barely to slow it. As it lunged forward, we beat a hasty retreat back into the open air, beyond the natural walls of the arbor, but the beast followed close behind.

In the open air, we started running, back the way we'd come. By this point, it was every man for himself. On and on we ran, we the three Europeans firing behind us as we went, the bearers abandoning their burdens in their flight. One of the bearers still carried a trunk across his shoulders, trying to run, his fellows shouting at him in their native language, calling for him to hurry, or to drop his load, or some such. The beast was on him the next instant, taking him up in its massive jaws, the saber-teeth doing their work, the pair of them ripping into his flesh.

We had a brief respite, then, as the monster busied himself eating the fallen bearer, but we all knew it would continue after us. We had to press on. Our place not slackening, we rushed on, side by side along the narrow forest tracks.

"What... was... that?" Culverton asked one syllable at a time, ragged and out of breath, feet pounding on the undergrowth.

"Its size is... ludicrous," I answered, as best I could, "but in every other respect... it appeared to be a rat."

"A... rat?" Culverton responded.

"Yes," I answered, "of a type... native... to this region."

"Nonsense," the baron shouted from behind, keeping up his steady pace. "I don't believe it."

"Perhaps," I said, calling over my shoulder, "you'd prefer to take it up with the giant rat?"

The baron kept quiet, and we raced on.

Letter to Frédéric Lerne, December 2, 1860

Success! I have successfully transfused the essential generative elements from one animal to another, and when the target subject bred it produced substantial changes.

I introduced specific traits of the Sumatran elephant (genus *Elephas*, species *maximus*, subspecies *sumatrensis*) into the "moon rat" native to these climes (genus *Echinosorex*, species *gymnura*). The resultant rat specimens are easily twice the size and weight of their parent, with an attendant increase in strength and resilience.

I have chosen the *Echinosorex gymnura* because, unlike other specimens available here, these rodents breed throughout the year, and typically produce at least two litters per year, with two young per litter being typical. I am working to modify the reproductive rate, though, to see if I can speed the process and introduce even greater degrees of improvement.

Yours, Francis

Abraham Van Helsing's Journal

6 Mar. Later – We raced on, knowing that the monstrous rat might be on us at any moment. We reached the river we'd passed the day before, just above the waterfall, the water cascading down to jagged rocks below.

"We are boxed in," the baron said, leaning over and with his hands on his knees, catching his breath. "We must stand and fight."

Culverton whimpered, summing up nicely my thoughts on our chances of survival facing the giant beast head on.

"No," I countered, recovering my composure. "There is a chance. If we ford the river here and cross to the far side, we'll have the river to act as a barrier between us and the monster."

"But if the rat can't cross this current, what makes you think we can?" The baron snapped.

"Because," I answered simply, "we are men and it is but an animal." I paused, considering the options. "You have strong cord among your supplies?"

"We did," the baron answered hotly. "But it was left somewhere far behind, when the bearers abandoned their duty."

"One didn't," Culverton said, his voice low.

"Yes," I said, "and he paid for his loyalty with his life. Very well, there is another option. We are now eight, and our outstretched arm-span reaches near six feet. The river at this point can't be much more than forty feet across. If we join hands in a human chain and then enter the water further upstream, one at a time, we can use those still on shore as anchors, inching our way to the farther shore."

The others were hesitant, but in the silence that followed my last words we could hear the sound of the monstrous rat crashing through the undergrowth, not far behind. Then, they were willing to try anything.

I was the first to enter the water. Before we'd begun, we all wrapped our firearms in our oilskin jackets and secured them over our shoulders, in the hopes they'd still fire on the far side. My rifle strapped across my shoulders, I entered the water, the baron holding my hand. He had to kick hard to keep from being dragged downstream and over the falls, but with the baron's strength pulling from shore to secure me, I managed to stay in position, my feet just barely touching bottom. I kicked further out as the baron slipped into the cold mountain water, and then the baron moved out as the next bearer in line plunged in, and so on.

I reached the opposite side just as the rat crashed through the trees. The rat paused at the river's edge and then plunged in with its mouth and forepaws, catching the last bearer in line in its teeth. It dragged the screaming man back on shore, dropped him on the ground, and then turned its attention back to the men still in the water. The baron and I were by now on dry land, trying to drag the rest of the men out after us. The baron left me to pull the men in alone and busied himself with unwrapping and loading his gun. The powder, fortunately, was still dry enough to fire, and without preamble he began shooting at the rat.

The rat plunged into the water, following us across the river. It must have been between ten and fifteen feet long, and once its rear legs were in the water, it began to drift downstream. By this point, nearly all of our party were on shore, and with our rifles unencumbered we began to fire and reload, fire and reload, and with every shot that hit home, the rat thrashed with less strength, red streamers of its monster's blood pouring downstream and over the falls.

Just as the rat was about to reach us, it drifted too far downstream and plunged over the falls, crashing into the jagged rocks down below.

When the giant rat had disappeared from view, we all of us collapsed onto the soft loam of the riverbank and breathed deep. It was a long hour before we rose, and longer yet before anyone spoke.

We made our slow way back to the plantation, having to divert miles out of our way to find a bridge across the river. We were bone weary and anxious for a fire and our beds, but we had no desire to try to cross the river in that fashion again, and so crossed the long distance in silence.

We returned to the plantation and relative safety. None of us has ventured out of doors in the days and hours since, the surviving bearers in their quarters, the staff and I in ours.

Letter to Frédéric Lerne, student, c/o University of Paris, Sorbonne, March 7, 1861

My most recent experiments have ended, and perhaps not on quite the note I'd have chosen. However, I have gathered the pertinent data and have to consider the project a resounding success. I am growing tired of island life and am eager to return to England. Well, for all of that, England is still an island, I suppose, isn't it. So I'll just be trading one island for another. But there my experiments will continue, and I will gain the notoriety and acclaim I so richly deserve.

Yours very truly, Francis Arnaud Moreau

Abraham Van Helsing's Journal

8 Mar. – I write now from my stateroom onboard the *Matilda Briggs*, bound for Calcutta on the western coast of India. I'm only too happy to be continuing my homeward journey. And, as glad as I am to be away from the monstrous creature that haunted the Sumatran forest, I'm just as glad to be quit of Francis. I never have recollected his name, though I now remember him more clearly from our school days. I recall him now an awkward and withdrawn youth, who failed to make the connection between his studies of the human body and the individual people who surrounded him at all times, able to obsess in minute detail over the functioning of some gland or minor bone, but unable to evince the slightest interest or concern in his fellow man, seeing them as little more than animals. Perhaps, then, his decision to practice medicine may, in the long run, be to his credit. Perhaps, forced into constant and close contact with the people around him, he will by turns become more "human" himself.

In my darker moments, though, I wonder. What if the reverse should happen, instead?

Unpossible

Daryl Gregory

Daryl Gregory (*darylgregory.com*) lives in State College, Pennsylvania, with his wife Kathy Bieschke and their two children, and works for a statistical software company. Formerly he has worked as an English teacher, a "telecom trainer," and a technical writer. He is one of the most striking new talents to emerge in fantasy and SF in the last few years. His first novel, *Pandemonium*, will be published by Del Rey in the fall of 2008.

"Unpossible" is a Bradburyesque revisiting of Peter Pan's territory, Never-Never-Land. But lost men don't have quite the same experience there as lost boys, and a midlife crisis just isn't a second childhood. This is a thematically complex moral tale directed at every adult's restless inner child and also perhaps a metaphorical representation of the legacy reading wonderful books as a child.

TWO IN THE MORNING and he's stumbling around in the attic, lost in horizontal archaeology: the further he goes, the older the artifacts become. The stuttering flashlight guides him past boxes of Christmas decorations and half-dead appliances, past garbage bags of old blankets and outgrown clothing stacked and bulging like black snowmen, over and around the twenty-year-old rubble of his son's treasures: Tonka trucks and science fair projects, soccer trophies and summer camp pottery.

His shoulder brushes against the upright rail of a disassembled crib, sends it sliding, and somewhere in the dark a mirror or storm window smashes. The noise doesn't matter. There's no one in the house below him to disturb.

Twenty feet from the far wall his way is blocked by a heap of wicker lawn furniture. He pulls apart the barricade piece by piece to make a narrow passage and scrapes through, straws tugging at his shirt. On the other side he crawls up and onto the back of a tilting oak desk immovable as a ship run aground.

The territory ahead is littered with the remains of his youth, the evidence of his life before he brought his wife and son to this house. Stacks of hardcover books, boxes of dusty-framed elementary school pictures – and toys. So many toys. Once upon a time he was the boy who didn't like to go outside, the boy who never wanted to leave his room. The Boy Who Always Said No.

Against the far wall, beside a rickety shelf of dried-out paint cans and rusting hardware, a drop cloth covers a suggestive shape. He picks his way through the crowded space. When he pulls aside the cloth, he grunts as if he's been elbowed in the stomach – relief and dread and wrenching sadness competing for the same throat.

Dust coats the Wonder Bike's red fenders, rust freckles its handlebars. The white-walled tires are flat, and stuffing sprouts from cracks in the leather saddle. But it's still here, still safe. And the two accessories he most needs, the things he'd almost convinced himself he'd imagined, are fastened to their places on the swooping crossbar: the five-pronged gearshift like a metal hand; and the glass-covered compass, its face scuffed white but uncracked.

The bike's heavier than he remembers, all old-fashioned steel, more solid than anything they'd bother to make today. He heaves it onto his shoulder and makes his way toward the attic door, handlebars snagging on unseen junk, errant wheels triggering miniature avalanches. Sweat pours down his back. He thinks about heart attacks. He's fifty-six now, a middle-aged man if he lives to a hundred and twelve. People younger than that die all the time. All the time.

The weight of the bike drags him down the attic stairs. He wheels it winging down the hall, then out the front door and across the frost-crackled lawn, aiming for the realtor sign. The sweat on his neck turns cold. Along the street his neighbors' houses are all dark. The moon stays tucked into its bed of clouds. He's grateful for the privacy. He lifts the front wheel and runs over the FOR SALE sign, flattens it.

In the garage he sets to work removing the accessories. The screws are rusted into place, so he puts aside the screwdriver and plugs in the power drill. The shifter comes free, but the screws holding the compass are stripped, spinning uselessly. He can't risk hammering it off, so he works a hacksaw blade between the handlebars and the bottom of the device and cuts it free. Gently he sets the Wonder Bike against the garage wall and gets into the car.

It takes much less time to attach the accessories to the dash. He screws them directly into the plastic, side by side above the radio.

He starts the engine and stares out the dirt-streaked windshield, trying to remember what to do next. It used to be automatic: pedal hard, thumb the gears, follow the compass. But something happened when he turned thirteen. He lost the knack and the bike stopped working for him. Or maybe, he's been thinking lately, he stopped working for the bike.

He sets the DeShifter to NOT RECOMMENDED. He taps the glass of the UnCompass and the needle quivers, stuck between UNFAMILIAR and UNKNOWN.

Sounds about right, he thinks.

Even with the compass it takes determination to get lost. He drives south out of town, past the tangle of interstate exchanges, toward the green empty parts of the map. He turns down the first road he doesn't recognize. He pays no attention to street names; he looks away when signs appear in his headlights.

Soon there are no signs. Forest swallows the highway. Switchbacks and the skulking moon conspire with him to disguise his direction.

Don't look in the rearview mirror, he tells himself. No trail of bread crumbs. As soon as he thinks of the road behind him, he realizes he left the front door of the house wide open. Maybe by morning robbers will have emptied the place. That would make it easier on the real estate agents. Too much clutter, they'd told him. They couldn't see that the home had been gutted a year ago.

He rolls down the window and lets the cold wind buffet him. When did he fall out of love with speed? He'd had adventures once. He'd rescued the Pumpkinhead Boys, raced the moto-crows, reunited the shards of the Glass Kingdom. His quick thinking had outwitted the Hundred Mayors of Stilt Town.

He nudges the DeShifter past INADVISABLE to ABSOLUTELY NOT and accelerates. The road ahead doesn't exist until it appears under his headlights; he's driving a plow of light through the dark, unrolling the road before him like a carpet.

A tiny yellow sign flashes past his right fender, too fast for him to read. He glances sideways – nothing but the dark – and turns back to the road just as the little purple house appears in his lights like a phantom.

The structure strikes the grille and explodes into a thousand pieces. The windshield pocks with white stars. He stomps on the brake and the car bucks, slides sideways. He jerks the wheel back to the right and suddenly the car's off the road, jouncing across ground. He bounces against the roof, ragdolling, unable to hold onto the wheel. The car bangs sideways against something invisible and immovable and then everything stops.

He stares out the cratered windshield. The engine coughs politely, shudders, and dies.

The DeShifter shows COMPLETELY OUT OF THE QUESTION. The UnCompass needle points straight at UNPOSSIBLE.

Later – he's as unsure of time as he is of location – he forces the car door open, pushing against tree limbs and thick brush, and climbs out and down. The driver-side wheels are two feet in the air. Trees surround the car as if they'd grown up around it.

He walks up a slight incline to the road, his pulse driving a headache deeper into his temples. The muscles of his neck burn; his chest aches where the seat-belt cut into him.

The surface of the road is littered with shattered plywood – and bits of silver. He stoops, drumming fresh pain into his head, and picks up a dime. There are coins all over the roadway.

The only thing remaining of the tollbooth is another of the child-sized yellow signs, miraculously erect: PLEASE HAVE YOUR DESTINATION IN MIND.

He drops the dime into his pocket and starts walking.

A farmhouse squats in the middle of the highway like a great toad, filling both lanes. He walks toward it in the inconstant moonlight, horrified. If he hadn't struck the tollbooth, he'd have slammed into the house at eighty miles per hour.

On closer inspection the house looks like it's been dropped there from a great height. Walls are askew, their wooden siding bowed, splintered, or blown out completely. Roofs cant at contrary angles.

He steps onto the porch and floorboards creak and shift under his weight like unstable ice. High-pitched barking erupts from inside. He knocks on the door and waits, hunched and shivering. A minute passes. The dog – a small, hyperactive thing by the sound of it – barks and barks.

He crouches next to the closest window but gauzy curtains obscure the view. He makes out a lamp, the suggestion of a couch, a dark rectangle that could be a bookshelf or a wardrobe. His teeth are on the edge of chattering.

He knocks again and sends the dog into fresh vocal frenzy. He considers trying the doorknob. It's warm in there. There could be a phone. How big can the dog be?

He backs off the porch and walks around the side of the house. It's nearly pitch black back there; the roof blocks the moon, and the windows at the back of the house, if there are windows at all, are unlit. He can't even tell if the road continues on the side. He moves in what he thinks is an arc, feeling for the scrape of pavement under his shoes, when suddenly he bangs his toes against something low and hard and stumbles forward. He catches his balance – and freezes, realizing where he's standing. He's in the middle of train tracks.

He doesn't hear anything, doesn't see anything but the eye-swallowing dark. Slowly he steps back over the rails, a chill in his stomach even though he'd see a train coming for miles.

The dog resumes barking, and the sound is different somehow. He circles around to the front of the house and sees that the front door is open now, light spilling around some dark shape filling the doorway.

"Hello?" he says. He holds out his hands as he steps toward the door. "I – I had a slight accident. A couple miles down the road."

"You came by car?" A woman's voice, low and rasping.

"I had an accident," he says again. "If you've got a phone, I could call someone...."

"The road's closed to your type." He's not sure if she's warning him or merely stating fact. Her shadow recedes. After a moment he approaches the door.

The dog, a tiny black terrier with an age-whitened snout, lies in a towel-lined wicker basket a few feet from the door. It bares its teeth at him and growls, but makes no move to leave its bed. He steps inside the room.

The woman's already sitting, leaning back in an old leather armchair the color of dried mud. The light is behind her so again her face is in shadow. She crosses her legs, sharp white shins over blood-red slippers. She pulls a foil pack from the pocket of her blue-checked housedress and taps out a cigarette.

He folds his arms across his chest and tries to stop shivering. At least the house is warm. He looks around for a phone but knows he won't find one – it's not that kind of house. It's been a long time, but the old instincts are coming back. He smiles thinly. "And what type would that be, ma'am?"

"Storm-chaser," she says. "Wardrobe-jumper." She flicks a cheap plastic lighter and holds the flame to the cigarette. "Mirror shards sticking to your coat, twigs in your hair. Little hard to squeeze that big ol' man-body through the hedgerow, eh?"

"You don't know me. You don't know who I am."

"Oh my goodness, you must be the *special* one," she says in mock recognition. "You must be the only traveler to see *lands beyond*." She taps cigarette ash onto the braided rug. "Let me guess – enchanted sailboat? Magic choo-choo train? Oh, that's right, you're a driver – electric kiddie car, then. The tollbooth boy."

"I had a bicycle," he says. "The most wonderful – "

She groans. "Spare me." She inhales on her cigarette, shakes her head. "At least you got rid of it. Most of you can't find your way back without the props." She sees his frown and laughs. Smoke spills from her mouth and hazes the lights.

"You think you're the first one to try to sneak back in?" she says. "You're not even the first one *tonight*." She laughs again. "Boo-hoo-hoo, my wife left me, whaaa, my daughters hate me. Life is meaningless, I'm gonna kill myself."

"I don't have a daughter," he says. "And my wife didn't leave me." But of course she had. She left him in the most absolute way, leaving behind a note like a set of driving directions, like a travel brochure to an exotic country. Two years later to the day, their son followed her. Tonight, come to think of it, is the anniversary of their deaths.

He takes a breath. "I'm just looking for a way back."

"Please. You couldn't find your shadow if it was stapled on. You think you can just waltz right back in there nursing your disappointments and diseases, your head stuffed full of middle-age sex fantasies and mortgage payments? You'd ruin everything. You'd stink the place up."

"You don't understand," he says. "I only need – "

"Stink. It. Up." She makes a tired shooing gesture. "Go home, you greedy little boy. No second helpings. You ought to be ashamed of yourself."

This is a test, he thinks. She's trying to throw him off, weigh him down with doubt and discouragement. He's met such trials before, and persevered. Once upon a time he was The Boy Who Always Said No.

As if in confirmation he hears a distant bell, a cheery *ding ding!* He recognizes that sound. He strides out of the room, into the dark kitchen, and flips open the hook to the back door.

"You'll never get on!" the woman calls. The dog begins to bark.

The dark, to his light-adjusted eyes, seems almost solid. He stops a few feet from the house and listens. The trolley must be close by. The little bell sounds again, but he can't tell if it's growing closer or more distant.

He moves forward slowly, arms out, feet sliding forward. The track is only a few yards from the house, he's sure of it. His feet drag through the unseen grass. After a few minutes he glances back, but now the house is gone as well. He turns in place, eyes wide. There's no sound, not even barking. A dank, dead-fish scent twists in the air.

When he completes his circle he notices a dark, fuzzed shape in the distance, barely distinguishable against a black sky edging toward indigo. It's the first hint since he left the attic that the night is not endless. He doesn't know what it is in the distance, but he recognizes the shape for what it is: unfamiliar, unknown.

The little boat lies at the bottom of the empty seabed, abandoned midway between the shore and the island. Sandy mud sucks at his shoes. He walks toward it, past stacks of smooth-headed boulders and stinking saltwater puddles in the shape of great clawed feet. He walks under a sky the color of pencil lead.

The island is shaped like a bowler hat. If not for the trees – a handful of curve-backed palms with outrageously broad leaves – and for the hunched figure silhouetted at the very crown of the hill, he'd have thought the island was huge but miles away. Instead he can see that it's ridiculously small, like a cartoon desert island.

He reaches the boat and rests a hand on the gunwales. The inside of the boat is an unmade bed, a white pillow and blue blankets and white sheets. Foot-shaped holes, human-size, stamp away from the boat toward the island. He follows them across the drained sea to the rim of the island, where his predecessor's mud-laden feet begin to print the grass. The trail leads up the slope, between bushes tinged yellow and brown. Only a few of the palm trees are standing; dozens of others are uprooted and lying on the ground, or else split and bent, as if savaged by a hurricane.

He climbs, breath ragged in his throat. The man at the top of the hill is facing away, toward the lightening sky. On his back is some kind of white fur shawl – no, a suit like a child's footie pajamas, arms tied around his neck. The yawning hood is a wolf's head that's too small for his grown-man's head.

He's huffing, making a lot of noise as he approaches, but the man with the wolf suit doesn't turn around.

When he's caught his breath he says, "Beautiful, isn't it?"

Above them the sky is fitful gray, but across the vast, empty sea in the land beyond, sunlight sparkles on the crystal minarets of the Glassine Palace. A great-winged roc dangling a gondola from its claws flaps toward its next fare. The rolling hills beyond the city are golden and ripe for harvest. It's all as he remembers.

"Look at those wild things go," the man in the wolf suit says. Who knows what he's seeing?

The sun crawls higher, but the clouds above the hill refuse to disperse. He glances at the man in the wolf suit, looks away. Tears have cut tracks down his muddy and unshaven face. The wolf man's older than he, but not by much.

What did the woman in the house say? *Not even the first one tonight.*

He nods at the man's wedding ring and says, "Can't take it off either?"

The man frowns at it. "Left me six months ago. I had it coming for years." He smiles faintly. "Couldn't quite stop making mischief. You?"

"She died a few years ago." But the damage hadn't stopped there, had it? He tilts his head, a half shrug. "Depression runs in her family."

"Sorry to hear that." He slowly shakes his head, and the upside-down wolf's head wags with him. "It's a disaster out there. Every day like an eraser. Days into months, months into years – gone, gone, gone." The man in the wolf suit stares at him without blinking. "Tell me I'm wrong. Tell me you were having a happy ending."

"No." He almost grins. "Not even close." But was that true? He'd had a dozen happy endings. A score of them.

Together they stare across the ocean of mud and squint into the brightness beyond.

"We can't get back in there," he says to the man with the suit. He's surprised by his certainty. But he can't imagine tracking that muck across the crystal streets. "And we can't stay here." He rubs a hand across his mouth. "Come with me."

The man doesn't answer.

"I could make you leave."

The man in the wolf suit laughs. "Don't you know who I am?" he says. "I'm their king!"

"No," he says. "Not anymore." He grips the edges of the white fur and yanks it over the man's head and off, quick as a magic trick. "I'm the king now."

He runs down the hill holding the suit above his head like a flag. The man roars a terrible roar. It's a chase down to the sea's edge and then they're tumbling in the muck, wrapped up and rolling like bear cubs, choking and half-blinded in mud. Hands claw for the suit. They tug it back and forth, the cloth rasping as threads stretch and tear. Then the zipper snaps and they fall away from each other, splash down on their asses.

They look at each other, too winded to get up.

The man clutches the scrap of fur he's regained. It's not white anymore. "Why'd you *do* that?" he says.

He's not sure. He flicks mud from his hands, wipes a hand clean on the inside of his shirt, runs a knuckle across his mouth. "It was the only thing I could think of."

The man looks at him. A smile works at the corners of his mud-spattered mouth. He makes a sound like a cough, and then he's laughing, they're both laughing. They sit in the mud, roaring.

Eventually they help each other out of the muck. "We screwed it up," the man says. "How did we screw it up?"

He's been wondering that himself for a long time. "I don't think we were supposed to keep them safe," he answers. He hands him the remnant of the suit. "This, the bed, the Wonder Bike – all that stuff. We weren't supposed to *hoard* them."

The man looks stricken. "What?"

"We were supposed to give them away."

"Oh my God," the man says quietly. "Oh my God."

They begin to trudge across the drained sea. They trade stories about their adventures. The man with the wolf suit takes out his wallet and shows him pictures. He has a granddaughter he's never met, six years old, a real hellion by all accounts. "She lives three states away," he says.

A dozen yards from the shore they see the trolley. The little car glides smoothly around the perimeter of the lake and stops in their path. It rolls a few feet forward, a few feet back. *Ding ding!*

They approach it carefully and without speaking, as they would a deer at a watering hole. It trembles as they step up onto the gleaming sideboards. They sit on the polished wooden benches. It's a shame their clothes are so filthy.

The trolley doesn't move.

"Wait," he says, and the man in the wolf suit watches him dig into his pocket. The dime he found on the roadway is still there. The coin clinks into the tin fare box and the car jerks into motion. Soon they're zipping across the plain toward the forest and the black ribbon of highway.

"And yourself?" the man with the suit says.

"No grandchildren," he says. "No children. Not anymore."

The man frowns and nods. "We'll find someone for the bike," he says. "The world is full of children."

Winter's Wife

Elizabeth Hand

Elizabeth Hand (*elizabethhand.com*) lives in a small town on the coast of Maine, which is the place where "Winter's Wife" takes place. She grew up in Westchester County in the New York City suburbs as part of a large Irish-Catholic family and lived for a while in Washington, D.C., before escaping to the Maine woods. In her website bio, she says, "I had my own encounter with the numinous in November 1974, when I had an epiphanic vision of a Dionysian figure I named 'the boy in the tree.' Several years later, on St. Patrick's Day 1978, I was abducted and raped while visiting my boyfriend in Washington, D.C. These two experiences, one of inexplicable transcendence, the other of random human violence, have shaped nearly all of my fiction."

"Winter's Wife," published in *Wizards*, tells of a man with the last name of Winter, who finds a strange Icelandic wife over the Internet and brings her to his home in small-town Maine. She becomes the magical embodiment of ecofeminism, a defender of Maine's old-growth trees.

WINTER'S REAL NAME was Roderick Gale Winter. But everyone in Paswegas County, not just me and people who knew him personally, called him Winter. He lived in an old schoolbus down the road from my house, and my mother always tells how when she first moved here he scared the crap out of her. It wasn't even him that scared her, she hadn't even met him yet; just the fact that there was this creepy-looking old schoolbus stuck in the middle of the woods with smoke coming out of a chimney and these huge piles of split logs around and trucks and cranes and heavy equipment, and in the summer all kinds of chainsaws and stuff, and in the fall deer and dead coyotes hanging from this big pole that my mother said looked like a gallows, and blood on the snow, and once a gigantic dead pig's head with tusks which my mother said was scarier even than the coyotes. Which, when you think of it, does sound pretty bad, so you can't blame her for being freaked out. It's funny now because her and Winter are best friends, though that doesn't mean so much as it does other places, like Chicago where my mother moved here from, because I think everyone in Shaker Harbor thinks Winter is their friend.

The schoolbus, when you get inside it, is sweet.

Winter's family has been in Shaker Harbor for six generations, and even before that they lived somewhere else in Maine.

"I have Passamaquoddy blood," Winter says. "If I moved somewhere else, I'd melt."

He didn't look like a Native American, though, and my mother said if he did have Indian blood it had probably been diluted by now. Winter was really tall and skinny, not sick skinny but bony and muscular, stooped from having to duck through the door of the schoolbus all those years. He always wore a gimme cap that said WINTER TREE SERVICE., and I can remember how shocked I was once when I saw him at Town Meeting without his hat and he had almost no hair. He'd hunt and butcher his own deer, but he wouldn't eat it – he said he'd grown up dirt poor in a cabin that didn't even have a wooden floor, just pounded earth, and his family would eat anything they could hunt, including snake and skunk and snapping turtle. So he'd give all his venison away, and when people hired him to butcher their livestock and gave him meat, he'd give that away too.

That was how my mother met him, that first winter fifteen years ago when she was living here alone, pregnant with me. There was a big storm going on, and she looked out the window and saw this tall guy stomping through the snow carrying a big paper bag.

"You a vegetarian?" he said when she opened the door. "Everyone says there's a lady from away living here who's going to have a baby and she's a vegetarian. But you don't look like one to me."

My mother said no, she wasn't a vegetarian, she was a registered certified massage therapist.

"Whatever the hell that is," said Winter. "You going to let me in? Jesus Q. Murphy, is that your woodstove?"

See, my mother had gotten pregnant by a sperm donor. She had it all planned out, how she was going to move way up north and have a baby and raise it – him, me – by herself and live off the land and be a massage therapist and hang crystals in the windows and there would be this good energy and everything was going to be perfect. And it would have been, if she had moved to, like, Huntington Beach or even Boston, someplace like that, where it would be warmer and there would be good skate parks, instead of a place where you have to drive two hours to a skate park and it snows from November till the end of May. And in the spring you can't even skate on the roads here because they're all dirt roads and so full of pot holes you could live in one. But the snowboarding is good, especially since Winter let us put a jump right behind his place.

But this part is all before any snowboarding, because it was all before me, though not much before. My mother was living in this tiny two-room camp with no indoor plumbing and no running water, with an ancient woodstove, what they call a parlor stove, which looked nice but didn't put out any heat and caused a chimney fire. Which was how Winter heard about her, because the volunteer fire department came and afterwards all anyone was talking about at the Shaker Harbor Variety Store was how this crazy lady from away had bought Martin Weed's old rundown camp and now she was going to have a baby and freeze to death or burn the camp down – probably both – which probably would have been okay with them except no one liked to think about the baby getting frozen or burned up.

So Winter came by and gave my mother the venison and looked at her woodpile and told her she was burning green wood, which builds up creosote which was why she had the chimney fire, and he asked her who sold her the wood, which she told him. And the next day the guy who sold her the wood came by and dumped off three cords of seasoned wood and drove off without saying a word, and the day after that two other guys came by with a brand-new woodstove which was ugly but very efficient and had a sheath around it so a baby wouldn't get burned if he touched it. And the day after *that* Winter came by to make sure the stove was hooked up right, and he went to all the cabin's windows with sheets of plastic and a hair dryer and covered them so the cold wouldn't get in, and then he showed my mother where there was a spring in the woods that she could go to and fill water jugs rather than buy them at the grocery store. He also gave her a chamber pot so she wouldn't have to use the outhouse, and told her he knew of someone who had a composting toilet they'd sell to her cheap.

All of which might make you think that when I say "Winter's wife" I'm referring to my mom. But I'm not. Winter's wife is someone else.

Still, when I was growing up, Winter was always at our house. And I was at his place, when I got older. Winter chops down trees, what they call wood lot management – he cuts trees for people, but in a good way, so the forest can grow back and be healthy. Then he'd split the wood so the people could burn it for firewood. He had a portable sawmill – one of the scary things Mom had seen in his yard – and he also mills wood so people can build houses with the lumber. He's an auctioneer, and he can play the banjo and one of those washboard things like you see in old movies. He showed me how to jump start a car with just a wire coat hanger, also how to carve wood and build a treehouse and frame a window. When my mother had our little addition put on with a bathroom in it, Winter did a lot of the carpentry, and he taught me how to do that too.

He's also a dowser, a water witch. That's someone who can tell where water is underground, just by walking around in the woods holding a stick in front of him. You'd think this was more of that crazy woo-woo stuff my mother is into, which is what I thought whenever I heard about it.

But then one day me and my friend Cody went out to watch Winter do it. We were hanging out around Winter's place, clearing brush. He let us use the hill behind the schoolbus for snowboarding, and that's where we'd built that sweet jump, and Winter had saved a bunch of scrap wood so that when spring came we could build a half-pipe for skating too.

But now it was spring and since we didn't have any money really to pay Winter for it, he put us to work clearing brush. Cody is my age, almost fourteen. So we're hacking at this brush and swatting blackflies and I could tell that at any minute Cody was going to say he had to go do homework, which was a lie because we didn't have any, when Winter shows up in his pickup, leans out the window and yells at us.

"You guys wanna quit goofing off and come watch someone do some real work?"

So then me and Cody had an argument about who was going to ride shotgun with Winter, and then we had another argument about who was going to ride in the truck bed, which is actually more fun. And then we took so long arguing that Winter yelled at us and made us both ride in the back.

So we got to the place where Winter was going to work. This field that had been a dairy farm, but the farm wasn't doing too good and the guy who owned it had to sell it off. Ms. Whitton, a high school teacher, was going to put a little modular house on it. There'd been a bad drought a few years earlier, and a lot of wells ran dry. Ms. Whitton didn't have a lot of money to spend on digging around for a well, so she hired Winter to find the right spot.

"Justin!" Winter yelled at me as he hopped out of the truck. "Grab me that hacksaw there – "

I gave him the saw, then me and Cody went and goofed around some more while Winter walked around the edge of the field, poking at brush and scrawny trees. After a few minutes he took the hacksaw to a spindly sapling.

"Got it!" Winter yelled, and stumbled back into the field. "If we're going to find water here, we better find a willow first."

It was early spring, and there really weren't any leaves out yet, so what he had was more like a pussy willow, with furry gray buds and green showing where he'd sawn the branch off. Winter stripped the buds from it until he had a forked stick. He held the two ends like he was holding handlebars, and began to walk around the field.

It was weird. Cause at first, me and Cody were laughing – we didn't mean to, we couldn't help it. It just looked funny, Winter walking back and forth with his arms out holding that stick. He kind of looked like Frankenstein. Even Ms. Whitton was smiling.

But then it was like everything got very still. Not quiet – you could hear the wind blowing in the trees, and hear birds in the woods, and someone running a chainsaw far off – but still, like all of a sudden you were in a movie and you knew something was about to happen. The sun was warm, I could smell dirt and cow manure and meadowsweet. Cody started slapping blackflies and swearing. I felt dizzy, not bad dizzy but like you do when the schoolbus drives fast over a high bump and you go up on your seat. A few feet away Winter continued walking in a very straight line, the willow stick held out right in front of him.

And all of a sudden the stick began to bend. I don't mean that Winter's arms bent down holding it: I mean the stick itself, the point that stuck straight out, bent down like it was made of rubber and someone had grabbed it and yanked it towards the ground. Only it wasn't made of rubber, it was stiff wood, and there was no one there – but it still bent, pointing at a mossy spot between clumps of dirt.

"Holy crap," I said.

Cody shut up and looked. So did Ms. Whitton.

"Oh my god," she said.

Winter stopped, angling the stick back and forth like he was fighting with it. Then it lunged down and he yelled "Whoa!" and opened his hands and dropped it. Me and Cody ran over.

"This is it," said Winter. He pulled a spool of pink surveyor's tape from his pocket and broke off a length. I stared warily at the willow stick, half-expecting it to wiggle up like a snake, but it didn't move. After a moment I picked it up.

"How'd you do that?" demanded Cody.

"I didn't do it," said Winter evenly. He took the stick from my hand, snapped off the forked part and tossed it; tied the surveyor's tape to what remained and stuck it in the ground. "Wood does that. Wood talks to you, if you listen."

"No lie," I said. "Can you show me how to do that sometime?"

"Sure," said Winter. "Can't today, got a towing job. But someday."

He and Ms. Whitton started talking about money and who had the best rates for drilling. The next time my mom drove past that field, the drill rig was there hammering at the ground right where Winter's stick had pointed, and the next time I ran into Ms. Whitton in the hall at school she told me the well was already dug and all geared up to pump 100 gallons a minute, once she got her foundation dug and her house moved in.

Not long after that, Winter announced he was going to Reykjavik.

It was after school one day, and Winter had dropped by to shoot the breeze.

"What's Reykjavik?" I asked.

"It's in Iceland," said my mother. She cracked the window open and sat at the kitchen table opposite Winter and me. "Why on earth are you going to Reykjavik?"

"To pick up my wife," said Winter.

"Your wife?" My eyes widened. "You're married?"

"Nope. That's why I'm going to Iceland to pick her up. I met her online, and we're going to get married."

My mother looked shocked. "In *Iceland?*"

Winter shrugged. "Hey, with a name like mine, where else you gonna find a wife?"

So he went to Iceland. I thought he'd be gone for a month, at least, but a week later the phone rang and my mom answered and it was Winter, saying he was back safe and yes, he'd brought his wife with him.

"That's incredible," said Mom. She put the phone down and shook her head. "He was there for four days, got married, and now they're back. I can't believe it."

A few days later they dropped by so Winter could introduce us to her. It was getting near the end of the school year, and me and Cody were outside throwing stuff at my treehouse, using the open window as a target. Sticks, a frisbee, a broken yo-yo. Stuff like that.

"Why are you trying to break the house?" a woman asked.

I turned. Winter stood there grinning, hands in the pockets of his jeans, his gimme cap pushed back so the bill pointed almost straight up. Beside him stood a woman who barely came up to his shoulder. She was so slight that for a second I thought she was another kid, maybe one of the girls from school who'd ridden her bike over or hopped a ride in Winter's truck. But she didn't have a kid's body, and she sure didn't have a kid's eyes.

"Justin." Winter squared his shoulders and his voice took on a mock-formal tone. "I'd like you to meet my wife. Vala, this is Justin."

"Justin." The way she said my name made my neck prickle. It was like she was turning the word around in her mouth; like she was tasting it. "*Gleour mig ao kynnast per.* That's Icelandic for 'I am glad to meet you.'"

She didn't really have an accent, although her voice sounded more English than American. And she definitely didn't look like anyone I'd ever seen in Maine, even though she was dressed pretty normal. Black jeans, a black t-shirt. Some kind of weird-looking bright blue shoes with thick rubber soles, which I guess is what people wear in Iceland; also a bright blue windbreaker. She had long straight black hair done in two ponytails – one reason she looked like a kid – kind of slanted eyes and a small mouth and the palest skin I've ever seen.

It was the eyes that really creeped me out. They were long and narrow and very very dark, so dark you couldn't even see the pupil. And they weren't brown but blue, so deep a blue they were almost black. I've never seen eyes that color before, and I didn't really like seeing them now. They were cold – not mean or angry, just somehow *cold*; or maybe it was that they made *me* feel cold, looking at them.

And even though she looked young, because she was skinny and her hair didn't have any gray in it and her face wasn't wrinkled, it was like she was somehow pretending to be young. Like when someone pretends to like kids, and you know they don't, really. Though I didn't get the feeling Vala didn't like kids. She seemed more puzzled, like maybe we looked as strange to her as she did to me.

"You haven't told me why you are trying to break the house," she said.

I shrugged. "Uh, we're not. We're just trying to get things through that window."

Cody glanced at Vala, then began searching for more rocks to throw.

Vala stared at him coolly. "Your friend is very rude."

She looked him up and down, then walked over to the treehouse. It was built in the crotch of a big old maple tree, and it was so solid you could live in it, if you wanted to, only it didn't have a roof.

"What tree is this?" she asked, and looked at Winter.

"Red maple," he said.

"Red maple," she murmured. She ran her hand along the trunk, stroking it, like it was a cat. "Red maple..."

She turned and stared at me. "You made this house? By yourself?"

"No." She waited, like it was rude of me not to say more. So I walked over to her and stood awkwardly, staring up at the bottom of the treehouse. "Winter helped me. I mean, your husband – Mr. Winter."

"Mr. Winter." Unexpectedly she began to laugh. A funny laugh, like a little kid's, and after a moment I laughed too. "So I am Mrs. Winter? But who should be Winter's proper wife – Spring, maybe?"

She made a face when she said this, like she knew how dumb it sounded; then reached to take my hand. She drew me closer to her, until we both stood beside the tree. I felt embarrassed – maybe this was how they did things in Iceland, but not here in Maine – but I was flattered, too. Because the way she looked at me, sideways from the corner of her eyes, and the way she smiled, not like I was a kid but another grownup...it was like she knew a secret, and she acted like I knew it, too.

Which of course I didn't. But it was kind of cool that she thought so. She let go of my hand and rested hers against the tree again, rubbing a patch of lichen.

"There are no trees in Iceland," she said. "Did you know that? No trees. Long long ago they cut them all down to build houses or ships, or to burn. And so we have no trees, only rocks and little bushes that come to here – "

She indicated her knee, then tapped the tree trunk. "And like this – lichen, and moss. We have a joke, do you know it?"

She took a breath, then said, "What do you do if you get lost in a forest in Iceland?"

I shook my head. "I dunno."

"Stand up."

It took me a moment to figure that out. Then I laughed, and Vala smiled at me. Again she looked like she was waiting for me to say something. I wanted to be polite, but all I could think was how weird it must be, to come from a place where there were no trees to a place like Maine, where there's trees everywhere.

So I said, "Uh, do you miss your family?"

She gave me a funny look. "My family? They are happy to live with the rocks back in Iceland. I am tired of rocks."

A shadow fell across her face. She glanced up as Winter put his hands on her shoulders. "Your mother home, Justin?" he asked. "We're on our way into town, just wanted to say a quick hello and introduce the new wife – "

I nodded and pointed back to the house. As Winter turned to go, Vala gave me another sharp look.

"He tells me many good things about you. You and he are what we would call *feogar* – like a father and his son, Winter says. So I will be your godmother."

She pointed a finger at me, then slowly drew it to my face until she touched my chin. I gasped: her touch was so cold it burned.

"There," she murmured. "Now I will always know you."

And she followed Winter inside. When they were gone, Cody came up beside me.

"Was that freaky or what?" he said. He stared at the house. "She looks like that weird singer, Boink."

"You mean Bjork, you idiot."

"Whatever. Where is Iceland, anyway?"

"I have no clue."

"Me neither." Cody pointed at my chin. "Hey, you're bleeding, dude."

I frowned, then gingerly touched the spot where Vala had pressed her finger. It wasn't bleeding; but when I looked at it later that night I saw a red spot, shaped like a fingerprint. Not a scab or blister or scar but a spot like a birthmark, deep red like blood. Over the next few days it faded, and finally disappeared; but I can still feel it there sometimes even now, a sort of dull ache that gets worse when it's cold outside, or snowing.

That same month, Thomas Tierney returned to Paswegas County. He was probably the most famous person in this whole state, after Stephen King, but everyone up here loves Stephen King and I never heard anyone say anything good about Thomas Tierney except after he disappeared, and then the only thing people said was good riddance to bad rubbish. Even my mom, who gets mad if you say something bad about anyone, even if they hit you first, never liked Thomas Tierney.

"He's one of those people who thinks they can buy anything. And if he can't buy it, he ruins it for everyone else."

Though the truth was, there wasn't much that he wasn't able to buy, especially in Paswegas. People here don't have a lot of money. They had more after Tierney's telemarketing company moved into the state and put up its telephone centers everywhere, even one not too far from Shaker Harbor, which is pretty much the end of nowhere. Then people who used to work as fishermen or farmers or teachers or nurses, but who couldn't make a living at it anymore, started working for International Corporate Enterprises. ICE didn't pay a lot, but I guess it paid okay, if you didn't mind sitting in a tiny cubicle and calling strangers on the phone when they were in the middle of dinner and annoying them so they swore at you or just hung up.

Once when she heard me and Cody ranking on people who worked at ICE, my mom took us aside and told us we had to be careful what we said, because even if we hated the company it gave people jobs and that was nothing to sneeze about. Of course a lot of those people who worked for ICE ended up not being able to afford to live here anymore, because Tierney gave all his friends from away the expensive jobs, and then they bought land here, which used to be cheap, and built these big fancy houses. So now normal people can't afford to live here, unless they were lucky enough to already own a house or land, like my mom and Winter.

But then Tierney got caught doing something bad, sneaking money from his company or something, and ICE got bought by a bigger company, and they shut down all their operations in Maine, and all the people who worked there got thrown out of work and a lot of them who did own their own houses or land got them taken away because they couldn't afford to pay their bills anymore. Then people *really* hated Thomas Tierney; but it didn't do any good, because he never even got in trouble for what he did, I mean he didn't go to jail or anything, and he didn't lose his money or his house down in Kennebunkport or his yacht or his private airplane.

As a matter of fact, the opposite happened: he bought the land next to Winter's. Winter dropped by the day he found out about it.

"That sumbitch bought old Lonnie Packard's farm!" he yelled.

Me and Cody looked at each other and sort of smirked, but we didn't say anything. I could tell Cody wanted to laugh, like I did – who the hell actually says "sumbitch"? – but at the same time it was scary, because we'd never seen Winter get mad before.

"I can't blame Lonnie," Winter went on, shifting from one foot to the other and tugging at his cap. "He had to sell his lobsterboat last year cause he couldn't pay his taxes, and then he had that accident and couldn't pay the hospital. And it's a salt farm right there on the ocean, so he never got much out of it except the view."

Cody asked, "Why didn't he sell it to you?"

Winter whacked his palm against the wall. "That's what I said! I told Lonnie long time ago, ever he wanted to sell that land I'd take it. But yesterday he told me, 'Winter, your pockets just ain't that deep.' I said, 'Well Lonnie, how deep is deep?' And he pointed out there at the Atlantic Ocean and said, 'You see that? You go out to the Grand Banks and find the deepest part, and I'm telling you it ain't deep as Thomas Tierney's pockets.'"

So that was that. Tell you the truth, I didn't give much thought to it. Where we snowboarded in the woods was safely on Winter's property, I knew that; besides which it was late spring now, and me and Cody were busy working on that half-pipe behind Winter's house and, once it was done, skating on it.

Sometimes Winter's wife would come out and watch us. Winter had made her a bench from a hunk of oak, laid slats across it and carved her name on the seat, VALA with carved leaves and vines coming out of the letters. The bench was set up on a little rise, so that you could look out across the tops of the trees and just catch a glimpse of the ocean, silver-blue above the green. Vala was so tiny she looked like another kid sitting there, watching us and laughing when we fell, though never in a mean way. Her laugh was like her eyes: there was a kind of coldness to it, but it wasn't nasty, more like she had never seen anyone fall before and every time it happened (which was a lot) it was a surprise to her. Even though it was warmer now, she always wore that same blue windbreaker, and over it a sweatshirt that I recognized as one of Winter's, so big it was like a saggy dress. It could get wicked hot out there at the edge of the woods, but I never saw her take that sweatshirt off.

"Aren't you hot?" I asked her once. She'd brought some water for us and some cookies she'd made, gingersnaps that were thin and brittle as ice and so spicy they made your eyes sting.

"Hot?" She shook her head. "I never get warm. Except with Winter." She smiled then, one of her spooky smiles that always made me nervous. "I tell him it's the only time winter is ever warm, when he is lying beside me."

I felt my face turn red. On my chin, the spot where she had touched me throbbed as though someone had shoved a burning cigarette against my skin. Vala's smile grew wider, her eyes too. She began to laugh.

"You're still a boy." For a moment she sounded almost like my mother. "Good boys, you and your friend. You will grow up to be good men. Not like this man Tierney, who thinks he can own the sea by buying salt. There is nothing more dangerous than a man who thinks he has power." She lifted her head to gaze into the trees, then turned to stare at me. "Except for one thing."

But she didn't say what that was.

I had always heard a lot about Thomas Tierney, and even though I had never seen him, there were signs of him everywhere around Shaker Harbor. The addition to the library; the addition to the school; the big old disused mill – renamed the ICE Mill – that he bought and filled with a thousand tiny cubicles, each with its own computer and its own telephone. The ICE Mill employed so many people that some of them drove two hours each way to work – there weren't enough people around Shaker Harbor to fill it.

But now it was empty, with big FOR SALE signs on it. Winter said it would stay empty, too, because no one in Paswegas County could afford to buy it.
"And no one outside of Paswegas County would want to buy it," he added. "Watch that doesn't drip – "

I was helping Winter varnish a crib he'd made, of wood milled from an elm tree that had died of the blight. He wouldn't say who it was for, even when I asked him outright, but I assumed it was a present for Vala. She didn't look pregnant, and I was still a little fuzzy about the precise details of what exactly might make her pregnant, in spite of some stuff me and Cody checked out online one night. But there didn't seem much point in making a trip to Iceland to get a wife if you weren't going to have kids. That's what Cody's dad said, anyway, and he should know since Cody has five brothers and twin sisters.

"I think they should make the mill into an indoor skate park," I said, touching up part of the crib I'd missed. "That would be sweet."

We were working outside, so I wouldn't inhale varnish fumes, in the shadow of a tower of split logs that Winter sold as firewood. I had to be careful that sawdust didn't get onto the newly varnished crib, or bugs.

Winter laughed. "Not much money in skate parks."

"I'd pay."

"That's my point." Winter shoved his cap back from his forehead. "Ready to break for lunch?"

Usually Winter made us sandwiches, Swiss cheese and tomato and horseradish sauce. Sometimes Vala would make us lunch, and then I'd lie and say I wasn't hungry or had already eaten, since the sandwiches she made mostly had fish in them – not tuna fish, either – and were on these tiny little pieces of bread that tasted like cardboard.

But today Winter said we'd go into town and get something from Shelley's Place, the hot dog stand down by the harbor. It was warm out, mid-August; school would start soon. I'd spent the summer hanging out with Cody and some of our friends, until the last few weeks when Cody had gone off to Bible camp.

That's when Winter put me to work. Because along with the crib, Winter had started building a house – a real house, not an addition to the schoolbus. I helped him clear away brush, then helped build the forms for the foundation to be poured into. Once the concrete cured, we began framing the structure. Sometimes Vala helped, until Winter yelled at her to stop, anyway. Then she'd go off to tend the little garden she'd planted at the edge of the woods.

Now I didn't know where Vala was. So I put aside the can of varnish and hopped into Winter's pickup, and we drove into town. Most of the summer people had already left, but there were still a few sailboats in the harbor, including one gigantic yacht, the *Ice Queen*, a three-masted schooner that belonged to Thomas Tierney. According to Winter she had a crew of ten, not just a captain and mate and deckhands but a cook and housekeeper, all for Tierney; as well as a red-and-white-striped mainsail, not that you'd ever have any trouble telling her apart from any of the other boats around here.

When he saw the *Ice Queen*, Winter scowled. But there was no other sign of Tierney, not that I could see. A few summer holdovers stood in line in front of Shelley's little food stand, trying to act like they fit in with the locals, even though the only other people were contractors working on job sites.

And Lonnie Packard. He was at the very front of the line, paying for a hot dog with onions and sauerkraut wrapped in a paper towel. It was the first time I'd seen Lonnie since I'd heard about him selling his farm to Thomas Tierney, and from the look on Winter's face, it was the first time he'd seen him, too. His mouth was twisted like he wasn't sure if he was going to smile or spit something out, but then Lonnie turned and nodded at him.

"Winter," he said. He pronounced it "Wintah" in this exaggerated way he had, like he was making fun of his own strong accent. "How's it hanging?"

Winter poked at the bill of his cap and gave his head a small shake. "Not bad." He looked at Lonnie's hot dog, then flashed me a sideways grin. "Now *that* looks like lunch. Right, Justin?"

So that's how I knew Winter wasn't going to stay pissed about Lonnie selling his farm, which was kind of a relief.

But Lonnie didn't look relieved. He looked uncomfortable, although Lonnie usually looked uncomfortable. He was a big rough-faced guy, not as tall as Winter but definitely plus-sized, with a bushy brown beard and baggy jeans tucked into high rubber fisherman's boots, which kind of surprised me since I knew he'd had to sell his boat. Then I remembered all the money he must have gotten from Thomas Tierney; enough to buy another boat, probably. Enough to buy anything he wanted.

"Gotta run," said Lonnie. "Got you an assistant there, eh, Winter?"

"Justin does good work," said Winter, and moved up to the window to place our order. For a moment Lonnie stared at him like he was going to say something else, but Winter was already talking to Shelley.

Instead Lonnie glanced at me again. It was a funny look, not like he was going to speak to me, more like he was trying to figure something out. Lonnie's not stupid, either. He puts on that heavy accent and acts like he's never been south of Bangor, but my mother said he actually has a law degree and fishes just because he likes it better than being a lawyer, which I think I would, too. I waited to see if he was going to talk to me, but instead he turned and walked quickly to where a brand-new SUV was parked in one of the spots reserved for fishermen, got inside and drove off. I watched him go, then angled up beside Winter to get my food.

Shelley gave me a quick smile and went back to talking to Winter. "See you're putting a house up by your place," she said, and handed him a paper towel with two hot dogs on it, a container of fried clams for Winter, and two bottles of Moxie. Winter nodded but didn't say anything, just passed her some money.

"Regular housing boom going on down there," Shelley added, then looked past us to the next customer. "Can I help you?"

We drove back to Winter's place and ate, sitting outside on a couple of lawn chairs and listening to woodpeckers in the pine grove. The air smelled nice, like sawdust and varnish and fried clams. When I was almost done, Vala stepped out of the schoolbus and walked over to me.

"*Ertu búinn?*" she said teasingly. "Are you finished? And you didn't save any for me?"

I looked uncertainly at Winter, still chewing.

"Mmm-mm," he said, flapping his hand at me. "None for her! Nothing unhealthy!"

"Hmph." Vala tossed her head, black ponytails flying. "Like I'd eat that – it's nothing but grease."

She watched disapprovingly as the last fried clam disappeared into Winter's mouth, then looked at me. "Come here, Justin. I want to show you something."

"Hey!" Winter called in mock alarm as Vala beckoned me towards the edge of the woods. "He's on the clock!"

"Now he's off," retorted Vala, and stuck her tongue out. "Come on."

Vala was strange. Sometimes she acted like my mother, grumpy about me forgetting to take my shoes off when I went into the schoolbus, or if me and Cody made too much noise. Other times, like now, she acted more like a girl my own age, teasing and unpredictable.

The way she looked changed, too. I don't mean her clothes – she pretty much wore the same thing all the time – but the way that sometimes she would look old, like my mom does, and other times she'd look the same age as me and my friends. Which creeped me out, especially if it was one of those times when she was acting young, too.

Fortunately, right now she was acting young but looking older, like someone who would be married to Winter. For one thing, she was wearing his clothes, a pair of jeans way too big for her and cuffed up so much you couldn't even see her shoes, and that baggy sweatshirt, despite it being so hot.

"I said *come*," she repeated, and whacked me on the shoulder.

I stood hastily and followed her, wondering if everyone in Iceland was like this, or if it was just Vala.

Under the trees everything was green and gold and warm; not hot like out in the full sun, but not cool, either. It made me sweat, and my sweat and the dim light made the mosquitoes come out, lots of them, though they never seemed to bother Vala, and after a few minutes I ignored them and (mostly) forgot about them. The ground was soft and smelled like worms, a good smell that made me think of fishing, and now and then we'd go by a kind of tree that smelled so good I'd stop for a second, a tree that Winter calls Balm of Gilead, because its buds smell like incense.

Winter owned a lot of land, more than a hundred acres. Some of it he cut for firewood or lumber, but not this part. This part he left wild, because it joined up with Lonnie's land – Thomas Tierney's land, now – and because it was old-growth forest. People think that all the woods in Maine are wild and old, but most of it isn't much older than what you'd find someplace like New Jersey – the trees were cut hundreds or maybe a thousand years ago by the Passamaquoddy or other Indians, and when those trees grew back they were cut by Vikings, and when those trees grew back they were cut by the English and the French and everyone else, all the way up till now.

So there's actually not a lot of true virgin forest, even if the trees look ancient, like what you see in a movie when they want you to think it's someplace totally wild, when it's really, like, trees that are maybe forty or fifty years old. Baby trees.

But these trees weren't like that. These were old trees – wolf trees, some of them, the kind of trees that Winter usually cuts down. A wolf tree is a big crooked tree with a huge canopy that hogs all the light and soil and crowds out the other trees. Wolf trees are junk trees, because they're crooked and spread out so much they're not much good for lumber, and they overwhelm other, smaller trees and keep them from growing up tall and straight so they can be harvested.

When I was little I'd go with Winter into the woods to watch him work, and I was always afraid of the wolf trees. Not because there was anything scary about them – they looked like ordinary trees, only big.

But I thought wolves lived in them. When I said that to Winter once, he laughed.

"I thought that too, when I was your age." He was oiling his chain saw, getting ready to limb a wolf tree, a red oak. Red oaks smell terrible when you cut them, the raw wood stinks – they smell like dog crap. "Want to know the real reason they call them that?"

I nodded, breathing through my mouth.

"It's because a thousand years ago, in England and around there, they'd hang outlaws from a tree like this. Wolf's-head trees, they called them, because the outlaws were like wolves, preying on weaker people."

Where the wolf trees grew here, they had shaded out most other trees. Now and then I saw an old apple tree overgrown with wild grape vines, remnants of Lonnie's family farm. Because even though this was old-growth forest, birds and animals don't know that. They eat fruit from the farm then poop out the seeds – that's how you get apple trees and stuff like that in the middle of the woods.

I was getting hot and tired of walking. Vala hadn't said anything since we started, hadn't even looked back at me, and I wondered if she'd forgotten I was even there. My mother said pregnancy makes women spacy, more than usual even. I was trying to think of an excuse to turn back, when she stopped.

"Here," she said.

We'd reached a hollow on the hillside above the farm. I could just make out the farmhouse and barn and outbuildings, some apple trees and the overgrown field that led down to the ocean. There was no real beach there, just lots of big granite rocks, also a long metal dock that I didn't remember having seen before.

It was still a pretty spot, tucked into the woods. A few yards from the farmhouse, more trees marched down to a cliff above the rocky beach. Small trees, all twisted from the wind: except for three huge white pines, each a hundred feet tall.

Winter called these the King's Pines, and they were gigantic.

"These trees are ancient," he'd told me, pointing up at one. "See anything up there?"

I squinted. I knew bald eagles nested near the ocean, but I didn't see anything that looked like a nest. I shook my head.

Winter put his hand on my shoulder and twisted me till I was staring almost straight up. "There, on the trunk – see where the bark's been notched?"

I saw it then, three marks of an axe in the shape of an arrow.

"That's the King's Mark," said Winter. "Probably dating back to about 1690. That means these were the King's Trees, to be used for masts in the King's naval fleet. See how high up that mark is? That's how old these trees are. Over three hundred years ago, this was a big tree. And it was probably at least three hundred years old then."

Now, with Vala, I could see the King's Pines jutting out above the other trees, like the masts of a schooner rising from a green sea. I figured that's what Vala was going to show me, and so I got ready to be polite and act like I already didn't know about them.

Instead she touched my arm and pointed just a few feet away, towards a clearing where trees had grown around part of the pasture.

"Whoa," I whispered.

In the middle of the clearing was a bush. A big bush, a quince, its long, thin branches covered with green leaves and small red flowers – brilliant red, the color of Valentines, and so bright after the dim woods that I had to blink.

And then, after blinking, I thought something had gone wrong with my eyes; because the bush seemed to be moving. Not moving in the wind – there wasn't any wind – but moving like it was breaking apart then coming back together again, the leaves lifting away from the branches and flickering into the air, going from dark-green to shining green like metallic paint, and here and there a flash of red like a flower had spun off, too.

But what was even more bizarre was that the bush made a noise. It was *buzzing*, not like bees but like a chainsaw or weed whacker, a high-pitched sound that got louder then softer then louder again. I rubbed my eyes and squinted into the overgrown field, thinking maybe Thomas Tierney had hired someone to clean up and that's what I was hearing.

There was no one there, just tall grass and apple trees and rocks, and beyond that the cliff and open sea.

"Do you see what they are?"

Vala's voice was so close to my ear that I jumped; then felt my skin prickle with goosebumps at her breath, cold as though a freezer door had opened. I shook my head and she touched my sleeve, her hand cold through the cloth, and led me into the clearing, until the bush rose above us like a red cloud.

"See?" she murmured.

The bush was full of hummingbirds – hundreds of them, darting in and out as though the bush were a city, and the spaces between the leaves streets and alleys. Some hovered above the flowers to feed, though most flew almost too fast to see. Some sat on the branches, perfectly still, and that was the weirdest thing of all, like seeing a raindrop hanging in the air.

But they didn't stay still; just perched long enough that I could get a look at one, its green green wings and the spot of red on its throat, so deep a red it was like someone had crushed its tiny body by holding it too hard. I thought maybe I could hold it too, or touch it, anyway.

So I tried. I stood with my palm open and held my breath and didn't move. Hummingbirds whizzed around like I was part of the quince, but they didn't land on me.

I glanced at Vala. She was doing the same thing I was, this amazed smile on her face, holding both arms out in front of her so she reminded me of Winter when he was dowsing. The hummingbirds buzzed around her, too, but didn't stop. Maybe if one of us had been wearing red. Hummingbirds like red.

Vala wasn't wearing red, just Winter's grubby old gray sweatshirt and jeans. But she looked strange standing there, eerie even, and for a second I had this weird feeling that I wasn't seeing Vala at all, that she had disappeared and I was standing next to a big gray rock.

The feeling was so strong that it creeped me out. I opened my mouth, I was going to suggest that we head back to Winter's house, when a hummingbird flickered right in front of Vala's face. Right in front of Vala's *eye*.

"Hey!" I yelled; and at the same instant Vala shouted, a deep grunting noise that had a word in it, but not an English word. Her hand flashed in front of her face, there was a greenish blur and the bird was gone.

"Are you okay?" I said. I thought the hummingbird's sharp beak had stabbed her eye. "Did it – ?"

Vala brought her hands to her face and gasped, blinking quickly. "I'm sorry! It frightened me – so close, I was surprised – "

Her hands dropped. She gazed at the ground by her feet. "Oh no."

Near the toe of one rubber shoe, the hummingbird lay motionless, like a tiny bright green leaf.

"Oh, I am sorry, Justin!" cried Vala. "I only wanted you to see the tree with all the birds. But it scared me – "

I crouched to look at the dead hummingbird. Vala gazed back into the woods.

"We should go," she said. She sounded unhappy, even nervous. "Winter will think we got lost and get mad at me for taking you away. You need to work," she added, and gave me a tight smile. "Come on."

She walked away. I stayed where I was. After a moment I picked up a stick and tentatively prodded at the dead bird. It didn't move.

It was on its back and it looked sadder that way. I wanted to turn it over. I poked it again, harder.

It still didn't budge.

Cody doesn't mind touching dead things. I do. But the hummingbird was so small, only as long as my finger. And it was beautiful, with its black beak and the red spot at its throat and those tiny feathers, more like scales. So I picked it up.

"Holy crap," I whispered.

It was heavy. Not heavy like maybe a bigger bird would have been, a sparrow or chickadee, but *heavy*, like a rock. Not even a rock – it reminded me of one of those weights you see hanging from an old clock, those metal things shaped like pine cones or acorns, but when you touch them they feel heavy as a bowling ball, only much smaller.

The hummingbird was like that – so little I could cradle it in my cupped palm, and already cold. I guessed that rigor mortis had set in, the way it does when you hang a deer. Very gently I touched the bird's wing. I even tried to wiggle it, but the wing didn't move.

So I dropped the bird into my cupped palm and turned it onto its stomach. Its tiny legs were folded up like a fly's, its eyes dull. Its body didn't feel soft, like feathers. It felt hard, solid as granite; and cold.

But it looked exactly like a live hummingbird, emerald green where the sun hit it, beak slightly curved; a band of white under the red throat. I ran my finger along its beak, then swore.

"What the frig?"

A bright red bead welled up where the dead bird's beak had punctured my skin, sharp as a nail.

I sucked my finger, quickly looked to make sure Vala hadn't seen me. I could just make her out in the distance, moving through the trees. I felt in my pocket till I found a wadded-up Kleenex, wrapped the hummingbird in it and very carefully put it into my pocket. Then I hurried after Vala.

We walked back in silence. Only when the skeletal frame of the new house showed brightly through the trees did Vala turn to me.

"You saw the bird?" she asked.

I looked at her uneasily. I was afraid to lie, but even more afraid of what she might do if she knew what was in my pocket.

Before I could reply, she reached to touch the spot on my chin. I felt a flash of aching cold as she stared at me, her dark eyes somber but not unkind.

"I did not mean to hurt it," she said quietly. "I have never seen a bird like that one, not so close. I was scared. Not scared – startled. My reaction was too fast," she went on, and her voice was sad. Then she smiled, and glanced down at my jeans pocket.

"You took it," she said.

I turned away, and Vala laughed. In front of the house, Winter looked up from a pile of two-by-sixes.

"Get your butt over here, Justin!" he yelled. "Woman, don't you go distracting him!"

Vala stuck her tongue out again, then turned back to me. "He knows," she said matter-of-factly. "But maybe you don't tell your friend? Or your mother."

And she walked over to kiss Winter's sunburned cheek.

I muttered, "Yeah, sure;" then crossed to where I'd left the varnish. Vala stood beside her husband and sighed as she stared at the cloudless sky and the green canopy of trees stretching down to the Bay. A few boats under sail moved slowly across the blue water. One was a three-masted schooner with a red-striped mainsail: Thomas Tierney's yacht.

"So Vala," said Winter. He winked at his wife. "You tell Justin your news yet?"

She smiled. "Not yet." She pulled up the sweatshirt so I could see her stomach sticking out. "Here – "

She beckoned me over, took my hand and placed it on her stomach. Despite the heat, her hand was icy cold. So was her stomach; but I felt a sudden heat beneath my palm, and then a series of small thumps from inside her belly. I looked at her in surprise.

"It's the baby!"

"*Eg veit*," she said, and laughed. "I know."

"Now don't go scaring him off, talking about babies," said Winter. He put his arm around his wife. "I need him to help me finish this damn house before it snows."

I went back to varnishing. The truth is, I was glad to have something to do, so I wouldn't think about what had happened. When I got home that evening I put the hummingbird in a drawer, wrapped in an old T-shirt. For a while I'd look at it every night, after my mother came in to give me a kiss; but after a week or so I almost forgot it was there.

A few days later Cody got back from Bible camp. It was September now. Labor Day had come and gone, and most of the summer people. School started up. Me and Cody were in eighth grade, we were pretty sick of being with the same people since kindergarten, but it was okay. Some days we skated over at Winter's place after school. It was getting crowded there with the piles of split firewood and all the stacks of lumber for the new house, and sometimes Winter yelled at us for getting in the way.

But mostly everything was like it usually was, except that Vala was getting more pregnant and everyone was starting to think about winter coming down.

You might not believe that people really worry about snow all the time, but here they do. My mother had already gotten her firewood from Winter back in August, and so had most of his other regular customers. Day by day, the big stacks of split wood dwindled, as Winter hauled them off for delivery.

And day by day the new house got bigger, so that soon it looked less like a kid's drawing of a stick house and more like a fairy tale cottage come to life, with a steep roof and lots of windows, some of them square and some of them round, like portholes, and scallop-shaped shingles stained the color of cranberries. I helped with that part, and inside, too, which was great.

Because inside – inside was amazing. Winter did incredible things with wood, everyone knew that. But until now, I had only seen the things he made for money, like furniture, or things he made to be useful, like the cabinets he'd done for my mother.

Now I saw what Winter did for himself and Vala. And if the outside of the little house looked like a fairy tale, the inside looked like something from a dream.

Winter usually carved from pine, which is a very soft wood. But he'd used oak for the beams, and covered them with faces – wind-faces with their mouths open to blow, foxes and wolves grinning from the corners, dragons and people I didn't recognize but who Vala said were spirits from Iceland.

"*Huldufolk*," she said when I asked about them. "The hidden people."

But they weren't hidden here. They were carved on the main beam that went across the living room ceiling, and on the oak posts in each corner, peeking out from carved leaves and vines and branches that made the posts look almost like real trees. There were *huldufolk* carved into the cupboards, and on benches and cabinets and bookshelves, and even on the headboard that Winter had made from a single slab of chestnut, so highly polished with beeswax that the entire bedroom smelled like honey.

So even though the house looked small from the outside, when you got inside you could get lost, wandering around and looking at all the wonderful carven things. Not just carved so the wood resembled something new, but so that you could see what was *inside* the wood, knots and whorls turned to eyes and mouths, the grain sanded and stained till it felt like soft, the way skin might feel if it grew strong enough to support walls and ceilings and joists, while still managing to remain, somehow, skin, and alive.

It was the most amazing house I've ever seen. And maybe the most amazing thing wasn't that it made me want to live in it, but that after spending hours working on it, I began to feel that the house lived in *me*, the way the baby lived inside Vala.

Only of course I could never tell anyone that, especially Cody. He would think I'd gone nuts from inhaling varnish fumes – even though I wore a dust mask, like Vala wore a fancy ventilating mask that made her look like Darth Vader.

She was working inside, too, building a stone fireplace. She found rocks in the woods and brought them up in a wheelbarrow. Big rocks, too, I was amazed she could lift them.

"Don't tell Winter," she whispered to me when I found her once, hefting a huge chunk of granite from the edge of the woods. "He'll just worry, and yell at me. And then I will yell at *you*," she added, and narrowed her spooky blue-black eyes.

Once the rocks were all piled inside she took forever, deciding which one would go where in the fireplace. When I made a joke about it she frowned.

"You do not want to make rocks angry, Justin." She wasn't kidding, either. She looked pissed off. "Because rocks have a very, very long memory."

It was early morning, just after seven on a Saturday. My mom had dropped me off at Winter's place on her way to see a client. It was a beautiful day, Indian summer, the leaves just starting to turn. I could see two sailboats on the water, heading south for the winter. I would rather have been skating with Cody, but Winter was anxious to get the inside of his house finished before it got too cold, so I said I'd come over and help trim up some windows.

Winter was outside. Vala, after yelling at me about the rocks, had gone up to the bedroom to get something. I yawned, wishing I'd brought my iPod, when upstairs Vala screamed.

I froze. It was a terrifying sound, not high-pitched like a woman's voice but deep and booming. And it went on and on, without her taking a breath. I started for the steps as Winter raced in. He knocked me aside and took the stairs two at a time.

"*Vala!*"

I ran upstairs after him, through the empty hall and into the bedroom. Vala stood in front of the window, clutching her face as she gazed outside. Winter grabbed her shoulders.

"Is it the baby?" he cried. He tried to pull her towards him, but she shook her head, then pushed him away so violently that he crashed against the wall.

"What is it?" I ran to the window. Vala fell silent as I looked out across the yellowing canopy of leaves.

"Oh no." I stared in disbelief at the cliff above the Bay. "The King's Pines – "

I rubbed my eyes, hardly aware of Winter pushing me aside so he could stare out.

"*No!*" he roared.

One of the three great trees was gone – the biggest one, the one that stood nearest to the cliff-edge. A blue gap showed where it had been, a chunk of sky that made me feel sick and dizzy. It was like lifting my own hand to find a finger missing. My chin throbbed and I turned, so the others wouldn't see me crying.

Winter pounded the windowsill. His face was dead white, his eyes so red they looked like they'd been smeared with paint. That frightened me more than anything, until I looked up and saw Vala.

She had backed against the wall – an unfinished wall, just gray sheetrock, blotched where the seams had been coated with putty. Her face had paled, too; but it wasn't white.

It was gray. Not a living gray, like hair or fur, but a dull mottled color, the gray of dead bark or granite.

And not just her face but her hands and arms: everything I could see of her that had been skin, now seemed cold and dead as the heap of fireplace rocks downstairs. Her clothes drooped as though tossed on a boulder, her hair stiffened like strands of reindeer moss. Even her eyes dulled to black smears, save for a pinpoint of light in each, as though a drop of water had been caught in the hollow of a stone.

"Vala." Winter came up beside me. His voice shook, but it was low and calm, as though he were trying to keep a frightened dog from bolting. "Vala, it's all right – "

He reached to stroke the slab of gray stone wedged against the wall, reindeer moss tangling between his fingers; then let his hand drop to move across a rounded outcropping.

"Think of the baby," he whispered. "Think of the girl..."

The threads of reindeer moss trembled, the twin droplets welled and spilled from granite to the floor; and it was Vala there and not a stone at all, Vala falling into her husband's arms and weeping uncontrollably.

"It's *not* all right – it's *not* all right – "

He held her, stroking her head as I finally got the nerve up to speak.

"Was it – was it a storm?"

"A storm?" Abruptly Winter pulled away from Vala. His face darkened to the color of mahogany. "No, it's not a storm – "

He reached for the window and yanked it open. From the direction of the cliff came the familiar drone of a chainsaw.

"It's Tierney!" shouted Winter. He turned and raced into the hall. Vala ran after him, and I ran after her.

"No – you stay here!" Winter stopped at the top of the stairs. "Justin, you wait right here with her – "

"No," I said. I glanced nervously at Vala, but to my surprise she nodded.

"No," she said. "I'm going, and Justin too."

Winter sucked his breath through his teeth.

"Suit yourself," he said curtly. "But I'm not waiting for you. And listen – you stay with her, Justin, you understand me?"

"I will," I said, but he was already gone.

Vala and I looked at each other. Her eyes were paler than I remembered, the same dull gray as the sheetrock; but as I stared at her they grew darker, as though someone had dropped blue ink into a glass of water.

"Come," she said. She touched my shoulder, then headed out the door after her husband. I followed.

All I wanted to do was run and catch up with Winter. I could have, too – over the summer I'd gotten taller, and I was now a few inches bigger than Vala.

But I remembered the way Winter had said *You stay with her, Justin, you understand me?* And the way he'd looked, as though I were a stranger and he'd knock me over, or worse, if I disobeyed him. It scared me and made me feel sick, almost as sick as seeing the King's Pine chopped down; but I had no time to think about that now. I could still hear the chainsaw buzzing from down the hill, a terrible sound, like when you hear a truck brake but you know it's not going to stop in time. I walked as fast as I dared, Vala just a few steps behind me. When I heard her breathing hard I'd stop, and try to keep sight of Winter far ahead of us.

But after a few minutes I gave up on that. He was out of sight, and I could only hope he'd get down to the cliff and stop whoever was doing the cutting, before another tree fell.

"Listen," said Vala, and grabbed my sleeve. I thought the chainsaw was still running, but then I realized it was just an echo. Because the air grew silent, and Vala had somehow sensed this before I did. I looked at her and she stared back at me, her eyes huge and round and sky-blue, a color I'd never seen them before.

"There is still time," she whispered. She made a strange deep noise in the back of her throat, a growl but not an animal growl; more like the sound of thunder, or rocks falling. "Hurry – "

We crashed through the woods, no longer bothering to stay on the path. We passed the quince bush shimmering through its green haze of feeding hummingbirds. Vala didn't pause but I slowed down to look back, then stopped.

A vehicle was parked by the farmhouse, the same new SUV I'd seen that day down at Shelley's hot dog stand: Lonnie Packard's truck. As I stared, a burly figure came hurrying through the field, the familiar orange silhouette of a chainsaw tucked under his arm. He jumped into the SUV, gunned the engine and drove off.

I swore under my breath.

"Justin!" Vala's anxious voice came from somewhere in the woods. "Come on!"

I found her at the head of the trail near the cliff. Through a broken wall of scrawny, wind-twisted trees I could just make out the two remaining pines, and the bright yellow gash that was the stump of the one that had fallen. The sharp scent of pine resin and sawdust hung in the air, and the smell of exhaust fumes from the chainsaw.

But there was no other sign of Lonnie, obviously, or of anyone else.

"Look," said Vala in a hoarse whisper. She clutched me and pulled me towards her, her touch so cold it was like I'd been shot up with novocaine. My entire arm went numb. "There! The boat – "

She pointed down to the boulder-strewn beach where the dock thrust into the bay. At the end of the dock bobbed a small motorboat, a Boston Whaler. Further out, the hulking form of the *Ice Queen* rose above the gray water, sails furled.

She was at anchor. Several small forms moved across the deck. I squinted, trying to see if I recognized any of them. A frigid spasm shot through my ribs as Vala nudged me, indicating the rocks below.

"Is that him?" she hissed. "This man Tierney?"

I saw Winter loping across the beach towards the dock, jumping from one boulder to the next. On the shore, right next to the end of the dock, stood two men. One was tall, wearing an orange life vest and a blaze-orange watch cap and high rubber boots. The other was shorter, white-haired, slightly heavy-set, wearing sunglasses and a red-and-white windbreaker, striped like the *Ice Queen*'s sails.

"That's him," I said.

Vala fixed her intense sky-blue gaze on me. "You're sure?"

"Yeah. I've seen his picture in the newspaper. And online."

She stood at the top of the trail and stared down. An angry voice rose from the rocks – Winter's – then another voice joined in, calmer, and a third, calm at first then laughing. I heard Winter curse, words I couldn't believe he knew. The third man, Tierney, laughed even harder.

I glanced at Vala, still staring at what was below us. One of her hands grasped the branch of a birch tree beside the path. She seemed to be thinking; almost she might have been daydreaming, she looked so peaceful, like somehow she'd forgotten where she was and what was happening. Finally she shook her head. Without looking back at me, she snapped the branch from the tree, dropped it, and started down the trail towards the beach.

I started after her, then hesitated.

The branch lay across the narrow path at my feet. Where Vala had touched them, the leaves had shriveled and faded, from yellow-green to the dull gray of lichen, and the white birch bark had blackened into tight charred-looking curls.

I tried to lift the branch. It was too heavy to move.

"It's *my* land now." Thomas Tierney's voice echoed from the cliff-face. "So I suggest you get the hell off it!"

I looked down to see Vala's small form at the bottom of the trail, hopping lightly from one boulder to the next as she headed for the dock. I scrambled down the path after her.

But I couldn't go as fast. For some reason, maybe because first Winter and then Vala had raced down before me, rocks had tumbled across the narrow trail. Not big rocks, but enough of them that I had to pick my way carefully to keep from falling.

Not only that: in spots a white slick of frost covered the ground, so that my feet slipped and once I almost fell and cracked my head. I stopped for a minute, panting. As I caught my breath I looked away from the beach, to where the cliff plunged into a deep crevice in the granite.

There, caught in the gigantic crack so that it looked as though it had grown up from the rocks, was the fallen pine. It tilted over the water, black in the shadow of the cliff, its great branches still green and strong-looking, the smell of pine sap overpowering the smell of the sea. In its uppermost branches something moved, then lifted from the tree and flew out above the bay – a bald eagle, still mottled brown and black with its young plumage.

I couldn't help it. I began to cry. Because no matter how strong and alive the tree looked, I knew it was dead. Nothing would bring it back again. It had been green when no one lived here but the Passamaquoddy, it had seen sailors come from far across the sea, and tourists in boats from Paswegas Harbor, and maybe it had even seen the *Ice Queen* earlier that morning with her red-and-white-striped mainsail and Thomas Tierney on the deck, watching as Lonnie Packard took a chainsaw to its great trunk and the tree finally fell, a crash that I hadn't heard.

But Vala had.

You stay with her, Justin, you understand me?

I took a deep breath and wiped my eyes, checked to make sure I could still see Vala on the rocks below, then continued my climb down. When I finally reached the bottom I still had to be careful – there were tidal pools everywhere between the granite boulders, some of them skimmed with ice and all of them greasy with kelp and sea lettuce. I hurried as fast as I could towards the dock.

"*You don't own those trees.*" Winter's voice rang out so loudly that my ears hurt. "Those are the King's Pines – no man owns them."

"Well, I own this land," retorted Tierney. "And if that doesn't make me the goddamn king, I don't know what does."

I clambered over the last stretch of rocks and ran up alongside Vala. Winter stood a few yards away from us, towering above Thomas Tierney. The other man stood uneasily at the edge of the dock. I recognized him – Al Alford, who used to work as first mate on one of the daysailers in Paswegas Harbor. Now, I guessed, he worked for Tierney.

"King?" Vala repeated. "*Hann er klikkapor.*" She looked at me from the corner of her eyes. "He's nuts."

Maybe it was her saying that, or maybe it was me being pissed at myself for crying. But I took a step out towards Tierney and shouted at him.

"It's against the law to cut those trees! It's against the law to do any cutting here without a permit!"

Tierney turned to stare at me. For the first time he looked taken aback, maybe even embarrassed or ashamed. Not by what he'd done, I knew that; but because someone else – a kid – knew he'd done it.

"Who's this?" His voice took on that fake nice tone adults use when they're caught doing something, like smoke or drink or fight with their wives. "This your son, Winter?"

"No," I said.

"Yes," said Vala, and under her breath said the word she'd used when I first met her: *feogar.*

But Winter didn't say anything, and Tierney had already turned away.

"Against the law?" He pulled at the front of his red-and-white windbreaker, then shrugged. "I'll pay the fine. No one goes to jail for cutting down trees."

Tierney smiled then, as though he was thinking of a joke no one else would ever get, and added, "Not me, anyway."

He looked at Al Alford, and nodded. Al quickly turned and walked – ran, practically – to where the Boston Whaler rocked against the metal railing at the end of the dock. Tierney followed him, but slowly, pausing once to stare back up the hillside – not at the King's Pines but at the farmhouse, its windows glinting in the sun where they faced the cliff. Then he walked to where Alford waited by the little motorboat, his hand out to help Tierney climb inside.

I looked at Winter. His face had gone slack, except for his mouth: he looked as though he were biting down on something hard.

"He's going to cut the other ones, too," he said. He didn't sound disbelieving or sad or even angry; more like he was saying something everyone knew was true, like *It'll snow soon* or *Tomorrow's Sunday*. "He'll pay the twenty-thousand- dollar fine, just like he did down in Kennebunkport, he'll wait and do it in the middle of the night when I'm not here. And the trees will be gone."

"No he will not," said Vala. Her voice was nearly as calm as Winter's. There was a subdued roar as the motorboat's engine turned over, and the Boston Whaler shot away from the dock, towards the *Ice Queen*.

"No," Vala said again, and she stooped and picked up a rock. A small gray rock, just big enough to fit inside her fist, one side of it encrusted with barnacles. She straightened and stared at the ocean, her eyes no longer sky-blue but the pure deep gray of a stone that's been worn smooth by the sea, with no pupil in them; and shining like water in the sun.

"Skammastu peî, Thomas Tierney. Farthu til fjandanns!" she cried, and threw the rock towards the water. *"Farthu! Låttu peog hverfa!"*

I watched it fly through the air, then fall, hitting the beach a long way from the waterline with a small thud. I started to look at Vala, and stopped.

From the water came a grinding sound, a deafening noise like thunder; only this was louder than a thunderclap and didn't last so long, just a fraction of a second. I turned and shaded my eyes, staring out to where the Boston Whaler arrowed towards Tierney's yacht. A sudden gust of wind stung my eyes with spray; I blinked, then blinked again in amazement.

A few feet from the motorboat a black spike of stone shadowed the water. Not a big rock – it might have been a dolphin's fin, or a shark's, but it wasn't moving.

And it hadn't been there just seconds before. It had never been there, I knew that. I heard a muffled shout, then the frantic whine of the motorboat's engine being revved too fast – and too late.

With a sickening crunch, the Boston Whaler ran onto the rock. Winter yelled in dismay as Alford's orange-clad figure was thrown into the water. For a second Thomas Tierney remained upright, his arms flailing as he tried to grab at Alford. Then, as though a trapdoor opened beneath him, he dropped through the bottom of the boat and disappeared.

Winter raced towards the water. I ran after him.

"Stay with Vala!" Winter grabbed my arm. Alford's orange life vest gleamed from on top of the rock where he clung. On board the *Ice Queen*, someone yelled through a megaphone, and I could see another craft, a little inflated Zodiac, drop into the gray water. Winter shook me fiercely. "Justin! I said, *stay with her* – "

He looked back towards the beach. So did I.

Vala was nowhere to be seen. Winter dropped my arm, but before he could say anything there was a motion among the rocks.

And there was Vala, coming into sight like gathering fog. Even from this distance I could see how her eyes glittered, blue-black like a winter sky; and I could tell she was smiling.

The crew of the *Ice Queen* rescued Alford quickly, long before the Coast Guard arrived. Winter and I stayed on the beach for several hours, while the search and rescue crews arrived and the Navy Falcons flew by overhead, in case Tierney came swimming to shore, or in case his body washed up.

But it never did. That spar of rock ripped a huge hole in the Boston Whaler, a bigger hole even than you'd think; but no one blamed Alford. All you had to do was take a look at the charts and see that there had never been a rock there, ever. Though it's there now, I can tell you that. I see it every day when I look out from the windows at Winter's house.

I never asked Vala about what happened. Winter had a grim expression when we finally went back to his place late that afternoon. Thomas Tierney was a multi-millionaire, remember, and even I knew there would be an investigation and interviews and TV people.

But everyone on board the *Ice Queen* had witnessed what happened, and so had Al Alford; and while they'd all seen Winter arguing with Tierney, there'd been no exchange of blows, not even any pushing, and no threats on Winter's part – Alford testified to that. The King's Pine was gone, but two remained; and a bunch of people from the Audubon Society and the Sierra Club and places like that immediately filed a lawsuit against Tierney's estate, to have all the property on the old Packard farm turned into a nature preserve.

Which I thought was good, but it still won't bring the other tree back.

One day after school, a few weeks after the boat sank, I was helping to put the finishing touches on Winter's house. Just about everything was done, except for the fireplace – there were still piles of rocks everywhere and plastic buckets full of mortar and flat stones for the hearth.

"Justin." Vala appeared behind me, so suddenly I jumped. "Will you come with me, please?"

I stood and nodded. She looked really pregnant now, and serious.

But happy, too. In the next room we could hear Winter working with a sander. Vala looked at me and smiled, put a finger to her lips then touched her finger to my chin. This time, it didn't ache with cold.

"Come," she said.

Outside it was cold and gray, the middle of October but already most of the trees were bare, their leaves torn away by a storm a few nights earlier. We headed for the woods behind the house, past the quince bush, its branches stripped of leaves and all the hummingbirds long gone to warmer places. Vala wore her same bright blue rubber shoes and Winter's rolled-up jeans.

But even his big sweatshirt was too small now to cover her belly, so my mother had knit her a nice big sweater and given her a warm plaid coat that made Vala look even more like a kid, except for her eyes and that way she would look at me sometimes and smile, as though we both knew a secret. I followed her to where the path snaked down to the beach, and tried not to glance over at the base of the cliff. The King's Pine had finally fallen and wedged between the crack in the huge rocks there, so that now seaweed was tangled in its dead branches, and all the rocks were covered with yellow pine needles.

"Winter has to go into town for a few hours," Vala said, as though answering a question. "I need you to help me with something."

We reached the bottom of the path and picked our way across the rocks, until we reached the edge of the shore. A few gulls flew overhead, screaming, and the wind blew hard against my face and bare hands. I'd followed Vala outside without my coat. When I looked down, I saw that my fingers were bright red. But I didn't feel cold at all.

"Here," murmured Vala.

She walked, slowly, to where a gray rock protruded from the gravel beach. It was roughly the shape and size of an arm.

Then I drew up beside Vala, and saw that it really was an arm – part of one, anyway, made of smooth gray stone, like marble only darker, but with no hand and broken just above the elbow. Vala stood and looked at it, her lips pursed; then stooped to pick it up.

"Will you carry this, please?" she said.

I didn't say anything, just held out my arms, as though she were going to fill them with firewood. When she set the stone down I flinched – not because it was heavy, though it was, but because it looked exactly like a real arm. I could even see where the veins had been, in the crook of the elbow, and the wrinkled skin where the arm had bent.

"Justin," Vala said. I looked up to see her blue-black eyes fixed on me. "Come on. It will get dark soon."

I followed her as she walked slowly along the beach, like someone looking for sea glass or sand dollars. Every few feet she would stop and pick something up – a hand, a foot, a long piece of stone that was most of a leg – then turn and set it carefully into my arms. When I couldn't carry any more, she picked up one last small rock – a clenched fist – and made her way slowly back to the trail.

We made several more trips that day, and for several days after that. Each time, we would return to the house and Vala would fit the stones into the unfinished fireplace, covering them with other rocks so that no one could see them. Or if you did see one, you'd think maybe it was just part of a broken statue, or a rock that happened to *look* like a foot, or a shoulder blade, or the cracked round back of a head.

I couldn't bring myself to ask Vala about it. But I remembered how the Boston Whaler had looked when the Coast Guard dragged it onshore, with a small ragged gash in its bow, and a much, much bigger hole in the bottom, as though something huge and heavy had crashed through it. Like a meteor, maybe. Or a really big rock, or like if someone had dropped a granite statue of a man into the boat.

Not that anyone had seen that happen. I told myself that maybe it really was a statue – maybe a statue had fallen off a ship, or been pushed off a cliff or something.

But then one day we went down to the beach, the last day actually, and Vala made me wade into the shallow water. She pointed at something just below the surface, something round and white, like a deflated soccer ball.

Only it wasn't a soccer ball. It was Thomas Tierney's head: the front of it, anyway, the one part Vala hadn't already found and built into the fireplace.

His face.

I pulled it from the water and stared at it. A green scum of algae covered his eyes, which were wide and staring. His mouth was open so you could see where his tongue had been before it broke off, leaving a jagged edge in the hole of his screaming mouth.

"*Loksins*," said Vala. She took it from me easily, even though it was so heavy I could barely hold it. "At last. . . ."

She turned and walked back up to the house.

That was three months ago. Winter's house is finished now, and Winter lives in it along with Winter's wife.

And their baby. The fireplace is done, and you can hardly see where there is a round broken stone at the very top, which if you squint and look at it in just the right light, like at night when only the fire is going, looks kind of like a face. Winter is happier than I've ever seen him, and my mom and I come over a lot, to visit him and Vala and the baby, who is just a few weeks old now and so cute you wouldn't believe it, and tiny, so tiny I was afraid to hold her at first but Vala says not to worry – I may be like her big brother now but someday, when the baby grows up, she will be the one to always watch out for me. They named her Gerda, which means Protector; and for a baby she is incredibly strong.

The King of the Djinn

David Ackert & Benjamin Rosenbaum

David Ackert (*davidackert.com*) lives in Los Angeles. He is a professional actor who grew up in an Iranian family in Virginia in the late '70s and early '80s, a situation he perceived at the time to be "life-threatening." He has starred in several independent films and appeared on a number of TV shows. Benjamin Rosenbaum (benjaminrosenbaum.com) lives with his wife Esther and their children in Virginia. He works for the National Science Foundation. His fine short stories have been published widely in science fiction and fantasy publications since 2001. "Strays," another Ackert/Rosenbaum collaboration, has recently been published, and several more may yet appear.

"The King of the Djinn" was published in *Realms of Fantasy* in the fall of 2007, although the magazine's cover date was February 2008, but it seemed to us an essential part of the 2007 year. According to Rosenbaum, this story was initially part of *Library of Souls*, a draft collaborative novel by Ackert and Rosenbaum that has since been "retired." It is the story of good and evil, and of a wish granted in the disturbingly complex world of today.

GRINDING AND ROARING, the sixteen-wheeler crested a great dune, and Musa rejoiced: there on the horizon, the Mediterranean glittered, blue as Heaven. "God is great!" he shouted as he shifted into second for the downgrade.

Each week, Musa made this trip, carrying a ton of devilish black carbonated soda from the bottling plant of El-Nasr to the decadent tongues of Cairo. And each week, when he reached the open road, his heart threw off its burdens.

In the town, the nights were empty and cold. He'd awaken again and again to the sudden emptiness of his house – his wife Suha dead, his son Jamal away at university. The days were full of packing and loading and tinkering, activity and worry. The men of the bottling plant were always asking Musa for blessings, for amulets, for the resolution of disputes. They'd found out, somehow, that he'd once studied Qur'an and Hadith in the great merkab in Cairo. Sometimes he even had the odd sense that they knew about his meetings with the King of the Djinn. He never knew what to say to them.

On the road, Musa was with God alone. He prayed without words as he drove, using only his breath, opening himself to God as the great bounty of the world came into focus. Every blinding white grain of sand reflected God's glory at Musa; the blue vault of the heavens was filled with God's breath. The roaring engine of the semi and the black ribbon of the highway testified to the great genius God had entrusted in man. Whenever Musa saw a camel or a goat or a date tree in the sand beyond the highway, it was full of life, full to bursting, and the life in it reached out into Musa's heart and whispered to him: we are one.

The King of the Djinn had been right. It was he who had told Musa to abandon the academy, that his soul was starving. Musa had given his inheritance to charity, dropped out of the merkab, and found this simple work. For forty years, he had devoted himself to the secret path of the breath. He slowed down enough for God to find him, and God took Musa in the palm of His hand and held him there. Even at Suha's death, God's love of Musa never wavered; Musa cried like a woman at her graveside, and God held him with strong arms and kept him safe from despair.

Now Musa could see tiny white flecks against the sea's blue. Whitecaps dancing. The road turned parallel to the shore.

As for the King of the Djinn: Musa was not sure, of course, that he really was the King of the Djinn. That was just a guess. He called himself "Gil."

But since 1952, when they had met in a café in the student quarter, Musa had become an old man, and Gil had not aged a day. Gil looked like a Persian, but he spoke a fluent and elegantly complex classical Arabic, the way no one had spoken it since the time of the Prophet. And in Gil's eyes, Musa saw the kind of fearlessness men had only when they were young and arrogant, or old and dying. Yet Gil possessed it all the time.

Given his instrumental role in turning Musa to the true knowledge of God, it was possible that Gil was an angel. But Gil did not act like an intimate of God's. Whenever he showed up, every few years, Gil would ask for Musa to talk of his discoveries, hanging hungrily on every word. It was the hunger of an unmarried youth asking about sex, or a poor man asking about luxury. There was something that kept Gil from embracing God's presence, from accepting God's love as Musa did. For this, Musa pitied him. Even so, Gil also had a majesty about him, an admirable depth and power. To call him just a Djinn seemed meager. Surely he was the King of the Djinn.

When Musa's thoughts turned to Gil like this, it was often a sign that he would be visiting soon. Musa's heart beat happily at the thought. If he had a friend in this world, with Suha gone, it was Gil.

The motor coughed a particularly agonized cough, and Musa looked quickly at the temperature gauge. It was in the red. Musa had no clock; he used the motor's periodic overheating to time his daily prayers. He pulled the truck off the road into a patch of sand packed down by the tracks of many tires.

Musa sloshed the remaining water in his canteen skeptically. He had drunk too much that morning; there was not enough for drinking and purification both. He clambered out of the cab and, in the shadow of the truck, did the ablutions with sand. Then he performed the prayers. How it lifted his heart, to be one with the millions of the faithful, all yearning towards the city where God had spoken to his best and final prophet. Thus had God completed the work of filling the world with his bounty: air to breathe, water to drink, food to eat, people to love, and finally the gentle and firm rules and the great poetry and wisdom of the Word of God.

His prayers done, his motor still smoking, Musa sat cross-legged in the shadow of the truck, on the sand, and allowed his soul to rise.

His soul ascended and saw the sand and the date palms, the ribbon of highway and the truck, the sea and cliffs beyond. It swept higher and he saw the fertile valley of the Nile and the teeming cities and the ships and cars and airplanes.

His soul descended into Cairo and flew through the streets, yearning for his only son Jamal. It was a Tuesday, when his son had no classes at the University. He would probably be watching soccer and drinking coffee at his favorite café.

Musa's soul entered the café. But there was no laughter, no shouting and no urging on of players running after a ball. The men sat in silence. The room was choked in anger.

On the television, Zionists were committing their atrocities in the camps of Palestine. Tanks fired at young men. Bulldozers tore houses open. Old women, old men, and children ran bleeding through the devastated and smoking streets.

Musa's soul found Jamal sitting in the corner, his fist clenched around his coffee glass. Jamal was full of fury. Why?, Jamal's heart cried. How can we bear our weakness, how can we bear to see the innocents suffer!

My son, Musa's soul called to him, do not be taken by hopelessness. There are always evildoers in the world, as long as men are weak. Take heart, God is great –

But Jamal's heart did not listen. It went on suffering and raging in its own misery and shame. I sit here in Cairo, it said, studying engineering, while America buys bullets to kill the children of Palestine. While my father delivers America's soda pop! To earn the money with which I buy this coffee. We are all slaves!

Musa's soul was struck as if his son had kicked him. It flew out of the café and out of Cairo, and back into his body where it sat by the road.

Musa prayed that his son would not be swept away by hatred and bitterness. As he prayed, his heart galloped like a horse, and he was aware of the thousands of bottles of Pepsi sitting in their crates in his truck, and he prayed that his son would not despise him.

At the sound of a car stopping, Musa opened his eyes. There, in the glare of the desert sun beyond the shadow of the truck, was the King of the Djinn getting out of a Jeep.

Musa got quickly to his feet. He bowed deeply in greeting.

The King of the Djinn walked into the shadow of the truck and bowed back. He was wearing a European-style suit and carrying a briefcase. Beneath his calm smile Musa could feel a great, empty yearning.

"It is good to see you," Musa said as they shook hands. He resisted the urge to embrace the King of the Djinn.

"And you."

Musa's heart was still thundering from his encounter with his son, and he was dizzy and sweating from the heat. He looked at the smile of the creature in the suit, and all of a sudden he found himself asking the question that was always on his tongue, but which he had told himself he would never ask. And so stupidly – he had not inquired as to the health of the other, had not offered him water or coffee or apologized for his inability to provide proper hospitality, had not told or heard any stories, had exchanged neither compliments nor proverbs. His stupid tongue simply jumped up and asked rudely: "Are you a Djinn?" Then he clapped his hands to his mouth in horror.

Gil grinned. As if he approved of the question, was proud of Musa for asking it. He squinted and pursed his lips as if deciding how to answer.

"I don't know what I am," he said finally. "But that is the best proposal I have heard so far."

Musa stood transfixed with embarrassment. He coughed and tried to think of what to say to return the conversation to its proper course.

"And since I am, for lack of a better word, a Djinn," said Gil, "I should offer you wishes."

"Oh no!" said Musa. "I could not accept!"

"Musa," said Gil, "our encounters have been valuable to me over the years. You deserve at least one wish. Would you like it for yourself, or for your son?"

"For my son!" gulped Musa. Old fool!, he shouted at himself silently. You did not even refuse three times! And yet he was so worried about Jamal.

"Very well," said Gil, smiling and handing Musa the briefcase. "Here is what your son wants most in the world."

A chill went through Musa's hands. He set the briefcase down in the sand and looked at the latches. They were shiny and brass.

"Well?" said Gil.

Musa reached out with shaking hands to open the latches.

Most of the contents of the briefcase were covered with a cloth of fine dark silk. But on top of the silk was a blue plastic booklet with a picture of an eagle, and western letters on it. An American passport. Musa opened it. There was his son's picture. He looked up at Gil, confused. Was this what Jamal wanted? To go to America? Musa did not know what to think. There would be dangers, temptations – but at the same time Jamal would learn much, and perhaps –

Gil's eyes were sad – though Musa thought, again, that the sadness was on the surface, like a mask; that beneath it was emptiness – and he gestured back to the briefcase.

Musa looked down again. He moved aside the black cloth.

The rest of the briefcase was filled with thick yellow cylinders of something that looked like clay, connected with electrical tape and wires.

"No!" shouted Musa. "No!"

With that passport, Jamal could go through the border at Taba, into Israel. He could go to the busiest café, the most crowded corner in Tel Aviv, and murder himself and a hundred Zionists – Zionists in baby carriages, Zionists in bridal gowns, Zionists with canes and false teeth – and join the Palestinian martyrs in their struggle.

But surely Jamal would never get through! He would be searched at the border. They would find the bomb, they would punish him! But the stillness in Gil's eyes told Musa that the King of the Djinn had granted far greater wishes, and that Jamal would not fail.

Musa prostrated himself at Gil's feet, burying his face in his hands. "No!" he cried. "Please! Please, sir – Gil – whatever you are – do not do this!"

"Musa, you have become complacent," Gil said. "You have a special gift, a special connection to God. But it is too easy for you. You drive your truck and have visions and take it for granted that it is enough. But God requires more. Sometimes God requires sacrifice."

Musa struggled to his feet, looked wildly around. "This isn't what God wants! Don't tell me God wants my only child martyred! To murder innocents along with the guilty, as the oppressors themselves do! Is that how the Prophet fought?"

"Musa," said Gil, and in his voice was an ancient, ancient cold, with ten thousand years of emptiness behind it, "there is nothing you can do about that. Here is what you can do."

Musa waited, watching Gil's bottomless, glittering eyes.

"Write an amulet," Gil said. "For the protection and redemption of your son's soul. If you think he is going into sin – write an amulet to protect him."

Musa wanted to protest more, to plead. But he found himself going to the cab of his truck and getting in, and taking his parchment and pens and ink out of the dashboard compartment. His tears mixed with the ink as he wrote the declaration of faith and he prayed, fervently, fervently. He no longer felt God's grace in every grain of sand. He felt as though God's grace was hidden at the end of a very long tunnel.

Gil came and took the amulet from him. "Thank you, Musa," he said, and walked to his Jeep and got in.

Musa started his motor. He would rush to Cairo, too, and talk to Jamal. He would persuade him of the wrongness of his actions. He released the clutch and eased onto the road as the Jeep pulled out ahead of him.

But Jamal would not listen. Musa could hear his arguments now. How else to strike at the powerful oppressor, he would say, but the only way we can? Could Musa say for certain he was wrong? But not my son!, Musa's heart shouted. God, God, not my only son! Jamal would look at him with contempt. Driver of sodas.

The road began a long, steep downgrade. Musa took his foot off the gas, lightly tapped the brake as he followed. The Jeep sped on ahead.

Jamal would not listen. He would be gone, and Musa's life would be empty. If Jamal could only get through this period of youth and fiery blood, if he could only learn patience and humility, learn to trust God and endure injustice... but he would not have time. The briefcase in the Jeep ahead would see to that.

Help me, God, help me, Musa prayed, with all his heart.

Was it God? Or was it His Adversary? Or simply desperation? Something took Musa's foot off the brake and slammed it down onto the gas and held it there.

The truck groaned and shuddered as it surged down the downgrade. It gained on the Jeep.

The distance closed.

Gil looked back over his shoulder, and in that instant Musa realized he loved the King of the Djinn as a dog loves his master, and he slammed on the brake. But the inertia of a ton of Pepsi would not entertain such indecision. The wheels of the cab locked and skidded, the trailer behind slammed it forward, and the nose of the semi smashed into the Jeep, flipping it into the air. Musa was thrown into the wheel; his jaw snapped and blood fountained across the windshield. He felt the truck fishtail off the road, and then roll; he heard the sound of ten thousand shattering Pepsi bottles fill the desert.

Then it stopped.

Then came the sound of ten thousand bottles slowly reassembling themselves.

The droplets of blood swam slowly back through the air into Musa's veins.

The glass of the windshield reassembled, each piece flying silently, gracefully, back to meet its brothers, glinting in the sunlight. Behind them, the sky rolled back to its proper place above Musa.

The Jeep swung down out of the sky, kissed the cab of the truck, and moved forward onto the road. The trailer of the rig drew back and the cab settled down. Musa's foot left the brake and landed on the gas.

Musa had never known what a gift the gentle movement of time was, the succession of each moment in its turn, each moment a wide-open field of freedom and of choice. He felt his heart beat backwards, his breath move backwards through his lungs. He wanted to shout, to cry, to escape the cab, but he could not: his limbs moved in their predetermined course as the Jeep and the truck crept backwards up the hill. Slowly, time dragged its Musa puppet back through the seconds, until he was in his cab parked at the side of the road handing the amulet to Gil. Then it released him.

Gil gasped and spat into the sand. He was shaking. So was Musa. The King of the Djinn looked up at him with a wild, feral grin.

Musa gripped the wheel, his heart exploding in terror.

"You surprised me, Musa," Gil said. "I'm amazed. It's been a very long time since any of my collection surprised me." He looked out over the desert horizon. "I think I've had you on too loose a leash. Your talents make you too hard to control."

Musa watched this King of the Djinn in silent terror. This creature who played with time as a child plays with dolls. Was this Satan himself?

Gil glanced back and saw Musa's face, and for a moment the chill, benign mask of the King of the Djinn slipped, and Musa saw what was under it: desperate rage. Then Gil smiled coolly again.

"You're a fool, Musa. I'm not Time's master. I'm its victim."

He looked down at the amulet and stroked it once, gently. Then he slipped it into his pocket.

He threw the briefcase into the Jeep but did not get in. He stood and watched Musa. "Well," he said finally, "there's nothing you can do to save Jamal. And you won't see me again. So all your earthly attachments are gone now, Musa. You're free to find God." Gil pointed out into the empty desert. "He's that way."

Musa looked in the direction the Djinn had pointed.

God's presence was everywhere, in every grain of sand. It was the same huge, infinite, bountiful light.

But how could he have misjudged it before, to think it gentle? It was alien, inhuman, immense beyond reason. If every human was burned alive, if every creature on earth was swallowed in the fire, the Divine Presence would not blink.

Musa began to walk.

He walked until his throat was dry and his breathing shallow. Then, after a while, he was crawling. It was only a spiritual exercise.

The sand was hot against his cheek.

The Sahara was a vast white page, and Musa's body one tiny, bent black letter written on it. Seen from above, seen from very far away.

Stilled Life

Pat Cadigan

Pat Cadigan (*fastfwd.livejournal.com* & *www.flickr.com/photos/cadigan*) lives with her husband Christopher Fowler in London where she has lived for the past decade and more, galvanizing the SF community. In the 1980s, she was cyberpunk's Dorothy Parker, the hip woman writer among the guys, and in 2002 edited the anthology *The Ultimate Cyberpunk*. Since then, she has published a number of books, including the novels *Synners* (1991), *Fools* (1992), and the collections *Patterns* (1989), *Home By the Sea* (1992), and *Dirty Work* (1993).

"Stilled Life" is from *Inferno*, edited by Ellen Datlow, the best dark fantasy anthology of the year. A middle-aged woman who works in an organic foods store (and is probably an alcoholic) is friends with a younger woman co-worker who is also a human statue in Hyde Park. Her friend falls under the sway of a sinister man, part Svengali and part pimp, and quits her job. And so our protagonist investigates.

WHEN THE WEATHER gets warm, the human statues come out in droves. In Covent Garden, especially. As you leave the tube station, turn right to go down to the covered piazza called the Apple Market and you'll see them every ten feet on either side. Young women and men painted white or silver or gold or even black, head to foot, clothes and all, standing on a stool or a box or an overturned bucket, holding impossibly still in some marvellous pose. Besides making a little money, a lot of them are hoping to get spotted by one of those agencies that provide entertainment for corporate parties or celebrity bashes. Either could be lucrative but Sophie was hoping more for the latter than the former. Corporate parties were good, steady gigs but even just one celebrity bash could make you a star. Sophie wanted stardom and she didn't bother hiding it.

Sophie was like that – unconditionally, sometimes brutally honest. Personally, I've always thought that excessive honesty was vastly overrated so exactly how we became friends is a mystery to me. We had very little in common – she was London-born-and-bred, I was a US ex-pat; she was in her late twenties, I was caught in the headlights of my oncoming fifties; she was a beauty, a classic English rose with fair hair, luminous eyes and porcelain skin...I was caught in the headlights of my oncoming fifties – go figure. Call it a chick thing – sisterhood is powerful.

Whatever our bond was, it was strong enough that we could accept each other even if we didn't always understand each other. I mean, I wouldn't have tried the human statue thing on the street even in my early twenties, and God knows I'd tried plenty back then. But I didn't mind helping her out with her paint and her costume and props when we both had the same day off from FRESH 4 U.

That was how we met – she'd been working at the health food store for almost a year when I was hired. We bonded among the organic produce and fair-trade chocolate when we weren't standing at adjacent cash registers and ringing up the lunch-time rush of health-conscious office-workers hoping that the anti-oxidants in the salads could counter the cumulative effects of twenty cigarettes a day. Some of them were also hoping to attract Sophie's attention, but she made it clear to all of them she wasn't interested.

"That kind of distraction would only interfere with the stillness," she told me once as I was helping her into her alabaster goddess get-up. This was a Grecian-style gown that she had bleached, starched, painted, and varnished to the point where it actually could have stood up without her. How she tolerated it next to her skin I couldn't imagine. She claimed that coating herself with several layers of greasepaint made it bearable; I didn't even like to touch the thing. The wig was even worse.

"If you say so," I replied.

She chuckled and handed me a tube of clown-white so I could touch up her back. "I don't expect you to understand, Lee. You're not a statue."

Neither are you, I wanted to tell her but I made myself shut up. Saying something like that to her just before she went into her act would screw her up completely and ruin the whole day – spoil her *stillness*. Ironic, I thought, that someone who worked as a statue could be so easily psyched out.

Besides the alabaster goddess, Sophie had two other personae: the bronze Amazon and the silver lady. The bronze Amazon wore more paint than clothing so she only came out in very warm weather, and only when Sophie was feeling particularly good about her body. The silver lady was, to my uncultured, American philistine's eye, a cross between a hood ornament and a second-place athletic trophy, which makes it sound a lot tackier than it looked. There was nothing tacky about the silver lady just as there was nothing sleazy about the bronze Amazon. I just couldn't take any of it as seriously as Sophie or her fellow statues and their helpers.

Chalk it up to my age. To me, the whole human-statue thing is the twenty-first century version of street mimes. It was less strenuous and it didn't involve someone in whiteface following you down the street making fun of the way you walked, which definitely counted in its favour. But anything done for pocket change was a paying-your-dues thing, not a vocational calling.

I did try talking to Sophie about her plans for the future; she was rather vague about everything. I supposed that only made sense. I mean, working as a human statue didn't suggest a specific next step, not like singing or dancing or riding a unicycle while juggling chainsaws.

"I have a pretty good singing voice," Sophie said when I finally managed to pin her down. We were restocking organic greens in the produce section. "But it's nothing special – one *of* a million, not one *in* a million and I'm not limber enough to be a real dancer. I'm not coordinated enough to even *look* at a unicycle. Hell, it took me most of a week just to learn how to ride a regular bike. And chainsaw juggling is *so* last century."

"So you're a human statue because holding still is something you can do?" I said, examining a head of crinkly green lettuce for spots.

"It's not just *holding still*. It's the *stillness*." She was smiling dreamily, distantly. "I like the stillness. I like the way it builds from a little tiny speck deep inside. It swells, spreads all through me. When I get it to go just right, the whole world is flowing around me while I just *stay*."

"Like a rock in a stream?"

Sophie shook her head. "Better than that."

"Sounds very...stoic."

"Does, doesn't it?" She beamed at me. "Stoic. That's a good word, stoic. *Stoic*. Strong. We shall not be moved."

I grinned. "Unmoved, an emperor is kneeling upon her mat.'"

She paused with a head of curly green in one hand and a softball-sized radicchio in the other. "Say again?"

"It's from a poem by Emily Dickinson. 'The soul selects her own society, then shuts the door; on her divine majority, obtrude no more.'"

"I love it," Sophie said. "'On her divine majority, obtrude no more.' That's a good mantra for stillness."

"Well, a long one, anyway." I shook my head and put a head of cos in the good pile. "Stillness is another thing I don't understand. When I was your age, I couldn't hold still for two seconds."

Sophie threw her head back and laughed. "Oh, man, what is this when-I-was-your-age shite? You make it sound like you're old enough to be my mother when I'm pretty sure you're not."

"Actually, I think I am," I said, wincing.

"Bollocks."

"Well, *technically* old enough if not really mature enough. If you know what I mean."

"Ah, right," she conceded, mirroring my wince. "Sometimes when people come in here with little kids it suddenly occurs to me that I'm old enough to be their mother." Sophie gave a small shudder. "Really weirds me out."

"What about when you're a statue? Does it weird you out then?"

"Nah. Statues can't have children." She looked down at the crate on the floor between us. "They don't have kids and they don't get older."

I gave a short laugh. "Everything that exists gets older. Statues are no exception."

Sophie tossed a wilted mass of curly red in the bad basket. "Not the same way people do."

"Oh, *no*, honey," I said unhappily. "*Please* don't tell me you're one of those people who thinks 'age' is a dirty word."

"Oh, come on, Lee – are you saying you wouldn't stay young if you could?"

"Got it in one, girlfriend."

"*Bollocks*."

"Why? Can you really not conceive of someone who doesn't want to stay young?"

She stared at me incredulously. "If I had the choice, I'd take it in a minute. And you'll never make me believe that you wouldn't, either."

I thought it over while we picked through some more greens. A dismaying amount of it was wilted. Stored too cold. Finally, I said, "Would you go back to high school? Pardon me, secondary school."

Sophie's lovely English Rose face took on a revolted expression. "I knew what you meant. And the answer is a resounding *hell, no, I'd rather die in a fiery car crash, thank you very much*."

"OK, how about elementary school? That was usually a lot more fun for most people."

"Uh-uh, not there, either."

"Well, all right, then," I said. "Now you know how I feel."

Her revulsion changed to puzzlement. "About what?"

"About staying young. I'm glad I *was* young, of course. I didn't waste much time being sensible, I took full advantage of my youth – I did all kinds of reckless, crazy things, I made a shitload of mistakes and generally made a right prat of myself, as you Brits put it. *Je ne regret rien*, pardon my French."

Sophie looked pained. "I will but the French wouldn't."

"I'm also glad I was young *when* I was young," I added. "Oh, what a time it was, there were giants in those days, blah-blah-blah. But I'm over it."

I could see she was mulling it over. "Staying young and going back to school *isn't* the same thing," she said finally. "Think about it. I mean, *really* think about it. Having a young body, more flexible, without so many aches and pains? No wrinkles? No grey hair? Never getting tired, having limitless amounts of energy? What about those things?"

I started to feel more than a little defensive. "I don't think I'm all that wrinkled. Grey hair – " I shrugged. "There are people who pay big money to get these highlights. And as for the rest of it, well, I don't remember having limitless amounts of energy and never getting tired, but then, I wasn't actually all that flexible back then so I wasn't wearing myself out doing gymnastics, either."

"But what about all those mistakes you claim you made?" Sophie gave me a sly grin. "You had to have a lot of energy for those, didn't you?"

I shrugged. "Sleep all day, party all night."

Her eyes widened. "Christ, what were you, a vampire?"

"Of course not. *Today* you'd have to be a vampire. Back then you only had to be a hippie. Never mind," I added in response to her puzzled look. "Different world." I tossed another wilted head of curly green into the bad pile and paused to massage the back of my neck.

"Did I mention aches and pains?" Sophie asked playfully, watching me.

"Hey, if people my age didn't have aches and pains, the ibuprofen companies might go out of business, which would lead to a worldwide economic crash and depression. You think we want that on our conscience?"

"Very funny," Sophie said, laughing. "But seriously – "

"But seriously, yourself, girlfriend. If that's what getting older means to you – aches and pains and grey hair and wrinkles, you're a lot shallower than I thought you were."

Sophie looked as if I had slapped her.

"I'm sorry, I didn't mean to call you shallow," I went on. "But that's not all there is to getting older."

"OK," she said. "So tell me some wonderful things."

I hesitated. "That's like you asking me to tell you how wonderful it is to be me and I just can't. It's my Catholic school education – I had modesty beaten into me by a succession of husky nuns with thick rulers."

We both laughed and went on sorting lettuce while I wondered if she knew just how badly I had copped out with my modesty excuse. Tell her what's so great about getting older. Well, Sophie, honey, first of all, you're still alive. Second, you're, uh, still alive. And third, uh...well, you see, girlfriend, whatever else might be good about getting older, still being alive trumps them all. The whole idea is to keep breathing and last as long as you can.

Sophie quit while I was off sick for a few days. I didn't find out till I came back and met the gangly eighteen-year-old guy replacing her. He was recently out of school, friendly and polite and reasonably intelligent, and everybody had already taken a liking to him. I felt betrayed and abandoned.

When my shift ended, I headed straight over to Covent Garden. I wasn't really expecting Sophie to talk to me, about the store or anything else. I just felt the overwhelming and rather selfish need to show her my unhappy face.

It was after three when I stepped out of the tube station and headed down toward the piazza. The intermittent sun had done a disappearing act and it was misting out (never turn your back on a London sky, as I heard a customer say once) but there were still a lot of people milling about on the street. No, not milling – they were assembled, watching something.

No, not merely watching – staring, hard. Transfixed.

There was only one human statue on the walkway but for a moment, I actually wasn't sure that it was Sophie. She was the bronze Amazon and there was no mistaking that – the spear, the helmet and wig, the torn cropped shirt, the modified swimsuit bottom, that perfect bronze-metal colour coating her well-conditioned body. She stood with her feet about shoulders' width apart, just starting to raise the spear in her right hand, as if she had glimpsed some hazard that had yet to show itself clearly. Her eyes never blinked, at least not that I saw, nor could I see any sign that she was taking even the shallowest of shallow breaths. Her other arm was by her side, bent slightly at the elbow, wrist starting to flex, ready to provide counterbalance if/when she threw her spear.

Perhaps it hadn't been the weather that had driven away all the other statues. The toy soldier, the clown, the rag doll, the fox, Marilyn Monroe – I could picture them stepping down from their boxes and stools, shouldering their gym bags and retreating, defeated by Sophie's power. It was something well beyond what the word *stillness* had meant to me, well beyond what I had seen Sophie do in the past. Maybe even well beyond the motionless nature of a real statue.

Fascinated, I eased my way forward through the crowd, which was also very still and quiet – so quiet, in fact, that it felt wrong even to move but I wanted to get up as close as possible. I was ten feet away from her when I saw something in her face change. It was barely there, not even so much as a shimmer in the heavy mist. I knew it meant that she had seen me.

Her stillness didn't crack for another ten or fifteen seconds, when I was almost within arm's reach. And that was exactly what happened: it cracked. Not visibly or audibly and yet it was, in a way – visible on the subliminal level, audible only to the subconscious. A few seconds later, her stillness flaked away and was gone, and the crowd was staring at nothing more than a scantily-clad woman in bronze body paint. The heavy mist deepened into rain.

Umbrellas went up and flapped open; voices murmured, rose, called to each other as people scattered, off to the piazza or the nearby shops and bars. I stayed where I was and watched Sophie come out of her pose like someone coming out of a dream.

"Dammit, Lee." Her shoulders slumped as she looked down at me. "This is all your fault."

"How?" I forced a laugh. "I didn't make it rain."

We both knew that wasn't what she meant but she let it go for the moment as she climbed down carefully from her pedestal. A real pedestal, or at least real enough. I rapped my knuckles on it.

"Where'd you get this?" I asked.

"Who ever heard of a statue on a stepladder?" Sophie said irritably.

"Good point," I said. "Does it help? With your stillness, I mean."

"Can't say, really." She eyed me darkly. "But I can tell you what *doesn't*."

"I'm sorry I broke your concentration," I told her. "Truly, I am. I didn't mean to."

Sophie said nothing as she took off her sandals and padded barefoot to the covered space in front of a clothing store to get her duffel bag. I was surprised that she had just left it sitting there and even more surprised that Covent Garden hadn't been closed down so the bag could be removed and blown up by the bomb squad.

"I'm sorry," I said again. "I was just upset when I came into work today and found out you quit."

Sighing, she removed the helmet and the wig. "You didn't really think I was going to devote my life to organic groceries, did you? Sorting wilted lettuces and spotty apples?" She reached into the bag and pulled out a towel to dry the helmet.

"Why don't you wipe off the bronze and let me buy you a pint?" I said. "Or even an early dinner?"

She bit her lip, staring at something over my right shoulder. I turned to follow her gaze and was startled to find a man leaning against a pillar. I thought he must have just sneaked up behind me because I couldn't believe I'd walked right past someone that close without noticing. He was an inch or two shorter than I was, dressed in an assortment of things, none of which went with anything else, a bit like an extra in a production of *Oliver!*, but without the theatrical flamboyance. His smile didn't reach his eyes. "Up to you, luv."

Sophie didn't answer. She had the apprehensive look of someone afraid of saying the wrong thing.

"You know that I've nothing against you eating," he added.

I leaned in toward her and lowered my voice. "Who's that? Have you got a manager now?"

"Something like that," she said, almost too softly for me to hear. She fiddled with the drawstring on the duffel bag. "Lee's a friend from the shop," she said to the guy, then added, "Someone I know, that I used to work with," as if she were correcting herself.

He frowned at me the way people do when they're measuring something.

"She used to help me out sometimes with my costumes and paint," Sophie went on, a bit urgently. "And she covered for me at the shop, too, before I quit."

"I told you, luv, I've nothing against you eating." All at once he was nose to nose with her before I could even register that he had moved. "Here, I'll take care of your bag so you don't have to lug it around."

Sophie was slightly taller than he was but she seemed to shrink under his gaze. "I won't be long," she said, still in that urgent, pleading tone. A knot gathered in my chest. I didn't see him nod or make any other sign but apparently Sophie had. She reached into the duffel bag, took out a loose shift, and slipped it over her head. "Right. So let's go, yes?"

She was still very bronze. If she didn't mind, I didn't, either, but she seemed to have forgotten she was barefoot. I pointed at her feet. A little flustered, she pulled the sandals out of her bag, stepping into them as we walked off together.

I had been thinking in terms of sandwiches but since her manager had gone to the trouble of saying not once but twice that he had nothing against her eating, I decided to blow the budget at a nearby brasserie. On my salary, that really was blowing the budget – I'd be living on the store's cast-offs for a while but I didn't care.

The brasserie hostess didn't even blink at Sophie's body paint although she did look significantly toward the loo. Sophie took the hint and excused herself while the hostess showed me to a table. I ordered a large platter of potato skins as a starter and two glasses of red wine while I waited. When she returned from the ladies', less bronze but still somewhat stained, she didn't look thrilled.

"I worked up quite an appetite today," I said as she sank into her chair, "and it's been a long time since I've indulged in comfort food. Hope you don't mind too much."

"I don't mind *you* indulging," she said, emphasizing the you slightly but pointedly. "But you really should have asked before ordering wine for me."

"Hey, my treat, remember?"

"And don't think I don't appreciate it. I do. It's just that I'm off alcohol completely."

I wondered if she realized she was holding the wine glass and gazing at the Shiraz with a longing that bordered on lust. "One glass of red wine with a meal is healthy," I said. "Didn't you read any of the nutritional propaganda at the store?"

She chuckled a little. "Red wine and potato skins? Very *haute cuisine.*"

"This is just the appetizer. Here comes our waitress to take the rest of our order."

"No!" She didn't actually yell but she spoke loudly enough to make the people on either side of us look up to see if someone was about to make a scene. "I mean – well, it's just that I don't know if I can eat more than what we've got right now," Sophie added, slightly apologetic. "That's a whole lot of potato skins."

"Give us a little while with our appetizer," I told the waitress, grabbing Sophie's menu before she could get rid of it. "I think we just have to make up our minds."

Sophie frowned annoyance at me as the waitress moved off to take someone else's order. "In case you've forgotten, I can't work if my stomach's too full."

"But it's the end of the day. You haven't taken to working after dark, have you?"

She sighed, put-upon. "Did it occur to you that I might have a gig this evening?"

Now I felt like a complete idiot. "Oh, shit, Sophie. No, it didn't. I'm so sorry."

Her grin was a bit mean as she pushed her wine glass over to me. "So you'll pardon me for not drinking this nice wine. And you won't try to force me to over-eat now, will you."

"No, of course not. But surely you've got to have a little something in your stomach to give you stamina – " I broke off and put my head in my hands. "Oh, Christ."

"What? What is it?" She sounded genuinely concerned.

I peeked through my fingers at her. "I sounded *exactly* like my mother just then."

Sophie burst into hearty giggles.

"I'm glad you think it's funny," I said, relieved that she still had a sense of humour. "But if you'd actually known my mother, you'd be making me crawl for forgiveness."

"That sounds ominous."

"You have no idea. But seriously, Sophie. If this – " I gestured at the potato skins " – is too heavy for you, what can you manage instead? A salad? Fruit? Yogurt?"

"I'm fine with a couple of these," she assured me, her expression softening. "Look, I didn't mean to be pissy. I'm just kind of nervous. This is my first big evening gig."

"What is it?" I asked. "Some corporate bash? Or have you hit the big time with a celebrity?"

Her smile faded away. "I'm not supposed to talk about it."

"Top secret, huh? Then it's either politics or royalty."

Sophie laughed uneasily. "I told you, I can't talk about it."

"OK," I said. "But that doesn't mean I can't let my imagination run away with me, right?"

"Sure, sure." She pulled one of the potato skins onto the small plate in front of her. "Knock yourself out."

My feeling that Sophie wouldn't be able to resist the appetizer proved correct. While I drank her wine and mine and then in a drunken folly ordered a third glass, Sophie ended up eating over half of the potato skins. Eating the first one seemed to loosen her up; after that, she was reaching for them casually, with no hesitation. When we got down to the last two, I helped myself to one and pushed the other one off the platter onto her plate. "That's yours," I said cheerfully.

She picked it up and then froze. "Oh, damn," she said, and practically threw it down. "Oh, no – *I didn't*." She put one arm across her stomach." Oh, Jesus, I *did*. Oh, God, I'm so *stupid*. How could I be so God damned *stupid*?"

"Sophie – " I started and then cut off. Tears were rolling down her cheeks. "My God, honey, don't *cry*."

"I'm *full*. No, it's worse – I'm *stuffed*."

"Sophie, don't – "

"That's what you should have said to me before, when I was stuffing my face," she said, hotly. "'Sophie, don't.' A *true* friend would have."

The people at the adjoining tables were staring at us. I ignored them. "That's an awful thing to say."

"The world weeps." She sat up straighter and took a deep breath. "Right. At least I know what to do about it." She got up.

"Wait," I said, reaching over and grabbing her wrist. "Where are you going?"

Her mouth tightened into a hard colourless line before she twisted out of my grip and headed toward the ladies' room. Because I was tipsy, it took me a little time to get it. Then I went stumbling across the brasserie after her but by the time I got there, she was finishing up.

"How could you do that?" I asked her as she came out of the stall, her face all red and sweaty.

"Finger down the throat, how do you think?" she said hoarsely, splashing water on her face from the sink. "It works." She drank from her cupped hands, swished the water around in her mouth and spat it out with a grunt.

"But you're not an adolescent girl, you're – what, twenty-seven? Twenty-eight?"

"Twenty-nine next month, actually." She splashed more water on her face and then straightened up to look at herself in the mirror. Her eyes were bloodshot.

"That's way too old for bulimia, Sophie."

She shut off the faucet and patted her face dry with a paper towel. "It's way too old for a whole lot of things, Lee. I'm fighting for my survival."

"Keep doing that shit and you'll lose," I said.

"Thanks for your support." She took a deep breath and let it out, putting her arm across her stomach again. "Empty. It's all right. I never should have done this but I'm going to be all right."

"Sophie – "

"Oh, shut up, Lee," she snapped. "This soul selects her own society and it's not you. Got that? Obtrude on someone else and stay the fuck away from me." She yanked open the door and left.

I started to go after her but the hostess intercepted me politely but firmly to make sure I wasn't trying to skip out on the bill. By the time I got outside, Sophie was nowhere to be seen. I went back to where we had left her manager but there was no trace of either of them. Even the pedestal was gone.

I stayed away from Covent Garden for over a week after that. When I finally did go back, I wasn't even sure that Sophie would be there anymore. Maybe the creep had packed her duffle bag for her and taken her away. I couldn't decide whether I was afraid I'd never see her again or hoping I wouldn't. But when I came out of the tube station, I knew Sophie was still there even before I spotted the bronze Amazon. The crowd was even larger and quieter than before.

This time, there were still a few other statues trying for attention – the weather was good and the tourists were out in force, enough to support a whole flock of statues, buskers, *Big Issue* vendors, and plain old beggars. But once again, Sophie had the lion's share.

"Oi. *Oi, you.*"

Something landed on my shoulder; it was Raggedy Andrew's blue ballet slipper, with his foot still in it. He was balanced on his other leg on a barrel painted to look like a very tall toy drum. It was a nice effect. No one was looking. He broke pose and sat down on the barrel. "You used to help out Miss Superstar over there." He jerked his chin in Sophie's direction.

"Not anymore."

The red yarn bobbed as he nodded his head. "Yeah, I know. You ain't been around lately so I guess the friendship's off between you two. You got no pull with her or anything, right?"

I spread my hands. "Why? Is there something you want?"

"Yeah. I want her to get the fuck outta here. We all do." He gestured at the other human statues.

I looked from him to Sophie's bronze form – even at a distance, that stillness was apparent. "I guess I can understand that."

Raggedy Andy gave a short, unpleasant laugh. "You think it's because she's getting all the money and attention. That's only part of it. But not all of it, or even most of it."

I raised my eyebrows. "So what is?"

"Stick around for a while, till she takes her break. You'll see then. *They* won't – the punters, I mean. I don't know why, but they don't. But us, we do." He waved at the other statues again. "I'm betting you will, too."

On the face of it, the idea that a grown man dressed as a ragdoll could scare me in broad daylight was laughable. But I wasn't laughing and neither was he. A chill went through me deep inside, where the warm sun couldn't reach. I turned away from him and started moving through the crowd again.

I didn't have to get that close to her to see that Sophie's body had gone from enviable to virtually perfect. Her muscle definition was better than I had ever seen on her or, for that matter, anyone else. But there was something strange about it, too. It was the kind of definition that wouldn't be apparent unless she were flexing and holding the pose like a bodybuilder, purposely displaying the muscles, and I knew she wasn't. A flexing pose would have shown off one set of muscles – arms or legs, back or stomach. Whereas Sophie's entire body was...well, an aerobics instructor would have wept at the sight of such an impossible ideal.

I heard the quiet *snick* of a camera shutter. The guy next to me was holding an elaborate digital SLR with an equally elaborate lens.

"Excuse me," I said, "but does that thing zoom in?"

It did. He took a close-up of Sophie and then showed me the image on the small screen on the back of the camera.

"I can't really see her face in any detail," I told him apologetically. "Would you mind terribly letting me look through the lens?"

He hesitated, then decided that I wasn't going to try to run off with it. He showed me which buttons to press and slipped the strap over my head; I put my eye to the view-finder.

The zoom went so fast that it took a moment for the focus to catch up with it and when it did, I wasn't sure I had aimed it at the right target. It seemed to be Sophie's face but the eyes were blank. Just blank featureless bronze. Like a statue's.

Shocked, I fumbled the camera; if the owner hadn't taken the precaution of putting the strap around my neck, I would have dropped it. Not trusting myself to handle it, I motioned for him to take it back and he did so, looking more than a little bemused.

As soon as it was around his neck again, I felt like a complete ass. I had glimpsed Sophie's face for barely a second and her head had been tilted slightly forward. If I had let my own middle-aged eyes adjust, I surely would have seen there was nothing wrong with hers. Should have followed my earlier impulse and gone home, I thought as I started working my way toward the front of the crowd. I didn't need to get up close and see whether her eyes were really blank or not. I already knew I'd imagined it, and I kept going anyway.

This time, I was twenty feet away from her when her stillness cracked. I froze where I was, thinking that I had done it again. But no, this was just her taking a break, like Raggedy Andy had said.

Or rather, it was her creepy manager telling her to take a break. I could see his hand resting on the back of her left calf, signalling her as if she were a trained dog. I felt a surge of anger that he would treat her like that.

Sophie seemed to shrink and fold in on herself, practically collapsing as she climbed down from the pedestal and disappeared behind the dispersing crowd. I got more than a few dirty looks as I forced my way through the people milling around in front of me. I had the strange feeling that they had all forgotten they'd just been staring at Sophie's bronze Amazon; like they'd been released from a trance with the command to remember nothing.

When I finally reached the pedestal, I thought Sophie had left, spirited away by her manager just like the night I had taken her to the brasserie. But that was ridiculous – no one could have gotten away so quickly with so many people clogging up every available walkway. I went over to where she had left her duffel bag the last time, then to the pillar where her creepy manager had appeared out of nowhere – nothing. People bumped into me on all sides as they passed, the crowd growing thicker and everyone in it apparently in a hurry; I started to feel a little unsteady, even disoriented.

And suddenly there she was, right next to her pedestal. She was wearing a loose-fitting robe printed with abstract shapes in various metallic browns and golds that complemented her body paint in such a way that made her seem somehow indistinct. A trick of light and colour?

"Sophie," I called. "Do you have a moment?"

Shoulders sagging, she turned away from me.

"Please, wait – " I rushed over to her and then stopped short, not just because her creepy manager appeared seemingly out of nowhere but at the sight of her face, close up. "Sophie?" I asked, suddenly unsure if it really was her.

Her face had the haunted, suffering look of someone who had been enduring years of torment and was now deteriorating under the strain. "Oh, Jesus, Sophie," I said. "What *happened* to you?"

"Leave me alone," she said dully, waving me off. I grabbed her arm.

"No, Sophie, talk to me! What the hell?"

She tried to pull away but I hung on to her. Her arm felt even worse than her face looked – the muscles were soft, practically limp, as if they had atrophied, while the bone underneath was oddly light, like it might have been hollow.

"I told you, *leave me alone,*" she growled, pushing at me. I managed to get hold of her robe and tore it open.

This could not have been the body that I had seen posing on that pedestal, I thought, staring in shock. There wasn't much flesh and what there was hung in loose little folds. Her midsection was abnormally concave, as if most of it had actually been removed, while her legs were little more than sticks. This could *not* have been the body that I had seen posing on that pedestal – and more than that, this could *not* have happened to her in the space of a week.

"Sophie, what did you do to yourself?" My gaze moved from her to the creep, who was standing beside her with a ghost of a smile on his evil face. "What did you do to her?"

He put his arm around her shoulders and closed up her robe.

"Sophie, *please* talk to me." I reached for her again but somehow he slipped her around to his other side and put himself between us.

"She told you to leave her alone," he said in a low, oily voice. "And now I'm telling you." Before I could answer, he turned Sophie and himself away from me and in the next moment, they were just *gone,* melting into the Covent Garden crowd of tourists without a trace.

I looked around and saw that the pedestal had disappeared as well.

"Certain things are impossible," said Raggedy Andy over a pint. "You can tell yourself this. You can learn it in school or by experience or both. Then they'll happen anyway and you won't be able to do a thing about it."

The toy soldier toasted that statement with a bottle of Beck's. "Right."

They weren't Raggedy Andy and the toy soldier anymore, of course. Raggedy Andy was now a ginger-haired, green-eyed fellow named Liam who was a few years older under the whiteface than I had estimated. The toy soldier was a very tall woman named Pauline whose olive features had a strangely ageless quality; she might have been seventeen or forty. I was sitting with them in a pub near the tube station.

"Maybe that's what 'impossible' really means," Pauline added. "Impossible to do anything about."

"You think it's impossible for me to help my friend?" I asked.

Liam gave a short, hard laugh. "You saw her. That's what's happened to her in a week. Can you honestly believe she's not beyond help?"

"What do you know about it?" I said. The words came out sounding defensive but at the same time, it was an honest question. "Do you know that guy she's with? Do you know anything about him?"

"No." He took a healthy gulp from the pint. "Not really." His eyes swivelled to Pauline in the chair beside him. She looked away.

I sat up straighter and grabbed his glass away from him. "Oh? What don't you really know?"

"Nothing to speak of," the other woman said, giving me an appalled look as she transferred her Beck's to the hand farther away from me. "Really. Liam doesn't know him and neither do I."

"No one does," Liam added in response to my skeptical look. "Nobody knows his name or where he comes from, who he works for if he works for anyone at all. And anyone who does know ain't talking. Like your friend." He reached for his glass; I held it away from him.

"When was the first time you saw this guy?" I asked.

"I don't know," he said irritably. "I see a few thousand people every day. After a while some faces get familiar but I couldn't tell you when I first saw most of them." He reached for the glass again but I still refused to give it to him. "And holding the last of my pint hostage isn't gonna improve my memory any. I can buy another." He started to get up; I waved him down and gave him back his glass.

"Did you ever see him do this with anyone else?" I asked.

Liam frowned thoughtfully. "No. But you hear things."

"No, *you* hear things," I corrected him. "So what have you heard?"

He looked at the woman again; she shrugged. "It was very vague. Something about a garden."

"Ah." I gave a harsh, humourless laugh. "Wait, don't tell me – could it be, oh, *Covent* Garden?"

"No, actually it wasn't," she said coolly. "Somewhere south of the river."

"Oh, yeah. That would be *New* Covent Garden, then." I made a disgusted noise. "Who do you think you're talking to, some clueless fuck of a tourist?"

They looked at each other, then got up and walked off. I slumped, resting my elbow on the table and staring at my own pint. Guinness Extra Cold; I couldn't remember whether it was my second or third. Or fourth? I was losing track and if I kept on, I was going to lose consciousness as well.

"Not New Covent Garden, either."

I jumped as the woman plopped down in the chair next to me.

"It's not any public place. A regular garden," she went on, "as in the place behind somebody's private residence."

"That's it?"

She tilted her head thoughtfully. "I got the impression it was a *big* garden.

Big garden behind a big house. Posh, lots of money."

"Wouldn't it belong to someone pretty well known, then?" I asked.

Pauline blinked at me. "Why?"

"Because that's how it seems to go in this country. If you're posh, you're famous."

Now she smiled faintly. "There's posh and then there's *posh* – too posh for lower life-forms like us to know anything about. Do you know all the very high-and-mighty in America, the rarefied elite?"

"No, but this is a much smaller country. Fewer people to keep track of."

She moved my pint away from me and pushed something else into its place. "Here. You need this."

I found myself staring at a large cup of coffee. There was no milk in it but I gulped it down anyway.

"Can't hold your liquor at all, can you?"

I shrugged. "On the other hand, I have the smallest bar bill in the country."

"All that means is you drink alone. A lot."

"That may be true," I said with another sigh, "but it's rather unkind to point it out. Isn't it?" I closed my eyes and waited for her response; nothing. "Well, isn't it?"

I opened my eyes. There was no one in the chair next to me.

I pulled myself together enough to gulp down another cup of coffee, even though I knew the whole sober-up-with-lots-of-coffee thing was just a myth. If I couldn't actually get sober, I would settle for drunk and wide awake. It would save me some time and trouble if I didn't fall asleep going home on the tube. Going home was really all I was thinking about when I finally stepped out of the pub. Then I saw the crowd and headed straight down to join it.

Sophie had changed into the silver lady and the persona was a lot different than the last time I had last seen it. Now she wore as little as the bronze Amazon – no, less. Her breasts were barely covered and I wasn't sure what she was wearing on the bottom but it looked like a modified doily, and a very small one at that.

Her body, however, had changed even more – i.e., it was better, if *better* was really the word to describe it. The impossible ideal of the bronze Amazon had somehow been surpassed. The silver lady's muscles were sleeker and better defined, her posture was so precise that she even looked *taller*. No, not just taller, but larger all the way around –

That couldn't be Sophie, I thought, goggling at her. There was a very strong resemblance but it wasn't her. This had to be someone else entirely, a bigger woman who was doing a variation on Sophie's silver lady. The creep manager's idea, no doubt. He probably had a whole stable of "clients" and made them trade off their costumes and personae all the time, just to make sure they knew who was boss.

After a bit, I realized she was moving; very, very slowly, all but imperceptibly, like the minute-hand on an old-fashioned clock, she was changing position. At the same time, I had the distinct impression of her figure *hardening*, becoming more statue-like rather than less. Her hands, held close together at waist level, began to descend, moving away from each other to the tops of her thighs; her head lifted, turned toward me as her weight shifted from one leg to the other.

Her eyes were blank. Smooth, featureless silver, just like a statue's.

Slowly, incredibly, painfully slowly, one arm began to rise and her weight shifted again as she reached forward. Her fingers were still curled softly inward toward her palm so she wasn't really pointing in my direction but for a few moments, I was sure she was going to. Instead, her arm went on rising and eventually stopped over her head, as if she meant to call down some power from heaven. Perhaps the silver lady was a goddess now.

This *was* a different woman; it was so obvious. She was several inches taller than Sophie and at least twenty pounds heavier. It couldn't have been Sophie.

Except that I knew it was.

It was practically dark by the time the silver lady broke and got down off the pedestal. In the whole time I had been watching her, I had barely moved myself. Now my legs hurt all the way up to my hips.

But at least I felt a lot more sober – sober enough to keep Sophie and the creep manager in sight despite the distance and the flow of people between me and them. I watched as the creep wrapped her up in a silver-grey robe but then carried out what seemed to be an inspection of her body. He felt her up with both hands, through the robe and then under the robe, as if she were a racehorse. Sophie submitted to it with no resistance that I could discern. Whatever he discovered apparently satisfied him. He put one arm around her shoulders and herded her away, talking intently while she hung on his every word.

I didn't make a decision to follow them – I just did it. They were so wrapped up in each other that they didn't bother to watch where they were going much less look back to see me trailing several yards behind them. Some instinct seemed to be guiding them along the street, stepping up or down as necessary, while people moved aside to let them pass without actually noticing. At a quick glance, they might have passed for any newly smitten couple enjoying the high of a new relationship. But what I saw in Sophie's face was an eaten-away-from-the-inside quality similar to terminal cancer patients, while the look in her creep manager's eyes was more like gluttony than desire.

They got into a black cab outside a theatre on Drury Lane; I grabbed the one behind it, unsure how the driver would react when I told him to follow that cab. He gave me an arch look but he didn't tell me to get out. I came up with a story about a sister with a large inheritance and a work-shy boyfriend I suspected was abusing her. It worked so perfectly I felt simultaneously relieved and ashamed.

I felt a lot more ashamed when we finally came to a stop in some tangle of streets whose names I'd never heard of, just around the corner from where Sophie and the creep were getting out – the fare was three and a half pounds more than I had. I asked for the cab driver's name and address so I could mail him the difference; he left me a couple of pound coins and drove away before I could even get his cab number.

From behind the low brick wall surrounding the front yard of the house on the corner, I watched Sophie waiting on the sidewalk while the creep paid the cab driver. Or argued with him – I couldn't really tell. Some kind of discussion was taking place; I didn't hear any raised voices but there was something about the way the creep was leaning in toward the driver that made me think it wasn't a friendly exchange. Maybe the creep was trying to beat *his* fare. Sophie remained motionless, not so much like a statue as just some inanimate object waiting to be picked up and carried away. Like a duffel bag. Finally, the creep stepped back and made an abrupt dismissing gesture with one hand, then turned to Sophie.

It was like he flipped a switch turning her on; she came to life and stood at attention. He put his hands on her shoulders, swivelled her around and steered her up the sidewalk in my direction.

I ducked down behind the wall quickly, almost cutting myself on the rough edge of a battered and bent metal sign screwed into the brick: *Foxtail Close*. Staying low, I risked peeking around the corner again just in time to see the two of them climbing the front steps of a house almost directly across from where I was crouching.

I hadn't noticed the place before; if I had, I would have taken it for derelict. It was large and dark, set back from the row houses stretching down the block, on a patch of ground that didn't really seem to belong with the rest of the street. Sophie and the creep went inside without turning on any lights. I waited but the house stayed dark.

After a while, I pushed myself upright and shook out each leg until my knees stopped screaming. And now that I knew where she was living – or where the creep was keeping her, anyway – what did I think I was going to do next? Take down the address and send her a card?

Abruptly, a big man came out of the shadows on the right side of the house. And I mean *big*, bouncer big, the kind of guy who handles "security" at a club. At first I thought the creep had seen me after all and had sent him out to settle my hash. But the man only stood on the sidewalk in front of the house. He was wearing a headset and holding a clipboard. He really was a bouncer, I realized, and he was on the job right now.

I'd thought the creep had taken Sophie home but he'd actually taken her clubbing, at one of those secret, members-only, you've-got-to-be-invited-to-find-it places –

No, she wasn't clubbing, I realized; she was *working*. This was Sophie's major night-time gig. The creep had her working all day and then working all night. No wonder she looked like the wreck of the *Hesperus*.

A cab pulled up at the curb and three people got out. The bouncer greeted them familiarly but looked them up on his clipboard all the same before directing them around the side of the house, where he had come from. The next cab arrived moments later; another was right behind it and a third pulled up behind that one. The bouncer seemed to know everyone but made a point of checking his clipboard anyway. He sent them all around the side of the house into the shadows and they all went without hesitation. Most of them were well-dressed; some were overly well-dressed and a few were more costumed than attired. I didn't recognize any of them but that didn't mean anything. Most celebrities aren't actually that recognizable in person. If the Royal Family had arrived I couldn't have been completely sure.

Eventually, the cabs came less frequently and then tapered off altogether. I waited for the bouncer to tuck his clipboard under his arm and vanish into the shadows again but he stayed where he was. Someone must have been fashionably late.

How late was it anyway? I had no idea. Late enough that I wasn't really drunk anymore. Still impaired, though – bad judgment and no cab fare. Even if I could find a tube station, it would be closed by now.

"Well? Are you just going to lurk there all night?"

I looked over at the bouncer to see who he was talking to, already knowing that he was calling to me.

"Come on, now. You came this far. Might as well come the rest of the way, yes?"

I made myself move forward, stopping at the corner. "How long have you known I was here?"

The bouncer laughed. "All along, luv. What do you think, we wouldn't have good security?"

I could run, I thought. Then I stepped off the curb and went over to him.

"This way." He tucked the clipboard under his arm.

"Aren't you going to check if I'm on the list?" I asked.

"Don't have to. Come along, now."

*

The party in the back yard had apparently been going on for some time. I sat in the chair where the big man had left me; it was next to the swimming pool, one of those silly, kidney-bean-shaped things, good only for getting your bathing suit wet rather than real swimming. It seemed to be much deeper than normal, however – even under the bright lights, I couldn't make out the bottom. Or maybe the water was tinted dark. To discourage guests from getting rowdy and pushing each other in, perhaps? It didn't seem to be that kind of crowd, I thought, watching the well-dressed people drift around chatting to each other and helping themselves to refreshments from a large round table.

A nondescript man in a nondescript waiter outfit materialized in front of me with a plate of hors d'oeuvres. He held it out with a faint smile. I pushed myself up out of the chair and walked away. The food smelled impossibly good, the way it does when you suddenly realize you haven't eaten all day but I didn't want to accept anything. I had it in my mind that if I did, it would be like accepting what had happened to Sophie, approving of it. They might have had my name on their list but I wasn't *at* this party. Not the way all the rest of these people were. Whoever they were. The nameless posh, perhaps, what the toy soldier had called the rarefied elite, and this was how they lived, one party after another, day after day, night after night. Wasn't there some old joke about people who would go to the opening of an envelope? I didn't see any envelopes here. Maybe they were in the house.

Or out in the garden.

Something about a garden. Big house, big garden.

I looked around but the lights were so bright and every one of them seemed to be shining right in my eyes.

"Not lost, are you?"

I knocked the creep's hand off my shoulder. "Where's the garden?"

He smiled. "You think that's where she is?"

"If she isn't, where is she? I want to talk to her."

"OK, you got me." A phony sheepish smile. "In the garden. But she won't talk to you. She's busy."

"When's her break?"

Now the creep acted surprised, as if I had asked him something completely absurd. "Her *break?* She doesn't take one."

"You've got her working without a break?"

"I said she was *busy*. I didn't say she was *working*."

I wasn't about to let him draw me into a word game. "Just tell me how to find her. If she's too busy to talk to me, I want to hear it from her. To my face."

"Yeah. Your face." He beckoned. "This way."

He led me around the pool and down some stone steps to another patio where even more people were sitting around eating finger-foods and talking in low murmurs about who knows what. This area was bounded on one side by a tall hedge with a wooden door in it. He stopped in front of the door, turned around and started to say something. Ignoring him, I reached for the handle; he pushed me back with a strength I hadn't suspected.

"Ladies and gentlemen," he said, raising his voice to address everyone there. "This is a little bit earlier than I had originally planned but I apparently underestimated the eagerness of some people – " he glanced at me " – to see what we've done with the reclaimed land. So without further delay, please follow me for your first look at the finished – "

I ducked around him and pushed through the door.

More bright lights hit me in the eyes along with the overpowering aroma of fresh flowers in massive quantities. The utter intense beauty of the smell was like being assaulted with bouquets.

Behind me, people were ooh-ing and aah-ing and I could hear the creep telling them to watch out for patches of uneven ground.

"Sophie?" I called hopefully.

"...statues are *perfect*," a man said, going past on my left.

I looked up. Yes, they were. And there were so many of them.

Every ten feet, there was a different figure standing on a pedestal about five feet off the ground. Men and women, gold, silver, bronze, black, alabaster, even marble. Warriors, kings and queens, fairies, gods and goddesses, shamans, witches, aliens and animal-hybrids – dog-people, cat-people, lion-people, lizard-, snake- and bird-people. Some nude, some nearly but not quite. All of them deeply still, completely wrapped in stillness.

"*Sophie!*" I ran along the row of statues on my right, looking up at each female. "*Sophie, answer me!*" I was expecting the bouncer to tackle me at any moment but no one tried to stop me. No one even came near me – when I looked over my shoulder, I saw that the creep and his party guests were staying up near the entrance. Giving the crazy woman a wide berth.

I slowed to a stop next to a woman made up like Marie Antoinette in marble. "Sophie, dammit, answer me or I'll start tearing things up! I swear I will, I'll rip all these flowers up by their roots!"

Nothing. I turned to see how the creep was taking this; he didn't look too worried.

"Sophie?" I started walking again, looking significantly at the flower beds on either side. This section was all tulips, every variety and colour. "Sophie, I'm not kidding. I'll tear this place apart, I really will."

I went another twenty feet before I stopped again. Just how big was this God damned yard anyway? Shading my eyes from the bright overhead lights, I tried to see where it ended. "Sophie?"

The rest of the people at the party looked ridiculously far away now, as if I were seeing them through the wrong end of a telescope. I couldn't hear the murmur of their voices or the music. I listened for traffic noises, the rustle of trees, any ambient night sounds but there was nothing. It was completely still.

"*Sophie!*" I bellowed her name at the top of my lungs. Still nothing.

I turned to look at the nearest statue. A young man who might have been either Robin Hood or Peter Pan. "You, in the jaunty hat," I called up to him. "Come down and help me out here or I'll pull you down."

He didn't twitch. I reached up and grabbed his ankles, intending to yank him off his perch. My hands closed around cold, hard stone. I let go with a yelp and staggered back, wiping my hands on my jeans. Great. I couldn't tell the difference between a human statue and a real statue. The creep and his party guests were probably very impressed. I moved to the next statue; Zorro. I didn't bother even touching him – the swirl of the whip was suspended in midair, like the lasso of the cowboy next to him.

I crossed over to the other side of the garden where a bronze-coloured matador stood with his face turned haughtily away from me. He held his cape low, the hem touching his feet. I put a hand on the cape. It was hard, cold, unyielding. Yet something about the set of his shoulders suggested he was human, not stone or metal. If only I could see his eyes, I thought.

I looked back over my shoulder at the other statues.

They had all moved, the matador, the cowboy, Zorro. Not much – barely noticeably – but I could tell.

"Sophie?" Dread rose inside me like cold water as I moved farther down the row of statues, away from the house. "Sophie, I really need you to answer me now. *Please.*"

A blank-eyed marble Cleopatra holding a snake to her breast stared through me.

"Where is she?" I demanded.

Next to her a chimney sweep was staring off to my right. I followed his gaze past a Victorian lady, past Oscar Wilde, a cricket player, a Madonna, a town crier, a jester, all the way down to the end of the garden.

The bronze Amazon stood on a pedestal in front of another hedge with a door in it.

She looked larger than life now, much larger – if I hadn't known better, I would have sworn she was seven feet tall, her perfectly sculpted muscles in flawless proportion.

"In metal, it would weigh several hundred pounds," said the creep, following me over to her.

"'It'?"

He ambled around me to stand in front of the pedestal, planting one elbow next to Sophie's foot. "And *it's* almost ready for the next garden," he added, glancing at the door.

"Sophie, come down," I begged.

"She doesn't hear you," he said cheerfully. "Once they're in the next garden, none of them hear anyone like you."

"But she's not in the next garden yet," I said, moving closer to her. "Sophie, you hear me, I know you do. Please, come down and let me take you out of here."

"Why should she? What can you offer her? Friendship in the monotony of a nothing job in a world where things ripen and then rot, to be discarded and forgotten." He laughed nastily. "You can go now, she doesn't care to listen to anything you have to say."

"That's not true, is it, Sophie?" I put a hand on her cold leg. "Please come down. I'll help you."

"Help her *what?*" The creep gave me a shove that sent me back a few steps. "Help her rot and convince herself she's happy about it? She's a star, now, she's my masterpiece and she'll stand in the next garden forever, unmoved and perfect. Take your spoiled meat out of my sight. You're not even mildly amusing anymore." He went to shove me again but I dodged around him and threw my arms around Sophie's pedestal.

I don't know whether it was the sight of the creep getting physical with me or just that the activity itself was a distraction, but she lost it.

This time, the cracking was quite audible. It came from deep inside of her and it was the sound of pure breakage, what you hear when something shatters that cannot be mended. Her body shuddered and began to collapse inward like a deflating balloon. Except her skin didn't hang on her now – there wasn't enough substance for that. This was what a living mummy would look like, wizened, dried up, little more than a husk. She wavered, trying to lift her torso and pull her rounding shoulders back but the cracking grew louder and more intense.

Suddenly the pedestal broke apart, dumping her down on the grass on her hands and knees in front of the creep.

"*What did you do?!*" His voice was as inhumanly shrill as a siren. I wasn't sure whether he was yelling at Sophie or me. "*What the hell is this, you were better than that, you told me you were better than that, what did you do?!*"

Sophie reached one hand toward him; he stepped back, revolted.

"Now you have to start all over!" he squealed.

Sophie was nodding her head, trying to speak. I wanted to sweep her up in my arms and rush her away from him but I was afraid to touch her, afraid that she would crumble to dust in my hands.

"Only I don't *have* another pedestal, you stupid cow!" he went on. "Every spot is taken! You'll have to wait! You'll have to wait and you'll never last that long!"

Sophie was gasping and wheezing as she tried to crawl toward him. Evading her, he turned to me with fury in his creep face. "This is your fault, you bitch! You had to come here and spoil everything! She was the best I'd ever had! I'll never get anyone else that good, *ever*! Get out of my garden before you spoil them all, get out of my garden *right now*!"

The bouncer and another equally burly man materialized on either side of me. I tried to twist away but one of them dug a fist into my hair and held on. I had one last, quick glance of Sophie flattened on the ground with the creep screaming at her before they rushed me out of the garden and into the darkness.

The sky was just getting light when the police woke me in Leicester Square. I was lying on a park bench in the garden, right next to a statue of the Little Tramp.

I tried to get him to tell me what had happened to Sophie but he wouldn't even twitch. I thought it was because the police were there but Chaplin was just as mute and still when I came back by myself later. All the statues are like that, everywhere I go – Leicester Square, Covent Garden, the West End, the South Bank. It doesn't matter what I say or how loud I yell, they're all unmoved. Like stone.

Poison

Bruce McAllister

Bruce McAllister (*mcallistercoaching.com*) lives in Redlands, California, with his wife Amelie Hunter. He works as a "writer, interdisciplinary writing coach, book and screenplay consultant, workshop leader and 'agent finder' for both new and established writers of non-fiction, fiction and screenplays." He taught writing for twenty years at the University of Redlands. A collection of his stories, *The Girl Who Loved Animals and Other Stories*, was published in 2007. And he had a story from *The Magazine of Fantasy & Science Fiction* reprinted in *The Best American Short Stories* in 2007.

"Poison" appeared in *Asimov's Science Fiction*. This is a contemporary fantasy but not urban. It is the story of an American boy who loves animals, living abroad in Italy in the neighborhood of a witch. It is an interesting contrast to the Gaiman story, earlier in this book.

In school that day the American boy, whose twelfth birthday was approaching, did just as well as his friends on the Roman history recitation and the spelling test, which included the word *stregheria* – *witchcraft* – which could, if you weren't careful, easily be confused with *straggaria*, an old-fashioned word for *respect*.

After school let out, he and his friends celebrated their good fortune by buying new plastic blowguns at the toy store in the fishing village and spending an hour making dozens of little paper cones with sewing needles taped to their points. Every boy in this country had at least one blowgun – they were cheap and no longer than a ruler – so the American boy had one too.

When the cones were finished, they went back up the hill and there, on the convent wall, not far from his family's *villetta*, hunted the lizards all boys in this country hunted. It wasn't easy hitting them. The bright green lizards weren't big and they moved like lightning, but he and his friends had gotten good at it. To keep things equal, they each stopped at six, leaving the bodies – which made the American boy sad if he looked at them too long – at the foot of the wall, where the convent cats might eat them if they were hungry enough.

The next night, after dinner, the American boy watched as his own cat – which he'd had for a year, slept with every night, and named "Nevis," the Latin word for "snow" – died in his bathtub, making little piglike sounds until he couldn't stand it any longer and he went outside to the flagstone patio to wait in darkness for the terrible sound to stop. When it finally did, he went back in, saw a strange shadow hovering over the tub, held his breath until it was gone, and then picked his cat up. When the limp but still-warm body made him cry, he let it. His parents were next door at their landlords, the Lupis, and wouldn't be back for a while. No one would hear him. No one would say, as his mother sometimes did, "You're too attached to your pets, John. Even your dad thinks so."

He knew who had done it. The three witches who lived in the olive groves that covered the hills around their house always put out poison for cats. If a cat died too suddenly for a doctor to help, and in great pain, everyone knew it was poison and who had put it out. It was what witches did – poisoning animals you loved. Everyone knew this.

Hand shaking, he found a paper bag under the kitchen sink just the right size for the body, put it in gently, twisted the top, and, though it hurt him to do it, left it in the bathtub where no one would notice it during the night. It was his bathroom, and no one would look in his tub until their maid came on Monday. If his parents asked where the cat was, he'd say he didn't know; and when he was finished with what he needed to do, he'd tell them what had happened. Or at least how the cat had died, poisoned by a witch, and how he'd buried it, which would indeed be true by the time he'd finished what he needed to do.

The next morning, as he ate breakfast with his mother and father, he asked, "What do witches do on Sunday?"

"They're not witches," his mother answered. "They're just old women, John, and if they had family – if they lived in town with their families – the entire village would call them *befane*, Christmas witches, and not *streghe*, which is so unkind." His mother was a teacher and was always teaching. She was wrong – they wouldn't be called *befane* – they'd be called *nonne* – *grandmothers* – but she was frustrated that she didn't know the language well enough to teach in this country, so she was always lecturing whenever she could.

"It doesn't matter whether they're witches or not," the boy answered, and, as he did, knew that it had begun and that he could not turn back. *The truth. The courage to speak it. The anger needed for such courage.* To stand before the witch who'd done it and talk to her about what was fair and what wasn't, to make her feel what he felt. And by doing so, free himself from an anger that was like a spell, one that might hold him forever if he did not find her in the olive groves and make her see what she had done.

"You could be more sensitive about the elderly," his mother was saying. "And you don't need to speak to me or your father in that tone of voice, John."

I had no tone, he wanted to say, but knew it would only make her madder and he would have to spend the morning undoing what he had done. He had his own anger now, and anger was a powerful thing. It could make you courageous. It could make people do what you wanted. But it was also a spell – like a song you couldn't get out of your head – and could make you a slave to it. He did not want to be a slave to it, but he did have a right to be angry, didn't he? His cat had died in his bathtub making that terrible sound; and as she'd died he'd stood there, seen the shadow, and watched it happen: The soul of his cat being pulled from its dying body by the ghostly hand of an old woman, the end of her pinky finger missing.

I will know the witch by her hand, he told himself again. *By her little finger....*

After breakfast, he went to his bathroom, picked up the bag carefully, and headed out into the great olive grove toward the place where the trees were dead and the witches lived in their stone huts. His friends would have told him not to – that only bad would come of it, "even if you are right to be sad and angry, Gianni" – and the boy was surprised he was doing it. He was supposedly "shy," wasn't he? This is what people said. Why did it take the death of his cat for him to be brave? And was it really bravery? Or was it simply the need to tell the truth – to stand before the old woman who'd done it and ask her, "Why did you poison my cat?" but also to say, "I would not kill what you love, *Signora.*"

He would begin, he'd decided, with the first stone hut, the one closest to his family's house on the hill. The witch who lived there would have found it easiest to poison his cat, wouldn't she? Whether she had put the poison by her hut or in the olive trees nearer his house wouldn't have mattered. Nevis had never gone far, so the chances she had traveled to the huts of the two witches higher up the hill made no sense. It was the closest witch who'd done it, he was sure. He had never laid eyes on her, but he had heard her in her hut when he and his friends had snuck in close one day, hiding in the little cave on the sunless side of the hill and watching from a distance, hoping to see her and yet afraid to. They never did, but they knew other boys who had.

Her teeth, a boy from the wharf had told them, were so bad you'd get nightmares if you looked at them. Yes, he'd seen her. Things were crawling in her mouth, and her tongue had made a noise like a viper's hiss. Another boy, Carlo – one who lived near the castle that overlooked the bay – hadn't seen her himself, but his older brothers had, years ago. They'd seen her hut turn green, tremble as if it were alive, even move toward them, just before she'd looked up, seen them, and shouted. They'd run, and as they had, they'd felt her green breath touch their backs. Days later they could still feel something crawling on them, and one of the brothers had scratched himself bloody trying to stop the itch.

When he glimpsed the hut through the trees, he stopped. It was green, yes, but that was because of the lichen. Everything in these groves – tree trunks, walls, and paths – had bright green lichen on it. And something moved, yes, but it was only an olive branch scraping across the hut's thatched roof. The trees here were not as dead as he remembered them. They had leaves. They were very alive. Why he remembered them as dead, he didn't know, unless it was that fear had made it seem so. He was not afraid today, so the trees were alive and the sunlight bright – was that the reason?

There was a vegetable garden he did not remember, and a stone path wandering from the hut's doorway into the grass, where it ended. He began toward it – under the trees, past a green lizard that watched him from a tree trunk, through the grass that reached his bare knees, through sudden yellow wildflowers, to the start of the path, its first flat stone, where he stopped. His heart jumped once in what felt like fear; but the sun was bright, and he clenched the paper bag, feeling his courage.

"*Strega!*" he wanted to shout, because it was true, but instead he said courteously, with only a little anger, "*Signora!*"

No one appeared in the doorway, which seemed small – even for a witch. Now he shouted it:

"*Signora!*"

He rattled the bag just a little. The body was stiff now, and he didn't want to do it; but maybe the old woman, because she was a witch, would hear it and know the reason he was here – even if she wanted to ignore him.

"*Addesso!*" he said, rattling the bag again, wondering how long it took maggots to grow.

"*Voglio parlare con Lei, Signora!*" *I wish to speak to you!*

Had Gian Felice been with him, they would never have come this close. They'd have stayed out under the nearest tree – or the second or third or fourth nearest – and thrown stones at the hut to get her attention, or shouted at her from a very safe distance. But he was too angry for that, and anger could make you feel safe. Gian Felice would have let his fear keep them in the trees, and the witch would know it, and it would give *her* courage – which the boy did not want. Witches had enough as it was.

Besides, he would not be able to see her hand if he stayed in the trees.

Something stirred in the darkness just inside the doorway, as he had known it would. *This is what witches do,* he told himself. They stir in the darkness – to scare you.

It was silly, the stirring. "Come out!" he shouted, in her language. "I am here to do business with you. Have the courage to come out, *Signora!*"

Had he really shouted that in her language? Had he really known what words to use? Yes, because he heard himself shouting it again:

"*Viene qui! Tiene corraggio, Signora!*"

After a moment the stirring spoke. "*Vengo!*" it said, and the shadow stepped outside.

"Che vuoi?" she asked, annoyed, her teeth indeed terrible. Even at this distance they were little yellow sticks, gaps between them, and how she ate (if she did eat) the boy didn't know. Her hair was long and gray, and she was as hunched as he'd imagined she'd be. But she was wearing black, as most old women in this country did, and this surprised him. The old women who wore black no longer had husbands, he knew. Their men were dead – from war, from heart attacks, from *fegato* problems – so they were widows, and widows wore black. But witches had no husbands. That is what Emilio had said more than once. "Witches never marry. They hate men and the boys who will become them!" A witch who wore black made no sense.

"I am here because of what it is in this bag," he said, holding it up, trying to keep his hand from shaking. But it shook, and worse, he was too far from her for his plan to work. He would have to be close enough that with just one step she could take the bag from him – to look inside – and when she did, he would see her hand.

He took a step toward her, stopped, took another, holding the bag out. No matter what he did – no matter how much anger he made himself feel – his hand would not stop shaking. Perhaps it wasn't fear? Perhaps it was only anger that made it shake?

When he was at last before her, he tried not to look at her teeth, but at her eyes – which were nearly closed, as if afraid of the light. If he stared at her eyes – if he made her feel his anger – perhaps the shaking would stop.

But then he smelled her. It was the smell of old women – old women at the Saturday market in town, old women on the wharf (when they didn't smell like fish), and also the smell of his own grandmother when he was little, before she died. It was the smell of vinegar – "She uses it on her hair," his mother had once said. He had loved his grandmother, but there were other smells to this old woman, too, and they were not his grandmother's.

Her eyes opened a little then and he saw that one was brown and one was green. This did not surprise him. Witches were not like ordinary people.

He was wrinkling his nose at her smell, he realized, but before he could stop himself she said:

"Do not come close if my body offends you, *ragazzo*."

His courage weakened then, and for a moment he could not find his anger.

"I am not here, *Signora*," he said as quickly as he could, "to discuss smells. I am here about what it is in this bag."

He thrust it at her. When she did not take it, he held his hand as steady as he could and waited. If he could not see her hand, he would not know!

When she spoke, he wasn't sure he'd heard her correctly.

"You wish to see my hand?" she repeated.

The bag was shaking even more now, but he made himself nod. "Yes, I wish to see your hand."

She made a sound like a snort, reached out and grabbed the bag. As she did, she shifted her weight to her other leg, which was shorter but just as skinny. For a moment he thought she might fall, and if she did, what would he do then? Should you touch a witch? Should you help her up?

But she didn't fall. She steadied herself, holding the bag in her hand, and stared at him. He still hadn't seen her hand, but he had to look away. Her eyes *knew* him – his bedroom, his cat, his parents' house – and the knowing made him afraid.

"I know what this bag holds, *ragazzo*. I do not need to look inside it. What dies deserves respect. Not to be put in a bag – not to be opened in the sunlight and stared at. Do you not agree?"

"Yes," the boy said, and then he saw the green lichen that covered, completely covered, the hut – its walls and thatch roof – begin to move. All of it. To wiggle. No, not wiggle, but to crawl, moving towards them slowly now even as the boy stopped breathing. The hut was moving. No – the lichen was.

But it wasn't lichen. It was –

Lizards.

It wasn't possible. *Lizards.* Hundreds – maybe thousands – of them. The green lizards that lived in these groves were all here somehow, sunning themselves on the roof and sunlit side of the hut, and now leaving their sunny places to move toward him and the old woman.

They were hers, he realized suddenly.

They were her pets.

They were coming to see what a boy might want with their mistress.

And then the movement stopped, and the roof and the sunny side of the hut fell still again. The lizards were waiting, he saw – but for what? It was like a dream, but it wasn't. It was real. She was a witch, after all, and with a witch anything was possible.

"Then why did you put what you loved – and what loved you – in a bag?" she was asking him, holding it but not looking in it.

He made himself find the words he had practiced.

"Because I wanted you to see it."

"Why?"

"Because I was angry."

"Why?"

"Because I knew that someone poisoned her. I saw the hand that did it. I wanted the person to see what she had done."

The old woman did not speak for a moment.

"Like all boys," she said at last with a sigh, "you understand nothing. But here is my hand, *ragazzo*."

Holding the bag, the hand came toward him, stopping so close to his face that he had to step back.

When a lizard crawled suddenly from the old woman's black sleeve, he almost screamed. The old woman snorted again and the lizard scampered down the side of the bag and back up again to her hand.

"*Via!*" she said to it. The creature returned to her sleeve, where three others were peering out now, watching him.

"Is this the hand you saw?"

It was. Two blue veins made a Y, with the end of the pinky finger missing, just as it had in the bathroom.

He nodded.

The old woman said nothing. It was up to him, he knew.

"Why did you want the soul of the animal I loved?" he asked.

When she spoke at last, it was with another sigh.

"It was not the soul of your cat I took," she said; and though he didn't want it to, it sounded true, and because it did, his anger left him once more, and with it his courage.

"I was taking another thing," she was saying, or at least that is what he heard. Whether she was actually speaking the words – out loud, in the air, in this sunlight – he could not be sure. He did not hear words in her language. He heard his own language and he could not even be sure she was speaking at all – with a throat. "I was taking back," her voice was saying, "the soul of my *lucertola* – my lizard."

It did not make sense. His cat was not a lizard. But then he saw it, because she wished him to: *his cat had eaten a lizard, and it had been one of hers. His cat had ventured into the grove too far, come upon her hut and her lizards, and, as cats do, eaten one of them.* It was true, he saw. It was not some lie she wanted him to believe.

She had poisoned his cat because his cat had killed her lizard? She had lost something she had loved, too, and had acted in anger?

He could have said, "Was *poison* the only way?"

But then she would say, "I chased your cat away many times, but she kept coming back, curious, ready to eat more of my lizards if I did not poison her."

He could say, "Why didn't you come to my house and tell me? You knew where I lived."

Then she would say, "You would have wanted a witch in your doorway? You would have believed her? You would not, in anger, have come with your friends to throw rocks at her house?"

Worst of all, she might even say, "I killed what you loved to save what I love," and what would his answer be then – except the silence of sadness? She was a witch and might be lying – to make him go away – but it would not feel like a lie, and so he would have no words.

Before he could say anything at all, the old woman – eyes on his, bag in her hand, the four lizards still peeking at him from her sleeve – said, "I know where you live, yes, but I could not have come to you. I cannot leave my house except at dark. But that is not the point of this. The point is that I did not poison your cat."

Now she was lying. He was sure of it. Witches did lie. They said and did what they needed to do and say to get what they wanted – to trip people up – especially children. They hated the happiness and lives of ordinary people – and "They hate the innocence of children," Antonio's mother had told him and his friends at dinner once – so they did whatever they could to trick you, to hurt you. It had been this way forever. World without end.

"My cat was poisoned," the boy said.

"Yes," the old woman answered, "but it was not poison."

"What?"

"Your cat ate my lizard."

"So?"

"My lizard was the poison."

"I do not understand you."

"My lizards are not ordinary lizards, and because they are not, they are poison to anything that eats them."

She was playing more tricks now. She was saying whatever she needed to say to make him lose his courage forever. It was like a spell, one that used logic to confuse the mind – to take away confidence. He could feel himself spinning within it, the spell, like a moth in a spider's cocoon.

He wanted to run, but he couldn't. He needed the bag back. How could he leave without it?

"You are putting a spell on me," he said, as if saying it might change it.

"Words have no power," she answered, "which the listener does not give them."

This was true. He had thought this himself when his mother, in an anger she would not let go of, used words that made him feel shame. Without her words, he knew, there could be no shame.

"That is true," he found himself saying, not wanting to but saying it anyway; and when he did, she made a little smile with her mouth. It was both wonderful and horrible. The little sticks showed against the dark hole of her mouth, and the skin of her lips pulled tight, as if on a corpse's skull, cracking. Little lines of blood appeared in the cracks, but the smile did not give up. It stayed.

If it was a spell that he was feeling, it was not a bad one.

"What are they," he asked suddenly, "if they are not lizards?"

After another snort, she said:

"They are what is left of the man I loved."

As he stared at her black dress, the one so many old women in this country wore, he knew that this too was true.

As if tired out from her smile, she frowned then, but said gently enough:

"Come in."

This was how the story always went, didn't it? The witch would get the boy or girl inside her hut, and that would be the end of it. As Perotto had told them once, a witch's spells are more powerful where she lives – in her own hut – where, like her smell or breath or bony hand, they are a part of her and have her power. She needed to get him inside to do what she wanted to him. Any witch would. The gentleness of her words was a lie, wasn't it?

"I cannot make you enter," she said. "I can only invite you."

This had to be a trick. This kindness; this honesty; this pretending she didn't have the power, the spells, to *make* him do what she wanted. "A witch," Emilio had told them, "will tell you anything she needs to tell you." Emilio knew because his own uncle had been killed by a witch's spell during the war. "With a lie she got him to sit beside her on a bench in the old cemetery, telling him she was there to grieve her sister. She touched his hand just once, but it was enough to put it on him. Fifteen days later he died in his bed like a dog!"

She was offering him the bag now. He could leave if he wanted.

"If you will not come in, you should have your cat back, to bury it as you wish, to say a blessing over it because it was something you loved."

This was not how witches were supposed to talk – such kindness. It was more trickery. It had to be. He would grab the bag and leave before she changed her mind.

But as he took the bag from her, the lizards in her sleeve scampered down her arm and onto his. He jumped and started turn – to run – but she was looking at him with her one brown eye and her one green eye, and the lizards did not feel wrong. They scampered down his arm again, back up, and stopped, watching him. He could not look away. They were green and beautiful and they seemed to like him. If they were a trick, they were not a trick from any story he had ever heard. They were not howling black cats or screeching owls or hissing vipers, the pets witches were known for. They were green and cheerful, and he was sorry he had ever killed the lizards of this country.

As he looked at the ones on his arm, the walls and roof of the hut began moving again like a slow green wave toward them. They flowed like water, down the path, under the old woman's feet, around them, to his own sandals. For a moment he felt a jerk of fear, but their toes and tails on his bare legs tickled, and he couldn't stop a smile.

When the wave stopped at last, he was covered with them. His arms and legs and shorts and shirt were green. He itched, yes, but it was fine.

"Come in," she said again; and walking carefully so as not to knock any of them from him, he followed her into the hut.

As he stood in the darkness with her, she touched his arm lightly and he didn't jump. Then she whistled once, as if calling a dog, but it was a witch's whistle – not just a sound in the air, for ears, but something more. As she whistled, a green light swirled like fog from her mouth, and the lizards that had followed them in, their tiny faces faintly by the dim light from her mouth, looked up at her from the floor.

She had begun to whisper, too, and it sounded like *"Ricordatelo"* – *"Remember him"* – and the lizards, in the light of the fog, their eyes like green stars, began to move toward the dark center of the room.

Beside him her voice said, "Can you see our bed?"

He could. In the dim green light he could see, in the middle of the floor, what looked like blankets, heavy wool ones, lying on a piece of lumpy canvas. What was inside the canvas he didn't know. Straw, rags, old clothes – anything to fill it. The bed was on the floor, and, except for blankets, it was empty. He was sure of it. But the lizards were gathering there; and as he looked at the green shadow that was the bed, it began to change. It was empty, yes, but *something* was taking shape there.

The lizards on his arms and legs moved once and fell still. He took a breath.

"This is where we slept when the war was over."

"Yes," the boy heard himself say, and a lizard moved from his neck to his ear.

"We lived here because we were poor," she was saying, though in what language he was not sure. "My husband, whose name was Pagano Lorenzo, picked grapes at Bocca di Magra. That was what he did."

"Yes," the boy said again.

"Do you see him?"

"What?"

"Do you see my husband?"

"No...."

"That is because my sister, who lives in Pozzuoli, the village of red doorways, killed him. She did not have a man. Her man, whom she did not really love, died at Monte Cavallo in the war, while mine returned. She hated me for my fortune and one day asked us to dinner. She made *dateri*, using the darkest clams, and the portion she gave to him was poisoned. It is easy to do if you know *stregheria*, if you are *strega*. You could poison your sister in jealousy – or at least try, witch to witch – but why bother? Why not instead take away what she loved, what you yourself do not have, so that you can watch her grieve forever? Do you see him now, *ragazzo?*"

The boy, who was shaking again, blinked and brushed a lizard's tail from his eye. He could see that the shadow on the bed was bigger now. He could feel the lizards on his arms and legs leaving him to join the others on the bed, where the shadow was growing.

"I – I..."

"Boys who tell stories about us do not understand. We cannot do *everything*. I could not save my husband. He died on this bed from the poison, the kind used for rats, and he died in great pain. With a spell she blinded his tongue to the taste of it and he ate it all."

The shadow on the bed was darkening and he could not stop shaking. It was not a ghost he was seeing, but something else.

"I did what I could, *ragazzo*. The lizards of these groves felt for us the affection we felt for them. They had lived with us, and we with them; and so, when my husband died, I gave his soul to them – a piece to each – a thousand pieces...."

The boy was shaking so hard he could barely stand. The shadow on the bed was complete, and the old woman, though her legs and hip hurt her, stepped to the window now to open it. As sunlight fell to the bed, he saw what the lizards had made, the shape they had taken: A man, sleeping peacefully on his stomach, green as lichen in the sunlight, but one that in the night would be real as a man needed to be for his wife, with her memories, to fall asleep.

She had wanted the piece of him back, that was all. He saw it now. She hadn't poisoned his cat. The lizard had. The lizard that was a piece of her husband's poisoned soul.

"I sleep well at night," the old woman was saying, "because we sleep well when we sleep with what we love. How do you sleep, *ragazzo?*"

As the boy walked back through the groves to his house, the bag in his hand, he could hear the grass rustling just behind him. How many there were, he did not know. A hundred perhaps, maybe more. He wanted to look, but did not want to scare them away. Even when he reached the steps to his house, he did not look back. He got a shovel from the shed, returned to the nearest trees, and dug a hole where his parents could not see him digging. There he buried the body, saying the blessing as he filled the hole with dirt. He used the Lord's Prayer, of course, because he had used it before when his pets had died; but also because he did not know another. They waited in the grass while he did this. Then he went back to the house, to his room – stepping quietly past the kitchen and his mother's anger, which did not have to be his anymore, he knew – and saw how it would go: He would open his bedroom window just enough that they could enter at will, sunning themselves on the windowsill when they wanted to, coming in when the sun had set. At night – and any night he wished it – he would need only lie down on his bed, whisper "*Remember her*" to the darkness, and wait to feel the tiny feet and tails moving over him as the animal – the one he had slept with every night for a year – took shape beside him, paws tucked neatly under it, body somehow warm, so that he could sleep at last.

Who Slays the Gyant, Wounds the Beast

Mark Chadbourn

Mark Chadbourn (*markchadbourn.net*) lives in Leicestershire, UK, where he pursues the adventurous life of a full-time writer. He prides himself on his methods of researching his fiction and describes in some detail on his website the lengths to which he goes to research his books, for example: "For his first novel *Underground*, set in an isolated mining community, he worked hundreds of feet beneath the earth, crawling along tunnels barely two feet high, experiencing the same kind of brutal lifestyle as his coal miner characters." He is the author of thirteen fantasy and horror novels to date, all published in the UK.

"Who Slays the Gyant, Wounds the Beast," published in *The Solaris Book of New Fantasy*, stems from the tradition of tales to be told 'round the fire at Christmas, that darkest time of the year: It is Christmas Eve, 1598, and the Queen's favorite poet is having an affair with the Faerie Queen. Elizabeth I is not amused.

CHRISTMAS EVE, 1598

The border between what is and what might be changes with the seasons, and with the hour. Homesteads and fields and lanes that have the hard, dusty air of the mundane on a hot summer afternoon can echo to the sly tread of something wild and irrational under the full moon. Whispers uttered by no human mouth are caught on the breeze on All Hallows Eve or Walpurgisnacht. At the great hall of Charlecote Park, lonely in the frozen landscape, the rules of the daylight world have long since dissipated with the setting sun.

There are whispers here too.

"*Now?*"

"*Soon.*"

And prints made by no human foot in the deep snow that lies heavy against the sturdy walls. Lights blaze in the many windows and the sound of viol, hautboy, and harpsichord drift out across the still countryside as the merrymakers prepare for the coming holy day.

"This is a pit of debauchery. We should be home in London, Will, not in dismal Warwickshire among these fornicators and cupshotten ne'er-do-wells. I would be at church when the first bell tolls, and keep the devil at my back." Nathaniel Colt huddled beneath the woolen blanket as he peered out of the carriage window at the approaching hall. His breath clouded and he had long since lost the feeling in his toes.

The man opposite did not appear to feel the chill. He lounged across the seat, cleaning his nails with a knife. His boots were polished to a shine, his clothes the latest fashionable cut from the tailors who supplied the court. An urbane air belied his true nature, which occasionally surfaced in the depths of his dark eyes.

"Fornicators and cupshotten ne'er-do-wells, Nathaniel? England's aristocracy may not take to such a description," he replied. "However true it may be."

"I am a God-fearing man. Unlike yourself," Nathaniel added sniffily. "But I would expect no less from someone who has intimate knowledge of every tavern and doxy on Cheapside."

"Life is short, Nat, and we are bounded by misery on all sides. We must seek out what jewels we can."

Nathaniel snorted.

The carriage jolted as it passed between the grand gates and made its way toward the entrance where servants waited to help them from the carriage.

"And when do you plan to tell me why the Queen has dispatched us to this devil-haunted spot?" Nathaniel added. "What could possibly demand the attention of the magnificent Will Swyfte, England's greatest spy?"

"That note of sarcasm is unbecoming, Nathaniel," Will said lightly. "I may have to find another assistant in future."

"My heavenly rewards come early."

The servants led them into the hall where they were greeted by the host, the newly knighted Sir Thomas Lucy, dressed in a black doublet.

"Will Swyfte, England's greatest spy," he said. Nathaniel rolled his eyes. "This is an honor, indeed." He paused. "Is the Queen – "

"Elizabeth has had to cancel her visit for the festivities," Will said. "And Walsingham sends his apologies. I am here on their behalf."

Lucy was crestfallen. He tugged at his beard for a moment and then said, "You will make merry with us, then, Mr. Swyfte? My house and staff are at your disposal. And I for one would take great pleasure in hearing of your famous exploits in your own words."

Lucy directed Will and Nathaniel toward the room where the festivities were taking place, before hurrying to the side of his wife. "I fail to see the value of a spy with a name and a face that is known by everyone in the realm," Nathaniel sighed.

"England needs its heroes, Nat. People must see that all is being done to keep them safe in their beds. It stops them asking difficult questions of their betters. More, it distracts them from the real nightmares threatening to steal their breaths. Philip of Spain was a small ogre in comparison."

"And what are these nightmares? Should not an assistant be trusted enough to know more than the common man?"

"Do not be so quick to shuck off the common life." A note of regret rose briefly in Will's voice. "Enough chat. I have work for you."

The ballroom was thronging with the cream of the aristocracy, dancing and drinking and carousing with the complete abandon of the carefree ruling class. On show were the finest gowns and cloaks and doublets, bright colors glowing in the Christmas candlelight. Each guest wore a mask, so that a man might have difficulty knowing if the woman with him were his wife; an added attraction. In the shadows, kisses were stolen, and dancers would occasionally vacate the floor to disappear to the rooms above.

"Somewhere in that morass of carnality is Sir Edmund Spenser."

"The Queen's favorite poet?"

"The same. Find him, Nat, and bring him to me. But with the politeness befitting his status, of course."

"What would you have me do?" Nathaniel said incredulously. "Snatch off every mask until I find the face we seek?"

"You are a resourceful man," Will said with a grin. "That is why I have elevated you to your high status."

"And where will you be while I risk the stocks or being thrown out into the winter cold?"

"I go in search of true love."

At the far end of the entrance hall, a hidden door revealed a tight, winding staircase that led to the guest bedrooms. Ice had formed on the inside of the windows and Will's breath plumed in the chill. He had memorized the layout of the house from the plans Walsingham had given him, but it was impossible to know which room had been set aside for Spenser.

The first door he tried revealed a couple in sweaty coitus. Though both naked, the man still wore a devil mask and the woman hid behind a cat's face. Lost to their rhythm, they did not see Will.

The next four rooms were empty, though fires crackled in the grate. The fifth was locked. From a hidden pouch, Will removed a roll of velvet containing a skeleton key. The lock turned with an irritatingly loud *clank*, but as he slipped inside the figure seated at the mirrored dressing table appeared not to have heard. It was a woman, though her reflected face was lost to the shadows of a hooded cloak. Ringlets of brown hair tumbled out on to her breast. She was still, like a moonlit pool, and at first Will thought she was asleep.

But then her voice rolled out, low and honeyed and as warm as the candlelight: "Leave now, uninvited guest, or face the inevitable repercussions." The soft tones betrayed no fear.

"You are the consort of Sir Edmund Spenser?"

She did not reply.

"It is not my habit to intrude into a lady's chamber..." Will paused. "At least, not without some degree of invitation."

"You did not leave your sword upon arrival," the woman noted. "You are expecting a threat? Here, in this house of celebration?"

Will found himself lulled by her soothing voice. "Weave no spells with me," he said. "I am aware of your tricks."

"Then there is no need for subterfuge." The woman turned to him and removed her hood. Though Will had encountered some of the most beautiful women in Europe, his breath caught in his throat. Her flawless skin appeared to exude a thin golden light and her hazel eyes flashed with an otherworldly light.

"Glamour?" he said.

"'Twould be an insult if I considered your opinion to carry any weight." She stood, and as the cloak shifted around her form the atmosphere became sexually charged.

"I can see why Spenser fell beneath your spell."

A shadow crossed her face. "No spell."

"What, then? True love?" Will expected a tart response to his mockery, but she turned from him and went to the window.

"I could not expect one such as you to understand," she said quietly as she gazed out across the frozen fields.

"You know we cannot allow it to continue."

"Is it so dangerous?"

"A man and a resident of Faerie? If the icy war between our two lands was not close to growing hot, you perhaps could make an argument for such a liaison. But – "

"War? You speak as if that means anything." She turned to him, her eyes blazing. For the first time, Will glimpsed the true power that he knew existed just beneath the otherworldly beauty. He drew his sword.

She strode toward him, the air crackling around her. "The events of tonight must reach their natural conclusion."

"Your profession of love does not ring true. You know well how much the information you both carry is of value to your kind. You cannot be allowed to cross over to the other side."

"My kind?" Her face grew cold and terrible. "My kind are fools and lovers." She snapped open her left hand to release a wild fluttering of wings. Within a second, Will fell to the floor, unconscious.

*

"Your master cuts a very dashing figure," Alice Lucy noted as she sent the eldest of her thirteen children back to bed. "Is it true he has personally dispatched one hundred Spaniards?"

Nathaniel masked his weariness at her question and the familiar, tiresome sparkle in the eye of the mistress of the house. "There are many stories surrounding my master, some of them even true."

"My husband has done his own duty to deal with the Catholic problem locally. Though, of course, not with the verve of Master Swyfte," she added hastily. "He is a God-fearing man?"

"I believe Master Swyfte does not know the meaning of fear," Nathaniel said with a tight smile.

"And no woman has yet led him up the aisle. How sad that he abides such a lonely existence."

Nathaniel's attention was drawn to some kind of disturbance on the far side of the whirling dancers. "Master Swyfte does not want for companionship. But Queen and Country demand much of him, and a wife would find her days and nights lacking."

A ripple moved across the ballroom as dancers came to a sudden halt. An animated group had grown near one of the windows looking over the formal gardens leading down to the river.

Alice peered at the growing crowd with irritation. "They are in their cups. Do not concern yourself."

"I fear, mistress, there is more to this than wine." Nathaniel deferentially edged through the dancers until he could hear the conversation of the knot of men and women move from jocularity to concern.

"Get him to a bedroom!" a rotund man in a pig mask squealed. "He holds up the festivities and the midnight hour draws near!"

"Hold. His chest does not move. Perhaps he has choked on a nut. Remove his mask."

Nathaniel could see a man prone on the floor, his white ruffle soaked in the red winc he had been drinking so that it appeared he had been shot. Fumbling fingers plucked his mask free and then all those around him recoiled as one.

"The Devil's work!" the pig-man exclaimed. He crossed himself as he staggered back onto the dance floor.

At first, Nathaniel was sure this was some joke to mark the festivities, for the man on the floor was not a man at all. Straw sprouted from ears and mouth like one of the figures farmers left in the cornfields after the harvest. Silver coins were embedded where the eyes should have been. Yet the skin still bloomed warm and the features were more real than any prankster could have constructed.

"Quick!" Nathaniel said. "Where was he before he fell?"

One of the guests pointed toward the window. "He looked out across the landscape as he drank his wine."

Those nearest the window backed away quickly, amid murmurs of "Witchcraft!" As the ripples of what had happened moved swiftly across the dance floor, Lucy rushed over aghast.

"A joke!" he cried. "A Christmas prank!" Hastily, he ordered his servants to remove the straw man. Circulating rapidly, he managed to calm the most anxious guests, but an atmosphere of unease still hung heavily over the hall.

"Is this why your Master is here?" Lucy asked as he pulled Nathaniel to one side. "If so, I would ask for his help before these matters worsen, for I fear they may."

"My Master's motives remain a mystery known only to himself. Though dress me in a cap and call me a fool if there were no connection, for bizarre occurrences follow my Master like a dog follows a wedding parade."

"Then I beseech you, bring him here, now, before we are all turned to straw."

Nathaniel bowed and disappeared into the crowd, though he was now niggled with the thought that Will had been gone for an undue amount of time.

Will woke on the cold, hard boards of the bedroom, his head filled with one memory constantly replaying: Jenny calling to him across the golden cornfield that lay beside her Warwickshire home. The image stung him so hard it had brought tears to his eyes while he slept. The remembrance had been planted there to teach him a lesson.

"Magicks," he muttered contemptuously.

"Many a time I have found you in such a position, but never without the consumption of wine." Nathaniel slipped in and helped Will to his feet. "You were attacked?"

"Not in the way you think." Will steadied himself. Jenny slipped from his mind, but she was not replaced by peace. "I fear I have a score to settle."

"I fear you have to listen to me prattle before you do another thing." Nathaniel quickly explained what had transpired in the ballroom. "What transpired here?" he added. "Is this the same threat?"

"In a way. Come – great danger draws near."

In the cold corridor, Will scraped the ice off the window to peer into the snow-bright night. The light from the great windows fell in large rectangles on rolling drifts. "Footprints," he mused.

"Someone is out there?" Nathaniel squeezed beside Will. "Those are the prints of animals," he said dismissively.

Beyond the pools of light, where the trees clustered, darkness lay heavily. Points of light appeared briefly here and there, as though fireflies moved among the branches. Will continued to watch until there was a sudden burst of fire; a torch igniting. Another, and then another, moving back and forth.

Will did not wait to hear Nathaniel's questions. He found Lucy passing brightly among the guests, splashing sack liberally into goblets while attempting to raise spirits with jokes and bawdy comments.

"Master Swyfte. Is the unfortunate incident now contained?"

Will drew him to one side. "The matter is just beginning. This hall is under siege."

Lucy cursed loudly. "'Tis the Catholics. The uprising we all feared has begun."

"You should find some warmth in your heart for the brotherhood of man," Will replied coldly. "There are worse things under heaven than Catholics."

"Moors?"

"We must make the hall secure by the midnight hour."

The grand clock squatting in the corner near the mantelpiece showed twenty minutes remaining. "There is time enow. I will order the servants to lock and bar the doors," Lucy said.

"That will not suffice. I will advise your kitchen servants to prepare a concoction of salt and other herbs. It must be sprinkled along every entrance into this place: doors, windows, hearths. To miss one opening could be the end of all of us."

Lucy blanched. "'Then you are saying this threat is witchcraft?"

"Best not discuss these things here and now for fear of frighting your guests, Sir Thomas. Trust in me and the authority of our Queen and we shall keep your home safe from all enemies." Lucy nodded. "One other thing: keep all guests away from the windows and anywhere they can be spied from without."

Deeply troubled, Lucy hurried off to find the cook. Will turned to Nathaniel. "Did you find Spenser?"

"I searched high and low, and met many who had spoken to him, or believed they had, but he always stayed one step ahead."

"Then back to it, Nat. The urgency is greater still. Spenser and his love must not be allowed to leave this place before the sun breaks."

"You fear for his life at the hands of whatever waits without?"

"I fear for all our lives, Nat, and the lives of every man, woman and child in England."

It took five minutes for the kitchen staff to prepare Will's salt-based concoction and a further thirteen minutes to draw a line of it before every entrance into the hall, and that was with every servant working fast with small leather pouches of the mixture. The final grains fell into place as the bell on the great clock began to chime midnight, and only then did Will ease slightly. Fuelled by more bottles brought up from Lucy's cellar, the guests continued to enjoy themselves oblivious to what was taking place around them, but Lucy himself wandered the party rooms ashen-faced.

And as the final chime echoed, every candle and lamp in the hall winked out.

Whoops and excited shrieks filled the room. "'Tis time for the great unmasking!" someone called. No one had noticed that even the roaring fire in the hearth had dimmed to a faint crackle. Through the gloom, Will quickly snatched a candle from the table and lit it with his flint. Another cheer rose up. With fumbling fingers, Lucy hastily lit another five sticks in a candelabrum on the other side of the room. The panic was clear in his face.

From an oblique angle, Will watched through the window, but there was no sign of anyone approaching. All around him, the drunken guests tore off their masks with great cheers. The women blushed and curtseyed. The men brayed and kissed their hands.

Except one. Will saw him at the same time the guests closest to him began to laugh and point. A large, fat-bellied man, he staggered around, feeling across the gray-furred surface of the wolf's mask he wore. Yet in his other hand, he clutched the same wolf mask that he had just removed.

"A mask beneath a mask! How novel," a freckle-faced woman cried.

Desperate to stop a panic that might drive the guests out into the night, Will ran to drag the guest to a more private place. He was too late. "This is no mask. It is my face!" the man howled. Those nearest peered closely and saw that it was true.

There was a gurgle and a swell that became a crashing wave as the guests swept toward the exit amid deafening cries for God to save them. Will was closer to the hall and made it to the grand oak door first. He drew his sword and brought the rush to a halt.

"You know me," he said firmly.

Silence.

"Do you know me?" he stressed in a tone that bordered on the threatening.

A few near the front quietly said that they did.

"Then you know that I will allow no further harm to come to loyal men and women of this realm. As long as you stay within my purview, and do not venture outside, for that is where the true danger awaits."

Several were still consumed with dread of the supernatural. They tore at their clothes and tore at their hair and for a moment Will thought they were going to rush him in the grip of their frenzy. But saner heads held them calm until the panic subsided and then the questions began in force. At the back of the hall, Nathaniel was trying to catch his attention. Shaking off the desperately clutching hands, Will left Lucy to maintain whatever calm he could and ran in pursuit of the figure Nathaniel had indicated.

At the foot of the rear staircase, Will caught up with a man with wavy brown hair above a high forehead that gave him the look of an intellectual, but it was marred by the desperation etched into his features.

Will took his arm. The man did not resist. "Sir Edmund?"

There was a long moment of silence before he relented. "Yes."

"You know who I am?"

"I have heard of your exploits, like every other person in this land."

"Then you know I am only charged with the gravest tasks."

Spenser nodded. Will saw no surprise that he was there, just a dismal resignation.

"Your wife, Elizabeth, has displayed remarkable fortitude during your repeated absences from the family home," Will continued, before adding knowingly, "while you were composing your poetry. She fears your latest absence may be longer than the others, Sir Edmund. Is she correct?"

Spenser bowed his head; his hands were shaking so much he appeared to be sick. "What is your intention?"

"To take you back to London. Our Queen wishes for you to spend some weeks...perhaps months... at the court."

"I cannot return." He grabbed Will's shoulders forcefully. "Please, you must understand. This is an affair of the heart. I seek freedom to let it breathe. I cannot return to the stifling fug of the court."

"You have one affair of the heart, Sir Edmund, the woman you wed four years past. There is no room for any other."

"What are you saying?"

"You will not be allowed to see your current associate, under orders of the Queen – "

"Walsingham, more like!"

"She will be returned to her former residence to continue the work she has carried out these last thirty years."

"No!" Spenser began to cry. "Not back to that cell. To the four walls and the gloom and the questions, the endless boredom. To one such as she, that is a living torture. Why do you not kill her and be done with it? Why do you not kill us both?"

The intensity of emotion in Spenser's face brought Will up sharp. "These are difficult times," he said, softening slightly, "and they require difficult measures.

The war between England and Faerie has blown hot and cold, and now it is cold, though no less dangerous. What you attempt here tonight will light a fire that could burn England to the ground. You know these things. Yet you persist."

"You call me traitor, but I am just a man in love. Can you not feel what I feel? Do you have no heart?"

"In the midst of this great struggle, there is no place for ones such as you or I to consider such things – "

"Such things? They are the reason we do what we do!" Spenser wrung his hands; he appeared on the verge of falling to his knees.

"You are a poet, Sir Edmund, and I am merely a spy. All I know is lies, whispered secrets, and the caress of a blade across the throat. Now, why here, this night? Why not return to Ireland?"

"There is a crossing point not far from the hall," Spenser said with bleak resignation. "At this time of year, it would allow me to travel with her without suffering the terrible fate of those who have ventured to the Far Lands in times past."

"Will! Come quick!" Nathaniel appeared at the door to the ballroom, his face pale.

"Stay by my side, Sir Edmund," Will cautioned. "Though a peer of the realm, 'twould not be fitting to ignore the Queen's decree." Spenser bowed his head at the implicit threat and followed silently.

In the ballroom, Will and Nathaniel turned one of the massive oak tables onto its side for cover. Outside, the torches were moving. They had emerged from the tree line and were slowly advancing on the house. As the snow flared in the torchlight, figures gradually came into view. Nathaniel caught his breath.

"Can this be true?" Then: "Is it the Devil and his followers, up from hell to claim our souls?"

"Not the Devil in name, Nat." The approaching group was led by tall, strong males with golden-tinged skin and beautiful but cruel faces. They wore black and silver helmets and breastplates that looked more like tropical shells than armor. But beyond them, still half-seen, were worse things that came with hooves and scales and bat-wings and horns, writhing in shadow, eyes glowing balefully. The approaching line reached across the entire back of the hall, and from the way it curved at the fringes, Will guessed the building was surrounded.

"What, then?" When Will did not reply, Nathaniel turned to him. "You knew of these things."

"For a long time."

"The Unseelie Court." Spenser stood to one side, his face ghostly in the gloom. "To them, humanity is like the cattle in the field. They have haunted our nightmares since Adam rose up in the Garden."

"*Hunted*, is the word, I think," Will said. "For an age, they saw us as playthings, Nat. Objects to torment, like the bears that dance in the inns on Cheapside. They would steal our children from the crib and leave misshapen things in their place. Or they would turn us into the stones that stand proud in the fields, or lure us to their land with the promise of gold, or magickal instruments." He glanced at Spenser. "Or love."

"No lure," Spenser said. "'Tis from the heart, Master Swyfte, I told you that."

"Your heart, perchance. But your paramour who has been at Her Majesty's convenience for many a year – "

"Imprisoned!"

"I would think she nurtures a little bitterness in her heart, would you not? A desire for revenge, say? To spew forth every detail of our magickal defenses that finally helped hold those foul creatures at bay?"

"No!"

Will grabbed Spenser roughly and thrust him behind the table so he could see clearly through the window. Nathaniel gasped at such rough treatment of a member of the aristocracy.

"Look deep into their faces, Sir Edmund, and tell me they would not make demands upon one of their own, even if she is as true and noble as you say. To prey upon us again, they would do anything to gain the information she holds."

Tears rimmed Spenser's eyes. "I could not bear to lose her, Master Swyfte. To you or them."

"Perhaps arrangements could be made for occasional access to her room – "

Spenser laughed bitterly. "Clearly you have never loved. "'Occasional access'? That would be more torment than reward."

"Where is she, Sir Edmund?"

"I know not. 'Struth." He smiled. "She could be standing an inch behind your shoulder and you would not know. Or she could already be away across the fields, free at last. The things she can do! It takes the breath away."

"Will?" Nathaniel's knuckles were white on the tabletop. Outside, the Unseelie Court had come to a halt just a few feet from the windows. Their torches cast a sickening ruddy glow into the hall. "The salt and herbs you spread at the entrances – it will prevent them gaining access?"

"They cannot cross it and survive."

"Then we are safe. We have but to wait till dawn."

Spenser snorted contemptuously.

"Whatever, we shall hold them at bay, Nat."

"They are so far beyond us, they are gods," Spenser said. "Old gods from the days of the Fall. Would you hold back an angel or a devil, Master Swyfte?"

"I would stand against hell itself if needs must."

*

Lucy's guests huddled on the floor near the walls furthest from the windows in the ballroom and the great hall. Some drank heavily to mask their fear, but most trembled and prayed. Will prowled the building in search of Spenser's Faerie Queen, but there was no sign of her in the ringing, empty bedrooms, or the vast, steaming kitchen.

"Perhaps Sir Edmund is right and she is long gone," Nathaniel ventured.

"If she were gone, our longtime tormentors would not continue to wait beyond the walls. No, Nat, she is still here, and we must find her before dawn. For when the Unseelie Court melts away, she will be gone from here, and all hope will be gone too."

"If she is as powerful as Sir Edmund says, what chance have we of finding her?"

A cry followed by a loud hubbub rose up from the rooms below. Will raced down to find several aristocrats wrestling one of their own to the flagstones of the entrance hall. He had the glassy-eyed look of a sleepwalker.

Lucy grabbed Will's arm. "He is possessed," he gasped. "My wife noticed him, in a dream, walking to the door where he proceeded to wipe away your concoction." Will turned toward the door, but Lucy continued, "We have replenished your magical barrier."

"Good. No barrier must be removed till dawn breaks. Do you hear?" Will heard the unintended lash in his voice, but Lucy did not appear to mind. He nodded anxiously.

Will inspected the glassy-eyed man who appeared to be coming to his senses. Others still pinned his arms and legs to the floor. Will motioned to them to free him. "The danger here has passed. But be vigilant in case others become pixie-led."

"The Unseelie Court controlled him?" Nathaniel asked when they had moved away to one side.

"They have the power to control weak minds for a short period," Will said.

"And unfortunately," Nat added tartly, "we are surrounded by the aristocracy."

Another cry rose up as a woman lurched toward the barrier at the fireplace in the ballroom. She was brought down in seconds.

"I fear it will be a long night, Nat."

By three o'clock, the party guests were whimpering and crying. Every few minutes one of their number would attempt to wander off, only to be brought down in a flurry of bodies. They were growing progressively more violent as the anxiety increased. One woman cried constantly with a broken arm. Blood streamed from the noses of others.

Will grabbed Spenser and hauled him next to the fire. "My patience wears thin, Sir Edmund. You must flush out your love."

"Or what, Master Swyfte? You will murder a favored subject of the Queen?"

"No threats. But death is not the worst thing."

"Will! Come quick!" Horrified, Nat appeared at the door followed by billowing smoke and a sickening smell of cooking meat. A tall, elderly man ran back and forth, squealing, as flames consumed him; he still clutched the lamp he had poured over himself, his hand now welded to the metal. Several men attempted to haul a tapestry to stifle the blaze, but the man in his death throes was too fast and random. Obstacles added to the chaos as women swooned across the floor and other guests stumbled in their crazed attempts to flee.

"They will kill us all!" one woman wailed repeatedly.

The blazing man was eventually forced to the ground and smothered by the tapestry, but it was too late for him. The smoke and the stink of burning filled the hall.

"Is this it, then?" Nathaniel said. "They will pick us off one by one?"

"They have nothing to gain by that." Will paced back and forth, attempting to count heads. "It was a diversion."

Lucy ran up, ashen-faced. "My wife," he said. "In the confusion, she departed."

"I saw her," a white-haired woman said. "She went towards the kitchens."

Will thought Lucy would faint. "They have taken her," he gasped.

Before Lucy could plead for his wife's return, Will was racing through the hall, with Nathaniel close behind. The deserted kitchen was filled with steam and the smell of Christmas spices, and from the scullery beyond came the sound of scraping. Hunched before the door that led to the kitchen yard, Lucy's wife had just finished removing the last of the salt mixture. Will vaulted the row of empty coppers, but it was too late. The door began to grind open and beyond an insane shrieking rose up that sounded like birds over the autumn fields.

Will dragged the dazed Lady Lucy back and thrust her into Nathaniel's arms. "Take her back, and put another line of the mixture beyond the kitchen door!"

"What about you?"

"They will be on us before we reach safety. I will hold them back as best I can."

Nathaniel looked aghast, but as the door swung open with a resounding crash, he took Lady Lucy's hand and ran. Will drew his sword and waited. Through the door, the dark was impenetrable and a deep, threatening silence had replaced the shrieking.

"Come, then, you foul and cowardly creatures," he said. "An Englishman with cold steel awaits."

The lights in the scullery and the kitchen beyond went out as one. The smell of wet fur and rotting fish filled the room. Holding his sword up, Will backed slowly across the room. A queasy dread began to rise in his stomach; he had felt it before, a by-product of the very nature of the otherworldly beings. They were so alien that simply being in their presence could reduce someone to tears or laughter or gibbering fear, the emotions pulled unbidden from the depths of the mind. What lay hidden before him was one of the Unseelie Court's outriders, sickeningly vicious but not as cunning or cruel as its golden-skinned masters.

Though he could see nothing in the gloom, Will was attuned to the slightest movement. The scrape of talons on the flags, the shiver of scales over the wooden table, an animal growl deep in the throat. When something lashed out toward his face, he was already responding to the shift of air currents. His sword flashed upwards, biting into meat. A high-pitched howl made his head ring. What felt like a falling tree crashed against his chest, flinging him back across the room. It opened up his shirt and the leather protector beneath, but only grazed his skin.

Rolling and springing back to his feet to avoid snapping, slavering jaws, he muttered, "Thank you, Master Dee, for the hidden armor. Your inventiveness will be my salvation."

For five long minutes, he danced in the pitch black, striking whenever he sensed his attacker near, clattering over pans and shattering crockery. He missed more blows than he hit, and it was clear his attacker was biding its time.

Finally something that felt like a vine wrapped tightly around his ankle and yanked him onto his back. The creature was on him in a second. Pinning him down with the weight of a horse, it lowered those snapping jaws to within six inches of Will's face. Its breath made his stomach churn and the scrambling effect of its nature left his thoughts fractured.

"Ah, Master Dee. One more time, I pray," he whispered. From the hidden pocket behind his belt, he managed to extricate a small pouch of tightly folded velvet. Screwing his eyes shut tight, he flicked the pouch into the face of the beast. With a searing flash, the velvet unfolded and the parchment container within burst to release the phosphorus.

Another deafening howl rang off the walls as the creature flung itself backward. "'Tis to my endless joy that some of your kind cannot abide the light," Will said as he scrambled across the scullery with the after-burn of the phosphorus still stinging his eyelids.

He pounded on the heavy oaken door to the hall. "Nat! Now would be a good time to admit your master! I have ambitions beyond being a tasty morsel."

Will heard the ferocious movement at his back as Nat threw the door wide. He bounded through and bolted it behind him as a tremendous force crashed against it. Nathaniel threw himself on to his back, but the hinges held.

"Come, I have had more than enough of these games," Will said.

Nat noted the many cuts visible through Will's ragged clothes. "You are hurt."

"Others will hurt more, trust me."

Will returned to the cowering, whimpering aristocrats where Lucy held his wife tightly to him. "For your own safety, you must retire to the bedrooms where I will lock you in," Will said.

"Never!" a man with bovine features exclaimed. "I will hear no such thing! Locked in? That will make us easy prey for those devils."

Will's hand fell to the hilt of his sword. The bovine man watched it uneasily. "You put each other at risk by roaming free. You must trust me to keep you safe."

The bovine man made to protest once more, but several hands pulled him back toward the stairs. "Look in his eyes," another hissed into his ear. "Best not to argue. Take this up with the Queen if we survive this night."

As Nathaniel herded the group up the stairs, Will called out politely, "Not you, Sir Edmund. We have unfinished business."

Hesitantly, Spenser returned to Will's side. The noises outside the house had grown louder, not just the menagerie cries but clanks and rattles as the Unseelie Court tested windows and doors or scurried up the walls to clatter across the roof.

"We have done well to survive till now," Spenser said as he eyed the torches moving past the windows. "They will not relent."

"Did you expect it to end like this when you fled London, Sir Edmund?"

"It has not ended. Not yet, at least."

"Oh, it has, Sir Edmund. For you, and your love. Sit." Will kicked a chair next to the dying fire and pressed Spenser into it; all pretense of deference for his station was now gone. Will pulled up a chair next to him.

"This is a damnable job I do, but to bemoan it is pointless. I accepted the responsibilities long ago, and there is no going back now," Will said as he looked deep into Spenser's face. "My service to Queen and Country precludes a life of my own. I live only to keep safe England and the Queen's subjects. Do you understand?"

Spenser nodded slowly.

Will laughed quietly. "I think not, Sir Edmund. There has been no sacrifice in your life. No loves lost. No good friends killed for reasons that always appeared trivial. I miss my Jenny with all my heart, and I miss Kit, murdered all those years ago in a small room. I regret so many things. Yet here I am."

"I fail to see where you are going with this, Master Swyfte."

"I speak by way of apology, Sir Edmund, for you should know that what I do is in no way personal, or colored by malice or bitterness. Though I have suffered hard, I have given my own happiness freely for the sake of great things." Will removed a small dagger from the back of his belt, and then he gripped Spenser's right wrist forcefully. "I am about to remove your little finger, Sir Edmund. And then I will move on to the next, and the next, and so on, until you have no digits left to write your grand works. And then I will take your ears, and your nose, and then your eyes. I will leave your tongue till last in the hope that at some point you will stop me to tell me of the whereabouts of your love, and then to order her to return with me to London. You will, then, of course, be free to go."

"I am the Queen's favored poet," Spenser gasped in horror.

"And I am the Queen's right arm, for better or worse. We are small people, all of us, and our individual lives are meaningless against the continued safety of all the good men and women of this land. They deserve to sleep soundly in their beds, and to raise their families, and earn their crust, free from fear and pain of death. I would gladly sacrifice myself for that cause. And so should you."

Will placed the blade against Spenser's finger. Spenser attempted to wrench his hand free, but Will's grip was too strong.

An aroma of honeysuckle filled the room. In one corner stood the Faerie Queen, her face terrifying.

Will quickly moved the blade to Spenser's throat. "He will be dead before you can act."

Tears rimmed Spenser's eyes. "Let him kill me. You must be free!"

The agony in the Queen's beautiful face was almost too much for Will to bear. He softened his tone. "Give me your word you will cause me no physical harm and he will live."

"I so do," she replied icily.

"No!" Spenser cried. "He will take you back to that cell! You will never see the sky again – "

The Queen raised her hand and Spenser slumped unconscious. Will hid his shock. "I see in your face you will not relent," she said. "I believe you will even follow us to the Far Lands."

"I do what I must to prevent all you know falling into the hands of the enemy."

She looked out at the flickering torchlight and the constant insectile movement. "I care nothing for the demands of my people. For this war, which has dragged on for so long. I want to be free." Her gaze fell fondly on Spenser. "The only meaning I have ever found has been in his presence."

"You are their Queen, and they want you back."

She nodded. "But even a Queen must do her duty or pay the price. They would extract the knowledge from me one way or another, however much I resisted. "'Who slays the gyant, wounds the beast,' that is what my love wrote, and it is true. Slay me, now, and you wound my people forever."

"You are more valuable to us alive. You have helped keep your people at bay for many a year. My Queen needs you."

She came over and gently caressed Spenser's neck. "If we are separated again, my love has only a few short days to live." The Queen's face remained impassive, but in her eyes Will saw raw emotion; human emotion, and this in itself was shocking. "He will die, at Westminster, on January the thirteenth. Three days later he will be interred at the Abbey, a burial fit for a true hero of the nation. And so easily is guilt assuaged," she added acidly.

"You know this?"

"I see it. There is no doubt." She smiled sadly. "Love is a terrible weapon. It can end a life as well as begin one."

Will hesitated.

"I was harsh," she continued. "I set the memory of your Jenny hard in your mind so it would haunt you every time your thoughts stilled. I wanted to show you what love truly meant."

"I know what it means," he snapped.

"How long since she died?" When he did not reply she continued, "I can remove it. Give you peace."

Will closed his eyes, and there was Jenny, smiling beneath the blue summer sky. His lips tingled from their final kiss. Her perfume filled his nose as if she were still there, close enough to take into his arms.

He opened his eyes. "Pain is the price we pay for what we do. I thank you for your gift, good lady. My Jenny will stay with me, and I will never know peace. That is how it should be. And in that I find some absolution."

Slipping the dagger back into his belt, he offered his chair to the Queen. "Dawn is not far away. Sit awhile, and make the most of this time."

With resignation, she took the chair, and Will knew from her face he had just consigned Spenser to death in a few short days.

The hideous sounds beyond the walls grew to a crescendo as dawn approached and then faded away like mist before the sun. The snow rolled out thick and heavy, now virginal as if no foot had ever touched it. As the Christmas bells tolled, Lucy and his guests descended, wringing their hands and crying their thanks to the Lord. Will watched them with contempt and then made his way to the main door where Nathaniel waited.

"Another victory for England's greatest spy," Nathaniel said with a tart smile that failed to mask his relief. "The tale of this night will only add to your fame."

"No one will speak of this again, on pain of death. The Queen will convey her wishes to her subjects herein. Let the people be content with stories of swordplay and rescues and assassinations foiled. They deserve no less."

Spenser still slept in his chair by the fire. The Queen, now hooded to hide her features, rose and came over.

Nathaniel cowered a step behind Will. "She is coming with us? Of her own free will?"

"Her love is fading and will soon be gone. There is nothing for her in this world or the next. Why should she not come?"

The Queen's eyes met Will's and an understanding lay between them. She walked silently past and across the snow to where the carriage awaited. Nathaniel followed, but Will stood on the threshold for a moment, listening to the words of his own love, seeing her smile, always dead, always alive. Only there when his thoughts were still, the Queen had said. There would be little of that. The war would continue as cold as that harsh winter, and there would be little rest for any of England's spies.

"Hurry up, Nat!" he called. "There are great works still to be done! No rest for the likes of you or I! To London, and the rest of it be damned!"

Under the Bottom of the Lake

Jeffrey Ford

Jeffrey Ford (*14theditch.livejournal.com*) lives in Medford Lakes, New Jersey, with his wife and sons. He is a professor of writing and literature at Brookdale Community College in New Jersey. He began publishing his fiction in 1988 and is the author of the Cley trilogy and a number of other books. His most recent book is the short story collection *The Empire of Ice Cream* (2006), and his latest novel *The Shadow Year* came out in early 2008.

"Under the Bottom of the Lake" was published in the last print issue, *Subterranean* 7, guest edited by Ellen Datlow, before that magazine became entirely an online publication. It is a metafiction about a writer writing a tale of dark fantasy and adventure, using lots of familiar material. Luckily the writer is talented and the tale is a good one. It is really fantastic.

UNDER THE BOTTOM of the lake, in a grotto guarded by stalactites and stalagmites, like the half-open maw of a stone dragon, on a pedestal that's a tall white mushroom, there sits a bubble of rose-colored glass, within which swirls a secret story, told once but never heard. It's been there for so long that no one remembers its existence. I'm not even sure how I'm able to tell it, but then I'm not really remembering it, I'm making it up as I go, which allows me to know it all in the moment that it comes to me. Perhaps in the grotto of my imagination there was a glass bubble, containing a secret story, the story of, but not in, the bubble of rose-colored glass, and I have inadvertently knocked it over while groping blindly through my thoughts and now that story, the story about the grotto under the lake, has been released into my mind and I'm hearing the words of the tale now as I tell them. This tale can tell me nothing about the story contained within the rose-colored bubble but only about its existence and about the grotto that was like a dragon's mouth. Still, there are methods to get at the story in that bubble under the lake. What's called for is someone to discover it. For this, we'll need a character.

Here's one, easy as could be – she comes toward me out of the shadows of my mind, a young lady, perhaps fifteen, maybe sixteen. One moment, please...OK, her name is Emily, and she has long red hair, green eyes, and freckles across her nose. She's dressed in denim overalls, and beneath them she wears a T-shirt, yellow, with the word AXIMESH in block, black letters showing just above the top of the pants bib. On her feet, she wears cheap, coral-colored beach sandals. She's got long eyelashes, a hemp necklace with a yin/yang pendant, and, in her back left pocket, for good luck, there's a piece of red paper folded into the figure of an angel. When you pull on its feet the wings flap and the ring that's the halo above its head separates at the front, and turns into two curved horns, sticking up.

I know she's walking along the sidewalk in her home town, moving her lips, silently talking to herself, staring at the cracked concrete beneath her feet, but I don't yet know where she's going. Wait...she lifts her head. She hears someone calling her name. "Emily!" She turns around and sees a boy of about her age approaching from behind. I see him, and the instant I do, the dim nature of my imagination pushes back in a circle with these two as its center to reveal a perfect blue day in a small town. I see and hear them talking within that portal of brightness, and he's asking her where she's going. "To the cemetery," she tells him. He nods and obviously decides to follow her.

The boy has large ears, that much is clear. His hair is cut close to his scalp, and his face could either be construed as dimwitted or handsome, depending on how you construe. I'm no judge of looks. He's got a name that begins with a "V," but I'm not sure what it is. It's sort of exotic, but since I can't think of it, I'll call him Vincent just to have something to call him. I know he knows the girl and she knows him. They more than likely go to school together. I think they're in the same math class. She's good at math. He's not very good at it, and the teacher, an old woman the students call "The Turkey" for the waddle beneath her chin, once gave him a zero for the day as a result of, as she said, his "gross ignorance." Emily felt badly for him, but she laughed along with the other students at the insult.

Emily's grandmother has recently passed away and Emily is telling Vincent that she's going to the cemetery to visit. Vincent's wearing the same expression as when The Turkey calls him to the black board and sticks a piece of chalk in his hand and tells him to solve a fantastical division problem – one number as long as his arm going into another number as long as his leg. He wants to do something in both instances – say the right thing, do what's appropriate – but he's not sure how to so he just keeps walking beside her. When they stop at a corner to check both ways before crossing, he reaches into his pocket and pulls out a pack of licorice gum and asks if she wants some. She says OK and takes a piece.

As they cross the street, I start to lose sight of them, so I lean in close to the circle of light in which they are walking, and...aghhh, shit, I've knocked it onto the floor of my imagination and it's cracked. Their story is leaking out and I'm missing some and knowing the rest too fast. The light that had been in the bubble of their scene slowly dissolves. Hold on while I try to find them again. I can't see at all, but I know there are cars going by on the street every now and then. I hear a dog bark and someone's using a lawn mower. I smell crumb cake. There's just a flash of light and in that moment I see the sun in the leaves of an oak tree. But now, darkness...

OK, they're now in the cemetery. They're walking among the gravestones and Vincent is telling Emily about how his father, whom he calls his "old man," is getting a divorce from his mother because he drinks too much. "My mom says he's screwed up because *his* old man was addicted to drugs from the war and was crazy, beating him and shit." Emily stops walking and looks at him. He's surprised that she's stopped and wonders why she did. "That's terrible," she says. "Which part?" he asks. "The whole thing," she says. He says, "Yeah," and then stares at a gravestone with the last name CAKE inscribed on it, and eventually, after a long time, a tear appears in the corner of his right eye. Emily steps close to him and puts her arm around him. Vincent blows a big black bubble with his licorice gum, and when it pops it reveals this scene that had been swirling inside of it:

Emily kneels on the ground in front of a headstone with the name JUDITH SOCHELL carved into it. This is the gravesite of her grandmother on her mother's side. Vincent stands a few feet behind her and chews his gum. He's watching the trees at the edge of the woods in the distance blowing in the wind and wondering how long it will be before his parents discover he hasn't given them his most recent report card. Every now and then he turns back to see if Emily is crying. She isn't, instead she's remembering her grandmother in her final days – wasted, wrinkled beyond recognition, and always shivering and shaking as if naked in a blizzard. The old woman had lost her mind four years earlier, had grown so feeble of intellect that at the time she died she could only speak one of four possible words – "eat," "no," "go," and "more." And the one she'd chosen for her final utterance, "more," was whispered to Emily as she stood holding her grandmother's boney hand. At the moment of the old woman's death, the girl remembered a story Grandma Judith had told her once about a man who'd exchanged his soul with that of a mythical bird – a strange story that made no sense but was full of tragedy and sorrow – but Emily doesn't think about that now. As bad as she'd gotten, though, and up until the very end, Grandma Judith was still capable, even with wildly shaking hands, to form the origami animals and figures she'd made from the time she was a little girl. During the wake, when she did remember the story, Emily put a specimen from her paper menagerie in the coffin with her grandmother, a piece of light blue paper folded into an amazing bird with wings that moved when its feet were pulled, and a head that bobbed up and down, a beak that opened and closed as if saying, "What a world. What a world."

Vincent's getting bored. "Come on, Em," he says. "Shut up," she tells him.

He walks over to and looks more closely at an old, jagged-topped tree stump jutting four feet out of the ground. Only when he's upon it does he realize that the stump is made of stone and that there's a name chiseled into it. In fact it's a marble grave marker lightly covered in moss.

It's later in the day now and Emily and Vincent are approaching a ruined mausoleum at the edge of the cemetery near the boundary of the woods. The columns of the marble structure, looking like the remains of a miniature savings and loan, are statues of women in togas, and their arms and faces, some with missing noses, are covered with green mold. Branching cracks run throughout the walls of the tomb, and pieces of it have crumbled off and fallen in chunks on the ground. The name above the portico where there's been a mishap of stone says AKE, but years ago it had once read CAKE. Don't ask me how, but I know this is the final resting place of Cassius Cake, a prominent member of the family of Cakes which still reside in Emily's town.

My imagination tells me that Cake made his fortune manufacturing medicines of an opiate nature, derived from giant mushrooms, to be used on battlefields, and that on his estate, which once lay by the lake, on the other side of the woods – the boundary of which his mausoleum now resides by the edge of – there was an aviary in which it was rumored that he kept a single exotic bird, so beautiful the sight of it could make you weep. The iron gate to his death chamber has long since rusted and been chewed by Time. The lock on the gate of the tomb is broken.

Vincent takes Emily by the hand and they enter that dim place of long-ago death turned to stone. The only light inside is offered by the setting sun seeping in through the diffuse colors of a stained-glass window at the back – a scene of a brightly feathered bird, rising from sharp-tipped, swirling flames. Once inside, the boy and girl turn to face each other and kiss, and it breaks across my consciousness like a wave that this is not their first kiss. I see them in another place, a small cedar attic in one of their homes, kissing. So they know each other better than I thought. At this very moment, she's thinking of her grandmother's skull under the ground, and he's thinking of his father's skull ablaze with liquid fire, no bird rising from it. He's about to move his hand down her back to rest it upon her rear end, but she turns away and points to a perfectly round hole in the floor, directly between the sarcophagi of Cassius Cake and his wife, Letti.

Emily gets down on all fours and peers into the hole in the marble floor. "There's steps," she says to Vincent. He nods. Then she stands up and takes a pack of cigarettes out of the bib pocket of her overalls. She takes a cigarette from the pack and she offers one to Vincent. He says no because he's a runner. He runs the 100 for the school track team. He's not the smartest kid in school, but he might be the fastest, save for Jordan Squires, who's the best at everything in the school, even kissing, as Emily well knows. "Let's go down there," she says, pointing to the hole in the floor, with the two fingers holding her cigarette. "Why?" asks Vincent. She doesn't have a ready answer, so I whisper to her just to coax things along, "There might be treasure." Instead she ignores my suggestion and says, "I want to see what's there."

Vincent smells danger, but the scent of the smoke from the cigarette confuses the acrid aroma for him and he thinks instead he smells the possible deepening of his bond with Emily. In a way he's right, because Emily's testing him, seeing if he'll follow her anywhere, even underground in a cemetery. They descend into the dark through the circle of nothing that's the hole in the floor. At the bottom of the steps, they find a passageway, and the rock walls glow with phosphorescent lichen. They...

I've lost them again, and instead I have a very strong vision of a soldier lying wounded on the battlefield, being administered, by a medic, a small cup, like a shot glass, of orange liquid. Now I see the soldier's right leg is half of its former self, the bottom half blasted off and blood and exposed bone showing through a shredded pant leg. The medic's shaking with fear and barely is able to get the medicine into his charge without spilling it. I see the man's face for an instant beneath his helmet with the red cross emblazoned on it and notice two weeks growth of beard and dark circles around the eyes, but that's all I see, because just then a bullet pierces his back, rips through muscle and bone, and deflates his heart. He falls backward, out of sight. Shells burst overhead. Machine gun fire and the screams of the dying echo across the misty marchland. The wounded soldier who's just been given the dose of Cake's Orixadoll thinks he's dying, but the feeling he has is just the hallucinogen kicking in. A feeling of warmth descends upon him. He no longer hears the sounds of war, but instead can make out, faintly, the voice of Judy Garland singing "Somewhere Over the Rainbow." When she sings the part about lemon drops melting, he realizes he feels no pain, and his vision sharpens into a circular field, a tunnel. He's flying through an underground tunnel, the walls of which are lit by phosphorescent lichen. Up ahead he sees a girl and boy in his path, and he blows around them, through them, lifting their hair and stealing their breath for a moment.

"What was that?" asks Emily. "Underground winds blowing up from Hell," says Vincent like he knows what he's talking about. Emily considers what he says, but then remembers that he's only good at kissing and running. They move on, and I'm stuck here watching them walk through a tunnel. I'm going to have a smoke while I wait for something to happen.

With my last drag I blow a smoke ring and inside it I see Vincent stop walking and say to Emily, "Let's go back." "No," she says, "this tunnel leads somewhere. Somebody made this tunnel. Don't you want to know what's at the end?" At this point I'm pretty sure they've traveled under the woods and are down under the bottom of the lake.

Oh, my god, a realization just exploded in my mind like one of those shells in the scene with the dying soldier. I get it now. I see Vincent's old man at the age Vincent is now, creeping through the woods at night. He comes clear of the trees and moves across a vast lawn in the moonlight. Ahead of him is a huge cage in the shape of a beehive where silvery beams from above glint off the thin brass bars. He approaches the cage, and inside he sees a beautiful bird of trailing plumage sitting on a perch. It has three long, thin feathers, ending in pink pompoms arcing off its forehead, and its beak is like that of a peacock. Even in the dark its colors are resilient – turquoise, orange, magenta, and a light, light blue like the oceans of story books. But Vincent's old man as a young man has a bow slung over his shoulder and he's holding one arrow. He sets the arrow and aims through the bars. He releases, the arrow pierces the chest of the bird, it screams once, a shrill cry like the sound of a newborn baby, and then all its beautiful feathers burst into flame. Vincent's old man turns and runs across the moonlit lawn, Cake wakes in his canopied bed and clutches his chest, Emily calls over her shoulder, "Look at this," and points ahead to a grotto surrounded by stalactites and stalagmites; a dragon's mouth inviting entry.

I'm so close now, but instead of following Emily and Vincent to the white mushroom and the rose-colored glass bubble, I'm in Cake's bedroom, and he's fallen onto the floor and is flopping around in pain, clutching his chest. His wife rolls over to his side of the bed, and says, "Cassius, dear, you're making a racket. I was having a perfectly delightful dream." "Letti," he croaks, "Letti, over in my dresser is a dose of Orixadoll. Get it. Hurry." "Oh, you're in pain?" she says and smiles. Slowly she gets out of bed, slips on her slippers and drapes her pink silk wrap around herself. Cake is still doing the landed bass, thumping the floor next to the bed, gurgling and grunting. Finally she returns. He reaches his hand up to her and into it she places, not the dose of his own medicine, but instead a tiny woman made of folded yellow paper. He holds it where he can see it. "Call her," says Letti, who then goes back to bed. A half hour later, after she's returned to her dream of a city with circular walls, he finally expires.

There is an enormous white mushroom, perfectly formed, that serves as a pedestal for a rose-colored glass bubble, and Emily and Vincent approach it cautiously. This is something I hadn't been aware of before, because I was seeing the scene under the bottom of the lake from a distance, but the white mushroom gives off a kind of perfume – a sweet, tantalizing scent, like the aroma of orchids, but more substantial, more delicious, so to speak. That fungal reek, I'm just realizing, also carries a soporific effect and Emily's long eyelashes are fluttering. Vincent yawns and forgets all about his anxiety at being underground and in a mysterious grotto. Instead, he's hungry and finds himself wanting to take a bite out of that big luscious white mushroom cap that's grown as high as his chest. Emily's more interested in the rose-colored bubble, and as she reaches for it, Vincent spits out his licorice gum, leans over, and sinks his teeth into the marshmallow meringue of the fungus. "What are you doing?" says Emily and, even though she knows what he's up to is dangerous, she finds it funny. Vincent reels backward, disoriented from the explosion of sweetness in his mouth. "It's awesome," he says in between chewing. She doesn't notice that he's now been brought to his knees by the overwhelming delight of the white morsel, because she's got the rose-colored bubble up to her eye and is staring inside where she sees something swirling.

What moves like a miniature twister within the see-through boundary is the tale once told but never heard. She puts the bubble to her ear but can hear nothing. She shakes it, taps it, and rolls it from palm to palm. Then she simply drops it, and I watch as it falls, slowly spinning in its descent. After an eternity, it explodes against the rock floor and scatters a fiery revelation, like a bird of flame careening off the walls within the grotto of my skull.

Once there was a yin/yang wizard who could perform great feats of magic that drew power from the balanced forces of the universe. Sometimes he worked for the sake of the good, and when that enjoyed too great an abundance he worked for the sake of evil. Swinging like a pendulum between the two extreme states of human nature, he spent his years conjuring and casting spells. His methods were always the same. A pilgrim would travel into the desert and visit his cave. That individual would ask him for assistance with some life problem. If the wizard decided to help, he would turn to a great fire that roared at the back of his cave and call for his ghostly assistants to bring him his blow-pipe. Turning whatever spell he was performing into a story, he'd speak it, so that none could hear it, into the glass blowing tube. In this way, when he was finished, the tale of his magic would be trapped within a rose-colored bubble. He didn't use ordinary glass, but instead his raw material was enchanted ice, crystal tears, and diamonds fallen from the moon. The pilgrim requesting the service would then have a spell cast in his or her behalf, and would be given the glass-bubble containing the story of their spell, which they were expected to hide in a safe place. If anything happened to that globe, the spell would be broken. One thing remained; the pilgrim never knew if the spell cast by the wizard was one of a positive or a negative nature.

It was to this very wizard that Cassius Cake came in the twenty-third year of his life. He had traveled the world, searching for release from the pain of an unrequited love. From Paris to Istanbul to Peking, he wandered the globe trying to outrun his sorrow, searching for some method or elixir by which he might again be able to feel anything but heartache. Nothing was able to help him. It seems that he had fallen in love with a young woman, Judith Sochell, who worked as kitchen help on his father's estate. She was stunningly beautiful, and he greatly admired the delicate little creatures and people she was capable of creating from folded paper. Judith also had feelings for Cassius, but when Cake's mother noticed him spending an inordinate amount of time in the kitchen and eventually caught wind of the romance, she bribed the girl to tell her son she did not love him. Judith could not lose her job, as too many at home depended upon her salary, so she complied with the old woman's plot. On the very day she gave Cassius the brush off, he fled home and booked passage on a steamship.

Two years of anguish had passed for Cake before he finally came to the cave in the desert. He begged for a cure, and the yin/yang wizard called for his blowpipe. The spell he cast upon Cake was one in which he took the young man's soul and placed it into a many-colored bird of beautiful plumage. Instantly, Cake's heartache dissipated, and for the first time in years he had a clear thought. In fact, his thinking processes were many times clearer now, for with the relief of his anguish also had come the negation of his emotions. He left the cave with the remarkable bird in a cage and the rose-colored bubble in his pocket. On his travels back home, he encountered the world with an exponentially increased intellect, and it was then that he realized that war was coming and that drugs for the battlefield would be worth a fortune.

He invented Orixadoll, a mixture of the narcotics he himself had tried in the international quest to ease his pain. His special elixir helped many soldiers to survive, even though they returned home horribly addicted. The black market sale of the drugs on the streets of his own country far outweighed what he made from sales to the military. He became wealthier than his father ever was. And, because it was a time period when the respectable needed to be married in order to move in certain circles of high society, he married. Letti Mane had not always been a self-interested windbag, but it soon became clear to her after the ceremony that her husband didn't really care for her; she was merely a decoration. He obviously cared more for the strange bird that was the sole inhabitant of an enormous aviary he'd had constructed on the grounds of his estate.

Cake was not happy, but happiness did not enter his mind. What filled his thoughts were new methods for increasing profit. This he did exceptionally well until one day when he found in the top drawer of an old dresser amidst useless keys, stopped watches, and foreign coins, a tiny, delicate woman made of yellow paper. The sight of this nudged his memory. It wasn't an emotion he felt, just a dull, distant pain, like the ghost of a toothache from a long-missing false tooth.

Later that month, he tracked down Judith Sochell, who was by this time married with one child, Emily's mother. He sent her large sums of cash in exchange for origami. He would send a note as to what he wanted, she would create it, send it back, and he would forward her a stack of money.

Emily blinks and the bird of fire she momentarily believes she sees emanating from the broken glass bubble vanishes into mist. She rubs her eyes and takes a few deep breaths. Then she helps Vincent to his feet and leads him out of the dragon's mouth grotto and into the tunnel. As she makes her way carefully up the dark passageway, with him stumbling behind, he tells her he's had a dream. "What was it?" she asks. "About my old man," he says. "In it we leave him and he goes away on a journey. He's gone a long time and he travels far until one day he comes to a cave in the desert where there's a man with a long mustache, smoking a cigarette, surrounded by ghosts. By the light of a huge fire that burns wildly at the back of the cave, this weird guy does magic on my father. With his bare hand he reaches through my old man's chest and removes a large turquoise feather from inside. 'Now there's room for your heart to grow back,' he says. My old man smiles and...that's all I remember."

At the end of the underground tunnel, they crawl back up into the mausoleum, and as they do, Emily notices that the marble lid to Cake's tomb has cracked and fallen in two large halves on the floor. The friends lean over and peer inside. Emily says, "Like your dream," and points into the remains of a feather, trapped by the rib cage where the heart is meant to be. Vincent, who has begun to come around, nods and says, "Look here," and reaches into the tomb to grab a skeletal wrist. As he lifts it, the boney fingers open, and a handful of creatures and figures made of folded paper fall out – a bird, a woman, a mushroom, a boy with a bow and arrow, a ship, and even one of a yin/yang wizard, who spoke this story into glass.

A Diorama of the Infernal Regions, or the Devil's Ninth Question

Andy Duncan

Andy Duncan (*beluthatchie.blogspot.com*) is an ex-journalist – for seven years a reporter and editor at the *News & Record* in Greensboro, North Carolina – and now a college teacher living in Frostburg, Maryland. In 1998 he was a finalist for the John W. Campbell Award for Best New Writer. His short fiction has made an immediate impression and in 2001 he won two World Fantasy Awards, one for a story and one for his first book, *Beluthahatchie and Other Stories* (2000). Duncan is a Southern writer; his settings have thus far characteristically been the American South, and his stories are revelations of character, often with a strongly ironic subtext. Duncan had an excellent literary short story, "Unique Chicken Goes in Reverse," in *Eclipses One* in 2007.

"A Diorama of the Infernal Regions, or the Devil's Ninth Question" appeared in *Wizards*. Set in the nineteenth century, the protagonist is an orphan girl raised in a carny-type museum on the East Coast, who halfway through the story is magically transported to the Winchester mansion in California. Quite a lot of fun, we think.

MY NAME is Pearleen Sunday, though I was always called Pearl, and this is the story of how I met the widow of Flatland House and her 473 dead friends and sang a duet with the Devil's son-in-law and earned a wizard's anger by setting that wizard free.

At the time I did these things, I was neither child nor woman, neither hay nor grass. I was like a cat with the door disease. She scratches to be let in or scratches to be let out, but when you open the door she only stands halfway and cocks her head and thinks deep cat thoughts till you could drown her. Had I been on either side of the door that summer, things might have turned out differently, but I could not decide, and so the door stood open to cold winds and marvels.

I grew up in Chattanooga in Professor Van Der Ast's Mammoth Cosmopolitan Musee and Pavilion of Science and Art. Musee is the French word for museum, and cosmopolitan means citified, and Professor Van Der Ast was born Hasil Bowersox in Rising Fawn, Georgia. Whether his were the quality Bowersoxes, who pronounce "Bower" to rhyme with "lower," or the common Bowersoxes, who pronounce "Bower" to rhyme with "scour," I cannot say, for Professor Van Der Ast never answered to either. The rest of the name of Professor Van Der Ast's

Mammoth Cosmopolitan Musee and Pavilion of Science and Art is self-explanatory, although the nature of science and art is subject to debate, and it was not a pavilion but a three-story brickfront, and I would not call it mammoth either, though it did hold a right smart of things.

You would not find the museum if you looked today. It sat in the shadow of the downtown end of the new Walnut Street Bridge across the Tennessee River. Years before, General Sherman had built a bridge there that did not last any time before God washed it away, but He seemed to be tolerating the new one for now.

I was told my parents left me in a hatbox in the alley between the museum and the tobacco warehouse. Two Fiji cannibals on their smoke break took pity and took me inside to the Professor, who made me a paying attraction before I was two years of age. The sign, I was told, read "Transparent Human Head! All Live and On the Inside!" What was inside was me, sucking a sugar tit with a bright lamp behind my head so my little brain and blood vessels could be seen. Every word on the sign was true.

A young girl like myself with no mother, father or schooling could do worse in those days than work in an educational museum, which offered many career opportunities even for girls with no tattoos or beards and all their limbs. Jobs for girls at Professor Van Der Ast's included Neptuna the Living Mermaid, who combed her hair and switched her tail in a pool all day, and the Invisible Girl, who hid behind a sheet and spoke fortunes into a trumpet, and Zalumma Agra the Circassian Princess, Purest Example of the White Race, who when snatched from the slave traders of Constantinople had left behind most of her clothes, though not enough to shut us down. Our Purest Example of the White Race in summer 1895 was my friend Sally Ann Rummage of Mobile, Alabama, whose mother had been a slave, though not in Constantinople. Sally Ann was ashamed of the museum and wrote her parents that she had become a teacher, which I suppose she had.

I had none of those jobs that summer because I was in that in-between age, and the Circassian Princess in particular was no in-between sort of job. No, I was so out of sorts with myself and the world that Professor Van Der Ast cast me entirely from the sight of the paying public, behind our Diorama of the Infernal Regions.

Now a diorama in those days was only a painting, but a painting so immense that no one ever would see it all at once. It was painted on a long strip of canvas ten feet high, and to see it, you rolled it out of a great spool, like a bolt of cloth in a dressmaker's shop for giants, and as it rolled out of the first spool it rolled back up in a second spool about twenty feet away. In between the spools the customers stood shoulder to shoulder and admired the sights that trundled past.

The spools were turned by an engine, but someone in the back had to keep the engine running and make sure the canvas threaded smooth, without snagging and tearing – for your town may have had a fine new Hell, but Chattanooga's was as ragged and patched as a family Bible. That someone in the back was me. I also had to work the effects. As the diorama moved past, and as Professor Van Der Ast stood on the public side and narrated the spiel, I opened and closed a bank of lanterns that beamed light through parts of the canvas – to make the flames of Hell flicker, and bats wheel through the air, and imps and satyrs wink in and out of existence like my evil thoughts as I sweated and strained like a fireman in a furnace-room. Every day in the spotty mirror over my washstand upstairs, I rubbed my arms and shoulders and wondered what man would ever want a woman with muscles, and what man she might want in return.

Ours was the only diorama I ever saw, but Professor Van Der Ast said that one famous diorama in New York City was a view of the riverbank along the entire length of the Mississippi, from Minnesota to New Orleans. Park Avenue swells in boater hats could lounge in air-cooled comfort and watch it all slide past: eagle-haunted bluffs, woodlands a-creep with Indians, spindly piers that stopped at the overalled butts of barefoot younguns, brawling river towns that bled filth for miles downstream. Professor Van Der Ast himself had been no farther north than Cleveland, Tennessee, but he described New York's Mississippi just as well as he described Chattanooga's Infernal Regions. You felt like you were there.

"Observe, my friends, from your safe vantage point this side of the veil, the ghastly wonders of the Infernal as they pass before you. I say, *as they pass before you!*" (The machinery was old and froze up sometimes.) "First on this ancient scroll, bequeathed us by the Chaldean martyrs, witness the sulfurous vapors of Lake Avernus, over which no sane bird will fly. Here is Briareus with his hundred arms, laboring to drag a chain the width of a stout man's waist, and at the end of that mighty leash snaps the hound Cerberus with his fifty heads, each of his fifty necks a-coil with snakes. Here is the stern ferryman who turns away all wretches who die without Christian burial. Next are the weeping lovers wringing their hands in groves of myrtle, never to be reunited with their soul-mates. Madame, my handkerchief. Your pity does you honor. Next is the whip of scorpions that flays those who believed their sins concealed in life. Here is the nine-acre giant Tityus, chained at the bottom of the abyssal gulf. Here are sufferers chin-deep in water they are doomed never to drink, while others are doomed to bail the water with sieves."

A weeping schoolmarm might ask: "But what about the realms of the blessed? the Elysian fields? the laurel groves?"

"For such consolations, madam, one must consult canvases other than mine. And here we have the writhing Pandaemonium of pleasure, where all noble and spiritual aims are forgotten in the base fog of sensation and lust. Next is the great – "

"Hey, buddy, could we have a little more light on that there Pandaemonium of pleasure?"

"This is the family show, friend, come back at ten. Here is the great winepress in which hundreds of the damned are crushed together until they burst. Here are the filthy, verminous infants of ingratitude, which spit venom even as they are hoisted with tongs over the fire. Note, ladies and gentlemen, that throughout this dreadful panorama, the plants in view are all thorny and rank, the creatures all fanged and poisonous, the very stones misshapen and worthless, the men and women all sick, feeble, wracked, and forgotten, their only music Hell's Unutterable Lament! Where all suffer horrid torments not for one minute, not for one day, not for one age, not for two ages, not for a hundred ages, not for ten thousand millions of ages, but forever and ever without end, and never to be delivered! Mind your step at the door, next show 2:30, gratuities welcome."

That was Professor Van Der Ast's side of the canvas, the public side. I told no one what I saw on my side: the patches and the stains, the backward paintings, the different tricks played by the light. I could see pictures, too, but only half-glimpsed, like those in clouds and treetops in leafy summertime. The pictures on my side were not horrible. I saw a man wrestling a lightning rod in a storm; and a great river catfish that sang to the crew in the gondola of a low-flying balloon; and a bespectacled woman pushing a single wheel down the road; and a ballroom full of dancing ghosts; and a man with a hand of iron who beckoned me with hinged fingers; and a farmer who waved goodbye to his happy family on the porch before vanishing and then, reappearing, waved hello to them again; and an angry face looking out of a boot; and a giant woman with a mustache throwing a man over the side of a riverboat; and a smiling man going over Niagara Falls in a barrel while around him bobbed a hundred hoodoo bottles, each with a rolled-up message for Marie Laveaux; and a hound dog with a pistol who was robbing a train; and a one-eyed man who lived in a gator hole; and a beggar presenting a peepshow to the Queen of Sheba; and a gorilla in a boater hat sitting in a deck chair watching a diorama of the Mississippi scroll past; and a thousand other wonders to behold. My Infernal Regions were a lot more interesting than Professor Van Der Ast's, and sometimes they lighted up and moved without my having to do a thing.

My only other knowledge of magic at the time was thanks to Wendell Farethewell, the Wizard of the Blue Ridge, a magician from Yandro Mountain, North Carolina, who performed at Professor Van Der Ast's for three weeks each summer. I never had the chance to see his act because, as the Professor liked to remind us, we were being paid to entertain and not to be entertained, but I was told that at the climax he caught in his teeth a bullet fired through a crystal pitcher of lemonade, and I believe it was so because sometimes when a pinhead was not available, the Professor asked me to go on stage after the show and mop up the lemonade and pick up the sharp splinters of glass.

The tricks I saw the wizard Farethewell perform were done after hours, when all the residents of the museum went to the basement for drinks and cold-meat sandwiches and more drinks. I squirmed my way into the front of the crowd around a wobbly table made of splinters and watched as he pulled the Queen of Hearts out of the air and walked coins across his knuckles and floated dollar bills. "Just like the government," he always said when he floated a dollar bill, and we always laughed. He showed us fifty-seven ways to shuffle a deck of cards and seventeen of the ways to draw an ace off the top whenever one was needed, even five times in a row. "Do this in a gambling hall," he said, "and you'll get yourself shot. Do it among you good people, and it's just a pleasant diversion, something to make Little Britches smile."

That was what Farethewell called me, Little Britches. He was the only one who called me that. Big Fred, who played our What-Is-It?, tried it once, and I busted his nose.

If the night wore on and Farethewell drank too much, he got moody and talked about the war, and about his friend, an older man he never named. "The 26th North Carolina mustered up in Raleigh, and I couldn't sleep that first night, without no mountains around to hold me, so I mashed my face into my bedroll and cried. I ain't ashamed of it, neither. The others laughed or told me to hush, but this man, he said, 'Boy, you want to see a trick?' Now, what boy don't want to see a trick? And after he's seen it, what boy don't want to know how it's done?" As he talked he stared into space, but his hands kept doing tricks, as if they were independent of the rest of him. "At New Bern he taught me the back palm, the finger palm, the thumb palm; at the Wilderness the Hindu Shuffle and the Stodart egg; at Spotsylvania the Biseaute flourish, the Miser's Dream, the Torn and Restored. I learned the Scotch and Soda and the Gin and Tonic before I drank either one; and all through the war, every day, I worked on the Three Major Vanishes: take, put, and pinch." As he said that, three coins disappeared from his hand, one by one. "So that was our war. It kept my mind off things, and maybe kept his mind off things, too. He had the tuberculosis pretty bad, toward the end. The last thing he taught me was the bullet catch, in the stockade at Appomattox, just before he died. I got one of his boots. The rest, they burned. When they turned out his pockets, it was just coins and cards and flash paper. It didn't look like magic no more. It just looked... It looked like trash. The magic went when he went, except the little he left to me."

Someone asked, "What'd you learn at Gettysburg?" and Farethewell replied:

"What I learned at Gettysburg, I will teach no man. But one day, living or dead, I will hold the Devil to account for what I learned."

Then he began doing tricks with a knife, and I went upstairs to bed.

My in-between summer came to an end after the last viewing of a Saturday night. As I cranked the diorama back into place, I heard the Professor talking to someone, a customer? Then the other voice got louder: "You ain't nothing but an old woman. She'll do just fine, you watch."

I could hear no more over the winding spool, and I did not want to stop it for fear of being caught eavesdropping. Then the Professor and the wizard Farethewell were behind the diorama with me.

"Shut off that engine, Little Britches. You can do that later. Right now, you got to help me." He had something in his hand, a tangle that glittered in the lamplight. He thrust it at me. "Go on, take it. Showtime was five minutes ago."

"What are you talking about?" It was a little sparkly dress with feathers, and a hat, and slippers with heels. I looked at Farethewell, who was drinking from a flask, and at the Professor, who was stroking his silver beard.

"Pearl, please mind Mr. Farethewell, that's a good girl. Just run along and put that on, and meet us in the theater, backstage." I held the costume up to the light: what there was of the light, and what there was of the costume. "Sukie can't help Mr. Farethewell with the ten o'clock show. She's sick."

"Dead drunk, you mean," Farethewell roared, and lifted his flask. The Professor snatched it away. Something spattered my cheek and burned.

"Get as drunk as you like at eleven," the Professor said. "Pearl, it'll be easy. All you have to do is wave to the crowd, climb into the box and lie there. Mr. Farethewell will do the rest."

"The blades won't come nowhere near you, Little Britches. The box is rigged, and besides, you ain't no bigger'n nothing. You won't even have to twist."

"But," I said.

"Pearl," said the Professor, like there were fifteen R's in my name. So I ran upstairs.

"What's wrong with you?" Sally Ann cried when I burst in.

I told her while she helped me out of my coveralls and my blue denims and into the turkey suit. "What in the world are they thinking?" Sally Ann said. "Hold still, Pearl, if I don't cinch this you'll walk plumb out of it."

"My legs are cold!" I yelled.

The hat was nothing I would have called a hat. In a rainstorm it would have been no cover at all. I finally snuggled it down over my hair and got the ostrich plume out of my face. Sally Ann was looking at me funny.

"Oh, my," she said.

"What?"

"Nothing. Come on, let's go. I want to see this. Clothes do make a difference, don't they?"

"Not to me," I said, and would have fallen down the stairs if she hadn't grabbed me. "Who can walk in any such shoes as this?"

There's no dark like the dark backstage in a theater, but Sally Ann managed to guide me through all the ropes and sandbags without disaster. I carried the shoes. Just inside the backdrop curtain, the Professor made a hurry-up motion. I hopped one-legged to get the shoes back on and peered through the slit in the curtain, but was blinded by the lamps shining onto the stage.

Farethewell was yelling to make himself heard over what sounded like a theater full of drunken men. "And now, my lovely assistant will demonstrate that no cutlass ever forged can cut her, that she can dodge the blade of any cavalryman, whether he be a veteran of the Grand Army of the Republic – "

The crowd booed and hissed.

" – or whether he fought for Tennessee under the great Nathan Bedford Forrest!"

The crowd whooped and stomped its approval.

"Here she is," muttered the Professor, as he held the curtain open.

I blinked in the light, still blinded. Farethewell's big callused hand grabbed mine and led me forward. "Ladies and gentlemen, I give you Aphrodite, the Pearl of the Cumberland!"

I stood frozen.

The crowd continued to roar.

Lying on a table in front of us was a long box like a coffin, open at the top. A pile of swords lay beside it.

"Lie down in the box, honey," Farethewell murmured. He wore a long blue robe and a pointed hat, and his face was slick with sweat.

I walked to the box like a puppet and looked down at the dirty pillow, the tatty blanket inside.

"And if you don't believe me when I tell you how amazingly nimble Aphrodite is, why when I am done shoving cutlasses into the box, those of you willing to pay an additional fifty cents can line up here, on the stage, and look down into the box and see for yourself that this young woman has suffered no injury whatsoever, save perhaps to her costume."

The crowd screamed with laughter. Blinking back tears, I leaned over the box, stepped out of the shoes: first left, then right. I looked up and into the face of a fat man in the front row. He winked.

In my head I heard the Professor say: "This is the family show, friend, come back at ten."

I turned and ran.

The noise of the crowd pushed me through the curtains, past Sally Ann and the Professor. In the sudden darkness I tripped over a sandbag, fell and skinned my knees, then stood and flailed my way to the door and into the corridor beyond.

"Pearl! Come back!"

My cheeks burned with shame and anger at myself and the crowd and Farethewell and the Professor and Sally Ann and those stupid, stupid shoes; I vowed as I ran barefoot like a monkey through the back corridors that I would never wear their like again. I ran as fast as I could – not upstairs, not to the room I slept in, but to the one place in the museum I felt was mine.

I slammed the door behind me and stood, panting, behind the Diorama of the Infernal Regions.

Someone, probably the Professor, had done part of my job for me, and shut down all the lamps. It was the job I liked least, snuffing the lights one by one like candles on a cake. But the Professor had not finished rolling up the canvas. It was backstage dark, but up there on the canvas, at eye level, was a little patch of light, flickering.

I'm sure that when I went missing, my friends thought I had run away, but they were wrong. I was running *away* from nothing. I was running *to* something, though I did not know what it was. Running to *what* is the rest of my story – is all my story, I reckon.

I walked right up to the flickering spot on my side of the canvas. The tip of my nose was an inch from the paint. When I breathed in, I smelled sawdust and walnuts. When I breathed out, the bright patch brightened just a little. If you blow gently on a flame, it does not go out, but flares up; that's how the canvas was. I almost could see a room through the canvas, a paneled room. Behind me, a woman's voice called my name, but in front of me, I almost heard music, organ music.

I closed my eyes and focused not on the canvas, but on the room beyond.

I stepped forward.

Have you ever stepped through a cobweb? That's how I stepped out of Professor Van Der Ast's Mammoth Cosmopolitan Musee and Pavilion of Science and Art and into a place without a ticket booth, into my own canvas, my own Infernal Regions.

Not a funeral, a ball. The organist was playing a waltz.

I opened my eyes.

I was in a ballroom full of ghosts.

I reached behind to feel the canvas, to feel anything familiar and certain.

Instead I felt a cold hard surface: a magnificent stained-glass window that ran the length of the wall, depicting mermaids and magicians and a girl at the lever of an infernal engine. Window and room spun around me. My knees buckled, and I sank onto a beautifully inlaid wooden floor.

The room wasn't spinning, but the dancers were. Fifty couples whirled through the room, the silver chandeliers and mahogany paneling and gold-leaf wallpaper visible through their transparent bodies. I never had seen such a beautiful room. The dancers were old and young, richly and poorly dressed, white and black and Indian. Some wore wigs and knee breeches, others buckskins and fur caps, others evening gowns or tailcoats. They didn't look like show people. All moved faster than their actual steps. No feet quite touched the floor. The dancers were waltzing in the air.

Against the far wall was a pump organ, and sitting at the bench with her back to me was a tiny gray-haired lady, shoulders swaying with the force of her fingers on the keys, her feet on the pedals. I tried to see the sheet music through her but could not. She was no ghost; she was substantial. I looked at my hand and saw through it the interlocking diamond pattern of the floor. That's when I screamed.

The music stopped.

The dancing stopped.

The old lady spun on her bench and stared at me.

Everyone stared at me.

Then the dancers gasped and stepped – no, floated – backward in the air, away from me. There was movement beside me. I looked up to see a skinny girl in a feathered costume step out of the stained-glass window. I screamed again, and she jumped and screamed, too.

She was me, and she also was becoming transparent.

"Five minutes break, please, everyone," trilled a little-old-lady voice. "When we return, we'll do the Virginia Reel."

The second Pearl had slumped onto the floor beside me. A third Pearl stepped out of the stained glass just as the old lady reached us. She wore an elaborate black mourning-dress with the veil thrown back to reveal chubby, ruddy cheeks and big gray eyes. "There, there," she said. "This won't do at all. The first rule of psychic transport is to maintain integrity, to hold oneself together." A fourth Pearl stepped from the glass as the old lady seized my hand and the second Pearl's hand and brought them together, palm to palm. It was like pressing my hand into butter; my hand began to sink into hers, and hers into mine. We both screamed and tried to pull back, but the old lady held our wrists in a grip like iron.

"Best to close your eyes, dear," the old lady said.

My eyes immediately shut tight not of my own doing but as if some unseen hand had yanked them down like windowshades. The old lady's grip tightened, and I feared my wrist would break. My whole body got warmer, from the wrist onward, and I began to feel better – not just calmer, but somehow fuller, more complete.

Finally the old lady released my wrist and said, "You can open your eyes now, dear."

I did, and it was my own doing this time. I stared at my hands, with their lines and calluses and gnawed-to-the-quick nails, and they were so familiar and so *solid* that I started to cry.

The ballroom was empty but for me – *one* of me – and the old lady kneeling beside me, and a single ghost bobbing just behind her, a little ferret-faced mustached man in a bowler hat and a checked waistcoat that might have been colorful once, but now was gray checked with gray.

"Beautifully done," said the floater. "You have the hands of a surgeon."

"The hands are the least of it, Mr. Dellafave, but you are too kind. Goodness, child, you gave me a fright. Six of you stranded in the glass. Good thing I was here to set things right. But I forget my manners. My name is Sarah Pardee Winchester, widow of the late William Wirt Winchester, and this is my friend Mr. Dellafave." She eyed my costume, reached over and tugged on my ostrich plume. "Too young to be a showgirl," she said, "almost."

I shuddered and wiped my nose with the back of my wonderful old-friend hand and asked: "Am I...Are you...Please, is this Heaven or Hell?"

The old lady and the bowler-hatted man both laughed. His laugh sounded like steam escaping, but hers was throaty and loud, like a much younger, much larger woman.

"Opinions differ," the old lady said. "We think of it simply as California."

She called the place Llanada Villa, which she said was Spanish for "Flatland House." I had never lived in a house before the widow took me in, so you might call Flatland House my introduction to the whole principle of houses. And what an introduction it was! No house I've seen since has been a patch on it.

There was the size, to start with. The house covered six acres. Counting the rooms that had been walled off and made unreachable except by ghosts, but not counting the rooms that had been demolished or merged into larger spaces, the house had a hundred and fifty rooms, mostly bedrooms, give or take a dozen. "I've slept in only seventy or eighty of them myself," the widow told me, "but that's enough to get the general idea."

Still the place was not finished. Workmen were always in the process of adding rooms, balconies, porches, turrets, whole wings; or in the process of dismantling or renovating what they had built just the month before. The construction had moved far away from the front of the house, where the widow mostly lived, but the distant sounds of saws and hammers and the men's voices calling to one another – "Steady! Steady! Move it just a hair to the right, please, Bill" – could be heard day and night. They worked in shifts around the clock. Once a week the foremen took off their hats and gathered in the carriage entrance for payday. The widow towed from the house a child's wagon full of heavy sacks, each full of enough gold pieces to pay each foreman's workers the equivalent of three dollars a day. The foremen were all beefy men, but even they strained to heft the bags and tote them away. They never complained, though.

"Aren't you afraid?" I asked the widow, that first payday.

"Of what, dear?"

"Of one of those men breaking into the house, and robbing you."

"Oh, Pearl, you are a caution! You don't need to worry about robbers, oh, no. Not in *this* house."

I suppose intruders would have gotten quickly lost, for many parts of the house simply did not make sense. Staircases led to ceilings and stopped. Doorways opened onto brick walls, or onto nothing, not even a balcony, just the outside air. Secret passageways no taller than the widow crisscrossed the house, so that she could pop in and out of sight without warning, as if she herself were a ghost. The widow told me the front door had never been opened, never even unlocked, since its hinges were hung.

I found the outside of the house even more confusing. If I walked around any corner, I found arched windows, recessed balconies, turrets and witch's caps and cupolas with red tile roofs, and miles of gingerbread trim. If I walked around the next corner, I found the same thing, only more of it. Many houses, I'm told, have only four corners to walk around, but Flatland House had dozens. Looking away from the house was no help, because no matter what direction I looked, I saw the same high cypress hedge, and beyond that, rolling hills of apricot, plum, and walnut trees stretching to the horizon. I never made it all the way around the place, but would give up and go back inside, and where I went inside always seemed to be the breakfast-room, with the widow knitting in the wicker chair just where I left her. She always asked, "Did you have a good trip, dear?"

In all those hundred and fifty rooms was not a single mirror. Which suited me just fine.

I did get lonely sometimes. Most of the ghosts had little to say – to the living, anyway – beyond "Lovely day, isn't it?" The few indoor servants seemed afraid of me, and none stayed in the house past sundown. The workmen I was forbidden to speak to at all.

"Do you never have any visitors," I asked the widow, "other than the workmen, and the ghosts, and the servants, and me?"

"Goodness, that's enough, wouldn't you say? I know there are 473 ghosts, not counting the cats, and Lord only knows how many workmen coming and going. And don't ever think of yourself as a visitor, Pearl dear. Consider this your home, for as long as you wish to stay."

The only ghost willing to spend time with me, other than the cats, was Mr. Dellafave. Three weeks into my stay at Flatland House, during a stroll around the monkey-puzzle tree, I asked him:

"Mr. Dellafave, what did you do before..."

His face had the look of someone expecting his feelings to be hurt but game not to let on.

"...before you came here," I finished.

"Ah," he said, smiling. "I worked for a bank, in Sacramento. I was a figure man. I added, mostly, and subtracted twice a week, and, on red-letter days, multiplied. Long division was wholly out of my jurisdiction, that was another floor altogether – but make no mistake, I could have done it. I was ready to serve. Had the third floor been swept away by fire or flood, the long division would have proceeded without interruption, for I'd had the training. But the crisis, like most crises, never came. I arrived at the bank every morning at eight. I went across the street to the saloon every day at noon for two eggs and a pickle and a sarsaparilla and the afternoon papers. I left the bank every day at five, and got back to the boarding house for supper at six. Oh, I was a clockwork, I was. 'You can set your watch by Dellafave,' that's what they said at the bank and the saloon and the boarding house and, well, those are the only places they said it, really, because those are the only places where anyone took any notice of me at all. Certainly that streetcar driver did not. He would have rung his bell if he had; it's in their manual. That was a sloppy business all around, frankly, a harsh thing to say but there it is. I know the time had to have been 12:47 precisely, because I walked out of the saloon at 12:46, and the streetcar was not due to pass until 12:49. I was on schedule, but the streetcar was not. I looked up, and there it was, and I flung up my arms – as if that would have helped, flinging up my arms. When I lowered them, I was standing in what I now know as Mrs. Winchester's potting shed. I was never an especially spiritual man, Pearl dear, but I considered myself fairly well-versed on all the major theories of the afterlife...none of which quite prepared me for Mrs. Winchester's potting shed. I didn't even bring my newspaper."

"But why – "

He held up a hand, like a serene police officer at an intersection. "I have no idea, Pearl, why I came here. None of us does. And I don't mean to imply that we're unhappy, for it is a pleasant place, and Mrs. Winchester is quite good to us, but our leaving here seems rather out of the question. If I were to pass through that cypress hedge over there, I would find myself entering the grounds through the hedge on the other side. It's the same front to back, or even up and down."

"I guess Mrs. Winchester is the magnet, and you and the others are..."

"The filings, yes. The tacks pulled from the carpet. I stand in the tower sometimes – if you can call it standing – and I look over all these rooftops and chimneys, all connected to the same house, and I'm forced to admit that this is more room than I allowed myself in life. If the boarding house were the front door of Llanada Villa, the bank would be at the carriage entrance, and the saloon would be at the third sun porch, the one that's been walled in and gets no sun. Which is such a small fraction of the house, really. And yet the whole house feels such a small part of the Earth, and I find myself wishing that I had ventured a bit farther, when I could."

We walked together in silence – well, I walked, anyway – while I reflected that the owner of the house seemed quite unable to leave it herself. And what about me? Could I leave Flatland House, and were I to leave it, where would I go? Professor Van Der Ast's seemed much farther away than a single continent.

"You'd best get inside, Pearl. The breeze from the bay is quite damp today."

I moved my face toward Mr. Dellafave's cheek, and when he began to blur, I figured I was close enough, and kissed the air.

"Shucks," he said, and dissipated entirely.

I felt no bay breeze, but as I ran back to the house I clutched my shawl more tightly anyway.

The next day, the earthquake struck.

The chandeliers swayed. The organ sighed and moaned. The crystal chittered in the cabinets. One nail worked its way free and rolled across the thrumming floorboards. A rumble welled up, not from below the house, but from above and around the house, as if the sound were pressing in from all sides. The ghosts were in a mad whirl, coursing through the house like a current of smoke overhead, blended and featureless but for the occasional startled face. I lurched along the walls, trying to keep my balance as I sought the exit nearest me, the front door. Once I fell and yelped as my palms touched the hot parquet.

Plaster sifted into my eyes as I stumbled through the entrance hall. I knew my mistake when I saw that massive front door, surely locked, the key long since thrown away or hidden in a far scullery drawer of this lunatic house. If the entire edifice were to shake down and crush me, this slab of swirling dark oak would be the last thing standing, a memorial to Pearl.

The grandfather clock toppled and fell just behind me, with the crash of a hundred heavy bells. I flung myself at the door and wrenched the knob. It turned easily, as if oiled every day, and I pulled the door open with no trouble at all.

Suddenly all was silent and still. A robin sang in the crepe myrtle as the door opened on a lovely spring day. A tall black man in a charcoal tailcoat stood on the porch, top hat in hand, and smiled down at me.

"Good morning," he said. "I was beginning to fear that no one was at home. I hope my knock didn't bring you too dreadfully far. I know this house is harder to cross than the Oklahoma Territory."

"Your knock?" I was too flabbergasted to be polite. "All that was your knock?"

He laughed as he stepped inside, so softly that it was just an open-mouthed smile and a hint of a cough. "That? Oh, my, no. That was just my reputation preceding me. Tell me, pray, might the mistress of the house be at home?"

"Where else would I be, Wheatstraw?" asked the widow, suddenly at my elbow and every hair in place.

"Hello, Winchester," the visitor said.

They looked at each other without moving or speaking. I heard behind me a heaving sound, and a muffled clang. I turned just as the grandfather clock resettled itself in the corner.

Then the widow and the visitor laughed and embraced. She kicked up one foot behind. Her head did not reach his chin.

"Pearl," the widow said, "this is Mr. Petey Wheatstraw."

"Pet-ER," he corrected, with a little bow.

"Mr. Wheatstraw," the widow continued, "is a rogue. My goodness," she added, as if something had just occurred to her. "How did you get in?"

We all looked at the front door. It was closed again, its bolts thrown, its hinges caked with rust. No force short of dynamite could have opened it.

The man Wheatstraw nodded toward me.

"Well, I'll be," the widow said. "She makes as free with my house as a termite, this one does. Well, you haven't come to see me, anyway, you old good-for-nothing," she said, swatting him as she bustled past. "It's a half-hour early, but you might as well join us for tea."

Wheatstraw offered me an arm and winked. This was far too fresh for my taste, but I was too shaken by the not-quite-earthquake to care. As I took hold of his arm (oak-strong beneath the finery), I felt my muscles complain, as if I had done hard work. I looked over my shoulder at the seized-up door as Wheatstraw swept me down the hallway.

"I heard you were here," Wheatstraw said.

"How?"

"Oh, you're a loud one, Miss Big Feet, clomp clomp clomp." He winked again. "Or is that just your reputation I heard?"

Something was wrong with the corridor, something I couldn't quite put my finger on. Then I realized that it was empty. Everything in the house was back to normal – paintings returned to their nails, plaster returned to the walls – except the ghosts, which were nowhere to be seen. I was so used to them flitting past me and over me and through me, even gliding through my bedroom wall and then retreating with apologies, like someone who didn't realize the train compartment was occupied, that their presence hardly bothered me at all. Their absence gave me a shiver.

"They'll be back after I'm gone," Wheatstraw said.

I laughed. "You telling me you scared off the haints? I mean, are you saying that Mrs. Winchester's, uh, guests don't like you?"

"I'm sure they have nothing against me personally. How could they? Once you get to know me, I'm really a fine fellow, full of learning and grace and wit, a decent dancer, a welcome partner at whist. I never snort when I laugh or drag my shirtsleeves in the soup. No, it must be my business affiliation. The company I represent. The Old Concern. My father-in-law's firm, actually, and my inheriting is out of the question. But these days we all must work for somebody, mustn't we?"

I thought of Sally Ann the Circassian Princess, and of Farethewell's hand on mine. "True enough," I said.

Wheatstraw set down his teacup and saucer with a clatter and said, "Well, enough chitchat. It's question time."

"Oh, Petey," the widow said. "Must you? We were having such a nice visit. Surely that can wait till later."

"I am in no hurry whatsoever, Winchester, but my father-in-law is another story. You might say that impatience rather defines my father-in-law. It is the cause of his, uh, present career. Pearl, please pay close attention."

I said nothing, having just shoved another chocolate cookie lengthwise into my mouth. I never quite realized that I was always a little hungry at Professor Van Der Ast's, until I came to Flatland House.

Wheatstraw rummaged in the inside pocket of his jacket and produced an atomizer. He opened his mouth and sprayed the back of his throat. "La la la la la," he said. "La la la la laaaaa. Pitch-perfect, as ever. Winchester?" He offered her the atomizer. "Don't, then. Now: Pearl."

He began to sing, in a lovely baritone:

Oh, you must answer my questions nine
Sing ninety-nine and ninety
Or you're not God's, you're one of mine
And you are the weaver's bonny.

"Now, Pearl, when I say, 'one of mine,' please understand that I speak not for myself but for the firm that I represent."

"And when you say 'God,'" I said, speaking carefully, "you speak of the firm that you do *not* represent."

"In a clamshell, yes. Now, if you're quite done interrupting – "

"I didn't interrupt!" I interrupted. "You interrupted yourself."

He slapped the table. "The idea! As if a speaker could interrupt himself. Why, you might as well say that a river could ford itself, or a fence jump itself."

"Or a bore bore himself," the widow said.

"You're not helping," Wheatstraw said.

"And I'm not the weaver's bonny," I said, becoming peevish now, "whatever a weaver's bonny is."

"Well," Wheatstraw said, "a weaver is a maker of cloth, such as aprons are made with, and gags, and a bonny is a beauty, a lovely creature, a precious thing."

"I don't know any weavers," I said, "except my friend Sally Ann taught me to sew a button. And I'm not beautiful, or lovely, or precious."

"Granted, that does seem a stretch at the moment," Wheatstraw said. "But we mustn't always take things so literally. When you say, 'I'm a silly goose,' you don't mean you expect to be plucked and roasted, and when you say, 'I'm fit to be tied,' you aren't asking to be roped and trussed, and when you say, 'Well, I'm damned,' you don't mean..."

His voice trailed off. A chill crept into the room. The sunlight through the bay window dimmed, as if a cloud were passing.

"...anything, really," Wheatstraw continued, and he smiled as the sun came out. "So, for purposes of this song, if *no other*, who are you?"

I folded my arms and forced my shoulders as far as I could into the padding of the loveseat and glared at Wheatstraw, determined to frown down his oh-so-satisfied smile.

"I'm the weaver's bonny," I mumbled.

Am not, I thought.

"Fine and dandy," Wheatstraw said. "Now, where was I? I'll have to go back to Genesis, as Meemaw would say." He cleared his throat.

Oh you must answer my questions nine
Sing ninety-nine and ninety
Or you're not God's, you're one of mine
And you are the weaver's bonny.

Ninety-nine and ninety *what?* I wondered, but I kept my mouth shut.

What is whiter than the milk?
Sing ninety-nine and ninety
And what is softer than the silk?

Oh you are the weaver's bonny
What is higher than a tree?
Sing ninety-nine and ninety
And what is deeper than the sea?
Oh you are the weaver's bonny
What is louder than a horn?
Sing ninety-nine and ninety
And what is sharper than a thorn?
Oh you are the weaver's bonny
What's more innocent than a lamb?
Sing ninety-nine and ninety
And what is meaner than womankind?
Oh you are the weaver's bonny

It was a short song, but it seemed to last a long time; as I sat there determined to resist, to be defiant and unamused, I realized I wasn't so much listening to it as being surrounded by it, filled by it, submerged in it. I was both sleepy and alert, and the pattern in the parquet floor was full of faces, and the loveseat pushed back and kneaded my shoulders, and the laces of my high-topped shoes led into the darkness like tracks in the Lookout Mountain tunnel. I could not vouch for Wheatstraw being a decent dancer as he claimed (though I suspected *decent* was hardly the word), but the man sure could sing. And somewhere in the second hour of the song (surely, I think now upon telling this, some lines were repeated, or extended, or elaborated upon), Wheatstraw's voice was joined by a woman's, his voice and hers twined together like fine rope. That voice was the widow Winchester's: *And you are the weaver's bonny.*

I sucked air and sat up as if startled from a dream, but felt less alert than a second before. The song was over. The widow pretended to gather up the tea things, and Wheatstraw pretended to study his fingernails.

"That part about womankind is insulting," the widow said.

"I didn't write it," he said. "The *folk* wrote it."

"Menfolk," she said.

"Eight," I said, and only after I said it did I realize why I had said it.

"Hm?" Wheatstraw asked, without looking up.

The widow held a tipped teacup, looking at nothing, as a thread of tea like a spider's descended to the saucer.

"Eight," I repeated. "Milk, silk, two; tree, sea, four; horn, thorn, six; lamb, kind, eight." I sang, rather than spoke, in surprise at my voice: "*Oh, you must answer my questions nine…* It ain't questions nine, it's questions eight. What's the ninth question?"

Wheatstraw looked at the widow, and the widow looked at Wheatstraw.

"Maybe that's it," Wheatstraw murmured. "'What's the ninth question,' maybe that's the ninth question."

"No," I said.

"Why no?" Wheatstraw cooed.

"Because," I said. "Because that would be stupid."

Wheatstraw laughed and slapped his thigh with his hat. The widow slammed two plates together.

"Indeed it would be," she snapped. "Petey, take these plates. Take them, I say. Do a lick of work for once in your lazy son-in-law of a life."

"So what's the ninth question?" I asked again.

"That's for you to tell us," Wheatstraw said.

"To tell *you*, you mean," the widow said, driving him from the room beneath a stack of dishes. "Don't drag *me* into this."

"Oh, excuse me, Lady Astor, whose house is it? The girl's a wizard, Sarah, and you can't stow a wizard in the china-cupboard like a play-pretty, like one of your ghosts, like Mr. Dellafave in there," he shouted as he passed a china-cupboard. Its door trembled, and someone inside squeaked.

"You know the rules," Wheatstraw continued as we all entered the kitchen in a clump. He dumped the dishes into the sink with a crash and whirled to face us. I tried to hide behind the widow, though she was a foot shorter. Wheatstraw pointed at her like he wanted to poke a hole in the air. His gentleman's fingernail was now long and ragged, with something crusted beneath, and his eyes were red as a drunkard's. "Just look at her," he said. "Just stand near her, for pity's sake! She's stoked with magic like a furnace with coal, and the wide world is full of matches. She's in a different world now, and she has got to learn." He turned to me. "Tea party's over, my dear. From now on, it's test after test, and you have your first assignment, your first nine questions."

"Eight," I said.

He threw back his head and roared like a bull. I clapped my hands over my ears and shrieked. Our dresses billowed as if in a strong wind. The cords stood out on Wheatstraw's neck. His hot breath filled the room. Then he closed his mouth, and the roar was gone. "All righty then," he said. "Eight it is. You owe the Old Concern eight answers – and one question." He jammed his hat two-handed onto his head down to his eyebrows, then sprang into the sink. He crouched there, winked, and vanished down the drain with a gurgle. His hat dropped to the porcelain and wobbled in place until it, too, was snatched into the depths. Wheatstraw's voice chuckled through the pipes, and ghosts flowed keening from the faucet.

"Showoff," the widow said. She squeezed my arm. "He's a liar, too. Absolutely terrible at whist."

"When he said I had to answer those questions, was that a lie, too?"

"Ah, no, that part was true enough."

"And the part about me being...a wizard?"

The widow smiled. "Truest of all," she said.

"All wizards have much the same talents," said the widow, as she washed the unbroken dishes and I dried them, "just as all carpenters, all painters, all landscapers do. But each wizard also has a specialty, some talent she is especially good at. Some work at the craft for decades before realizing what their specialty is. Some realize what it was only in hindsight, only on their deathbeds, if they ever realize it at all. But other wizards have their talents handed to them, almost from birth, the way we all are granted the earth and the sky.

"I myself was no taller than a turnip when I realized that many of the little friends I played with every day, in the attic and beneath the grape arbor and in the bottom of the garden, were children that others could not see, and I realized, too, that my parents did not like for me to speak of them, to say, 'Oh, Papa, how funny! Little Merry just passed through your waistcoat, as you were stirring your tea.' How cross he became that day."

She wrung dry a dishcloth in her tiny fists. I blew soap bubbles from my palm into the face of a sleeping tabby as it floated past. The bubbles bobbed through the cat, or was it the other way around? The widow had been scrubbing dishes with pumice, so the bubbles were reddish in color and seemed more substantial than the wholly transparent cat. Then the bubbles vanished, and the tabby remained.

The widow continued: "And so I began keeping my talent secret, and once you start keeping your talents secret, why, you're well along the path of the wizard."

"My talents are a secret even from me," I said.

"There now, you see how wrong you can be?" said the widow. She popped my shoulder with the dishtowel. "You play with dead cats. You converse with all my boarders. You unbind the front door and then bind it again without half trying. You come here from Tennessee in a single step, as if the world were a map you could fold. My goodness, that's a step even Paul Bunyan couldn't take, and Paul is a big, big man." After a moment's reverie, she shook her head and with a great splash yanked free the plug. "Well, that's done!" she cried over the rush of the emptying sink. "May it all go down Wheatstraw's gullet." She stood on tiptoe and kissed my cheek. Her kiss was quick, dry, and powdery, like the dab of a cotton swab. "Never you fret, child," she said, taking my arm and leading me down the steps into the garden. "You've got talent to burn, as Mr. Winchester would have said. And now that you've begun to focus, well, you'll tumble across a specialty or three very soon, I daresay."

"Mr. Wheatstraw said I'm in a different world now."

The widow snorted. "Different world, indeed! You can't change worlds like garters, my dear. This is the same world you were born into, the same world you are stuck with, all the days of your life. Never forget that. But the older you get, and the more traveling you do, why, the more of this world you inevitably will see – and inevitably be *able* to see, I daresay."

"Because I walked through the diorama, you mean?"

"That was a powerful bit of traveling, indeed it was. Doubtless it broadened your mind a bit. Who knows? A few weeks ago you might have been as ignorant of the spirit world as my carpenters, might have looked right through Mr. Dellafave without even seeing him, much less being able to converse with him. And what a shame that would have been," she said, not sounding quite convinced.

I considered telling her that Mr. Dellafave was in love with her, but decided she knew that already. Instead, I finally dared to ask a question.

"Mrs. Winchester. In all these years since Mr. Winchester died, has he ever, well...visited?"

"Ah, that's sweet of you to ask, child," said the widow, with a sniff and a toss of her head. "No, not yet, though early on I looked for him and listened for him, by day and by night. Especially by night. I confess I even hired a medium or two to conduct a séance – for those were all the rage, a few years ago." She waved absently as we passed a headless brakeman, who raised his lantern to her. "A phantom herd of buffalo might have stampeded through the parlor without those frauds noticing. And the mess! We mopped up ectoplasm for days." She leaned against the trunk of an English yew and stared, not unhappily, into the sky. "I finally concluded that Mr. Winchester – like my Mama and Papa, and my old nurse, and my little dog, Zip, that I had when we were first wed, and my poor child Annie – that I will be reunited with none of them until I'm as insubstantial as that lady in the pond over there."

In silence, we watched the woman as she rose from the water, stood a few moments on the surface, then sank out of sight amid the lily pads, her face unreadable. Her dress was from an earlier time. Where had all her lovers got to, I wondered, and what did she remember of them?

"I'll tell you the puzzle that worries me," the widow Winchester abruptly said, "and it's not Mr. Winchester, and it's not where all the dogs go. What worries me is that in all these years of receiving the dear departed in my home, I have met not one – not one – who was, in life, a wizard."

"Sarah!" the man yelled. "Sarah!"

The widow and I ran to the bay window in the parlor. I knew that voice.

A two-horse wagon had pulled up in front of the house, and a big man in a black suit and black hat was climbing out of it. It was a warm fall day, but his hat and shoulders were dusted with snow, and ice clung to the spokes of the wheels. The wagon was faded blue and covered with painted stars and crescent moons. The side read:

WIZARD OF THE BLUE RIDGE

MAGICIAN OF THE OLD SOUTH

PURVEYOR OF MAGIC AND MIRTH

He removed his hat and called again: "Sarah! I got him! I finally got him!"

It was Mr. Farethewell.

By the time we reached the front door – which the widow opened with a wave of her hand – a horse and rider had galloped up. It was Petey Wheatstraw, dressed like a fox hunter in red coat, white breeches and high boots.

"Winchester, do something!" he yelled as he dismounted. "Farethewell's gone crazy."

"Crazy, nothing," Farethewell said. "He's trapped like a bug in a jar."

"Who is?" the widow asked.

"Old Scratch himself!" Farethewell replied. "Here's your Devil."

He went to the back of the wagon and began dragging out something heavy, something we couldn't yet see.

The widow looked to Wheatstraw. "Is this true?"

He threw up his hands. "Who knows? No one's seen the Old Man in days."

Farethewell dragged the whatever-it-was a little closer to the end of the wagon, and an old boot thumped to the gravel. I stepped closer, out of the shadow of the porch.

"Well, hello, Little Britches," said Farethewell. "Sarah told me you were here. So you decided to pull some magic after all?" He pulled a flask from his jacket, looked at it, then laughed and flung it across the yard. It landed in the rosebushes with a clank.

"She told you?" I cried. I got behind a pillar. Just the sight of Farethewell made me feel flushed and angry. "You *know* each other?"

"Well, he *is* a wizard," Wheatstraw said.

Farethewell stood there, hands on hips, and looked pleased with himself. The widow peered into the wagon.

"Where is he? Is that his boot?"

Farethewell snatched her up and hugged her and spun her around. "That ain't his boot. That's him! He's in the boot! Come look, Little Britches!"

"Don't you call me that," I yelled, but I stepped off the porch anyway. Farethewell took hold of the boot with both rough hands and walked backward, hunched over, dragging the boot toward the house as if he dragged a big man's corpse. The boot tore a rut in the gravel.

"Couldn't be," Wheatstraw said.

"It is!" Farethewell said.

"Blasphemy," the widow said.

"Bad for business, anyway," Wheatstraw said.

Farethewell let go of the boot and stepped back, gasping, rubbing the small of his back with his hands. "I run him down in the Sierras," he said. "He'd a got away from me, if he had just let go of that chicken. Seven days and seven nights we fought up and down them slopes. The avalanches made all the papers. I've had this boot since Appomattox. It's my teacher's boot, hexed with his magic and with his blood. On our eighth day of wrestling, I got this jammed down over the Devil's head, and just kept on jamming till he was all inside, and now the Devil will pay!"

We all gathered around the boot.

"It's empty," the widow said.

Wheatstraw cackled. "Sure is. Farethewell, you are crazier than a moonstruck rat."

I did not laugh. Peering out through the laces of the boot was a face. The two blue eyes got wider when they saw me. The face moved back a little, so that I could see more of it.

It was Farethewell in the boot.

I looked over my shoulder. Yes, big Farethewell stood behind me, grinning. But the tiny man in the boot was Farethewell also, wearing a robe and pointed hat, as I last had seen him at Professor Van Der Ast's.

The little Farethewell hugged himself as if he were cold and began silently to cry.

"What's the matter, child?" the widow asked. I shrugged off her little spindly hand of comfort. It was like twitching free of a spider.

"What you see in there?" Wheatstraw asked.

"Tell them, Little Britches!"

"Don't take on so, dear. What could you possibly see? This has nothing to do with you."

"Maybe it does," said Farethewell. "Who you see in there, girl? What's this varmint to you?"

"What's his name this time?" Wheatstraw asked. "The Old Man answers to more names than the Sears and Roebuck catalog."

I didn't answer. Little Farethewell was backing up, pressing himself flat against the heel of that old floppy boot. I stepped forward to see him better, and he shook so, the whole boot trembled.

"He's scared," I said, more loud and fierce than I meant to sound, for in fact this scared me worse than anything – not that I was faced with a second Farethewell the size of a kewpie you could win with a ball toss, but that I was more fearsome to him than his larger self was. What kind of booger did he take me for? This scared me but made me mad, too. I snarled and made my fingers into claws like Boola the Panther Boy and lunged.

"Yah!"

Little Farethewell twitched so hard the boot fell over. The sole was so worn you could see through it nearly, and a gummy spot at the toe treasured a cigarette butt and a tangle of hair.

"He's ours," big Farethewell hissed into my ear. "Whatever face he's showing you, girl, whoever he once was to you, he is ours now and no mistake. All the way here, off the slopes and down the river and through the groves, it was all I could do to keep him booted and not kicking the boards out of the wagon, but now you got him broken like a pony. And a girl loves a pony. He's mine and yours together now."

"Don't listen," the widow said.

"Sarah. You forgetting what we got in there? You forgetting Gettysburg, Cold Harbor, Petersburg? The tuberculosis that carried off your William, the marasmus that stole Annie from the cradle? Don't you care what this *thing* has done to the world, what it still could do? Ain't you learned nothing?"

"Some things ain't fit to be learned," the widow said, "and some wizards breathing God's free air are cooped up worse than this creature is. Petey, tell him. You've seen worse than Cold Harbor, worse any of us."

Wheatstraw did not answer at once. He did not seem to be listening. He was in the act of dusting a metal bench with his handkerchief. He slowly re-folded the handkerchief, then flicked off one last spot of dust and sighed and settled himself on the bench, perched on the edge as if delicacy alone could keep his breeches away from the iron. The moment he sat, a transparent cat jumped onto his lap and settled itself. Wheatstraw scratched between its ears as it sank out of sight, purring, until Wheatstraw was scratching only his leg.

"What I see," Wheatstraw finally said, "is that whatever half-dead thing you dragged in, Farethewell, it ain't yours anymore. It's Pearl's."

"Pearl's!" said Farethewell and the widow, together.

"Pearl's," Wheatstraw repeated. "Otherwise she couldn't see it, could she? So it's hers to do with as she will. And there ain't no need in y'all looking like you just sucked down the same oyster. Folks making up their own minds – why, that's the basic principle of the Old Concern, the foundation of our industry. And besides," he added, as he leaned back and tipped his felt hat over his eyes and crossed his legs at the ankles, "she's done made it up anyhow."

When he said that, I realized that I had.

"No," Farethewell said.

I picked up the boot. It was no heavier for me than a dead foot. The thought made me shiver.

"Wheatstraw," said Farethewell. "What have you done to me, you wretch? I can't move."

"It ain't my doing."

"Nor mine," said the widow.

"Pearl. Listen to me."

I held up the boot and looked at it, eye to eyelet. The trembling shape no longer looked much like Farethewell – more like a bad memory of him, or a bad likeness of him, or just a stain on a canvas that put you in mind of him, if you squinted just right. To whatever it was, I said, "Go home."

Then I swung the boot three times over my head and let it fly.

"*Noooo!*" Farethewell yelled.

The boot sailed over the fence and past the point where it ought to have fallen back to earth and kept on going, a tumbling black dot against the pale sky like a star in reverse, until what I thought was the boot was just a floater darting across my eye. I blinked it away, and the boot was gone.

Mr. Farethewell stared into the sky, his jaw working. A tear slid down his cheek. He began to moan.

"Whoo! Don't reckon we need wait supper on him tonight," Wheatstraw said.

"I knew it," the widow said. She snapped her fingers in Wheatstraw's face. "I knew it the moment she and her fetches stepped out of the ballroom window. Her arrival was foretold by the spirits."

"Foretold by the spirits, my eye," Wheatstraw said. "She's a wizard, not the 3:50 to Los Angeles."

Farethewell's moan became a howl.

I suddenly felt dizzy and sick and my breath was gone, like something had hit me in the gut. I tried to run, without quite knowing why, but Farethewell already had lunged across the distance between us. He seized my shoulders, shook me like a rag, howled into my face.

"I'm sorry!" I cried. "I had to do it. I had to!"

He hit me then, and I fell to the grass, sobbing. I waited for him to hit me again, to kill me. Instead the widow and Wheatstraw were kneeling beside me, stroking my hair and murmuring words I did not understand. Farethewell was walking jerkily across the yard, like a scarecrow would walk. He fell to his knees in the rosebushes and scrabbled in the dirt for his flask, the thorns tearing his face.

⋆

I stayed in bed a few days, snug beneath layers of goosedown. The widow left the room only to fetch and carry for me. Mr. Dellafave settled into a corner of the ceiling and never left the room at all.

When she felt I was able, the widow showed me the note Mr. Farethewell had left.

I never should have hit you, Little Britches, and I am sorry for it, but you never should have got between me and the Devil. Many women and children in Virginia got between the armies and died. Hear me. Farethewell.

"His fist didn't hurt you," the widow said.

"I know," I said. "Doing what I did with the boot, that's what hurt me. I need to find out what I did, and how to do it right. Mrs. Winchester?"

"Yes, child."

"When I am better, I believe I shall take a trip."

"Where, child?"

"All over," I said. "It was Mr. Dellafave's idea, in a way. I need to see some of the other things in the diorama, and I need to meet some other wizards. As many as I can. I have a lot to learn from all of them."

She pulled a handkerchief out of her sleeve and daubed her eyes. "I can't go with you," she said.

"But I'll always come back," I said. "And you mustn't worry about me. I won't be alone."

I considered walking back through the ballroom window, but I had been there before. I ran my finger over the pebbled face of the stained-glass girl to say good-bye.

When I walked out the front gate of Flatland House, toting an overstuffed carpetbag, I half-expected to find myself walking in at the back, like Mr. Dellafave. But no, there were the orchards, and the lane leading over the hill to San Jose, and Petey Wheatstraw sitting cross-legged on a tall stump like a Hindu fakir.

I waved. He waved, and jumped down. He was dressed like a vagabond, in rough cloth breeches and a coarse shirt, and his belongings were tied up in a kerchief on the end of a stick.

"You're a sight," I said.

"In the future," he replied, "they'll call it *slumming*. Which way?"

"That way, to the top of the hill, and then sideways."

We set off.

"Also, Mr. Wheatstraw, I have some answers for you."

"Are you prepared to sing them? Anything worth saying is worth singing."

"I am."

"You're so agreeable this morning. It can't last." He sang:

Oh you must answer my questions nine
Sing ninety-nine and ninety
Or you're not God's, you're one of mine
And you are the weaver's bonny.

I sang back:

Snow is whiter than the milk
Sing ninety-nine and ninety
And down is softer than the silk
And I am the weaver's bonny.
Heaven's higher than a tree
Sing ninety-nine and ninety
And Hell is deeper than the sea
And I am the weaver's bonny
Thunder's louder than a horn
Sing ninety-nine and ninety
And death is sharper than a thorn
And I am the weaver's bonny
A babe's more innocent than a lamb
Sing ninety-nine and ninety
And the Devil is meaner than womankind

– "And MAN kind too," I said, interrupting myself –

And I am the weaver's bonny.

Wheatstraw gave me a half-mocking salute and sang:

You have answered my questions nine
Sing ninety-nine and ninety
And you are God's, you're none of mine
And you are the weaver's bonny.

Then I asked him the ninth question, and he agreed that it was the right question to ask, so right that he did not know the answer, and together we reached the top of the hill and walked sideways, right off the edge of the world.

Just this year I made it back to Chattanooga. The town was so changed I hardly recognized it, except for the bend in the river and the tracks through the tunnel and Lookout Mountain over everything.

The new bridge is still hanging on, though it's no longer new and carries no proper traffic anymore, just visitors who stroll along it and admire the view and take photographs. Can you call them photographs anymore? They need no plates and no paper, and you hardly have to stand still any time to make one.

At the end of my visit I spent a good hour on the bridge, looking at the river and at the people, and enjoying walking my home city on older, stronger legs and seeing it with better eyes and feeling more myself than I had as a girl – though I'm still not as old-looking as you'd expect, thanks to my travels and the talents I've picked up along the way.

How you'd *expect* me to look at my age, I reckon, is *dead*, but I am not that, not by a long shot.

I wondered how many of these young-old people creeping along with the help of canes, and candy-faced children ripping and roaring past me, and men and women rushing along in short pants, my goodness, their stuck-out elbows going up and down like pistons – how many of them dreamed of the world that I knew. But what had I known myself of the invisible country all around, before I passed into the Infernal Regions?

Up ahead, sitting on one of the benches along the bridge, was a girl who put me in mind of my old Chattanooga friend Sally Ann Rummage, with her red hair and her long neck and her high forehead like a thinker. Probably about sixteen, this girl was, though it's hard to tell; they stay younger so much longer now, thank goodness. She didn't look very happy to be sixteen, or to be anything. A boy was standing over her, with one big foot on the bench like he was planting a flag, and he was pointing his finger in her face like Petey Wheatstraw was known to do, and his other hand was twisting her pretty brown jacket and twisting her shoulder, too, inside it, and she looked cried-out and miserable. He was telling her about herself, or presuming to, and when he glanced my way – no more seeing me than he would a post or a bird or a food wrapper blowing past – I saw that he was Farethewell. He was high-cheeked and eighteen and muscled, where Farethewell was old and jowly, and had a sharp nose unlike Farethewell, and had nothing of Farethewell's shape or face or complexion, but I recognized him just the same. I would recognize Farethewell anywhere.

I stood behind him, looking at her, until she looked up and met my gaze. This is a good trick, and one that even non-wizards can accomplish.

The boy said to me something foul that I will not lower myself to repeat, and I said, "Hush," and he hushed. Of all the talents I've learned since I left Flatland House, that may be the handiest.

The girl frowned, puzzled, her arms crossed tight to hold herself in like a girl I once knew in a California parlor long ago. I smiled at her and put in her head the Devil's ninth question:

Who am I?

And while I was in there, in a thousand places, I strewed an answer like mustard seeds: *I am the weaver's bonny.*

Then I walked on down the bridge. The sun was low, the breeze was sharp, and a mist was forming at the river bend, a mist only I could see. The mist thickened and began to swirl. The surface of the water roiled. In the center of the oncoming cloud, twin smokestacks cleaved the water, then the wheelhouse, then the upper deck. The entire riverboat surfaced, water sluicing down the bulkheads, paddle-wheel churning. I could read the boat's bright red markings. It was the *Sultana*, which blew up in 1865 just north of Memphis, at the islands called the Hen and Chickens, with the loss of 1,700 men. And my, did she look grand!

At the head of the steps to the riverfront, I looked back – for wizards always look back. Have I not been looking back since I began this story, and have you not been looking back with me, to learn the ways of a wizard? I saw the girl striding away from the boy, head held high. He just stood there, like one of Professor Van Der Ast's blockheads with a railroad spike up his nose. The girl whirled once, to shout something at him. The wind snatched away all but one word: " – ever!" Then she kept on walking. The mustard was beginning to sprout. I laughed as loudly as the widow Winchester, and I ran down the slick steps to the river, as giddy as a girl of ninety-nine and ninety.

Don't Ask

M. Rickert

M. Rickert lives in Cedarburg, Wisconsin. Her short fiction has appeared often in recent years in F&SF, and in both our *Year's Best SF* and *Year's Best Fantasy* volumes. She said in an interview (*www.ideomancer.com/ft/Rickert/Rickert.htm*), "My stories are not factual but the factual existence is not the only one and they are, really, a truer record of my soul than a photograph or a journal could ever be." We see her fantasy as somewhere in the range of Kit Reed's and in the tradition of Shirley Jackson's work. Her first story collection, *Map of Dreams*, appeared in 2006. In 2007 she began to win awards for her fiction.

"Don't Ask" was published in F&SF, which had an excellent year in fantasy. It is another version of a "lost boys" story, very different from Daryl Gregory's earlier in this book. A group of mothers whose sons were abducted by wolves, then ultimately returned, tries to understand what has happened to their boys. It is perhaps an allegory of mothers whose sons go to war, but with truly strange twists towards the end.

WHEN THE LOST BOYS returned with their piercings, tattoos, and swagger, we rejoiced and greeted them with balloons, bubble gum, chocolate chip cookies, and bone-crunching hugs, which they did not resist. Only later did we realize that this was one of their symptoms, this acquiescence, not a sign of their affection for us, though we do not doubt their affection.

How could wolves slope through town, unseen, and steal our boys from bicycles, from country roads, from the edge of the driveway, from our kitchen tables, dank with the scent of warm milk and soggy cereal; from our arms – wasn't it just yesterday that we held our boys close and sang them lullabies? How could they be taken from us?

Yet they were, and we wept and gnashed our teeth, tore our hair and screamed their names into the dark. Through the seasons we searched for them so thoroughly that even in our dreams we could not rest and often awoke to find dewy grass stuck to the soles of our feet, dirt beneath our fingernails, our hair matted by the wind. We continued to search even after the Sheriff, with his hound dog face and quivering hands, said he would never stop looking but couldn't keep meeting with us and the very next day we woke up and no one waited at the door with pots of coffee and boxes of sticky, bright-colored doughnuts, and we sat at our kitchen tables and listened to school buses pass, not even slowing down for the memory of our sons.

But why speak about sorrow now that our boys have returned? They are home again, sleeping with hairy feet hanging over the edges of little boy beds, wearing the too small T-shirts, the split pants that reveal their long bones and taut muscles which quiver and spasm while they dream.

Of course we realized that in the years our boys were gone they had grown, this was the hope at least, this was the best possibility of all the horrible scenarios, that our lost boys were growing in the wolves' den and not slaughtered by them – so yes, we are happy, of course we are, but what is this strange sorrow we discover in the dark? Why can't we stop weeping during this, the happiest of times?

Years before our boys returned there was the return of the famous lost boy, stolen from the end of his driveway, the wheels of his blue bicycle still spinning when his mother went to the door to call him in for dinner and saw the bike there but did not immediately comprehend it as a sign of catastrophe. He was missing for eight years, and was a hero for a while, until he started committing petty crimes in the neighborhood.

The famous lost boy, a man now, explains that he has been observing our behavior and the behavior of our sons. We cannot help but feel squeamish about the whole thing, we are uncomfortable with the notion that, after everything that happened, we have been studied and observed and did not know it. We discuss this in whispers in the high school auditorium, where the famous lost boy has come to speak. The therapists have their theories but we assume only one person has the truth and we are eager to hear what he can tell us about all our suffering, because, we say, nodding our heads and hugging ourselves in the cold auditorium, this happened to all of us.

"No," the famous lost boy (now a grown man with long, stringy hair) says. "It didn't."

We have been advised by therapists and counselors, experts beyond the meager fourth grade education of the famous lost boy (by the time he came back, he was too angry and unruly for school) not to ask what happened. "They will tell you when they are ready," the experts say.

We ask them if they want maple syrup for their pancakes, what show they'd like to watch, what games they'd like to play. We spoil them and expect them to revel in it, the way they did before they were taken, but oddly, in spite of all they've been through, and the horrors they have endured, they behave as though our servitude and their eminence is a given. Yet, sometimes we ask a question, so innocent, "chocolate chip or peanut butter?" which they respond to with confusion, frowning as if trying to guess a right answer, or as though unfamiliar with the terms. Other times they bark or growl like angry dogs being taunted, but it passes so quickly we are sure it's been imagined.

The famous lost boy wants us to give him our sons. "You can visit whenever," he says.

What is he, crazy? What does he think we are?

"You don't understand them. Nobody does. Except me."

We are not sure if this is true. The part about him understanding them. Perhaps. We know that we don't. The therapists say, "Give it time. Don't ask."

We ask them if they want meatloaf or roast chicken and they stare at us as if we have spoken Urdu. We show them photographs of the relatives who died while they were gone and find it disturbing that they nod, as if they understand, but show no grief. We stock the refrigerator with soda, though we know they should drink juice, and Gatorade, remembering how they used to gulp it down in great noisy swallows (and we scolded them for drinking right out of the bottle) after games of little league and soccer, though now they are happy to sit, listlessly, in front of the computer for hours, often wandering the house in the middle of the night. We ask them if their beds are comfortable enough, are they warm enough, are they cool enough, but we never ask them what happened because the therapists have told us not to. When we explain this to the famous lost boy (though why do we feel we have to explain ourselves to him? He can't even hold down a job at McDonald's) he says, "You don't ask, because you don't want to know."

We hate the famous lost boy, he sneers and ridicules and we do not want our sons to turn out like him. He is not a nice man. We just want him to go away, but he won't. Notoriously reclusive for years, he is now, suddenly, everywhere. Walking down Main Street. Hanging out at the coffee shops. Standing on the street corner, smoking. We are sorry to see that our boys seem to like him. Sometimes we find them, running together, like a wild pack. We call them home and they come back to us panting, tongues hanging out. They collapse on the couch or the floor and when they fall asleep they twitch and moan, cry and bark. We don't know what they dream about, though we think, often, they dream of running.

They run all the time now. In the morning they run down the stairs and around the kitchen table. We tell them to sit, or calm down, but it doesn't really work. Sometimes we open the door and they tear into the backyard. We have erected fences but they try to dig out, leaving potholes where tulips and tiger lilies and roses blossomed through all those years of our grief. We stand at the window wondering at the amazing fact of their tenacity in trying to escape us when (and this is public knowledge, much discussed and debated by newscasters and talk show hosts in those first heady weeks after they were found) they never tried to escape their beasts.

Sometimes we feel our neck hairs tingle and we find the lost boys staring at us like animals in a cage, frightened and wary, then they smile, and we smile in return, understanding that they will have these bad memories, these moments of fear.

The famous lost boy sighs, and right there, in the high school auditorium, lights a cigarette, which Hymral Waller, the school board president, rushes to tell him must be extinguished. "What?" the word sounds angry in the bite of microphone. "This?" Hymral's words drift from the floor, hollow, balloon-like, "fire," and "sorry." The famous lost boy drops the cigarette to the stage floor and stamps it out with the toe of his sneaker. We gasp at his impertinence and he squints at us.

"Okay. So, right. You're protecting your children by worrying about me and my friggin' cigarette?" He shakes his head, laughing a little jagged laugh, and then, without further comment, turns and walks out the fire exit door.

We should have just let him walk away. We should have gone home. But instead, we followed him, through the icy white streets of our town.

He walks down the cold sidewalk (neatly shoveled, only occasionally patched with ice) beneath the yellow street lamps, hunched in his flimsy jean jacket, hands thrust in his pockets, acrid smoke circles his head. We cannot see his face, but we imagine the nasty, derisive curl of his lips, the unruly eyebrows over slit eyes, the unshaved chin stubbled with small black hairs as though a minuscule forest fire raged there.

We walk on the cold white sidewalks, beneath the blue moon and we breathe white puffs that disappear the way our sons did. We keep our distance. We are sure he does not realize we have followed him, until, suddenly, he leaps over the winter fence (meant to discourage errant sleigh riding from this dangerous hill) into the park. A shadow passes overhead, just for a second we are in darkness, and then, we are watching the shape of a lone wolf, its long tail down, its mouth open, tongue hanging out, loping across what, in spring, will be the baseball diamond. We all turn, suddenly, as if broken from some terrible spell, and, careful because of those occasional patches of ice, we run home where our lost boys wait for us. (Or so we like to think.) We find them sprawled, sleeping, on the kitchen floor, draped uncomfortably across the stairs, or curled, in odd positions, in the bathroom. We don't wake them. Any sleep they find is sorely needed and any interruption can keep them up for days, running in circles and howling at all hours. The doctors have advised us to give them sleeping pills but we are uncomfortable doing so; we understand that their captors often drugged them.

"It's not the same thing," the experts say.

Well, of course not. The experts are starting to get on our nerves.

And now, we realize, as we stand in the dark rooms of our miracle lives, we have been consulting the wrong professionals all along. We don't need psychologists, psychiatrists, medical doctors, or the famous lost boy. We need a hunter, someone who knows how to kill a wolf.

We find her on the Internet and pool our resources to pay her airfare and lodging at the B & B downtown. We wish we had something more appropriate, fewer stuffed bears and fake flowers, more hunting lodge, but we don't.

When she arrives we are surprised at how petite she is, smaller than our boys, with an amazingly chipmunky voice and an odd xylophone laugh. She comes into the high school auditorium bearing the strong scent of the B & B roses soap, and we think we've been duped somehow, but, once we adjust our positions, craning our necks to see between shoulders, scooting over to the edges of the cold hard chairs, adjusting to her unexpected size, she commands our attention.

"Now, wait a minute," she says, laughing (and we resist the temptation to cover our ears). "Why are you all making this so complicated?"

We explain to her again how a werewolf roams amongst us, a monster! We shout and interrupt each other. We try to tell her how the werewolf was once one of our own. "We don't really want to hurt him," someone says. "We just want him gone."

At this she looks at us in such a way that we are all victims of her gaze. "Now wait a minute, why did you send for me? What am I doing here? Are you hunting, or starting a zoo?"

There is a moment's silence. After all, a zoo might be nice, a perfect addition to our town, but from the back of the room, a voice cries out, "Hunting!" The cry is taken up by all of us. Our boys have been through enough. We will protect them at any cost.

The small pink tip of her tongue protrudes between her pretty lips and she nods slowly, smiling. "He's not necessarily a werewolf. Not all men who turn into wolves are, uh, wait a minute. I'd like to get my fee now."

Duped! We've been duped after all. Suddenly it seems we have found ourselves in the middle of a bad joke, we'll pay her and she'll say something pithy and, all right, perhaps a little funny. Here's how you do it, she'll say, and tell us something completely useless. We begin to argue this plan, what does she think we are, country hicks? Until finally she shrugs and nods at Hymral, who has volunteered to be her chauffeur and local guide. He has reported that she asked him if there are any good vegetarian restaurants in the area, which we consider further evidence against her. A vegetarian hunter, who ever heard of such a thing? But when we confront her with all the evidence, her small frame, her flowered suitcases, her lack of weapons, she just shrugs. "What's going on here, folks," she chirrups. "I've got ten jobs waiting for me right now and I ain't gonna stay another night, lovely as it is. If you want my expert guidance, you are going to have to pay me up front, 'cause the fact is, catching a wolf just ain't that hard, but I have to earn my living somehow."

"You gonna use your feminine wiles?"

She fixes such a look in the general direction of that question that we all shiver and step back as if separating ourselves from the inquisitor.

"I ain't no prostitute," she says, disgusted.

Well, what were we going to do? Consult more therapists with their various opinions and modalities? Call the Sheriff who did everything he could to help us find our sons though none of it was enough and they came home only after a freak series of events? Pray, as we did for all those nights and all those days and all those hours upon minutes upon seconds when our sons were being torn apart? Or pay this little Goldilocks person to rid us of the danger that resided amongst us?

We pay her, of course.

He lives in a shack at the edge of town and he does not expect our arrival, though certainly he sees all our cars coming up the long, deserted road, headlights illuminating the taloned branches of trees and the swollen breasts of snow. Certainly he hears the car doors open and shut. We stand there whispering in the dark, observe the light go on in the small upstairs window and observe it go out again. We suspect he is watching us through the web of old lace curtain there. We feel horrible, just terrible about what we have come to do but we don't even consider not doing it. At last he opens his front door. He is wearing plaid flannel pajamas, boots, and that old jean jacket again, which, later, some of us recall, was the coat his parents bought him when he first came back, all those years ago. "What's up?" he says.

We don't look at each other, embarrassed, and then at last someone says, "Sorry, Jamie, but you've got to come."

He nods, slowly. He turns to look back into his house, as though fondly, though later, when we went in there, we all agreed it was nothing to feel sentimental about, a beat-up couch, an ancient TV, a three-legged kitchen table, and, both disturbing and proof of our right course, enormous stacks of children's books, fairy tales, and comics. To think he wanted us to send our boys here!

He shuts the door gently, thrusts his hands into his pockets, sniffs loudly. He works his mouth in an odd manner, the way boys do when they are trying not to cry.

He walked right to us, as though he had no say in the matter, as though he could not run, or shout, or lock himself in the house, he came to us like a friendly dog to kibble, like a child to sugar, he came to us as though there was no other possible destination. He didn't ask why or protest in any way. It was so strange. So inhuman.

She was giggling when she told us how to do it, as though it were all just a joke, but she was also counting a big stack of money at the time. "How you catch a wolf is you catch the man. This is something the French knew. You don't have to wait until he turns and his teeth are sharp and he has claws."

We live tidy lives; ice-free sidewalks, square green lawns, even our garages, so clean you could eat in them (and some of us do, using them as summer porches). We are not eager to do something so sloppy, but for our sons we make the sacrifice.

We cut and cut looking for the pelt.

"The wolf rests within," she said before she wiggled her red nail-polished fingers at us and nodded for Hymral to take her to the airport.

We have grown sensitive now to the sound of screams. Our boys run through the town, playing the way boys do, shouting and whatnot, but every once in a while they make a different sort of sound, blood-curdling, we always thought that was an expression, but when a man screams while being cut, his blood is dotted with bubbles as though it is going sour.

Once it was begun, it was impossible to stop.

"Wolf! Hair!" someone shouted holding up a thatch, which caused a tremendous amount of excitement until we realized it was scalp.

All we needed was the hair of the wolf trapped within the famous lost boy to redeem ourselves. There was no redemption.

Our boys slam the doors and kick the cats. We scold them. We love them. They look at us as though they suspect the very worst. They ask us about the famous lost boy and we say, "Don't ask," but they do, they ask again and again and again, they ask so much and so often that each of us, separately, reach a breaking point and turn on them, spitting the words out, the dangerous words, "What happened to you, while you were lost?"

They tell us. They tell us everything about the years upon months upon days upon hours upon minutes upon seconds. We sweat and cry. They gnash their teeth, pull their hair, scratch themselves incessantly. We try to hold them but they pull away. The sun sets and rises. We sleep to the drone of this terrible story and wake to another horrible chapter. We apologize for our need for sleep, but the recitation continues, uninterrupted, as if we are not the reason for it. We become disoriented, we have waking dreams, and in sleep we have death. Our boys change before us, from the lost sons we kissed on freckled noses to sharp-toothed beasts. We shake our heads. We readjust.

And we know now that what we said for all those years was not just a promise, but a curse; we will always be searching for the boys that were taken from us. We will never find them, for they are lost, no grave to mark their passing and passage by which they can return, like dreams or the memory of sunshine in the dark. We fill their bowls with water, and they come in slobbering, tongues hanging out, collapsing on the floor or couch, shedding hair and skin and we would do anything for them, but still, some days, when the sun is bright or clear, you can find us staring out at the distant horizon. We have discovered that if we look long enough and hard enough we can see them again, our lost boys, their haircuts ragged with youth, their smiles crooked. They are riding bicycles, jumping over rocks, playing with their friends, shoving hamburgers into their mouths, gulping soda, eating cake, running out the door, running down the sidewalk; the sun shining on them as if they were not just our sons, but sons of the gods and then, suddenly, we are brought back to the present, by that feeling at the back of our necks, and we turn to find them watching us with that look, that frightened, wary look of an animal caged by an unkind human. At moments like these, we smile, and sometimes, on good days, they smile back at us, revealing sharp white teeth in the tender red wounds of their mouths.

The Stranger's Hands

Tad Williams

Tad Williams (*tadwilliams.com*) lives in the vicinity of San Francisco, California, with his wife, former SF editor Deborah Beale, and their children. He began publishing fiction in 1985 with the novel *Tailchaser's Song*. For the most part, he writes long fantasy novels of high quality, sometimes in series: the Memory, Sorrow, and Thorn trilogy, the Shadowmarch trilogy, and the Otherland series. A collection of his short fiction, *Rite: Short Work*, was published in 2006. His most recent novel is *Shadowplay* (2007) which *Publishers Weekly* described as "sweeping spellbinder full of mystical wonder." Several of his books are to be reprinted in 2008.

"The Stranger's Hands" is from the anthology *Wizards*. Reviewer Don D'Ammassa describes the story as "a 'Monkey's Paw' variation," summarizing its moral as, "If you get what you wish for, you might discover that it's not what it's cracked up to be." It is interesting to compare this story to Ackert and Rosenbaum's "The King of the Djinn" in this volume.

PEOPLE IN THE VILLAGE had been whispering for days about the two vagabonds in Squire's Wood, but the boy Tobias was the first to speak to them.

Tobias was a somewhat wayward lad, and the fact that he should have been grazing his father's sheep on the hill above the forest at that hour more or less assured the sheep in question would be wandering along the shady edges of the wood instead, with Tobias wandering right behind them.

It was not until he saw a drift of smoke twining like a gray scarf through the trees that the boy remembered that strangers had been seen in the wood. He felt a moment of fear: Why would anyone live out of doors in the cold nights and flurries of autumn rain if they were God-fearing folk? Only robbers and dangerous madmen dwelt under the unsheltered sky. Everyone knew that. If he had been a fraction less headstrong, Tobias would have turned around then and hurried back to the hillside, perhaps even remembering to take his father's sheep with him, but there was a part of him, a strong part, that hated *not knowing things* worse than anything. It was the part that had once caused him to pull the leg off a frog, just to find out what it would do. (It did very little, and died soon after with what Tobias felt guiltily certain was an accusatory look in its bulging eyes.) It was also the reason he had dented his father's best scythe when he had used it to try to cut down a tree, and why he had dumped the contents of his mother's precious sewing basket all over the ground – a search for knowledge that ended with

Tobias spending all afternoon in the fading light on his hands and knees, locating every last needle and pin he had spilled. Once this rebel voice had even led him several miles out of the village, on a quest for the town of Eader's Church, which he had heard was so big that the streets actually had names. His father and two other men had caught up to him an hour after sunset as he sat exhausted and hungry by the side of the road. He had got a whipping for it, of course, but for young Tobias whippings were part of the cost of doing business.

So now, instead of turning and leaving the woods and its perilous inhabitants behind (for the sake of his father's livestock if nothing else) he followed the trail of smoke back to its source, a small cookfire in a clearing. A small man with a ratlike face was tending the flames, his wrinkles made so deep and dark by grime he looked like an apple-doll. His large companion, who sat on a stone beside the fire and did not look up even when Tobias stepped on a twig and made the little man jump, was so odd to look at that the boy could not help shivering. The large man's head was shaved, albeit poorly in some places, and the skull beneath the skin bulged in places that it should not. His bony jaw hung slack, the tongue visible in the space between top and bottom teeth, and although he did not seem blind, the eyes in the deep sockets were dull as dirty stones.

If the big man was paying no attention, the little man was. He stared at Tobias like a dog trying to decide whether to bark or run.

"Your wood's too wet," the boy told him.

"What?"

"You'll get mostly smoke and little fire from that. Do you want smoke?"

The small man frowned, but in dismay, not anger. "I want to cook this fish." He had the sound of a southerner, the words stretched and misshapen. Tobias wondered why they couldn't learn to speak properly.

He squinted at the man's supper with the eye of an experienced angler. "It's small."

"It's better than starving," the man pointed out.

"Well, then, I'll show you." Tobias quickly found enough dry wood to rebuild the fire and within a short time the little man was cooking the fish over it on a long stick. His large companion still had not moved or spoken, had not even seemed to notice the newcomer in their camp.

"Thanks for your kindness," the small man said. "I am Feliks. We are new to this."

"My name's Tobias," the boy said, basking in the glow of his own helpfulness. "What does that mean, new?"

"We have been living somewhere there was food." Feliks shrugged. "The food ran out."

Tobias stared at the other man, who still gazed at nothing, only the slow movement of his chest behind his dark, travel-worn robe showing that he was something other than a statue. "What's *his* name?"

Feliks hesitated for a moment. "Eli." He said it in the southern way, the last syllable rising like a shorebird's cry – Eh-*lee*. "He was my master, but he...something happened to him. He lost his wits."

Tobias now examined the big man with unhidden interest – if he had no wits, it couldn't be rude to stare, could it? "What happened?"

"The roof fell on him." Feliks took the fish from the stick, burning his fingers so that he almost dropped it – Tobias was amused by how many things the man didn't know how to do – and then cut it into two pieces with a knife, handing the larger piece to the silent giant. Eli moved for the first time; he took the fish without looking at it, put it in his mouth, and chewed with bovine patience. Feliks began to eat the other piece, then turned shamefacedly to Tobias. "I should offer some to you, for your kindness."

Tobias was old enough to understand this would not be a small sacrifice for Feliks. "No, I'll eat at home. And I'd better go now or Father will have the strap out." He looked through the trees to the angle of the sun, which was definitely lower than he would have liked. "He'll have the strap out, anyway." The boy stood. "I'll come back tomorrow, though. I can help you catch better fish than that one." He hesitated. "Have you been to other places? Other villages, even towns?"

Feliks nodded slowly. "Many places. Many cities all over the Middle Lands."

"Cities!" Tobias swayed a little, faint-headed at the thought. "Real cities? I'll be back!"

The tall man named Eli suddenly put out his hand, a gesture so startling after his hour of near-immobility that Tobias recoiled as though from a snake.

"He...I think he wants to thank you," Feliks said. "Go ahead, boy – take his hand. He was a great man once."

Tobias slowly extended his own small hand, wondering if this might be the beginning of some cruel or even murderous trick – if he had been too trusting after all. Eli's hand was big, knob-knuckled and smudged with dirt, and it closed on the boy's slim fingers like a church door swinging closed.

Then Tobias vanished.

When two days had passed with no sign of the boy, suspicion of course fell on the two strangers living in Squire's Wood. When the man named Feliks admitted that they had seen the child and spoken to him, the shireward and several local fellows dragged them out of the forest and chained them in wooden stocks beside the well in the center of the village, where everyone could see them and marvel at their infamy. Feliks tearfully continued to insist that they had done nothing to harm the boy, that they did not know where he had gone – both things true, as it turned out – but even if the two men had not been strangers and thus naturally suspect, the villagers could see that the big one was plainly touched, perhaps even demon-possessed, and almost no one felt anything for them but horror and disgust.

The lone exception was Father Bannity, the village priest, who felt that it was a troubling thing to imprison people simply because they were strangers, although he dared not say so aloud. He himself had been a stranger to the village when he had first arrived twenty years earlier (in fact, older villagers still referred to him as "the new priest") and so he had a certain empathy for those who might find themselves judged harshly simply because their grandfathers and great-grandfathers were not buried in the local churchyard. Also, since in his middle-life he had experienced a crisis of faith, leading him to doubt many of the most famous and popular tenets of his own religion, he was doubly unwilling to assume the guilt of someone else simply because they were not part of the familiar herd. So Father Bannity took it on himself to make sure the two prisoners had enough food and water to survive. It would be a long wait for the King's Prosecutor General to arrive – his circuit covered at least a dozen villages and lasted a full cycle of the moon – and even if the two were guilty of killing the poor child and hiding his body, Father Bannity did not want them to die before this could be discovered for certain.

As the small man, Feliks, grew to trust him, he at last told Bannity what he swore was the true story of what had happened that day, that the boy had touched big Eli's hand and then disappeared like a soap bubble popping. Father Bannity was not quite certain what to think, whether this was a true mystery or only the precursor to a confession, a man easing gradually into a guilty admission as into a scalding bath, but he stuck by his resolution to treat them as innocent until they told him otherwise, or events proved the worst to have happened.

One day, as he was holding a ladle of water to Eli's dry lips, the big man suddenly looked at him almost as if seeing him for the first time, a flash of life in the dull, bestial eyes that Bannity had not seen before. Startled, the priest dropped the ladle. The big man lifted his hand as far as he could with his wrist restrained by the stocks and spread his long fingers like some strange flower blooming.

"Don't," whispered Feliks. "That's what the boy did."

Father Bannity hesitated for only a moment. Something in the big man's strange gaze, something solemn and distant but not unkind, convinced him. He reached out and allowed Eli's hand to fold around his.

For a startling moment Bannity thought he had become a fish, jerked thrashing out of the river and up into the daylight, blinded by the sun and its prismatic colors, dazzled by the burning air. Then, a half-instant later, he realized it was as though he had been out of the water for years, and now had suddenly been plunged back *into* it: everything that had withered in him suddenly sprang back to life, all the small losses of the passing days and months – color, feeling, ecstasy. The feeling was so strong, so overwhelming, that he could not even answer Feliks' worried questions as he staggered away.

Bannity *knew* again. He had forgotten what it felt like, but now he remembered, and the thunderous force of belief returning betrayed how much he had lost. God had sent him a miracle in the person of the silent giant, and with that single touch, a world which had slowly turned gray around him over the years had been kindled back into flaming life.

God was in everything again, just as He had been when Bannity had been a child, when he had been able to imagine nothing better than to serve Him.

God was alive inside him. He had experienced a miracle.

It was only when the first surge of ecstatic happiness had become a little more ordinary, if no less pleasurable, that Father Bannity realized nothing tangible had actually changed. It wasn't so much that God had shown him a miracle, a sign, it was more as if touching the giant's hand had reawakened him to the love of God he had once had, but which had slipped away from him.

It was Eli, he realized, although undoubtedly acting as God's messenger, who had given him back his love of the Lord, his belief in a living Creation, and most of all, his certainty that what *was*, was meant to be.

The silent, damaged man had given Bannity his heart's desire, even though the priest himself had not known what it was.

Grateful, renewed, the priest resolved to speak on behalf of the two prisoners when the Prosecutor General returned to the village, to tell the truth even if it meant admitting that he had, for a time, lost his own faith. Father Bannity would undoubtedly have been their only defender, except that on the day before the traveling lawspeaker rode into town, the boy named Tobias came back.

He had been, the boy told the villagers (and very gleefully too) in the town of Eader's Church, and it was just as big and wonderful as he had imagined. "They have lots of dogs!" he said, his eyes still bright with the spectacle he had seen. "And houses that go up and up! And people!" He seemed to feel that the whipping his father had just given him – on general principles, since the actual mechanics of the boy's disappearance were still a mystery – was a small price to pay for all he'd seen.

Tobias knew nothing about how he had got from the village to the far-off town – it had happened in an instant, he said, from clasping Eli's hand to finding himself in the middle of the Eader's Church marketplace – but unfortunately there had been no equally magical way of returning. It had taken him all the days since he'd been gone to walk home.

When the Prosecutor General arrived the next day, there was no longer a case for murder to be tried, although several of the villagers were talking darkly of witchcraft. The Prosecutor General, a small, round, self-important fellow with a beard on his chin as small and sharp as an arrowhead, insisted on being taken to see the two former prisoners, who had been released to their campsite in Squire's Wood, if not to their previous state of anonymity.

Holding out his rod of office, the lawspeaker approached Eli and said, "In the name of the State and its gracious Sovereign, His Majesty the King, you must tell me how you sent the boy to Eader's Church."

The big man only looked at him, unbothered. Then he extended his hand. The Prosecutor General, after a moment's hesitation, extended his own small plump hand and allowed it to be grasped.

When Father Bannity and the other men watching had finished blinking their eyes, they saw that instead of his prosecutor's tunic, the Prosecutor General was now unquestionably wearing a judge's robes, cowl, and wreath, and that a judge's huge, round, golden emblem of office now hung on a chain around his neck. (Some also suggested that he had a stronger chin as well, and more penetrating eyes than he had heretofore possessed.) The ex-Prosecutor General, now a full-fledged Adjudicator, blinked, ran his fingers over the leafy wreath on his head, then fell down on his knees and uttered a happy prayer.

"Twelve years I've waited!" he said, over and over. "Thank you, Lord! Passed over and passed over – but no more!"

He then rose, and with fitting jurisprudential gravity, proclaimed, "These men have not practiced any unlicensed witchcraft. I rule that they are true messengers of God, and should be treated with respect."

Finding that his pockets were now richer by several gold coins – the difference between his old salary and new – the new-minted Adjudicator promptly sold his cart and donkey to Pender the village blacksmith and left town in a covered carriage, with a newly hired driver and two new horses. Later rumors said that he arrived home to find he had been awarded the King's Fourteenth Judicial Circuit.

In the wake of the Prosecutor General's astonishing transformation, Squire's Wood began to fill with people from the village and even some of the surrounding villages – for news travels fast in these rural areas – turning the two men's camp into a site of pilgrimage. The size of the gathering grew so quickly that Father Bannity and some of the wood's nearer and soberer neighbors worried that the entire forest soon would be trampled flat, but the squireward could not turn the newcomers away any more than he could have held back the tide at Landsend.

Although none of this swarm of postulants was turned away, not all received their heart's desire, either – Eli's hand opened only to one in perhaps three or four and it was impossible to force the issue. One man, a jar maker named Keely, tried to pry the big man's fingers apart and shove his own hand in, and although he succeeded, nothing magical happened to him except that he developed a painful boil in the middle of his forehead the following day.

Some of the pilgrims' wishes turned out to be surprisingly small and domestic: a man whose sick cow suddenly recovered, a woman whose youngest son abruptly discovered he could hear as well as he had before the fever. Others were more predictable, like the man who after clasping Eli's hand discovered a pot of old coins buried under an ancient wall he was rebuilding.

To the astonishment of many, two blighted young folk who lived on neighboring farms, a young man with a shattered leg and a girl with a huge strawberry blotch on her face, both went to Eli, and both were gifted with a handclasp, but came out again looking just the same as they had before. But within the next few days the young man's drunkard father died of a fit, leaving him the farm, and the girl's cruel, miserly uncle who treated her like a servant fell under the wheels of a cart and died also, leaving her free to marry if anyone would have her. The two young people did indeed marry each other, and seemed quite happy, although they both still bore the disfigurements that had made them so pitiable to the rest of the village.

The only apparent failure of Eli's magical touch was Pender, the blacksmith, who went to the campsite a massive, strapping man with a beard that reached halfway down his chest, and went away again with the shape and voice and apparently all the working parts of a slender young woman. He left town the same night, trading the Prosecutor General's old cart for a pair of pretty dresses before setting off on the donkey toward the nearest city to start his life over (at least so he told his neighbors), so no one was ever able to find out exactly how such a strange thing had happened when others had been served so well.

Soon the lame youth and other grateful folk came and built a great tent in Squire's Wood for Eli and Feliks to shelter in, and began bringing them daily offerings of food and drink. People were coming to see the two strangers from all around, and even the villagers who had not obtained a supernatural gift from the silent giant came to realize how valuable his presence was: the village was full of pilgrims, including some quite well-to-do folk who were willing to pay exorbitant prices to be fed and housed near the miracle worker.

Father Bannity, still basking in the joyful light of his newly recovered faith, did not doubt that Eli and Feliks were gifts from God, but he had not lost all caution or good sense, either, and he was worried by what was happening to his quiet village. He sent a messenger describing recent events to Dondolan, the nearest accredited wizard, who had an eyrie near the top of Reaching Peak. The wizard had not passed through the village for years – but he and the priest had met several times, and Bannity liked the mage and trusted his good sense, certainly beyond that of the village elders, who were growing as greedy of pilgrimage gold as children tumbled into a treacle vat, happily eating themselves to death.

Dondolan the Clear-Eyed, as he had been named back in his Academy days, took one look at the priest's letter, then leaped out of his chair and began packing (a task which takes a wizard a much shorter time than the average traveler.) The messenger asked if there would be any reply, and Dondolan told him, "I will be there before you." Then, suiting deed to word, he promptly vanished.

He appeared again in the village at the base of the mountain, and took his horse from the livery stable there – even an accomplished wizard will not travel by magic for twenty leagues, not knowing what he will find at the other end, for it is a fierce drain on the resources – and set out. Other than an ill-considered attempt by some local bandits to waylay him just outside Drunken Princes' Pass, an interaction which increased the frog population of the highlands but did not notably slow Dondolan's progress, it was a swift journey, and he reached the nameless village within two days. Spurning more ordinary couriers, he had sent a raven ahead, and as a result Father Bannity waited at the crossroads outside of town to meet him.

When they had greeted each other – fondly, for the respect was mutual, despite their differences on the theological practicalities – Bannity led Dondolan through the fields around the outskirts of the village, so as not to cause more ruckus and rumor than was necessary: already the village practically breathed the stuff, and the pilgrims arriving daily from all over only made things more frantic.

"Do you wish to speak to the two of them?" Bannity asked. "It will be difficult, but I might persuade the village elders to let us close off the camp, although it will not be easy to remove all the addled folk who are living there now – they have practically made a new town in the middle of the forest."

"We should decide nothing until I see these miracle men," Dondolan said. "Although I must say that the description of them in your letter gave me an unpleasant feeling in the pit of my stomach."

"Why?" asked Bannity with some alarm. "Do you think they mean harm? I worried mainly that so many pilgrims would jeopardize the safety of our little town, drawing thieves and confidence tricksters and such. But surely God has sent those two to us – they have done so much good!"

"Perhaps. That is why I will restrain my conjectures until I have seen them."

They made their way through the woods, between groups of revelers singing and praying, gathered around so many campfires it seemed more like the eve of a great battle than twilight in the woods outside a quiet village too unassuming even to have its own name. As they grew close to the great pale tent and the crowd of people waiting there – some patiently, others loudly demanding that they be allowed to be next to see the wonder-workers because their need was so great – Bannity found it increasingly difficult to make headway through the throng. It was a mark of how many of these people were strangers to the area that the village's well-respected priest almost got into two fights, and only Dondolan's discreet use of a quelling-charm got them past those at the front of the line without real violence.

They slipped through the tent's flap-door. Dondolan peered across the big tent at the miraculous pair sitting like minor potentates on high-backed chairs the villagers had built them, the small man Feliks and the big man with the misshapen skull. Feliks was scratching himself and laughing at something. Eli was staring down at one of the kneeling postulants before him, his expression as emptily self-absorbed as a bullfrog waiting for a fly of sufficient size to happen past. Dondolan swallowed, then stepped back out of the tent again, and Bannity followed him. Even by torchlight, the priest could see the wizard had gone quite pale.

"It is indeed as I feared, Bannity. That is no poor traveler, innocently touched by God – or at least that is not how he began. The large man is the dark wizard Elizar the Devourer, scourge of the southern lands, and greatest enemy of the archmage Kettil of Thundering Crag."

"Elizar?" Bannity suddenly found swallowing difficult. Even a village priest knew the Devourer, who had burned whole towns because he liked the gloomy skies their smoking ruins provided, who had performed vile rites to turn men into beasts and beasts into men, and whose campaign of violent conquest had only been stopped by Kettil himself, the greatest wizard of the age, who had come down from his great ice caverns atop Thundering Crag and helped the young King defeat Elizar's vast army of slavering beast-men at the field of Herredsburn. Kettil himself had dueled Elizar before the gathered forces of both armies – the skies above Herredsburn, everyone remembered, had lit up as if with half a dozen simultaneous thunderstorms, and although neither had managed definitively to best the other, it had been Elizar who had fled the field, his plans in ruins, and who had retreated into a dark obscurity that had covered him for years – an absence that had lasted until this very moment. "*That* Elizar?" murmured Father Bannity. "*Here?*"

"I would stake my life on it," said Dondolan, "and may be doing so. Even if his mindlessness is real, just seeing someone like me that he has known might shock him back to his prior self."

"But we cannot simply...leave it. We cannot leave things this way."

"No, but I dare not go near him. His miracles, you tell me, are real, so he still wields mighty powers. Even if he stays witless, I cannot afford the chance he might decide to give *me* my heart's desire." Dondolan shook his head, his white beard wagging. "The heart of a wizard, even a relatively decent one like myself, is full of dark crevices. It is the world we inhabit, the wisdoms we study, the powers we have learned to harness, if not always to understand." He smiled, but there was not much pleasure in it. "I truthfully do not know my heart's desire, and have no urge to discover it this way."

"I'm...I'm not certain what you mean."

"What if my heart's desire is to be the greatest wizard of my age? I felt that way once, when I was young and first entering the Academy. What if that desire has not gone, only hidden?" He shook his head again. "I dare not risk it."

"But what if an ordinary mortal – someone not a wizard – has the same thing as *his* heart's desire? Or something worse, asking for the end of the world or something."

Dondolan gave the priest a shrewd, sober look. "So far, that has not happened. In fact, the power Elizar wields seems not to have harmed much of anybody, except, by your account, a pair of nasty old folk who deliberately stood in the way of their children's happiness. And even there, we cannot prove that coincidence did not carry them away. Perhaps there is something to Elizar's magic that is self-limiting – something that prevents him from granting any but mostly benign wishes. I do not know." He looked up. "I *do* know that we must discover more before we can make up our minds. We cannot, as you said, simply leave things be, not with Elizar the Devourer here, surrounded by eager supplicants, busily creating miracles, however kind-hearted those miracles may seem." Dondolan ran his fingers through his long beard. "Not to mention the evil chance that this is all some cruel trick of Elizar's – that he only shams at having lost his mind, and plots to seize the Middle Lands again." He frowned, thinking. "When do they stop for the night?"

"Soon. When my sexton rings the church bell for evening prayer."

"Wait until that bell rings, Father, then bring me the man Feliks."

The small man seemed almost relieved to have been found out. "Yes, it is true. He was once Elizar, the greatest wizard of all."

"After Kettil the archmage, you mean," said Dondolan.

Feliks waved his hand. "My master poured his soul into five thousand beastmen at Herredsburn, animating them throughout the battle. Even so, he duelled Kettil Hawkface to a standstill."

"This is neither here nor there," said Father Bannity impatiently. "Why is he the way we see him? Is this some new plot of his, some evil device?"

"Tell the truth, minion, and do not think to trick me," Dondolan said harshly. "Even now, Kettil himself must be hearing news of this. He will not take longer than I did to deduce that your Eli is in fact his old arch-enemy."

Feliks sighed. "Then we must be moving on again. Sad, that is. I was enjoying it here."

"Damn it, man, one of the most dangerous men in the world sleeps twenty paces away! Talk to us!"

"Dangerous to you, perhaps." Feliks shook his head. "No, not even to you – not now. There is no trick, wizard. What you see is the truth. The old Elizar is gone, and dumb Eli is what remains.

"It was after Herredsburn, you see, when the King and your Wizard's Council turned us away. With all his beast-men dead or changed back to their former selves, my master left the field and retreated to his secret lair in the Darkslide Mountains."

"We suspected he had a bolthole there," murmured Dondolan, "but we could never find it."

"He was determined to have his revenge on Kettil and the others," continued Feliks. "I have never seen him thus. He was furious, but also weary, weary and distraught." The small man peered at the priest and the wizard for a moment. "Once, in middle-night when I was awakened from sleep by a strange noise, I found him weeping."

"I cannot believe that," said Dondolan. "Elizar? The Devourer?"

"Believe what you will. There was always more to him than you folk on the Council understood. Whatever the case, he became fixed on the idea of securing the Amulet of Desire, which can grant its possessor whatever gift he most wants. He spent many months – a year, almost – pursuing its legend down many forgotten roads, in old books and older scrolls. He spoke to creatures so fearsome I could not even be under the same roof while they were conversing." The memory still seemed to make Feliks fearful, and yet proud of his bold master. "At last the time came. Deep in our cavern home in the Darkslide Mountains, he prepared the spells. I helped him as best I could, but I am just a servant, not a necromancer. I stoked the fires, polished the alembics, brought the articles he needed from our reliquary. At last the hour came when the spheres were in alignment, and he began the Summoning of the Empty Gods.

"He had been nights on end without sleep, in the grip of a fever that I had never seen in him before, even on the night before Herredsburn, when dominion over all the world was still at his fingertips. Pale, wide-eyed, talking to himself as though I was not even present, he was like a prisoner desperate for release, whether that release came from the opening of the prison door or from the hangman's rope."

Feliks sighed and briefly wiped his eyes while Dondolan tapped impatient fingers.

"The spell went on for hours," the small man continued, "names shouted into the darkness that hurt my ears. At one point I fled, terrified by the shadows that filled the room and danced all around me. When I came back, it was because I heard my master's hoarse cry of triumph.

"He stood in the center of his mystical diagram, holding up something I could barely see, something that gleamed red and black..."

"Something cannot gleam black," Dondolan said – a trifle querulously, Bannity thought. "It makes no sense."

"Little of what had happened that night made sense, but I will not change my tale. It gleamed red and black. Elizar held it over his head, crying out with a ragged voice, 'My greatest wish made real...!' – and then the roof collapsed."

"Collapsed?" said Bannity. "How? I thought you were in some mountain cavern."

"We were," Feliks agreed. "I still am not certain how it happened – it was like being chewed in a giant's mouth, chewed and chewed and then spit out. When I woke up, we both lay on the slope beneath the entrance to the lair, which was choked with fallen rock. Elizar was as you see him now, crushed and silent, his head all bloody, poor fellow. The Amulet was gone. Everything was gone. I helped him up and we stumbled and crawled down the hill to a cotsman's deserted shack – the owner had fled when the mountain began to shake. I shaved my master's head and doctored his wounds. We ate what supplies the cotsman had laid in, but when we ran out, we had no choice but to become wandering beggars." The small, wrinkled man spread his hands. "I can do no magic, you see."

"Was the boy in the village, the one Elizar sent to Eader's Church, the first to be...touched?"

Feliks shook his head. "My master took a few people's hands, mostly folk who gave generously to our begging bowl, and sometimes things happened. None were harmed, all profited," he added, a little defensively.

"And you," Dondolan demanded. "You must have touched his hands many times since this occurred. What of you?"

"What could happen? I already have my heart's desire. All I have ever wanted was to serve him. From the first moment I saw him outside the Academy, I knew that he was my destiny, for good or bad."

Dondolan sighed. "For bad, certainly, at least until now. You are not a true villain, Feliks, but you have served an evil man."

"All great men are thought evil by some."

"Not all great men graft the heads of wild boars onto the shoulders of peasant farmers," Dondolan pointed out. "Not all great men wear the skins of other wizards for a cloak."

"He killed only those who turned against him," said Feliks stubbornly. "Only those who would have killed him."

Dondolan stared at him for a moment. "It matters little now," he said at last. "As I said, Kettil will have heard by now, and guessed who is here. The archmage will come, and things will change."

"Then we must go," said Feliks, rising to his feet with a weary grunt. "We will move on. There are still places we can live in quiet peace, if I only help my poor master to keep his hands to himself."

"I dare not try to stop you," Dondolan said. "I fear to wake your master if he really sleeps inside that battered skull – I admit I was never his match. But even if you flee, you will not outrun Kettil's power."

It does not matter. What will be, will be, Bannity thought to himself, but a little of his newfound peace had gone with Eli's unmasking. *Whether Elizar is a man transformed or a villain disguised, surely what happens next will be as God wills, too. For who can doubt His hand when He has shown us so many miracles here?*

But Eli would not leave the wood, despite Feliks' urging. The mute man was as resistant as a boulder set deep in mud: none of his servant's pleas or arguments touched him – in fact, he showed no sign of even hearing them.

Dondolan and Bannity, armed with the knowledge of the miracle worker's true identity convinced the suddenly terrified village elders that for a while at least, the crowds should be kept away. With a contingent of solders from the nearest shirepost, hired with a fraction of the profits from the long miracle-season, they cleared the forest of all the supplicants, forcing them out into the town and surrounding fields, where local sellers of charms and potions gleefully provided them with substitute satisfaction, or at least the promise of it.

Even as the last of the camps were emptied, some of the latest arrivals from beyond the village brought news that Kettil Hawkface himself was on the way. Some had seen nothing more than a great storm swirling around Thundering Crag while the sky elsewhere was blue and bright, but others claimed to have seen the archmage himself speeding down the mountain on a huge white horse, shining as he came like a bolt of lightning. In any case, those who had been turned away from Squire's Wood now had something else to anticipate, and the great road that passed by the nameless village was soon lined with those waiting to see the most famous, most celebrated wizard of all.

Father Bannity could not help wondering whether Elizar sensed anything of his great rival's coming, and so he walked into Squire's Wood and across the trampled site of the camp, empty now but for a couple of hired soldiers standing guard.

Inside the tent wrinkled little Feliks looked up from eating a bowl of stew and waved to Bannity as if they were old friends, but Elizar was as empty-faced as ever, and seemed not to notice that the crowds of pilgrims were gone, that he and Feliks were alone. He sat staring at the ground, his big hands opening and closing so slowly that Father Bannity could have counted a score of his own suddenly intrusive heartbeats between fist and spread fingers. The man's naked face and shaved scalp made the head atop the black robe seem almost like an egg, out of which anything might hatch.

Why did I come here? he asked himself. *To taunt the blackest magician of the age?* But he felt he had to ask.

"Are you truly gone from in there, Elizar?" The priest's voice trembled, and he prayed to God for strength. He now realized, in a way he had not before, that here sat a man who of such power that he had destroyed whole cities the way an ordinary man might kick down an ant-hill. But Bannity had to ask. "Are you truly and completely empty, or is there a spark of you left in that husk, listening?" He had a sudden thought. "Did you bring this on yourself, with your magical amulet? When the time came for your heart's desire to be granted, did God hear a small, hidden part of you that was weary of death and torment and dark hatreds, that wanted to perform the Lord's work for your fellow men instead of bringing them blood and fire and terror?"

Eli did not look up or change expression, and at last Father Bannity went out. Feliks watched him go with a puzzled expression, then returned to his meal.

He came down the main road with crowds cheering behind him as though he were a conquering hero – which, after all, he was. Bannity watched the people shouting and calling Kettil's name as the wizard rode toward the village on his huge white horse, the same people who only days before had been crouched in the dirt outside Eli's tent, begging to be let in, and the priest wondered at God's mysterious ways.

Kettil Hawkface was younger than Bannity would have guessed, or else had spelled himself to appear so. He seemed a man in the middle of life, his golden hair only touched with gray, his bony, handsome face still firm in every line. His eyes were the most impressive thing about him: even from a distance, they glittered an icy blue, and up close it was difficult to look at him directly, such was the chilly power of his gaze.

Bannity and Dondolan met the archmage at the edge of the wood. Kettil nodded at his fellow wizard, but hardly seemed to see the priest at all, even after Dondolan introduced him.

"He is in there..." Dondolan began, but Kettil raised his hand and the lesser mage fell silent.

"I know where he is." He had a voice to match his eyes, frosty and authoritative. "And I know what he is. I have battled his evil for half my long life. I do not need to be told where to find him – I smell him as a hound smells his quarry."

Strange, then, that you did not find him before, thought Bannity, then regretted his own small-minded carping. "But he is not the monster you knew, Archmage..."

Kettil looked at him then, but only a moment, then turned away. "Such creatures do not change," he said to Dondolan.

Bannity tried again. "He has done much good...!"

Kettil smirked. "Has he revived all those he killed? Rebuilt the cities he burned? Do not speak to me of things you do not understand, priest." He slid down off his massive white horse. "I will go, and we will see what devilry awaits."

Bannity had to admit the archmage was as impressive as legend had promised. He strode into the forest with no weapon but his staff of gnarled birch, his long hair blowing, his sky-blue robes billowing as though he still stood on the heights of Thundering Crag. Bannity looked at Dondolan, whose face bore a carefully composed expression that betrayed nothing of what he was thinking, then they both followed the Archmage Kettil into Squire's Wood.

To Bannity's astonishment, Eli himself stood in the doorway of the tent, looking out across the great clearing.

"Ho, Devourer!" Kettil's voice echoed, loud as a hunting horn, but Eli only looked at him incuriously, his large hands dangling from his sleeves like roosting bats. "I have found you again at last!"

The hairless man blinked, turned, and went back into the tent. Kettil strode after him, crossing the clearing in a few long paces. Bannity started to follow, but Dondolan grabbed his arm and held him back.

"This is beyond me and beyond you, too."

"Nothing is beyond God!" Bannity cried, but Dondolan the Clear-Eyed looked doubtful. A few moments later little Feliks came stumbling out of the tent, flapping his hands as if surrounded by angry bees.

"They stand face to face!" he squawked, then tripped and fell, rolling until he stopped at Bannity's feet. The priest helped him up, but did not take his eyes off the tent. "They do not speak, but stare at each other. The air is so thick!"

"It seems..." Dondolan began, but never finished, for at that instant the entire clearing – in fact, all the woods and the sky above – seemed to suck in a great breath. A sudden, agonizing pain in Bannity's ears dropped him to his knees, then everything suddenly seemed to flow sideways – light, color, heat, air, everything rushing out across the face of the earth in all directions, pushing the priest flat against the ground and rolling him over several times.

When the monstrous wind died, Bannity lay for a long, stunned instant, marveling at the infinite skills of God, who could create the entire universe and now, just as clearly, was going to dismantle it again. Then a great belch of flame and a roar of rushing air made him roll over onto his knees and, against all good sense, struggle to sit up so he could see what was happening.

The tent was engulfed in flame, the trees all around singed a leafless black. As Father Bannity stared, two figures staggered out of the inferno as though solidifying out of smoke, one like a pillar of cold blue light, with flame dancing in his pale hair and beard, the other a growing, rising shadow of swirling black.

"I knew you but pretended, demon!" shouted Kettil Hawkface, waving his hands in the air, flashes of light crackling up from his fingertips. "Devourer! I know your treachery of old!"

The shadow, which had begun to fold down over the archmage like a burning blanket, instead billowed up and away, hovering in the air just above Kettil's head. A face could be seen in its roiling, cloudy midst, and Bannity could not help marveling even in his bewildered horror how it looked both like and unlike the silent Eli.

"I will make sure your dying lasts for centuries, Hawkface!" shrieked the dark shape in a voice that seemed to echo all the way to the distant hills, then it rose up into the air, flapping like an enormous bat made of smoke and sparks, and flew away into the south.

"Master!" screamed Feliks, and stumbled off through the woods, following the fast-diminishing blot of fiery blackness until he, too, disappeared from sight.

Kettil Hawkface, his pale robes smeared with ash, his whiskers and hair singed at the edges, strode away in the other direction, walking back toward the village with the purposeful stride of someone who has completed a dangerous and thankless job and does not bother to wait for the approbation he surely deserves.

As he emerged at the forest's edge, he stood before the hundreds of onlookers gathered there and raised his hands. "Elizar the Devourer's evil has been discovered and ended, and he has flown in defeat back to the benighted south," the archmage cried. "You people of the Middle Lands may rest safely again, knowing that the Devourer's foul plan has been thwarted."

The crowd cheered, but many were confused about what had happened and the reception of his news was not as whole-hearted as Kettil had perhaps expected. He did not wait to speak again to his colleague Dondolan, but climbed onto his white horse and galloped away north toward Thundering Crag, followed by a crowd of children crying out after him for pennies and miracles.

Bannity and Dondolan watched in silence as the ramrod-straight figure grew smaller, and then eventually disappeared. The crowds did not immediately disperse, but many seemed to realize there would be little reason to collect here anymore, and the cries of the food sellers, charm hawkers, and roving apothecaries became muted and mournful.

"So all is resolved for good," Father Bannity said, half to himself. "Elizar's evil was discovered and thwarted."

"Perhaps," said Dondolan. "But a part of me cannot help wondering whose heart's desire was granted here today."

"What do you mean? Do you think...they clasped hands?"

Dondolan sighed. "Do not misunderstand me. It is entirely possible that the world has been spared a great evil here today – Elizar was always full of plots, many of them astoundingly subtle. But if they *did* touch hands, I think it is safe to say that only one of them was granted his heart's desire."

"I don't understand."

"Elizar may not have seemed entirely happy as Eli the dumb miracle-worker," Dondolan said, "but he did seem peaceful. Now, though, he is the Devourer again, and Kettil once more has an enemy worthy of his own great pride and power."

Bannity was silent for a long time, watching the sky darken as the sun settled behind Squire's Wood. "But surely God would not let Elizar's evil back into the world simply because his enemy missed it – God must have a better plan for mankind than that!"

"Perhaps," said Dondolan the Clear-Eyed. "Perhaps. We will think on it together after we return to the church and you find the brandy you keep hidden for such occasions."

Father Bannity nodded and took a few steps, then turned. "How did you know about the brandy?"

The priest thought Dondolan's smile seemed a trifle sour. "I am a wizard, remember? We know almost everything."

Soul Case

Nalo Hopkinson

Nalo Hopkinson (*nalohopkinson.com*) lives in Toronto, Canada. In an interview a few years ago with Gavin Grant, she explained, "I am a writer living in Toronto; I've lived there for the past, oh, twenty-four years now. I went to Canada from the Caribbean. I was born in Jamaica to Jamaican and Guyanese parents and lived in Jamaica, Trinidad, and Guyana." She is the daughter of poet and playwright Slade Hopkinson. She began publishing her fiction in 1996 and in 2007 published her fourth novel, *The New Moon's Arm*. A collection of her short fiction, *Skin Folk*, appeared in 2001. She has also edited three anthologies, most recently *So Long Been Dreaming: Postcolonial Science Fiction & Fantasy* (2004) with Uppinder Mehan.

"Soul Case" appeared in *Foundation* 100, the special fiction issue (and hundredth issue) of the British SF Foundation's journal. In this story of the magical defense of a village attacked, old-fashioned magic works slowly, like old-fashioned slow cooking.

MOMENTS AFTER the sun's bottom lip cleared the horizon, the brigade charged down the hill. Kima stood with the rest of the maroons, ready to give back blow for blow.

The pistoleers descended towards the waiting village compong. Their silence unnerved. Only the paddy thump of the camels' wide feet made any sound. Compong people murmured, stepped back. But Mother Letty gestured to them to the maroons defending them to stand still. So they did. Kima felt her palm slippery on her sharpened hoe.

The pistoleers advanced upon them in five rows; some tens of impeccably uniformed men and women posting up and down in unison on their camels. Each row but the last comprised seven gangly camels, each camel ridden by a soldier, each soldier kitted out a la zouave, in identical and pristine red-and-navy with clean white shirts. Near on four muskets for each of them, and powder, carried by a small boy running beside each camel. There were only twelve muskets in the compong.

Now the first rows of camels stepped onto the pitch road that led into the village. The road was easily wide enough for seven camels across. The cool morning sun had not yet made the surface of the pitch sticky. The camels didn't even break stride. Kima made a noise of dismay. Where was the strong science that the three witches had promised them? Weeks and weeks they'd had them cart-ing reeking black pitch from the deep sink of it that lay in the gully, re-warming it on fires, mixing it with stones and spreading it into this road that led from nowhere to the entrance of the compong, and stopped abruptly there. Had they done nothing but create a smooth paved surface by which the army could enter and destroy them?

From her position at the head of the cimarrons, the black witch, the Obe Acotiren, showed no doubt. She only pursed her lips and grunted, once. Standing beside her, white Mother Letty and the Taino witch Maridowa did not even do that. The three should have been behind the cimarrons, where they could be protected. If the villagers lost their Knowledgeables, they would be at the mercy of the whites' fish magic. Yet there the three stood and watched. Acotiren even had her grandson cotched on her hip. So the cimarrons took their cue from the three women. Like them, they kept their ground, ready but still.

"Twice five," whispered Mother Letty. "Twice six." She was counting the soldiers as they stepped onto the black road. Kima thought it little comfort to know exactly how many soldiers had come to kill them, but she found herself counting silently along with Mother Letty.

The leading edge of the army was almost upon them, scant yards from the entrance to the compong. Camels covered almost the full length of the road. A few of the cimarrons made ready to charge. "Hold," said Mother Letty. Her voice cut through the pounding of the camels. They held.

Maridowa turned her wide, brown face to the maroons and grinned. "Just a little more," she said. She was merry at strange times, the young Taino witch was.

The soldiers had their muskets at the ready. The barrels gleamed in the sun. The cimarrons' muskets were dull and scorched. "So many of them," whispered Kima. She raised her hoe, cocked it ready to strike. Beside her, the white boy Carter whimpered, but clutched his cutlass at the ready, a grim look on his face. He'd said he would rather die than be press-ganged onto the ships once more as a sailor. He had fourteen years. If he survived this, the village would let him join the boys to be circumcised; let him become a man.

Thrice six...

The thrice seventh haughty camel stepped smartly onto the battlefield, a little ahead of its fellows. "That will do it," pronounced the Obe Acotiren. It wasn't quite a question.

The pitch went liquid. Camels began to flounder, then to sink. The villagers gasped, talked excitedly to each other. They had laid the pitch only four fingers deep! How then was it swallowing entire camels and riders?

The pitch swamp had not a care for what was possible and what not. It sucked the brigade into its greedy gullet like a pig gobbling slops. Camels mawed in dismay, the pitch snapping their narrow ankles as they tried to clamber out. They sank more quickly than their lighter riders. Soldier men and women clawed at each other, stepped on each others' heads and shoulders to fight free of the melted pitch. To no avail. The last hoarse scream was swallowed by the pitch in scarce the time it took the Obe Acotiren's fifth grandchild – the fat brown boy just past his toddling age, his older sisters and brothers having long since joined the cimarron fighters – to slip from her arms and go running for his favourite mango tree.

The black face of the road of tar was smooth and flat again, as though the army had never been.

One meager row of uniformed soldiers stared back at the cimarrons from the other side of the pitch. Their weapons hung unused from their hands. Then, together, they slapped their camels into a turn, and galloped hard for the foot of the hill.

All but one, who remained a-camelback at the bank of the river of pitch.

The pistoleer slid off her beast. She stood on the edge of where her fellows, suffocated, were slowly hardening. She bent her knees slightly, curling her upper body around her belly. Fists held out in front of her, she screamed full throat at the villagers; a raw howl of grief that used all the air in her lungs, and that went on long after she should have had none remaining. She seemed like to spit those very lungs up. Her camel watched her disinterestedly for a while, then began to wander up the hill. It stopped to crop yellow hog plums from a scraggly tree.

On the hill above, the general sounded the retreat. In vain; most of his army had already dispersed. (Over the next few weeks, many of them would straggle into cimarron compongs – some with their camels – begging asylum. This they would be granted. It was a good land, but mostly harsh scrub. It needed many to tend it.)

Some few of the cimarrons probed the pitch with their weapons. They did not penetrate. Cautiously, the cimarrons stepped onto the pitch. It was hard once more, and held them easily. They began to dance and laugh, to call for their children and their families to join them. Soon there was a celebration on the flat pitch road. An old matron tried to show Carter the steps of her dance. He did his best to follow her, laughing at his own clumsiness.

The Obe Acotiren watched the soldier woman, who had collapsed onto her knees now, her scream hiccoughing into sobs. While the army was becoming tar beneath the feet of the villagers, Acotiren had pushed through the crowd and fetched her fearless grandchild from the first branch of the mango tree. He'd fallen out of it thrice before, but every day returned to try again. She hitched him up onto her hip. He clamped his legs at her waist and fisted up a handful of her garment at the shoulder. He brought the fist happily to his mouth.

Acotiren's face bore a calm, stern sadness. "Never you mind," Kima heard her mutter in the direction of the grieving woman. "What we do today going to come back on us, and more besides." Maridowa glanced at the Obe, but said nothing.

Then Acotiren produced her obi bag from wherever she had had it hidden on her person, and tossed it onto the pitch. Mother Letty started forward. "Tiren, no!" cried Mother Letty, her face anguished.

She was too late to intercept the obi bag. It landed on the road. It was a small thing, no bigger than a guinea fowl's egg. It should have simply bounced and rolled. Instead, it sank instantly, as though it weighed as much in itself as the whole tarred army together.

Maridowa was dancing on the road, and hadn't noticed what was happening. It was Kima who saw it all. Acotiren pressed her lips together, then smiled a bright smile at her grandchild. "Come," she said. "Make I show you how to climb a mango tree."

Tranquil, as though she hadn't just tossed her soulcase away to be embalmed forever in tar, she turned her back to go and play with the boy, leaving Mother Letty kneeling there, tears coursing through the lines on her ancient face as she watched her friend go.

In less than a year Acotiren was frail and bent. There was no more climbing trees for her. Her eyes had grown crystalline with cataracts, her hands tremulous, her body sere and unmuscled. One morning she walked into the bush to die, and never came out again. But by then her daughter's child, Acotiren's fifth grandchild, was so sure-footed from skinning up gru-gru bef palms and mamapom trees with his nana, that he never, ever fell. Wherever he could plant his feet, he could go. His friends called him Goat.

Sir Hereward and Mister Fitz Go to War Again

Garth Nix

Garth Nix (*garthnix.com*) lives in Clovelly near Sydney, Australia and works for Creative Enclave, an online games company of which he is co-founder. He is also an Executive Producer for Cartwheel Partners, an independent film company. He has worked extensively in publishing and in public relations. He is a bestselling fantasy writer whose books have sold more than 4.5 million copies. His most recent book is the latest installment in his successful Keys to the Kingdom fantasy series (*www.keystothekingdom.com.au*), *Lady Friday*.

"Sir Hereward and Mister Fitz Go to War Again" was published in *Jim Baen's Universe*, online, and this is perhaps its first appearance in print. It is a full-scale complex fantasy adventure set in a detailed fantasy world in which every city has a godlike entity at its heart. Sir Hereward is a mercenary soldier and his companion, Mister Fitz, is a magical self-aware puppet, deadly and witty. They are on a quest. This is classic sword & sorcery in the great tradition of Fritz Leiber.

"Do you ever wonder about the nature of the world, Mister Fitz?" asked the foremost of the two riders, raising the three-barred visor of his helmet so that his words might more clearly cross the several feet of space that separated him from his companion, who rode not quite at his side.

"I take it much as it presents itself, for good or ill, Sir Hereward," replied Mister Fitz. He had no need to raise a visor, for he wore a tall lacquered hat rather than a helmet. It had once been taller and had come to a peak, before encountering something sharp in the last battle but two the pair had found themselves engaged in. This did not particularly bother Mister Fitz, for he was not human. He was a wooden puppet given the semblance of life by an ancient sorcery. By dint of propinquity, over many centuries a considerable essence of humanity had been absorbed into his fine-grained body, but attention to his own appearance or indeed vanity of any sort was still not part of his persona.

Sir Hereward, for the other part, had a good measure of vanity and in fact the raising of the three-barred visor of his helmet almost certainly had more to do with an approaching apple seller of comely appearance than it did with a desire for clear communication to Mister Fitz.

The duo were riding south on a road that had once been paved and gloried in the name of the Southwest Toll Extension of the Lesser Trunk. But its heyday was long ago, the road being even older than Mister Fitz. Few paved stretches remained, but the tightly compacted understructure still provided a better surface than the rough soil of the fields to either side.

The political identification of these fallow pastures and the occasional once-coppiced wood they passed was not clear to either Sir Hereward or Mister Fitz, despite several attempts to ascertain said identification from the few travelers they had encountered since leaving the city of Rhool several days before. To all intents and purposes, the land appeared to be both uninhabited and untroubled by soldiery or tax collectors and was thus a void in the sociopolitical map that Hereward held uneasily, and Fitz exactly, in their respective heads.

A quick exchange with the apple seller provided only a little further information, and also lessened Hereward's hope of some minor flirtation, for her physical beauty was sullied by a surly and depressive manner. In a voice as sullen as a three-day drizzle, the woman told them she was taking the apples to a large house that lay out of sight beyond the nearer overgrown wood. She had come from a town called Lettique or Letiki that was located beyond the lumpy ridge of blackish shale that they could see a mile or so to the south. The apples in question had come from farther south still, and were not in keeping with their carrier, being particularly fine examples of a variety Mister Fitz correctly identified as emerald brights. There was no call for local apples, the young woman reluctantly explained. The fruit and vegetables from the distant oasis of Shûme were always preferred, if they could be obtained. Which, for the right price, they nearly always could be, regardless of season.

Hereward and Fitz rode in silence for a few minutes after parting company with the apple seller, the young knight looking back not once but twice as if he could not believe that such a vision of loveliness could house such an unfriendly soul. Finding that the young woman did not bother to look back at all, Hereward cleared his throat and, without raising his visor, spoke.

"It appears we are on the right road, though she spoke of Shumey and not Shome."

Fitz looked up at the sky, where the sun was beginning to lose its distinct shape and ooze red into the shabby grey clouds that covered the horizon.

"A minor variation in pronunciation," he said. "Should we stop in Lettique for the night, or ride on?"

"Stop," said Hereward. "My rear is not polished sandalwood, and it needs soaking in a very hot bath enhanced with several soothing essences...ah...that was one of your leading questions, wasn't it?"

"The newspaper in Rhool spoke of an alliance against Shûme," said Mister Fitz carefully, in a manner that confirmed Hereward's suspicion that didactic discourse had already begun. "It is likely that Lettique will be one of the towns arrayed against Shûme. Should the townsfolk discover we ride to Shûme in hope of employment, we might find ourselves wishing for the quiet of the fields in the night, the lack of mattresses, ale and roasted capons there notwithstanding."

"Bah!" exclaimed Hereward, whose youth and temperament made him tend toward careless optimism. "Why should they suspect us of seeking to sign on with the burghers of Shûme?"

Mister Fitz's pumpkin-sized papier-mâché head rotated on his spindly neck, and the blobs of blue paint that marked the pupils of his eyes looked up and down, taking in Sir Hereward from toe to head: from his gilt-spurred boots to his gold-chased helmet. In between boots and helm were Hereward's second-best buff coat, the sleeves still embroidered with the complicated silver tracery that proclaimed him as the Master Artillerist of the city of Jeminero. Not that said city was any longer in existence, as for the past three years it had been no more than a mass grave sealed with the rubble of its once-famous walls. Around the coat was a frayed but still quite golden sash, over that a rare and expensive Carnithian leather baldric and belt with two beautifully ornamented (but no less functional for that) wheel-lock pistols thrust through said belt. Hereward's longer-barreled and only slightly less ornamented cavalry pistols were holstered on either side of his saddle horn, his saber with its sharkskin grip and gleaming hilt of gilt brass hung in its scabbard from the rear left quarter of his saddle, and his sighting telescope was secured inside its leather case on the right rear quarter.

Mister Fitz's mount, of course, carried all the more mundane items required by their travels. All three feet six and a half inches of him (four-foot-three with the hat) was perched upon a yoke across his mount's back that secured the two large panniers that were needed to transport tent and bedding, washing and shaving gear and a large assortment of outdoor kitchen utensils. Not to mention the small but surprisingly expandable sewing desk that contained the tools and devices of Mister Fitz's own peculiar art.

"Shûme is a city, and rich," said Fitz patiently. "The surrounding settlements are mere towns, both smaller and poorer, who are reportedly planning to go to war against their wealthy neighbor. You are obviously a soldier for hire, and a self-evidently expensive one at that. Therefore, you must be en route to Shûme."

Hereward did not answer immediately, as was his way, while he worked at overcoming his resentment at being told what to do. He worked at it because Mister Fitz had been telling him what to do since he was four years old and also because he knew that, as usual, Fitz was right. It would be foolish to stop in Lettique.

"I suppose that they might even attempt to hire us," he said, as they topped the low ridge, shale crunching under their mounts' talons.

Hereward looked down at a wasted valley of underperforming pastures filled either with sickly-looking crops or passive groups of too-thin cattle. A town – presumably Lettique – lay at the other end of the valley. It was not an impressive ville, being a collection of perhaps three or four hundred mostly timber and painted-plaster houses within the bounds of a broken-down wall to the west and a dry ravine, that might have once held a river, to the east. An imposing, dozen-spired temple in the middle of the town was the only indication that at some time Lettique had seen more provident days.

"Do you wish to take employment in a poor town?" asked Mister Fitz. One of his responsibilities was to advise and positively influence Hereward, but he did not make decisions for him.

"No, I don't think so," replied the knight slowly. "Though it does make me recall my thought...the one that was with me before we were interrupted by that dismal apple seller."

"You asked if I ever wondered at the nature of the world," prompted Fitz.

"I think what I actually intended to say," said Hereward," is 'do you ever wonder why we become involved in events that are rather more than less of importance to rather more than less people?' as in the various significant battles, sieges, and so forth in which we have played no small part. I fully comprehend that in some cases the events have stemmed from the peculiar responsibilities we shoulder, but not in all cases. And that being so, and given my desire for a period of quiet, perhaps I should consider taking service with some poor town."

"Do you really desire a period of quiet?" asked Mister Fitz.

"Sometimes I think so. I should certainly like a time where I might reflect upon what it is I do want. It would also be rather pleasant to meet women who are not witch-agents, fellow officers or enemies – or who have been pressed into service as powder monkeys or are soaked in blood from tending the wounded."

"Perhaps Shûme will offer some relative calm," said Mister Fitz. "By all accounts it is a fine city, and even if war is in the offing, it could be soon finished if Shûme's opponents are of a standard that I can see in Lettique."

"You observe troops?" asked Hereward. He drew his telescope, and carefully leaning on his mount's neck to avoid discomfort from the bony ridges (which even though regularly filed-down and fitted with leather stocks were not to be ignored), looked through it at the town. "Ah, I see. Sixty pike and two dozen musketeers in the square by the temple, of no uniform equipment or harness. Under the instruction of a portly individual in a wine-dark tunic who appears as uncertain as his troops as to the drill."

"I doubt that Shûme has much to fear," said Mister Fitz. "It is odd, however, that a town like Lettique would dare to strike against such a powerful neighbor. I wonder..."

"What?" asked Hereward as he replaced his telescope.

"I wonder if it is a matter of necessity. The river is dry. The wheat is very thin, too thin this close to harvest. The cattle show very little flesh on their ribs. I see no sign of any other economic activity. Fear and desperation may be driving this mooted war, not greed or rivalry. Also..."

Mister Fitz's long, pale blue tongue darted out to taste the air, the ruby stud in the middle of what had once been a length of stippled leather catching the pallid sunlight.

"Their godlet is either asleep or...mmm...comatose in this dimension. Very strange."

"Their god is dead?"

"Not dead," said Mister Fitz. "When an other-dimensional entity dies, another always moves in quickly enough. No...definitely present, but quiescent."

"Do you wish to make a closer inquiry?"

Hereward had not missed the puppet's hand tapping the pannier that contained his sewing desk, an instinctive movement Mister Fitz made when contemplating sorcerous action.

"Not for the present," said Mister Fitz, lifting his hand to grasp once again his mount's steering chains.

"Then we will skirt the town and continue," announced Hereward. "We'll leave the road near those three dead trees."

"There are many trees that might be fairly described as dead or dying," remarked Fitz. "And several in clumps of three. Do you mean the somewhat orange-barked trio over yonder?"

"I do," said Hereward.

They left the road at the clump of trees and rode in silence through the dry fields, most of which were not even under attempted cultivation. There were also several derelict farmhouses, barns, and cattle yards, the level of decay suggesting that the land had been abandoned only in recent years.

Halfway along the valley, where the land rose to a slight hill that might have its origin in a vast and ancient burial mound, Hereward reined in his mount and looked back at the town through his telescope.

"Still drilling," he remarked. "I had half thought that they might dispatch some cavalry to bicker with us. But I see no mounts."

"I doubt they can afford the meat for battlemounts," said Mister Fitz. "Or grain for horses, for that matter."

"There is an air gate in the northeastern temple spire," said Hereward, rebalancing his telescope to get a steadier view. "There might be a moonshade roost behind it."

"If their god is absent, none of the ancient weapons will serve them," said Mister Fitz. "But it would be best to be careful, come nightfall. Lettique is reportedly not the only town arrayed against Shûme. The others may be in a more vigorous condition, with wakeful gods."

Hereward replaced his telescope and turned his mount to the north, Mister Fitz following his lead. They did not speak further, but rode on, mostly at the steady pace that Hereward's Zowithian riding instructor had called "the lope," occasionally urging their mounts to the faster "jag." In this fashion, several miles passed quickly. As the sun's last third began to slip beneath the horizon, they got back on the old road again, to climb out of the wasted valley of Lettique and across yet another of the shale ridges that erupted out of the land like powder-pitted keloid scars, all grey and humped.

The valley that lay beyond the second ridge was entirely different from the faded fields behind the two travelers. In the warm twilight, they saw a checkerboard of green and gold, full fields of wheat interspersed with meadows heavily stocked with fat cattle. A broad river wound through from the east, spilling its banks in several places into fecund wetlands that were rich with waterfowl. Several small hillocks in the valley were covered in apple trees, dark foliage heavily flecked with the bright green of vast quantities of emerald fruit. There were citrus groves too, stone-walled clumps of smaller trees laden with lemons or limes, and only a hundred yards away, a group of six trees bearing the rare and exquisite blue-skinned fruit known as *serqa* which was normally only found in drier climes.

"A most pleasant vista," said Hereward. A small smile curled his lip and touched his eyes, the expression of a man who sees something that he likes.

Shûme itself was a mile away, built on a rise in the ground in the northwestern corner of the valley, where the river spread into a broad lake that lapped the city's western walls. From the number of deep-laden boats that were even now rowing home to the jetties that thronged the shore, the lake was as well stocked with fish as the valley was with livestock and produce.

Most of the city's buildings were built of an attractively pale yellow stone, with far fewer timber constructions than was usual for a place that Hereward reckoned must hold at least five thousand citizens.

Shûme was also walled in the same pale stone, but of greater interest to Hereward were the more recent earthworks that had been thrown up in front of the old wall. A zigzag line of revetments encircled the city, with respectably large bastions at each end on the lakeshore. A cursory telescopic examination showed several bronze demicannon on the bastions and various lesser pieces of ordnance clustered in groups at various strong points along the earthworks. Both bastions had small groups of soldiery in attendance on the cannon, and there were pairs of sentries every twenty or thirty yards along the earthen ramparts and a score or more walked the stone walls behind.

"There is certainly a professional in charge here," observed Hereward. "I expect...yes...a cavalry piquet issues from yonder orchard. Twelve horse troopers under the notional command of a whey-faced cornet."

"Not commonplace troopers," added Mister Fitz. "Dercian keplars."

"Ah," said Hereward. He replaced his telescope, leaned back a little and across and, using his left hand, loosened his saber so that an inch of blade projected from the scabbard. "They are in employment, so they should give us the benefit of truce."

"They should," conceded Mister Fitz, but he reached inside his robe to grasp some small item concealed under the cloth. With his other hand he touched the brim of his hat, releasing a finely woven veil that covered his face. To casual inspection he now looked like a shrouded child, wearing peculiar papery gloves. Self-motivated puppets were not great objects of fear in most quarters of the world. They had once been numerous, and some few score still walked the earth, almost all of them entertainers, some of them long remembered in song and story.

Mister Fitz was not one of those entertainers.

"If it comes to it, spare the cornet," said Hereward, who remembered well what it was like to be a very junior officer, whey-faced or not.

Mister Fitz did not answer. Hereward knew as well as he that if it came to fighting, and the arts the puppet employed, there would be no choosing who among those who opposed them lived or died.

The troop rode toward the duo at a canter, slowing to a walk as they drew nearer and their horses began to balk as they scented the battlemounts. Hereward raised his hand in greeting and the cornet shouted a command, the column extending to a line, then halting within an easy pistol shot. Hereward watched the troop sergeant, who rode forward beyond the line for a better look, then wheeled back at speed toward the cornet. If the Dercians were to break their oath, the sergeant would fell her officer first.

But the sergeant halted without drawing a weapon and spoke to the cornet quietly. Hereward felt a slight easing of his own breath, though he showed no outward sign of it and did not relax. Nor did Mister Fitz withdraw his hand from under his robes. Hereward knew that his companion's molded papier-mâché fingers held an esoteric needle, a sliver of some arcane stuff that no human hand could grasp with impunity.

The cornet listened and spoke quite sharply to the sergeant, turning his horse around so that he could make his point forcefully to the troopers as well. Hereward only caught some of the words, but it seemed that despite his youth, the officer was rather more commanding than he had expected, reminding the Dercians that their oaths of employment overrode any private or societal vendettas they might wish to undertake.

When he had finished, the cornet shouted, "Dismount! Sergeant, walk the horses!"

The officer remained mounted, wheeling back to approach Hereward. He saluted as he reined in a cautious distance from the battlemounts, evidently not trusting either the creatures' blinkers and mouth-cages or his own horse's fears.

"Welcome to Shûme!" he called. "I am Cornet Misolu. May I ask your names and direction, if you please?"

"I am Sir Hereward of the High Pale, artillerist for hire."

"And I am Fitz, also of the High Pale, aide de camp to Sir Hereward."

"Welcome...uh...sirs," said Misolu. "Be warned that war has been declared upon Shûme, and all who pass through must declare their allegiances and enter certain...um..."

"I believe the usual term is 'undertakings,'" said Mister Fitz.

"Undertakings," echoed Misolu. He was very young. Two bright spots of embarrassment burned high on his cheekbones, just visible under the four bars of his lobster-tailed helmet, which was a little too large for him, even with the extra padding, some of which had come a little undone around the brow.

"We are free lances, and seek hire in Shûme, Cornet Misolu," said Hereward. "We will give the common undertakings if your city chooses to contract us. For the moment, we swear to hold our peace, reserving the right to defend ourselves should we be attacked."

"Your word is accepted, Sir Hereward, and...um..."

"Mister Fitz," said Hereward, as the puppet said merely, "Fitz."

"Mister Fitz."

The cornet chivvied his horse diagonally closer to Hereward, and added, "You may rest assured that my Dercians will remain true to their word, though Sergeant Xikoliz spoke of some feud their...er...entire people have with you."

The curiosity in the cornet's voice could not be easily denied, and spoke as much of the remoteness of Shûme as it did of the young officer's naïveté.

"It is a matter arising from a campaign several years past," said Hereward. "Mister Fitz and I were serving the Heriat of Jhaqa, who sought to redirect the Dercian spring migration elsewhere than through her own prime farmlands. In the last battle of that campaign, a small force penetrated to the Dercians' rolling temple and...ah...blew it up with a specially made petard. Their godlet, thus discommoded, withdrew to its winter housing in the Dercian steppe, wreaking great destruction among its chosen people as it went."

"I perceive you commanded that force, sir?"

Hereward shook his head.

"No, I am an artillerist. Captain Kasvik commanded. He was slain as we retreated – another few minutes and he would have won clear. However, I did make the petard, and...Mister Fitz assisted our entry to the temple and our escape. Hence the Dercians' feud."

Hereward looked sternly at Mister Fitz as he spoke, hoping to make it clear that this was not a time for the puppet to exhibit his tendency for exactitude and truthfulness. Captain Kasvik had in fact been killed before they even reached the rolling temple, but it had served his widow and family better for Kasvik to be a hero, so Hereward had made him one. Only Mister Fitz and one other survivor of the raid knew otherwise.

Not that Hereward and Fitz considered the rolling temple action a victory, as their intent had been to force the Dercian godlet to withdraw a distance unimaginably more vast than the mere five hundred leagues to its winter temple.

The ride to the city was uneventful, though Hereward could not help but notice that Cornet Misolu ordered his troop to remain in place and keep watch, while he alone escorted the visitors, indicating that the young officer was not absolutely certain the Dercians would hold to their vows.

There was a zigzag entry through the earthwork ramparts, where they were held up for several minutes in the business of passwords and responses (all told aside in quiet voices, Hereward noted with approval), their names being recorded in an enormous ledger and passes written out and sealed allowing them to enter the city proper.

These same passes were inspected closely under lanternlight, only twenty yards farther on by the guards outside the city gate – which was closed, as the sun had finally set. However, they were admitted through a sally port and here Misolu took his leave, after giving directions to an inn that met Hereward's requirements: suitable stabling and food for the battlemounts; that it not be the favorite of the Dercians or any other of the mercenary troops who had signed on in preparation for Shûme's impending war; and fine food and wine, not just small beer and ale. The cornet also gave directions to the citadel, not that this was really necessary as its four towers were clearly visible, and advised Hereward and Fitz that there was no point going there until the morning, for the governing council was in session and so no one in authority could hire him until at least the third bell after sunrise.

The streets of Shûme were paved and drained, and Hereward smiled again at the absence of the fetid stench so common to places where large numbers of people dwelt together. He was looking forward to a bath, a proper meal and a fine feather bed, with the prospect of well-paid and not too onerous employment commencing on the morrow.

"There is the inn," remarked Mister Fitz, pointing down one of the narrower side streets, though it was still broad enough for the two battlemounts to stride abreast. "The sign of the golden barleycorn. Appropriate enough for a city with such fine farmland."

They rode into the inn's yard, which was clean and wide and did indeed boast several of the large iron-barred cages used to stable battlemounts complete with meat canisters and feeding chutes rigged in place above the cages. One of the four ostlers present ran ahead to open two cages and lower the chutes, and the other three assisted Hereward to unload the panniers. Mister Fitz took his sewing desk and stood aside, the small rosewood-and-silver box under his arm provoking neither recognition nor alarm. The ostlers were similarly incurious about Fitz himself, almost certainly evidence that self-motivated puppets still came to entertain the townsfolk from time to time.

Hereward led the way into the inn, but halted just before he entered as one of the battlemounts snorted at some annoyance. Glancing back, he saw that it was of no concern, and the gates were closed, but in halting he had kept hold of the door as someone else tried to open it from the other side. Hereward pushed to help and the door flung open, knocking the person on the inside back several paces against a table, knocking over an empty bottle that smashed upon the floor.

"Unfortunate," muttered Mister Fitz, as he saw that the person so inconvenienced was not only a soldier, but wore the red sash of a junior officer, and was a woman.

"I do apolog – " Hereward began to say. He stopped, not only because the woman was talking, but because he had looked at her. She was as tall as he was, with ash-blond hair tied in a queue at the back, her hat in her left hand. She was also very beautiful, at least to Hereward, who had grown up with women who ritually cut their flesh. To others, her attractiveness might be considered marred by the scar that ran from the corner of her left eye out toward the ear and then cut back again toward the lower part of her nose.

"You are clumsy, sir!"

Hereward stared at her for just one second too long before attempting to speak again.

"I am most – "

"You see something you do not like, I think?" interrupted the woman. "Perhaps you have not served with females? Or is it my face you do not care for?"

"You are very beautiful," said Hereward, even as he realized it was entirely the wrong thing to say, either to a woman he had just met or an officer he had just run into.

"You mock me!" swore the woman. Her blue eyes shone more fiercely, but her face paled, and the scar grew more livid. She clapped her broad-brimmed hat on her head and straightened to her full height, with the hat standing perhaps an inch over Hereward. "You shall answer for that!"

"I do not mock you," said Hereward quietly. "I have served with men, women...and eunuchs, for that matter. Furthermore, tomorrow morning I shall be signing on as at least colonel of artillery, and a colonel may not fight a duel with a lieutenant. I am most happy to apologize, but I cannot meet you."

"Cannot or will not?" sneered the woman. "You are not yet a colonel in Shûme's service, I believe, but just a mercenary braggart."

Hereward sighed and looked around the common room. Misolu had spoken truly that the inn was not a mercenary favorite. But there were several officers of Shûme's regular service or militia, all of them looking on with great attention.

"Very well," he snapped. "It is foolishness, for I intended no offence. When and where?"

"Immediately," said the woman. "There is a garden a little way behind this inn. It is lit by lanterns in the trees, and has a lawn."

"How pleasant," said Hereward. "What is your name, madam?"

"I am Lieutenant Jessaye of the Temple Guard of Shûme. And you are?"

"I am Sir Hereward of the High Pale."

"And your friends, Sir Hereward?"

"I have only this moment arrived in Shûme, Lieutenant, and so cannot yet name any friends. Perhaps someone in this room will stand by me, should you wish a second. My companion, whom I introduce to you now, is known as Mister Fitz. He is a surgeon – among other things – and I expect he will accompany us."

"I am pleased to meet you, Lieutenant," said Mister Fitz. He doffed his hat and veil, sending a momentary frisson of small twitches among all in the room save Hereward.

Jessaye nodded back but did not answer Fitz. Instead she spoke to Hereward.

"I need no second. Should you wish to employ sabers, I must send for mine."

"I have a sword in my gear," said Hereward. "If you will allow me a few minutes to fetch it?"

"The garden lies behind the stables," said Jessaye. "I will await you there. Pray do not be too long."

Inclining her head but not doffing her hat, she stalked past and out the door.

"An inauspicious beginning," said Fitz.

"Very," said Hereward gloomily. "On several counts. Where is the innkeeper? I must change and fetch my sword."

The garden was very pretty. Railed in iron, it was not gated, and so accessible to all the citizens of Shûme. A wandering path led through a grove of lantern-hung trees to the specified lawn, which was oval and easily fifty yards from end to end, making the center rather a long way from the lanternlight, and hence quite shadowed. A small crowd of persons who had previously been in the inn were gathered on one side of the lawn. Lieutenant Jessaye stood in the middle, naked blade in hand.

"Do be careful, Hereward," said Fitz quietly, observing the woman flex her knees and practice a stamping attack ending in a lunge. "She looks to be very quick."

"She is an officer of their temple guard," said Hereward in a hoarse whisper. "Has their god imbued her with any particular vitality or puissance?"

"No, the godlet does not seem to be a martial entity," said Fitz. "I shall have to undertake some investigations presently, as to exactly what it is – "

"Sir Hereward! Here at last."

Hereward grimaced as Jessaye called out. He had changed as quickly as he could, into a very fine suit of split-sleeved white showing the yellow shirt beneath, with gold ribbons at the cuffs, shoulders and front lacing, with similarly cut bloomers of yellow showing white breeches, with silver ribbons at the knees, artfully displayed through the side-notches of his second-best boots.

Jessaye, in contrast, had merely removed her uniform coat and stood in her shirt, blue waistcoat, leather breeches and unadorned black thigh boots folded over below the knee. Had the circumstances been otherwise, Hereward would have paused to admire the sight she presented and perhaps offer a compliment.

Instead he suppressed a sigh, strode forward, drew his sword and threw the scabbard aside.

"I am here, Lieutenant, and I am ready. Incidentally, is this small matter to be concluded by one or perhaps both of us dying?"

"The city forbids duels to the death, Sir Hereward," replied Jessaye. "Though accidents do occur."

"What, then, is to be the sign for us to cease our remonstrance?"

"Blood," said Jessaye. She flicked her sword towards the onlookers. "Visible to those watching."

Hereward nodded slowly. In this light, there would need to be a lot of blood before the onlookers could see it. He bowed his head but did not lower his eyes, then raised his sword to the guard position.

Jessaye was fast. She immediately thrust at his neck, and though Hereward parried, he had to step back. She carried through to lunge in a different line, forcing him back again with a more awkward parry, removing all opportunity for Hereward to riposte or counter. For a minute they danced, their swords darting up, down and across, clashing together only to move again almost before the sound reached the audience.

In that minute, Hereward took stock of Jessaye's style and action. She was very fast, but so was he, much faster than anyone would expect from his size and build, and, as always, he had not shown just how truly quick he could be. Jessaye's wrist was strong and supple, and she could change both attacking and defensive lines with great ease. But her style was rigid, a variant of an old school Hereward had studied in his youth.

On her next lunge – which came exactly where he anticipated – Hereward didn't parry but stepped aside and past the blade. He felt her sword whisper by his ribs as he angled his own blade over it and with the leading edge of the point, he cut Jessaye above the right elbow to make a long, very shallow slice that he intended should bleed copiously without inflicting any serious harm.

Jessaye stepped back but did not lower her guard. Hereward quickly called out, "Blood!"

Jessaye took a step forward and Hereward stood ready for another attack. Then the lieutenant bit her lip and stopped, holding her arm toward the lanternlight so she could more clearly see the wound. Blood was already soaking through the linen shirt, a dark and spreading stain upon the cloth.

"You have bested me," she said, and thrust her sword point first into the grass before striding forward to offer her gloved hand to Hereward. He too grounded his blade, and took her hand as they bowed to each other.

A slight stinging low on his side caused Hereward to look down. There was a two-inch cut in his shirt, and small beads of blood were blossoming there. He did not let go Jessaye's fingers, but pointed at his ribs with his left hand.

"I believe we are evenly matched. I hope we may have no cause to bicker further?"

"I trust not," said Jessaye quietly. "I regret the incident. Were it not for the presence of some of my fellows, I should not have caviled at your apology, sir. But you understand...a reputation is not easily won, nor kept..."

"I do understand," said Hereward. "Come, let Mister Fitz attend your cut. Perhaps you will then join me for small repast?"

Jessaye shook her head.

"I go on duty soon. A stitch or two and a bandage is all I have time for. Perhaps we shall meet again."

"It is my earnest hope that we do," said Hereward. Reluctantly, he opened his grasp. Jessaye's hand lingered in his palm for several moments before she slowly raised it, stepped back and doffed her hat to offer a full bow. Hereward returned it, straightening up as Mister Fitz hurried over, carrying a large leather case as if it were almost too heavy for him, one of his standard acts of misdirection, for the puppet was at least as strong as Hereward, if not stronger.

"Attend to Lieutenant Jessaye, if you please, Mister Fitz," said Hereward. "I am going back to the inn to have a cup...or two...of wine."

"Your own wound needs no attention?" asked Fitz as he set his bag down and indicated to Jessaye to sit by him.

"A scratch," said Hereward. He bowed to Jessaye again and walked away, ignoring the polite applause of the onlookers, who were drifting forward either to talk to Jessaye or gawp at the blood on her sleeve.

"I may take a stroll," called out Mister Fitz after Hereward. "But I shan't be longer than an hour."

Mister Fitz was true to his word, returning a few minutes after the citadel bell had sounded the third hour of the evening. Hereward had bespoken a private chamber and was dining alone there, accompanied only by his thoughts.

"The god of Shûme," said Fitz, without preamble. "Have you heard anyone mention its name?"

Hereward shook his head and poured another measure from the silver jug with the swan's beak spout. Like many things he had found in Shûme, the knight liked the inn's silverware.

"They call their godlet Tanesh," said Fitz. "But its true name is Pralqornrah-Tanish-Kvaxixob."

"As difficult to say or spell, I wager," said Hereward. "I commend the short form, it shows common sense. What of it?"

"It is on the list," said Fitz.

Hereward bit the edge of his pewter cup and put it down too hard, slopping wine upon the table.

"You're certain? There can be no question?"

Fitz shook his head. "After I had doctored the young woman, I went down to the lake and took a slide of the god's essence – it was quite concentrated in the water, easily enough to yield a sample. You may compare it with the record, if you wish."

He proffered a finger-long, inch-wide strip of glass that was striated in many different bands of color. Hereward accepted it reluctantly, and with it a fat, square book that Fitz slid across the table. The book was open at a hand-tinted color plate, the illustration showing a sequence of color bands.

"It is the same," agreed the knight, his voice heavy with regret. "I suppose it is fortunate we have not yet signed on, though I doubt they will see what we do as being purely a matter of defense."

"They do not know what they harbor here," said Fitz.

"It is a pleasant city." said Hereward, taking up his cup again to take a large gulp of the slightly sweet wine. "In a pretty valley. I had thought I could grow more than accustomed to Shûme – and its people."

"The bounty of Shûme, all its burgeoning crops, its healthy stock and people, is an unintended result of their godlet's predation upon the surrounding lands," said Fitz. "Pralqornrah is one of the class of cross-dimensional parasites that is most dangerous. Unchecked, in time it will suck the vital essence out of all the land beyond its immediate demesne. The deserts of Balkash are the work of a similar being, over six millennia. This one has only been embedded here for two hundred years – you have seen the results beyond this valley."

"Six millennia is a long time," said Hereward, taking yet another gulp. The wine was strong as well as sweet, and he felt the need of it. "A desert might arise in that time without the interference of the gods."

"It is not just the fields and the river that Pralqornrah feeds upon," said Fitz. "The people outside this valley suffer too. Babes unborn, strong men and women declining before their prime...this godlet slowly sucks the essence from all life."

"They could leave," said Hereward. The wine was making him feel both sleepy and mulish. "I expect many have already left to seek better lands. The rest could be resettled, the lands left uninhabited to feed the godlet. Shûme could continue as an oasis. What if another desert grows around it? They occur in nature, do they not?"

"I do not think you fully comprehend the matter," said Fitz. "Pralqornrah is a most comprehensive feeder. Its energistic threads will spread farther and faster the longer it exists here, and it in turn will grow more powerful and much more difficult to remove. A few millennia hence, it might be too strong to combat."

"I am only talking," said Hereward, not without some bitterness. "You need not waste your words to bend my reason. I do not even need to understand anything beyond the salient fact: this godlet is on the list."

"Yes," said Mister Fitz. "It is on the list."

Hereward bent his head for a long, silent moment. Then he pushed his chair back and reached across for his saber. Drawing it, he placed the blade across his knees. Mister Fitz handed him a whetstone and a small flask of light, golden oil. The knight oiled the stone and began to hone the saber's blade. A repetitive rasp was the only sound in the room for many minutes, till he finally put the stone aside and wiped the blade clean with a soft piece of deerskin.

"When?"

"Fourteen minutes past the midnight hour is optimum," replied Mister Fitz. "Presuming I have calculated its intrusion density correctly."

"It is manifest in the temple?"

Fitz nodded.

"Where is the temple, for that matter? Only the citadel stands out above the roofs of the city."

"It is largely underground," said Mister Fitz. "I have found a side entrance, which should not prove difficult. At some point beyond that there is some form of arcane barrier – I have not been able to ascertain its exact nature, but I hope to unpick it without trouble."

"Is the side entrance guarded? And the interior?"

"Both," said Fitz. Something about his tone made Hereward fix the puppet with an inquiring look.

"The side door has two guards," continued Fitz. "The interior watch is of ten or eleven...led by the Lieutenant Jessaye you met earlier."

Hereward stood up, the saber loose in his hand, and turned away from Fitz.

"Perhaps we shall not need to fight her...or her fellows."

Fitz did not answer, which was answer enough.

The side door to the temple was unmarked and appeared no different than the other simple wooden doors that lined the empty street, most of them adorned with signs marking them as the shops of various tradesmen, with smoke-grimed night lamps burning dimly above the sign. The door Fitz indicated was painted a pale violet and had neither sign nor lamp.

"Time to don the brassards and make the declaration," said the puppet. He looked up and down the street, making sure that all was quiet, before handing Hereward a broad silk armband five fingers wide. It was embroidered with sorcerous thread that shed only a little less light than the smoke-grimed lantern above the neighboring shop door. The symbol the threads wove was one that had once been familiar the world over but was now unlikely to be recognized by anyone save a historian...or a god.

Hereward slipped the brassard over his left glove and up his thick coat sleeve, spreading it out above the elbow. The suit of white and yellow was once again packed, and for this expedition the knight had chosen to augment his helmet and buff coat with a dented but still eminently serviceable back- and breastplate, the steel blackened by tannic acid to a dark grey. He had already primed, loaded and spanned his two wheel-lock pistols, which were thrust through his belt; his saber was sheathed at his side; and a lozenge-sectioned, armor-punching bodkin was in his left boot.

Mister Fitz wore his sewing desk upon his back, like a wooden backpack.

He had already been through its numerous small drawers and containers and selected particular items that were now tucked into the inside pockets of his coat, ready for immediate use.

"I wonder why we bother with this mummery," grumbled Hereward. But he stood at attention as Fitz put on his own brassard, and the knight carefully repeated the short phrase uttered by his companion. Though both had recited it many times, and it was clear as bright type in their minds, they spoke carefully and with great concentration, in sharp contrast to Hereward's remark about mummery.

"In the name of the Council of the Treaty for the Safety of the World, acting under the authority granted by the Three Empires, the Seven Kingdoms, the Palatine Regency, the Jessar Republic and the Forty Lesser Realms, we declare ourselves agents of the Council. We identify the godlet manifested in this city of Shûme as Pralqornrah-Tanish-Kvaxixob, a listed entity under the Treaty. Consequently, the said godlet and all those who assist it are deemed to be enemies of the World, and the Council authorizes us to pursue any and all actions necessary to banish, repel or exterminate the said godlet."

Neither felt it necessary to change this ancient text to reflect the fact that only one of the three empires was still extant in any fashion; that the seven kingdoms were now twenty or more small states; the Palatine Regency was a political fiction, its once broad lands under two fathoms of water; the Jessar Republic was now neither Jessar in ethnicity nor a republic; and perhaps only a handful of the Forty Lesser Realms resembled their antecedent polities in any respect. But for all that the states that had made it were vanished or diminished, the Treaty for the Safety of the World was still held to be in operation, if only by the Council that administered and enforced it.

"Are you ready?" asked Fitz.

Hereward drew his saber and moved into position to the left of the door. Mister Fitz reached into his coat and drew out an esoteric needle. Hereward knew better than to try to look at the needle directly, but in the reflection of his blade, he could see a four-inch line of something intensely violet writhe in Fitz's hand. Even the reflection made him feel as if he might at any moment be unstitched from the world, so he angled the blade away.

At that moment, Fitz touched the door with the needle and made three short plucking motions. On the last motion, without any noise or fuss, the door wasn't there anymore. There was only a wood-paneled corridor leading down into the ground and two very surprised temple guards, who were still leaning on their halberds.

Before Hereward could even begin to move, Fitz's hand twitched across and up several times. The lanterns on their brass stands every six feet along the corridor flickered and flared violet for a fraction of a second. Hereward blinked, and the guards were gone, as were the closest three lanterns and their stands.

Only a single drop of molten brass, no bigger than a tear, remained. It sizzled on the floor for a second, then all was quiet.

The puppet stalked forward, cupping his left hand over the needle in his right, obscuring its troublesome sight behind his fingers. Hereward followed close behind, alert for any enemy that might be resistant to Fitz's sorcery.

The corridor was a hundred yards long by Hereward's estimation, and slanted sharply down, making him think about having to fight back up it, which would be no easy task, made more difficult as the floor and walls were damp, drops of water oozing out between the floorboards and dripping from the seams of the wall paneling. There was cold, wet stone behind the timber, Hereward knew. He could feel the cold air rippling off it, a chill that no amount of fine timber could cloak.

The corridor ended at what appeared from a distance to be a solid wall, but closer to was merely the dark back of a heavy tapestry. Fitz edged silently around it, had a look, and returned to beckon Hereward in.

There was a large antechamber or waiting room beyond, sparsely furnished with a slim desk and several well-upholstered armchairs. The desk and chairs each had six legs, the extra limbs arranged closely at the back, a fashion Hereward supposed was some homage to the godlet's physical manifestation. The walls were hung with several tapestries depicting the city at various stages in its history.

Given the depth underground and the proximity of the lake, great efforts must have been made to waterproof and beautify the walls, floor and ceiling, but there was still an army of little dots of mold advancing from every corner, blackening the white plaster and tarnishing the gilded cornices and decorations.

Apart from the tapestry-covered exit, there were three doors. Two were of a usual size, though they were elaborately carved with obscure symbols and had brass, or perhaps even gold, handles. The one on the wall opposite the tapestry corridor was entirely different: it was a single ten-foot-by-six-foot slab of ancient marble veined with red lead, and it would have been better situated sitting on top of a significant memorial or some potentate's coffin.

Mister Fitz went to each of the carved doors, his blue tongue flickering in and out, sampling the air.

"No one close," he reported, before approaching the marble slab. He actually licked the gap between the stone and the floor, then sat for a few moments to think about what he had tasted.

Hereward kept clear, checking the other doors to see if they could be locked. Disappointed in that aim as they had neither bar nor keyhole, he sheathed his saber and carefully and quietly picked up a desk to push against the left door and several chairs to pile against the right. They wouldn't hold, but they would give some warning of attempted ingress.

Fitz chuckled as Hereward finished his work, an unexpected noise that made the knight shiver, drop his hand to the hilt of his saber, and quickly look around to see what had made the puppet laugh. Fitz was not easily amused, and often not by anything Hereward would consider funny.

"There is a sorcerous barrier," said Fitz. "It is immensely strong but has not perhaps been as well thought out as it might have been. Fortuitously, I do not even need to unpick it."

The puppet reached up with his left hand and pushed the marble slab. It slid back silently, revealing another corridor, this one of more honest bare, weeping stone, rapidly turning into rough-hewn steps only a little way along.

"I'm afraid you cannot follow, Hereward," said Fitz. "The barrier is conditional, and you do not meet its requirements. It would forcibly – and perhaps harmfully – repel you if you tried to step over the lintel of this door. But I would ask you to stay here in any case, to secure our line of retreat. I should only be a short time if all goes well. You will, of course, know if all does not go well, and must save yourself as best you can. I have impressed the ostlers to rise at your command and load our gear, as I have impressed instructions into the dull minds of the battlemounts – "

"Enough, Fitz! I shall not leave without you."

"Hereward, you know that in the event of my – "

"Fitz. The quicker it were done – "

"Indeed. Be careful, child."

"Fitz!"

But the puppet had gone almost before that exasperated single word was out of Hereward's mouth.

It quickly grew cold with the passage below open. Chill, wet gusts of wind blew up and followed the knight around the room, no matter where he stood. After a few minutes trying to find a spot where he could avoid the cold breeze, Hereward took to pacing by the doors as quietly as he could. Every dozen steps or so he stopped to listen, either for Fitz's return or the sound of approaching guards.

In the event, he was midpace when he heard something. The sharp beat of hobnailed boots in step, approaching the left-hand door.

Hereward drew his two pistols and moved closer to the door. The handle rattled, the door began to move and encountered the desk he had pushed there. There was an exclamation and several voices spoke all at once. A heavier shove came immediately, toppling the desk as the door came partially open.

Hereward took a pace to the left and fired through the gap. The wheel locks whirred, sparks flew, then there were two deep, simultaneous booms, the resultant echoes flattening down the screams and shouts in the corridor beyond the door, just as the conjoining clouds of blue-white smoke obscured Hereward from the guards, who were already clambering over their wounded or slain companions.

The knight thrust his pistols back through his belt and drew his saber, to make an immediate sweeping cut at the neck of a guard who charged blindly through the smoke, his halberd thrust out in front like a blind man's cane. Man and halberd clattered to the floor. Hereward ducked under a halberd swing and slashed the next guard behind the knees, at the same time picking up one edge of the desk and flipping it upright in the path of the next two guards. They tripped over it, and Hereward stabbed them both in the back of the neck as their helmets fell forward, left-right, three inches of saber point in and out in an instant.

A blade skidded off Hereward's cuirass and would have scored his thigh but for a quick twist away. He parried the next thrust, rolled his wrist and slashed his attacker across the stomach, following it up with a kick as the guard reeled back, sword slack in his hand.

No attack – or any movement save for dulled writhing on the ground – followed. Hereward stepped back and surveyed the situation. Two guards were dead or dying just beyond the door. One was still to his left. Three lay around the desk. Another was hunched over by the wall, his hands pressed uselessly against the gaping wound in his gut, as he moaned the god's name over and over.

None of the guards was Jessaye, but the sound of the pistol shots at the least would undoubtedly bring more defenders of the temple.

"Seven," said Hereward. "Of a possible twelve."

He laid his saber across a chair and reloaded his pistols, taking powder cartridges and shot from the pocket of his coat and a ramrod from under the barrel of one gun. Loaded, he wound their wheel-lock mechanisms with a small spanner that hung from a braided-leather loop on his left wrist.

Just as he replaced the pistols in his belt, the ground trembled beneath his feet, and an even colder wind came howling out of the sunken corridor, accompanied by a cloying but not unpleasant odor of exotic spices that also briefly made Hereward see strange bands of color move through the air, the visions fading as the scent also passed.

Tremors, scent and strange visions were all signs that Fitz had joined battle with Pralqornrah-Tanish-Kvaxixob below. There could well be other portents to come, stranger and more unpleasant to experience.

"Be quick, Fitz," muttered Hereward, his attention momentarily focused on the downwards passage.

Even so, he caught the soft footfall of someone sneaking in, boots left behind in the passage. He turned, pistols in hand, as Jessaye stepped around the half-open door. Two guards came behind her, their own pistols raised.

Before they could aim, Hereward fired and, as the smoke and noise filled the room, threw the empty pistols at the trio, took up his saber and jumped aside.

Jessaye's sword leapt into the space where he'd been. Hereward landed, turned and parried several frenzied stabs at his face, the swift movement of their blades sending the gun smoke eddying in wild roils and coils. Jessaye pushed him back almost to the other door. There, Hereward picked up a chair and used it to fend off several blows, at the same time beginning to make small, fast cuts at Jessaye's sword arm.

Jessaye's frenzied assault slackened as Hereward cut her badly on the shoulder near her neck, then immediately after that on the upper arm, across the wound he'd given her in the duel. She cried out in pain and rage and stepped back, her right arm useless, her sword point trailing on the floor.

Instead of pressing his attack, the knight took a moment to take stock of his situation.

The two pistol-bearing guards were dead or as good as, making the tally nine. That meant there should only be two more, in addition to Jessaye, and those two were not immediately in evidence.

"You may withdraw, if you wish," said Hereward, his voice strangely loud and dull at the same time, a consequence of shooting in enclosed spaces. "I do not wish to kill you, and you cannot hold your sword."

Jessaye transferred her sword to her left hand and took a shuddering breath.

"I fight equally well with my left hand," she said, assuming the guard position as best she could, though her right arm hung at her side, and blood dripped from her fingers to the floor.

She thrust immediately, perhaps hoping for surprise. Hereward ferociously beat her blade down, then stamped on it, forcing it from her grasp. He then raised the point of his saber to her throat.

"No you don't," he said. "Very few people do. Go, while you still live."

"I cannot," whispered Jessaye. She shut her eyes. "I have failed in my duty. I shall die with my comrades. Strike quickly."

Hereward raised his elbow and prepared to push the blade through the so-giving flesh, as he had done so many times before. But he did not, instead he lowered his saber and backed away around the wall.

"Quickly, I beg you," said Jessaye. She was shivering, the blood flowing faster down her arm.

"I cannot," muttered Hereward. "Or rather I do not wish to. I have killed enough today."

Jessaye opened her eyes and slowly turned to him, her face paper white, the scar no brighter than the petal of a pink rose. For the first time, she saw that the stone door was open, and she gasped and looked wildly around at the bodies that littered the floor.

"The priestess came forth? You have slain her?"

"No," said Hereward. He continued to watch Jessaye and listen for others, as he bent and picked up his pistols. They were a present from his mother, and he had not lost them yet. "My companion has gone within."

"But that...that is not possible! The barrier – "

"Mister Fitz knew of the barrier," said Hereward wearily. He was beginning to feel the aftereffects of violent combat, and strongly desired to be away from the visible signs of it littered around him. "He crossed it without difficulty."

"But only the priestess can pass," said Jessaye wildly. She was shaking more than just shivering now, as shock set in, though she still stood upright. "A woman with child! No one and nothing else! It cannot be..."

Her eyes rolled back in her head, she twisted sideways and fell to the floor. Hereward watched her lie there for a few seconds while he attempted to regain the cold temper in which he fought, but it would not return. He hesitated, then wiped his saber clean, sheathed it, then despite all better judgment, bent over Jessaye.

She whispered something and again, and he caught the god's name, "Tanesh," and with it a sudden onslaught of cinnamon and cloves and ginger on his nose. He blinked, and in that blink, she turned and struck at him with a small dagger that had been concealed in her sleeve. Hereward had expected something, but not the god's assistance, for the dagger was in her right hand, which he'd thought useless. He grabbed her wrist but could only slow rather than stop the blow. Jessaye struck true, the dagger entering the armhole of the cuirass, to bite deep into his chest.

Hereward left the dagger there and merely pushed Jessaye back. The smell of spices faded, and her arm was limp once more. She did not resist, but lay there quite still, only her eyes moving as she watched Hereward sit down next to her. He sighed heavily, a few flecks of blood already spraying out with his breath, evidence that her dagger was lodged in his lung though he already knew that from the pain that impaled him with every breath.

"There is no treasure below," said Jessaye quietly. "Only the godlet, and his priestess."

"We did not come for treasure," said Hereward. He spat blood on the floor. "Indeed, I had thought we would winter here, in good employment. But your god is proscribed, and so..."

"Proscribed? I don't...who..."

"By the Council of the Treaty for the Safety of the World," said Hereward. "Not that anyone remembers that name. If we are remembered it is from the stories that tell of...god-slayers."

"I know the stories," whispered Jessaye. "And not just stories...we were taught to beware the god-slayers. But they are always women, barren women, with witch-scars on their faces. Not a man and a puppet. That is why the barrier...the barrier stops all but gravid women..."

Hereward paused to wipe a froth of blood from his mouth before he could answer.

"Fitz has been my companion since I was three years old. He was called Mistress Fitz then, as my nurse-bodyguard. When I turned ten, I wanted a male companion, and so I began to call him Mister Fitz. But whether called Mistress or Master, I believe Fitz is nurturing an offshoot of his spiritual essence in some form of pouch upon his person. In time he will make a body for it to inhabit. The process takes several hundred years."

"But you..."

Jessaye's whisper was almost too quiet to hear.

"I am a mistake...the witches of Har are not barren, that is just a useful tale. But they do only bear daughters...save the once. I am the only son of a witch born these thousand years. My mother is one of the Mysterious Three who rule the witches, last remnant of the Council. Fitz was made by that Council, long ago, as a weapon made to fight malignant gods. The more recent unwanted child became a weapon too, puppet and boy flung out to do our duty in the world. A duty that has carried me here...to my great regret."

No answer came to this bubbling, blood-infused speech. Hereward looked across at Jessaye and saw that her chest no longer rose and fell, and that there was a dark puddle beneath her that was still spreading, a tide of blood advancing toward him.

He touched the hilt of the dagger in his side, and coughed, and the pain of both things was almost too much to bear; but he only screamed a little, and made it worse by standing up and staggering to the wall to place his back against it. There were still two guards somewhere, and Fitz was surprisingly vulnerable if he was surprised. Or he might be wounded too, from the struggle with the god.

Minutes or perhaps a longer time passed, and Hereward's mind wandered and, in wandering, left his body too long. It slid down the wall to the ground and his blood began to mingle with that of Jessaye, and the others who lay on the floor of a god's antechamber turned slaughterhouse.

Then there was pain again, and Hereward's mind jolted back into his body, in time to make his mouth whimper and his eyes blink at a light that was a color he didn't know, and there was Mister Fitz leaning over him and the dagger wasn't in his side anymore and there was no bloody froth upon his lips. There was still pain. Constant, piercing pain, coming in waves and never subsiding. It stayed with him, uppermost in his thoughts, even as he became dimly aware that he was upright and walking, his legs moving under a direction not his own.

Except that very soon he was lying down again, and Fitz was cross.

"You have to get back up, Hereward."

"I'm tired, Fitzie...can't I rest for a little longer?"

"No. Get up."

"Are we going home?"

"No, Hereward. You know we can't go home. We must go onward."

"Onward? Where?"

"Never mind now. Keep walking. Do you see our mounts?"

"Yes...but we will never...never make it out the gate..."

"We will, Hereward...leave it to me. Here, I will help you up. Are you steady enough?"

"I will...stay on. Fitz..."

"Yes, Hereward."

"Don't...don't kill them all."

If Fitz answered, Hereward didn't hear, as he faded out of the world for a few seconds. When the world nauseatingly shivered back into sight and hearing, the puppet was nowhere in sight and the two battlemounts were already loping toward the gate, though the leading steed had no rider.

They did not pause at the wall. Though it was past midnight, the gate was open, and the guards who might have barred the way were nowhere to be seen, though there were strange splashes of color upon the earth where they might have stood. There were no guards beyond the gate, on the earthwork bastion either, the only sign of their prior existence a half-melted belt buckle still red with heat.

To Hereward's dim eyes, the city's defenses might as well be deserted, and nothing prevented the battlemounts continuing to lope, out into the warm autumn night.

The leading battlemount finally slowed and stopped a mile beyond the town, at the corner of a lemon grove, its hundreds of trees so laden with yellow fruit they scented the air with a sharp, clean tang that helped bring Hereward closer to full consciousness. Even so, he lacked the strength to shorten the chain of his own mount, but it stopped by its companion without urging.

Fitz swung down from the outlying branch of a lemon tree, onto his saddle, without spilling any of the fruit piled high in his upturned hat.

"We will ride on in a moment. But when we can, I shall make a lemon salve and a soothing drink."

Hereward nodded, finding himself unable to speak. Despite Fitz's repairing sorceries, the wound in his side was still very painful, and he was weak from loss of blood, but neither thing choked his voice. He was made quiet by a cold melancholy that held him tight, coupled with a feeling of terrible loss, the loss of some future, never-to-be happiness that had gone forever.

"I suppose we must head for Fort Yarz," mused Fitz. "It is the closest likely place for employment. There is always some trouble there, though I believe the Gebrak tribes have been largely quiet this past year."

Hereward tried to speak again, and at last found a croak that had some resemblance to a voice.

"No. I am tired of war. Find us somewhere peaceful, where I can rest."

Fitz hopped across to perch on the neck of Hereward's mount and faced the knight, his blue eyes brighter than the moonlight.

"I will try, Hereward. But as you ruminated earlier, the world is as it is, and we are what we were made to be. Even should we find somewhere that seems at peace, I suspect it will not stay so, should we remain. Remember Jeminero."

"Aye." Hereward sighed. He straightened up just a little and took up the chains, as Fitz jumped to his own saddle. "I remember."

"Fort Yarz?" asked Fitz.

Hereward nodded, and slapped the chain, urging his battlemount forward. As it stretched into its stride, the lemons began to fall from the trees in the orchard, playing the soft drumbeat of a funerary march, the first sign of the passing from the world of the god of Shûme.

Debatable Lands

Liz Williams

Liz Williams (*mevennen.livejournal.com*) lives in Glastonbury, England, where she is co-director of a witchcraft supply business. She is the author of the Detective Inspector Chen series and five other novels. Most years she publishes several short stories of very high quality. Her short fiction is collected in *The Banquet of the Lords of Night and Other Stories* (2004). *The Shadow Pavilion*, a Detective Inspector Chen book, will be out in 2008 as will a novel entitled *Winterstrike*. In 2007 she served on the editorial board of the SF magazine *Interzone*.

"Debatable Lands," which appeared in *Asimov's*, treads on that edge between fantasy and science fiction. Historically, the Debatable Lands were a strip of territory between England and Scotland, for 300 years owned by neither. Perhaps that's a metaphor for the story's genre placement. The setting of this story is richly fantasy, but its creature would not be out of place in the movie *Alien*.

HE CHASED IT through the rushes at the water's edge, late spring, with the dark-mist twilight coming down around him. It was as though he had been chasing it lifelong, all through the racing years of childhood, past the time when he was initiated as a warrior and warlord's man, past the battles of Cadon and Burn, the years of love and the years of war. He knew that it was barely a short span since the hounds had put up the scent and begun the chase, but that was what it felt like. And already he was exhausted by it, bone weary, as though the day was already at its end. The thing he was chasing had sapped him: he could feel it sipping at his strength, leaching into marrow and sinew, spooling him out like the thread from a dropped spindle. Then it raised its unnatural head and gave a pealing cry and the sound brought him to his knees.

He was somewhere else. There were towers all around, made of red stone, higher than any building he had ever seen before. They reached up into cloudy greyness, rain on the way, and he felt dizzy and disconnected. Hastily he looked down and around. He stood on a grassy circle but the grass was not green, as it should be, but yellow and sere, as though the summer had been hot and long. It did not feel like summer to him, but there were no trees to show him the season.

There was, however, a plank of wood on a ball, tilted so that one end of the plank rested on the ground. A smaller plank hung from a frame, creaking in the rising wind. He blinked. A child was sitting on the plank, swinging to and fro. The child was staring at him, her face as blank as an egg.

"Where am I?" he cried. "What is this place?"

But the child's face cracked and she laughed and laughed, not kind laughter but cold, and he knew her for one of the Changing, or thought he did. Then the child and the towers were gone and there were only the rushes and the marsh's edge, with the wind whistling through the reeds.

That night, he dreamed of Less Britain.

He had been born there, on the sea's edge. First memories were of the salt wind whipping his face, the ocean thundering in and lashing against the granite cliffs until exhausted into froth. His father had died young, in Broceliande, but Broceliande was too often a word they used when they did not want you to know how a man had died, the magic in the name weaving a spell over blood and shattered bone, making death into music. A forest code and he had never found out how his father had met his end.

His mother had gone under the protection of his uncle shortly afterward – not willingly, but she had little choice and he had rejoiced, seeing his uncle's fort as a safe place, true, but also the court in which he would become a man. He had been made welcome, his mother less so, and as she faded and sank in the shadows of the tower, he was trained in arms. There was little doubt as to what kind of man he would be: a warrior, but silent-souled, loving the woods and marshes, the sea's edge, solitude. When he took his totem, it was not raven or gull, but curlew, the sad cry in the dark, always at the edge of things. The other boys, and, later, men, recognized this: he was left alone.

When he was thirteen, he killed his first man, a raider from the northeast. By the time he was seventeen, he had killed more, a man for every year of his age. Shortly after that, the call came from the High Court and he left the sea-churned shores and the cold cliffs for the milder, wetter marshlands around the island kingdoms, in Britain-the-More.

He was initiated, all the same. They sent him out into the lake villages, the lands that had belonged to the king's queen Whiteshadow, that she had brought with her as dowry. He saw the marsh homes of the small dark people, the ones who had been there since time began and the moon was set on its track. He did not understand them, and they did not trust him, although they admired the iron spear he carried and he saw them looking at it with longing. They were covered in blue markings, allowing them to disappear against the reeds and the coiling mist. He painted himself with the same, and went out into the marsh when the early sun was a brass circle in the east.

That was when he saw the thing, but that came later. When he first took the coracle out into the rushes that marked the channel, a curlew flew across his path, calling its ghost-cry, and he knew it would be a good killing day. He speared a heron shortly after that, laying its striped corpse on the slats of the coracle, admiring the beauty of it. Then a crested duck, but never the totem he was seeking: hunting was a pastime, nothing more, but it was preparation for the initiation feast. He had no intention of being unsuccessful.

He heard it before he saw it. At first he thought it was one of the booming birds that rose like reeds, with their necks stretched up from the marsh. It was a long, belling cry, similar to bird or hound, but with a strange pattern to it, like someone crying out in a language that he did not understand. Maybe it was one of the lake people themselves, come stealing after him to take the iron spear, and he jolted round in the coracle. No one was there.

It came again and it was desolate, a spirit's cry. He reached for the charm around his neck, hazel bound with bronze to keep him safe from fire and water, and he thought it had worked because the cry was cut off, suddenly, as if choked. Then he swung the oar, took the coracle around a bend in the channel into a wide flat pool, and saw it.

It looked like death. It was all sinew and bone, with more legs than a natural beast, and a face made of spines, that as he stared, aghast, shifted to become something else, something human and ancient and sad. Then it bounded high in the air. He saw a twisting tail, ending in a spiked club, and all of it was the color of summer roses, or the inside of a dead man on the battlefield's earth. It was gone and he was left gaping after it.

He knew then that his initiation was complete: he had seen what he was supposed to see, yet he did not know what that was. He could not take this for his totem; it was no natural thing. And so, wondering, he paddled the coracle back through the channel of reeds, to the banks of alder through which a white sun was rising.

It was early, but he had seen enough. There was a bursting pressure in his head, the sense of a summer storm. He put his hands to his ears to block out thunder, then realized that it was within. It was not until he stumbled back into the alder groves that the pressure lessened and even then his head rang to the end of the day.

The high king's oak-man was silent, when he spoke of what he had seen. At first, Curlew thought that he was not believed. But yarrow thrown smoldering into the fire sent smoke into the oak-man's rafters and the oak-man passed a knife across the palm of Curlew's hand and proclaimed him a man of the high court.

That night, the high king asked him to tell the court what he had seen. He did so grudgingly, but the warriors did not laugh; something about his quietness, perhaps, or the black haunt in his eyes. The thing he had seen had left a scar on his soul, something he did not want to tell the other warriors, but perhaps they saw it in him all the same.

His account of the creature, his quest beast, excited them. Knives were stuck into the tabletop; toasts were made. The king watched with guarded interest; by his side, Whiteshadow's face was avid. They wanted to set out that night, run the beast to ground in the marshes, capture it and bring it back – living or dead, or so the head of the king's warriors boasted. Curlew did not think that was as easy a choice as it might seem, but he said nothing.

The king was indulgent, but held them back. Curlew, watching the king's face closely, thought he saw something pass across it, a shadow like the knowledge of a man's death, but he was not sure. The king was a young man, who looked old, and Curlew did not know what the king had or had not seen.

That night, he dreamed he was back in the marshes. It was afternoon, the day glowing, but when he looked up he could see the stars and he knew that the glow was not coming from the sun. The beast came out of the light, walking on two legs like a man, but the rest of its legs were coiled around it, drifting like seaweed in the shining air. Curlew reached for the iron spear but it was no longer by his side and anyway, there was no need. His fear had drained into the light, leaving him empty and calm.

"What are you?" he said, and the beast replied with that belling cry that seemed to be made of words. He had the sudden glimpse of a great plain, grey and shivering with grasses, mountains in the distance that were the color of old ale. Home, but not his. Then it was gone and the beast and the dream with it.

Next morning, nine warriors rode to the marsh, leaving their rough-coated ponies restless at the water's edge. Curlew went with them, but did not follow them into the reeds. Instead, he waited, standing alongside the oak-man as the sun came up through the alder groves.

"That boy, the one they call Lamb," the oak-man said. "You know him?"

Curlew nodded. "I've seen him at the court."

"He is older than he looks. Lamb is his child-name; he has not yet seen his totem."

"Perhaps this will be it," Curlew said, with an idleness that he did not feel, for suddenly the back of his neck prickled like nettle-sting. The oak-man gave him a sharp glance.

"I will be surprised if he comes back."

"Do you know of this thing, this quest beast?" Curlew asked, echoing the previous day.

"No. I told you truth," the oak-man said. "But I have heard of things like the thing you have seen. They come after dark stars; war comes in their wake, and famine. They love the blood of men. There were a lot of things like that, in the wake of the great comet that swept the land a hundred years ago, bringing iron cold, disease. This is why I will be surprised if Lamb comes back on his own two feet."

"I will be sorry," Curlew murmured.

"If Lamb dies, it could lead to war."

"Why so? Is he a warlord's son?"

The oak-man nodded. "Bennek of the north marshes, beyond Broceliande. Your country."

"I know Bennek. Not an easy man." Curlew chose words carefully.

"Lamb is the only one left; he was fostered here. Bennek thinks it will bring advantage, that there will be the possibility of a land-claim. "

"But not if the boy dies."

"Oh no. Not then. I told you. War comes in the wake of such beasts, and famine."

They fell silent, gazing out over the marsh. Curlew could barely see the rushes through the mist. One of the horses shifted, uneasy, and then the cry came, belling out over the water. Curlew looked at the oak-man and saw that his face had grown strained and old.

"I have not – " he started to say. Curlew put a hand on the man's arm, felt the trembling, did not answer.

Lamb did not come back. He had gone down into the water, along with four of the others. The ones who remained spoke of horror, their faces twisting with a lack of understanding, but Curlew had seen the thing in the marsh and knew how it crept into the head. He remembered his glowing dream and nearly smiled, but the slack, terrified faces before him drove the smile away and he could only think of the dead.

They rode back to the high court in silence and Curlew went straight to the chamber in the tower, leaving the oak-man to tell the king of what had taken place. He was bone-tired, as if the heat had been leached from his marrow, leaving him a thin dry stick. He thought that they might blame him for the tragedy, but they did not. The king said only, "We must find it. Find it and kill it." Curlew agreed, but the thought of going after the belling thing was a dreadful one.

Not long after that, word came from Lamb's father Bennek, demanding reparation.

"He wants land," the oak-man said, as they walked together on the ridge of the fort.

"Of course he does," Curlew said, surprised. "What else would he want?"

The oak-man shrugged. "A woman, perhaps."

"No woman is worth a son," Curlew said. "Unless she brings land with her."

"Well, that is the way of it, isn't it?" the oak-man said. "The lands he wants are not the ones that fostering might have brought. They are the swamplands, the ones that belonged to the queen, to Whiteshadow."

"That makes no sense. Half of that is swamp," Curlew said.

"And half is fertile water meadow. Good grazing."

"Her father took those lands in war, reparation in turn."

The oak-man gave Curlew a glance that was filled with amusement as well as curiosity. "You have learned a lot since you came here, and not just of war."

"Land is part of war," Curlew said. "What use is war else, if not for land?"

"What use indeed? But the lands that Lamb's father wants have always been debatable lands in consequence, subject to constant dispute."

"And now, more dispute. Will Bennek come here, do you think?"

"Almost certainly," the oak-man said. "The king will want you near, I think. You speak the language, and you know him. Ordinarily, he would not come; he would send warriors."

"And they would be sent back to him. Or their hands would." Curlew thought of the limed heads that marked the doorway of the fort, set into the lintel so that the voices of their spirits might carry the message out through all the worlds, that this was not a place to dishonor.

"Of course. But this is a matter of pride; the boy was the only son, the heir. He was in the high king's charge."

"I hold myself responsible," Curlew said, after a pause. "I was the one who saw the beast, whatever it is. I was the one who started things."

The oak-man sighed. "Who is to say who starts things? You did not make the creature. You did not summon it. Unless there is something you're not telling me."

Curlew laughed. "A quick enough head and my sword arm, that's the kind of power I've got. Not the sort of power that brings nightmares to life. The land is full enough of nightmares as it is. Keeps that come and go, spirits who pass between human and animal, warriors conjured from the trees...."

"But nothing like the thing in the marshes."

"No. Nothing like that."

After that, there seemed little else to say. Three days later, Lamb's father arrived from Less Britain.

Curlew was the one designated to take the warlord out to the debatable lands. He did so without reluctance, glad to get away from the stifling fright of the court. Four deaths, bad enough, but since then the tale had grown until it was as though the cold clamminess of the marshes had crept into the stone of the fort, and into the bones and minds of men.

But when they reached the borders of Whiteshadow's lands, beyond the lake villages, Curlew realized that it was no better. At this time of the year, with the mist rising up from the stagnant water, black and slow between the reed-beds, there was more marsh than water meadow. The willows were straggling and rotten, and the alders, which otherwise would have gone to make good shields, seemed stunted. Yet Bennek slapped Curlew on the back, handed him a swig of Breton mead from his own leather flask, declared himself well pleased.

"Sure, now?" Curlew said. "It's a bit wet. No good for growing, if you ask me, whatever the summer grazing might be like."

"No matter," Bennek replied. He seemed remarkably cheerful, given his recent loss. "I have plans."

Curlew waited, but he didn't say any more. They rode around the bounds, then back to the court, arriving half a day later.

"What did you think?" the oak-man asked Curlew, that night.

"Of Bennek? Or of the lands?"

"Both."

"I think Bennek must be a madman or a fool and yet I know him to be neither. Nor does he seem so deeply grieved, for one who has lost his only son, and that recently. I think the lands are a wasteland, and Whiteshadow would do well to get rid of them."

"Whiteshadow does not think so, and nor does her husband. I heard her say that she wished Bennek had chosen almost anywhere else."

"They were her dowry," Curlew said. "I always wondered why."

Next day, he was given another chance to find out.

The high king asked him to ride through the lands, assess damage to the meadows, and the number of sheep and pigs still present. He was to talk to shepherd and swineherd. Bennek trusted him, it seemed, because he was his uncle's man: a good intermediary, between the warlord and the high king.

He was halfway across the marsh, riding hock-high through dark water with the willows whipping in the wind, when he heard it, the same dreadful, belling cry. He felt his guts turn watery, his head begin to pound. He did not want to see it again. He drove the pony on but the pony needed no urging: it screamed as the cry rang out again. And then, somehow, the thing was ahead of him, standing under the willows, beckoning. It threw its cry over his head and around his shoulders, roping him in. The pony reared, throwing him backward into the water, then bolted. He stumbled to his feet and followed the thing, which was loping through the swamp but leaving no ripples in its wake. It is a spirit, he thought, but he could smell it, a sweet rankness like rotting roses.

Then it was gone and he was among towers and a child's cold laughter, ending in dreams.

*

Back at the fort, he was summoned to the king's own chamber to tell his story. Bennek watched him all the while, with little light eyes, as though sipping the story from him. The king was summoned briefly away, to take a message, and, as soon as he was out of the room, Curlew said to Bennek, swiftly, in their own language.

"Have nothing to do with this place. Ask for any other lands; he will give them to you. This is an ill totem, and it has already taken your son."

"You are a good man," Bennek said, in the same tongue. "Loyal to your countrymen. I won't forget that. But it is none of your concern."

Curlew knew when he was being dismissed and he was only a warrior, no statesman. It was Bennek's business, not his own. He turned to the narrow window of the fort and looked out across the hearth fires, waiting until the high king returned. Bennek was due to depart on the following day, having secured his lands. Curlew hoped that was the last of it.

"It is a temporary thing only," the king said, once Bennek had gone. "He has asked for you, by name and by oath."

"I am no steward, lord," Curlew said. His sinews ached, as though his body was drawing in on itself. "And – I have a horror of the place." It was not a confession he would have made to anyone else.

"His son was slain," the high king said. "It is an honor bond. He trusts you."

"I wish he did not." But he knew he would be going, all the same.

Whiteshadow's lands – now Bennek's – did not have a fort to secure them and the people would not have accepted him into the lake villages. Curlew took up his stewardship in a shepherd's broch, a circle of old stone on a slight rise. This was foul land, he thought as he surveyed his new domain: the waters brackish, seeping in from the estuary of the great river, winter flooded and too low for frost to whiten and crack and kill any marsh breeding thing. It was no wonder to him that the creature had taken up residence there: that was foul, too, unnatural. And he wondered whether Whiteshadow had kept it because of her dowry, simply because it was her own land, or whether there was some other purpose. The high king was surrounded by witches – Whiteshadow herself, his sister Sea, her mother Grain, all of them prone to jealousies and silences, spinning endless spell webs between them, sometimes to weave them together, sometimes to separate. Curlew had no time for women, apart from the usual thing. Whiteshadow's motives in keeping the land were suspect, and so was her release of it. He thought of the place of the great red towers and of the child, laughing as it swung, and shivered.

The day after that he rode around the bounds, with a dutiful reluctance that felt echoed in the pony's nervous, plodding steps. He saw nothing worse than ducks. The day after that, he did the same thing, and the day after. On that third day, he saw a white swan drifting across a mere like a cloud and next moment it was gone. Only a white feather spiraled down to show where it had been but there were no ripples in the water. Curlew watched the spot for a long time, but the bird did not reappear and as twilight drew on, he went back to the broch.

The broch was clammy and damp. He longed to light a fire, or a lamp, anything to keep the encroaching darkness at bay, but instinct told him not to do so, because once he did that, it would separate him from the night, creating a barrier that something might long to cross. He crouched by the small window of the broch, his sword across his knees, looking outward.

A blink. The red tower was back, blazing with light, a caer. He looked out onto a world of stone. There was a rushing sound as a sudden wind hurled something past, scaled, gleaming. Curlew jerked back. Blue light glowed high in the windows of the caer; Curlew knew magic when he saw it. He made a sign, hoping the blue light would go away, but it flickered and changed, grew brighter. That was when he knew he was doomed.

And soon after that, it came. It moved quickly through the stone world, standing upright on two legs, like a warrior. It was carrying something, a small form. Perhaps the child he had seen, or perhaps a lamb. Curlew could not tell. But it had the unmistakable scent of a hunter: blood and metal, he could smell it from inside the broch. It came up to the window of the broch and stared in: Curlew looked into eyes the color of bloody fire.

That was all he remembered. He woke the next morning to find himself lying by the window. He had pissed himself in the night and the earth stank of it. That was when he decided to ride back to court – to Less Britain if necessary – and tell the king to find another man. But he did not have to. On that day, Bennek came back.

Curlew glimpsed them riding through the reeds and for a moment, in the early morning mist, he thought they were the beast. He flinched back against the wall of the broch, but then the ring of metal harness across the water reassured him and he went out to meet them. Bennek had the self-satisfied look of a man who has pulled off a great trick.

"My Lord?" Curlew said.

Bennek dismounted and clapped him on the shoulder. "None of that, boy. You're one of us and you've played your part. You deserve a share of what's to come." A grey glaze, opaque as mist, Curlew thought. But he could not fail to deliver the warning. Devious Bennek may be, but he was still a fellow countryman and the friend of kindred; there had been foster ties in the past and that made him almost blood-kin.

"I have seen the beast," he told Bennek now. "And there is something else, something you should know. This is a gateway to the otherworld, a great red caer. I have seen it. It is set in a wasteland."

He expected fear to fill Bennek's face, anxiety at the least of it, but the warlord only laughed and again struck Curlew on the shoulder.

"Why, so it is as I had hoped."

"Hoped?" Curlew said.

"You think I wanted the land for *this*?" Bennek's sweeping hand indicated the rustling reeds, the glistening peaty waters of the mere. "There's nothing here except sallie willow and eels. The pasture Whiteshadow speaks about is as much of a myth as one of old Myrddin's stories. What I want is what you saw."

Curlew stared at him, disbelieving. "The wasteland?"

"The *key* to the wasteland, boy. The questing beast."

"The beast is a horror," Curlew said. He felt unreal, as though the world was drifting away from him, diminishing through the mists. "What can you possibly want with it? It killed your son."

"This is worth even a son," Bennek said and that cold grey glaze crept even further across his eyes, like ice in winter, and that was when Curlew knew he was mad. "The beast opens the lock of time, it unlocks the gateway to all the times that are, in this place and maybe more. That caer you saw is what will come, perhaps centuries from now when the water has drawn back toward the estuary and this has become solid ground. My oak-man has seen the past – a great swamp, with dragons moving through it. Imagine the riches that lie even in this meager place, that the beast can lead us to."

"Bennek," said Curlew, despairingly. "What *is* the beast?"

"A monster. A god. Who can say? My oak-man has looked into a dark glass and tells me that it is a spirit from the skies, but he does not know for certain. Help me capture it, now that these lands are mine, and perhaps we will find out."

"My lord – Bennek – I do not think it will be easily captured." *If at all*, but Curlew did not want to say that. You had to be careful when speaking with the mad; they could take your words and turn them against you, and Bennek was his lord, with armed men at his back. Curlew wondered what they thought, but did not look at them. "But you agree with me, don't you, you do see, that it *can* be captured, can be taken? All that is needed is the right kind of net and I have such a net, made out of bronze, fashioned with golden threads from the fire islands far to the south, my oak-man had it made for me. See? Do you see?" He reached into a fold of his tunic and took out something that glittered and sparked, only for a moment, before thrusting it back. Curlew did not have time to see if it was really a net, but the forge-smell of spell work hung about it and he felt his scalp prickle. One of the horses stirred uneasily and blew a cloud of breath into the freezing air.

"And you can take us to it," Bennek said.

Curlew was sure, then, that this would be the day on which his death would come. He had known it ever since the beast had looked in through the window with its red eyes and its voice of a thousand hounds. Perhaps he had known it even before that, but he could not turn back. To run from your death is a shameful thing, postpones the inevitable, makes things worse. So he nodded only, mounted the pony and led Bennek and his men into the marsh.

A dark day, with the mist and the cloud seeming to meet at the tops of the reeds and brush them with wet. Nothing moved in the water under the pony's feet, except the black swirls of peat as the sudden boom of a bittern caused the pony to shy. They rode for a morning and the sun rose no higher, then more than half a day and still the cloud hung low over the land and there was little light behind it. That was when Curlew knew that they had crossed into the Otherworld and left time behind. He also knew that the beast would be close.

When it came, it was without warning. There was a stifled cry from the last man in the group. His pony stumbled, he went down into the water and did not rise, even though the water was not deep at that point. Curlew's spear was in his hand as the beast rose from the mere, bloody water streaming from its red sinew sides. It gave its belling cry as it saw the warriors, and sprang backward into the marsh like an acrobat.

"After it!" Bennek cried, and Curlew shouted, "No, it wants you to follow!" But it was too late. Bennek was racing ahead, driving his pony through the mist with the spell-net drifting after him like a swarm of golden bees. Curlew caught a last glimpse of the questing beast, a red spiny form hurtling through the reeds, and of the warriors in pursuit. The eight men, with Bennek at their head, seemed already insubstantial, the mist coiling through their bodies and swallowing them whole. Curlew hesitated for only a moment before bolting after them. If this was to be the day of his death, then best it came quickly.

He did not die. He did not find Bennek or the warriors, either, although a long way ahead there was a dusting of gold on the fleecy heads of the bulrushes and a bloody curl in the waters around. Curlew broke off one of the rush heads and rode on, not knowing what else to do, and gradually the light grew brighter. The reeds thinned and the channels opened out to a great shallow pool.

In the middle of the pool lay an iron boat. At least, this was what Curlew thought it must be: it lay overturned, with the hull upward, and it was made of a black-gleaming metal, tinged with green. Like a dragonfly's armor, perhaps, or the dragon of which mad Bennek had spoken. The metal surface was covered with knots and coils, spirals and signs, and Curlew knew it for magic even before he saw the beast.

It was crouching in the lee of the hull, in an opening. It held a human hand in its fist and was gnawing at the stump. It looked at Curlew from quiet red eyes and grinned at him with long curving teeth. Curlew stared at it, while the pony quivered beneath him, but the beast made no move. Then, it set the hand carefully on the metal beside it and opened its mouth, wider and wider, and Curlew hauled the pony's head around and kicked it crashing through the reeds while the baying of a thousand hounds tumbled through the air around him and opened up the worlds.

He did not look back. He rode on as the light rose and did not look right or left, although he thought he heard a child's cold laughter as he rode, and a strange splitting wail. He rode straight past the broch and over the willow border of Whiteshadow's lands, and into the long reaches of water meadow that sloped to the small snaking rivers. He rode all the way back to the high court and did not stop until the gates slammed shut behind him.

The high king was not there, but Whiteshadow was, sitting in her own carved chair at the table's head. She looked the same as ever, sad blue gaze and asphodel hair, but when he dropped the golden fleece of the bulrush head onto the table in front of her, saying not a word, she smiled.

"He failed," she said.

"He died," said Curlew.

"And the beast?"

"It lives yet. I think it will always live."

Whiteshadow shrugged, but with an effort. "It came with the comet, my father thought. Those were rich enough lands before then, if wet. Perhaps one day it will go back where it came from."

"Perhaps," Curlew said, and he sat down beside her, staring at the gilded rush until the heat from the fire reached his bones and the last of the golden dust rose into the smoking air and was gone.

The Forest

Laird Barron

Laird Barron (*benjamindesign.com/lairdbarron*) lives in Olympia, Washington, with his wife Erin. He moved to Seattle from Alaska in the mid '90s and began to concentrate on writing poetry and fiction. He has published a body of excellent horror stories since 2000, in *Sci Fiction* and *F&SF*, and has been reprinted in *The Year's Best Fantasy and Horror* and in earlier editions of this anthology. The best of them were collected in 2007 in *The Imago Sequence and Other Stories.*

"The Forest" is another story from *Inferno.* A cinematographer is summoned from California by a mysterious old friend to his New England estate, there to be introduced to some very strange ideas, but also to see his former lover and fulfill both of their desires. This is a dark science fantasy, a horrific variant on transhumanism, immortality, and the idea of a conscious ecosystem, dense with ideas and with menace.

AFTER THE DRIVE had grown long and monotonous, Partridge shut his eyes and the woman was waiting. She wore a cold white mask similar to the mask Bengali woodcutters donned when they ventured into the mangrove forests along the coast. The tigers of the forest were stealthy. The tigers hated to be watched; they preferred to sneak up on prey from behind, so natives wore the masks on the backs of their heads as they gathered wood. Sometimes this kept the tigers from dragging them away.

The woman in the cold white mask reached into a wooden box. She lifted a tarantula from the box and held it to her breast like a black carnation. The contrast was as magnificent as a stark Monet if Monet had painted watercolors of emaciated patricians and their pet spiders.

Partridge sat on his high, wooden chair and whimpered in animal terror. In the daydream, he was always very young and powerless. The woman tilted her head. She came near and extended the tarantula in her long, gray hand. "For you," she said. Sometimes she carried herself more like Father and said in a voice of gravel, "Here is the end of fear." Sometimes the tarantula was a hissing cockroach of prehistoric girth, or a horned beetle. Sometimes it was a strange, dark flower. Sometimes it was an embryo uncurling to form a miniature adult human that grinned a monkey's hateful grin.

The woman offered him a black phone. The woman said, "Come say goodbye and good luck. Come quick!" Except the woman did not speak. Toshi's breathless voice bled through the receiver. The woman in the cold white mask brightened then dimmed like a dying coal or a piece of metal coiling into itself.

Partridge opened his eyes and rested his brow against window glass. He was alone with the driver. The bus trawled through a night forest. Black trees dripped with fog. The narrow black road crumbled from decades of neglect. Sometimes poor houses and fences stood among the weeds and the ferns and mutely suggested many more were lost in the dark. Wilderness had arisen to reclaim its possessions.

Royals hunted in woods like these. He snapped on the overhead lamp and then opened his briefcase. *Stags, wild boar, witches. Convicts.* The briefcase was nearly empty. He had tossed in some traveler's checks, a paperback novel and his address book. No cell phone, although he left a note for his lawyer and a recorded message at Kyla's place in Malibu warning them it might be a few days, perhaps a week, that there probably was not even phone service where he was going. Carry on, carry on. He had hopped a redeye jet to Boston and once there eschewed the convenience of renting a car or hiring a chauffeur and limo. He chose instead the relative anonymity of mass transit. The appeal of traveling incognito overwhelmed his normally staid sensibilities. Here was the first adventure he had undertaken in ages. The solitude presented an opportunity to compose his thoughts – his excuses, more likely.

He'd cheerfully abandoned the usual host of unresolved items and potential brushfires that went with the territory – a possible trip to the Andes if a certain Famous Director's film got green-lighted and if the Famous Director's drunken assertion to assorted executive producers and hangers-on over barbequed ribs and flaming daiquiris at the Monarch Grille that Richard Jefferson Partridge was the only man for the job meant a blessed thing. There were several smaller opportunities, namely an L.A. documentary about a powerhouse high school basketball team that recently graced the cover of *Sports Illustrated*, unless the documentary guy, a Cannes Film Festival sweetheart, decided to try to bring down the Governor of California instead, as he had threatened to do time and again, a pet crusade of his with the elections coming that fall, and then the director would surely use his politically savvy compatriot, the cinematographer from France. He'd also been approached regarding a proposed documentary about prisoners and guards at San Quentin. Certainly there were other, lesser engagements he'd lost track of, these doubtless scribbled on memo pads in his home office.

He knew he should hire a reliable secretary. He promised himself to do just that every year. It was hard. He missed Jean. She'd had a lazy eye and a droll wit; made bad coffee and kept sand-filled frogs and fake petunias on her desk. Jean left him for Universal Studios and then slammed into a reef in Maui learning to surf with her new boss. The idea of writing the want-ad, of sorting the applications and conducting the interviews and finally letting the new person, the stranger, sit where Jean had sat and handle his papers, summoned a mosquito's thrum in the bones behind Partridge's ear.

These details would surely keep despite what hysterics might come in the meanwhile. Better, much better, not to endure the buzzing and whining and the imprecations and demands that he return at once on pain of immediate career death, over a dicey relay.

He had not packed a camera, either. He was on vacation. His mind would store what his eye could catch and that was all.

The light was poor. Partridge held the address book close to his face. He had scribbled the directions from margin to margin and drawn a crude map with arrows and lopsided boxes and jotted the initials of the principles: Dr. Toshi Ryoko; Dr. Howard Campbell; Beasley; and Nadine. Of course, Nadine – she snapped her fingers and here he came at a loyal trot. There were no mileposts on the road to confirm the impression that his destination was near. The weight in his belly sufficed. It was a fat stone grown from a pebble.

Partridge's instincts did not fail him. A few minutes before dawn, the forest receded and they entered Warrenburgh. Warrenburgh was a loveless hamlet of crabbed New England shop fronts and angular plank and shingle houses with tall, thin doors and oily windows. Streetlights glowed along Main Street with black gaps like a broken pearl necklace. The street itself was buckled and rutted by poorly tarred cracks that caused sections to cohere as uneasily as interleaved ice floes. The sea loomed near and heavy and palpable beneath a layer of rolling gloom.

Partridge did not like what little he glimpsed of the surroundings. Long ago, his friend Toshi had resided in New Mexico and Southern California, did his best work in Polynesia and the jungles of Central America. The doctor was a creature of warmth and light. *Rolling Stone* had characterized him as "a rock star among zoologists" and as the "Jacques Cousteau of the jungle," the kind of man who hired mercenaries to guard him, performers to entertain his sun-drenched villa, and filmmakers to document his exploits. This temperate landscape, so cool and provincial, so removed from Partridge's experience of all things Toshi, seemed to herald a host of unwelcome revelations.

Beasley, long-standing attendant of the eccentric researcher, waited at the station. "Rich! At least you don't look like the big asshole *Variety* says you are." He nodded soberly and scooped Partridge up for a brief hug in his powerful arms. This was like being embraced by an earth mover. Beasley had played Australian-rules football for a while after he left the Army and before he came to work for Toshi. His nose was squashed and his ears were cauliflowers. He was magnetic and striking as any character actor, nonetheless. "Hey, let me get that." He set Partridge aside and grabbed the luggage the driver had dragged from the innards of the bus. He hoisted the suitcases into the bed of a '56 Ford farm truck. The truck was museum quality. It was fire engine red with a dinky American flag on the antenna.

They rumbled inland. Rusty light gradually exposed counterchanged shelves of empty fields and canted telephone poles strung together with thick, dipping old-fashioned cables. Ducks pelted from a hollow in the road. The ducks spread themselves in a wavering pattern against the sky.

"Been shooting?" Partridge indicated the .20 gauge softly clattering in the rack behind their heads.

"When T isn't looking. Yeah, I roam the marshes a bit. You?"

"No."

"Yah?"

"Not in ages. Things get in the way. Life, you know?"

"Oh, well, we'll go out one day this week. Bag a mallard or two. Raise the dust."

Partridge stared at the moving scenery. Toshi was disinterested in hunting and thought it generally a waste of energy. Nadine detested the sport without reserve. He tasted brackish water, metallic from the canteen. The odor of gun oil and cigarette smoke was strong in the cab. The smell reminded him of hip waders, muddy clay banks, and gnats in their biting millions among the reeds. "Okay. Thanks."

"Forget it, man."

They drove in silence until Beasley hooked left onto a dirt road that followed a ridge of brambles and oak trees. On the passenger side overgrown pastures dwindled into moiling vapors. The road was secured by a heavy iron gate with the usual complement of grimy warning signs. Beasley climbed out and unlocked the gate and swung it aside. Partridge realized that somehow this was the same ruggedly charismatic Beasley, plus a streak of gray in the beard and minus the spring-loaded tension and the whiskey musk. Beasley at peace was an enigma. Maybe he had quit the bottle for good this time around. The thought was not as comforting as it should have been. If this elemental truth – Beasley the chronic drunk, the lovable, but damaged brute – had ceased to hold, then what else lurked in the wings?

When they had begun to jounce along the washboard lane, Partridge said, "Did T get sick? Somebody – think Frank Ledbetter – told me T had some heart problems. Angina."

"Frankie...I haven't seen him since forever. He still working for Boeing?"

"Lockheed-Martin."

"Yah? Good ol' L&M. Well, no business like war business," Beasley said. "The old boy's fine. Sure, things were in the shitter for a bit after New Guinea, but we all got over it. Water down the sluice." Again, the knowing, sidelong glance. "Don't worry so much. He misses you. Everybody does, man."

Toshi's farm was more of a compound lumped in the torso of a great, irregular field. The road terminated in a hardpack lot bordered by a sprawl of sheds and shacks, gutted chicken coops and labyrinthine hog pens fallen to ruin. The main house, a Queen Anne, dominated. The house was a full three stories of spires, gables, spinning iron weathercocks, and acres of slate tiles. A monster of a house, yet somehow hunched upon itself. It was brooding and squat and low as a brick and timber mausoleum. The detached garage seemed new. So too the tarp and plastic-sheeted nurseries, the electric fence that partitioned the back forty into quadrants, and the military drab shortwave antenna array crowning the A-frame barn. No private security forces were in evidence, no British mercenaries with submachine guns on shoulder slings, nor packs of sleek, bullet-headed attack dogs cruising the property. The golden age had obviously passed into twilight.

"Behold the Moorehead Estate," Beasley said as he parked by slamming the brakes so the truck skidded sideways and its tires sent up a geyser of dirt. "Howard and Toshi bought it from the county about fifteen years ago – guess the original family died out, changed their names, whatever. Been here in one form or another since 1762. The original burned to the foundation in 1886, which is roughly when the town – Orren Towne, 'bout two miles west of here – dried up and blew away. As you can see, they made some progress fixing this place since then."

Partridge whistled as he eyed the setup. "Really, ah, cozy."

There were other cars scattered in the lot: a Bentley; a Nixon-era Cadillac; an archaic Land Rover that might have done a tour in the Sahara; a couple of battered pickup trucks and an Army surplus Jeep. These told Partridge a thing or two, but not enough to surmise the number of guests or the nature of Toshi's interest in them. He had spotted the tail rotor of a helicopter poking from behind the barn.

Partridge did not recognize any of the half-a-dozen grizzled men loitering near the bunkhouse. Those would be the roustabouts and the techs. The men passed around steaming thermoses of coffee. They pretended not to watch him and Beasley unload the luggage.

"For God's sake, boy, why didn't you catch a plane?" Toshi called down from a perilously decrepit veranda. He was wiry and sallow and vitally ancient. He dressed in a bland short sleeve button-up shirt a couple of neck sizes too large and his omnipresent gypsy kerchief. He leaned way over the precarious railing and smoked a cigarette. His cigarettes were invariably Russian and came in tin boxes blazoned with hyperbolic full-color logos and garbled English mottos and blurbs such as "Prince of Peace!" and "Yankee Flavor!"

"The Lear's in the shop." Partridge waved and headed for the porch.

"You don't drive, either, eh?" Toshi flicked his hand impatiently. "Come on, then. Beasley – the Garden Room, please."

Beasley escorted Partridge through the gloomy maze of cramped halls and groaning stairs. Everything was dark: from the cryptic hangings and oil paintings of Mooreheads long returned to dust, to the shiny walnut planks that squeaked and shifted everywhere underfoot.

Partridge was presented a key by the new housekeeper, Mrs. Grant. She was a brusque woman of formidable brawn and comport; perhaps Beasley's mother in another life. Beasley informed him that "new" was a relative term as she had been in Campbell's employ for the better portion of a decade. She had made the voyage from Orange County and brought along three maids and a gardener/handyman who was also her current lover.

The Garden Room was on the second floor of the east wing and carefully isolated from the more heavily trafficked byways. It was a modest, L-shaped room with low, harshly textured ceilings, a coffin wardrobe carved from the heart of some extinct tree, a matching dresser, and a diminutive brass bed that sagged ominously. The portrait of a solemn girl in a garden hat was centered amidst otherwise negative space across from the bed. Vases of fresh-cut flowers were arranged on the window sills. Someone had plugged in a rose-scented air freshener to subdue the abiding taint of wet plaster and rotting wood; mostly in vain. French doors let out to a balcony overlooking tumbledown stone walls of a lost garden and then a plain of waist-high grass gone the shade of wicker. The grass flowed into foothills. The foothills formed an indistinct line in the blue mist.

"Home away from home, eh?" Beasley said. He wrung his hands, out of place as a bear in the confined quarters. "Let's see if those bastards left us any crumbs."

Howard Campbell and Toshi were standing around the bottom of the stairs with a couple of other elder statesmen types – one, a bluff aristocratic fellow with handlebar mustaches and fat hands, reclined in a hydraulic wheelchair. The second man was also a corn-fed specimen of genteel extract, but clean-shaven and decked in a linen suit that had doubtless been the height of ballroom fashion during Truman's watch. This fellow leaned heavily upon an ornate blackthorn cane. He occasionally pressed an oxygen mask over his mouth and nose and snuffled deeply. Both men stank of medicinal alcohol and shoe polish. A pair of bodyguards hovered nearby. The guards were physically powerful men in tight suit-jackets. Their nicked-up faces wore the perpetual scowl of peasant trustees.

Toshi lectured about a so-called supercolony of ants that stretched six thousand kilometers from the mountains of Northern Italy down along the coasts of France and into Spain. According to the reports, this was the largest ant colony on record; a piece of entomological history in the making. He halted his oration to lackadaisically introduce the Eastern gentlemen as Mr. Jackson Phillips and Mr. Carrey Montague and then jabbed Campbell in the ribs, saying, "What'd I tell you? Rich is as suave as an Italian prince. Thank God I don't have a daughter for him to knock up." To Partridge he said, "Now go eat before cook throws it to the pigs. Go, go!" Campbell, the tallest and gravest of the congregation, gave Partridge a subtle wink. Meanwhile, the man in the wheelchair raised his voice to demand an explanation for why his valuable time was being wasted on an ant seminar. He had not come to listen to a dissertation and Toshi damned-well knew better...Partridge did not catch the rest because Beasley ushered him into the kitchen whilst surreptitiously flicking Mr. Jackson Phillips the bird.

The cook was an impeccable Hungarian named Gertz, whom Campbell had lured, or possibly blackmailed, away from a popular restaurant in Santa Monica. In any event, Gertz knew his business.

Partridge slumped on a wooden stool at the kitchen counter. He worked his way through what Gertz apologetically called "leftovers." These included sourdough waffles and strawberries, whipped eggs, biscuits, sliced apples, honey dew melon, and chilled milk. The coffee was a hand-ground Columbian blend strong enough to peel paint. Beasley slapped him on the shoulder and said something about chores.

Partridge was sipping his second mug of coffee, liberally dosed with cream and sugar, when Nadine sat down close to him. Nadine shone darkly and smelled of fresh-cut hayricks and sweet, highly polished leather. She leaned in tight and plucked the teaspoon from his abruptly nerveless fingers. She licked the teaspoon and dropped it on the saucer and she did not smile at all. She looked at him with metallic eyes that held nothing but a prediction of snow.

"And...action," Nadine said in a soft, yet resonant voice that could have placed her center stage on Broadway had she ever desired to dwell in the Apple and ride her soap-and-water sex appeal to the bank and back. She spoke without a trace of humor, which was a worthless gauge to ascertain her mood anyhow, she being a classical Stoic. Her mouth was full and lovely and inches from Partridge's own. She did not wear lipstick.

"You're pissed," Partridge said. He felt slightly dizzy. He was conscious of his sticky fingers and the seeds in his teeth.

"Lucky guess."

"I'm a Scientologist, Grade-Two. We get ESP at G-2. No luck involved."

"Oh, they got you, too. Pity. Inevitable, but still a pity."

"I'm kidding."

"What...even the cultists don't want you?"

"I'm sure they want my money."

Nadine tilted her head slightly. "I owe the Beez twenty bucks, speaking of. Know why?"

"No," Partridge said. "Wait. You said I wouldn't show – "

" – because you're a busy man – "

"That's the absolute truth. I'm busier than a one-armed paper hanger."

"I'm sure. Anyway, I said you'd duck us once again. A big movie deal, fucking a B-list starlet in the South of France. It'd be something."

" – and then Beasley said something on the order of – "

"Hell yeah, my boy will be here! – "

" – come hell or high water!"

"Pretty much, yeah. He believes in you."

Partridge tried not to squirm even as her pitiless gaze bore into him. "Well, it was close. I cancelled some things. Broke an engagement or two."

"Mmm. It's okay, Rich. You've been promising yourself a vacation, haven't you? This makes a handy excuse; do a little R&R, get some *you* time in for a change. It's for your mental health. Bet you can write it off."

"Since this is going so well...How's Coop?" He had noticed she was not wearing the ring. Handsome hubby Dan Cooper was doubtless a sore subject, he being the hapless CEO of an obscure defense contractor that got caught up in a Federal dragnet. He would not be racing his classic Jaguar along hairpin coastal highways for the next five to seven years, even assuming time off for good behavior. Poor Coop was another victim of Nadine's gothic curse. "Condolences, naturally. If I didn't send a card..."

"He *loves* Federal prison. It's a country club, really. How's that bitch you introduced me to? I forget her name."

"Rachel."

"Yep, that's it. The makeup lady. She pancaked Thurman like a corpse on that flick you shot for Coppola."

"Ha, yeah. She's around. We're friends."

"Always nice to have friends."

Partridge forced a smile. "I'm seeing someone else."

"Kyla Sherwood – the Peroxide Puppet. Tabloids know all, my dear."

"But it's not serious."

"News to her, hey?"

He was boiling alive in his Aspen-chic sweater and charcoal slacks. Sweat trickled down his neck and the hairs on his thighs prickled and chorused their disquiet. He wondered if that was a massive pimple pinching the flesh between his eyes. That was where he had always gotten the worst of them in high school. His face swelled so majestically people thought he had broken his nose playing softball. What could he say with this unbearable pressure building in his lungs? Their history had grown to epic dimensions. The kitchen was too small to contain such a thing. He said, "Toshi said it was important. That I come to this...what? Party? Reunion? Whatever it is. God knows I love a mystery."

Nadine stared the stare that gave away nothing. She finally glanced at her watch and stood. She leaned over him so that her hot breath brushed his ear. "Mmm. Look at the time. Lovely seeing you, Rich. Maybe later we can do lunch."

He watched her walk away. As his pulse slowed and his breathing loosened, he waited for his erection to subside and tried to pinpoint what it was that nagged him, what it was that tripped the machinery beneath the liquid surface of his guilt-crazed, testosterone-glutted brain. Nadine had always reminded him of a duskier, more ferocious Bettie Page. She was thinner now, probably going gray if not for the wonders of modern cosmetics. Her prominent cheekbones, the fragile symmetry of her scapulae through the open-back blouse, registered with him as he sat recovering his wits with the numb intensity of a soldier who had just clambered from a trench following a mortar barrage.

Gertz slunk out of hiding and poured more coffee into Partridge's cup. He dumped in some Schnapps from a hip flask. "Hang in there, my friend," he said drolly.

"I just got my head beaten in," Partridge said.

"Round one," Gertz said. He took a hefty pull from the flask. "Pace yourself, champ."

Partridge wandered the grounds until he found Toshi in D-Lab. Toshi was surveying a breeding colony of cockroaches: Periplaneta americana, he proclaimed them with a mixture of pride and annoyance. The lab was actually a big tool shed with the windows painted over. Industrial-sized aquariums occupied most of the floor space. The air had acquired a peculiar, spicy odor reminiscent of hazelnuts and fermented bananas. The chamber was illuminated by infrared lamps. Partridge could not observe much activity within the aquariums unless he stood next to the glass. That was not going to happen. He contented himself to lurk at Toshi's elbow while a pair of men in coveralls and rubber gloves performed maintenance on an empty pen. The men scraped substrate into garbage bags and hosed the container and applied copious swathes of petroleum jelly to the rim where the mesh lid attached. Cockroaches were escape artists extraordinaire, according to Toshi.

"Most folks are trying to figure the best pesticide to squirt on these little fellas. Here you are a cockroach rancher," Partridge said.

"Cockroaches…I care nothing for cockroaches. This is scarcely more than a side effect, the obligatory nod to cladistics, if you will. Cockroaches…beetles… there are superficial similarities. These animals crawl and burrow, they predate us humans by hundreds of millions of years. But…beetles are infinitely more interesting. The naturalist's best friend. Museums and taxidermists love them, you see. Great for cleansing skeletal structures, antlers and the like."

"Nature's efficiency experts. What's the latest venture?"

"A-Lab – I will show you." Toshi became slightly animated. He straightened his crunched shoulders to gesticulate. His hand glimmered like a glow tube at a rock concert. "I keep a dozen colonies of dermestid beetles in operation. Have to house them in glass or stainless steel – they nibble through anything."

This house of creepy-crawlies was not good for Partridge's nerves. He thought of the chair and the woman and her tarantula. He was sickly aware that if he closed his eyes at that very moment the stranger would remove the mask and reveal Nadine's face. Thinking of Nadine's face and its feverish luminescence, he said, "She's dying."

Toshi shrugged. "Johns Hopkins…my friends at Fred Hutch…nobody can do anything. This is the very bad stuff; very quick."

"How long has she got." The floor threatened to slide from under Partridge's feet. Cockroaches milled in their shavings and hidey holes; their tick-tack impacts burrowed under his skin.

"Not long. Probably three or four months."

"Okay." Partridge tasted breakfast returned as acid in his mouth.

The technicians finished their task and began sweeping. Toshi gave some orders. He said to Partridge, "Let's go see the beetles."

A-Lab was identical to D-Lab except for the wave of charnel rot that met Partridge as he entered. The dermestid colonies were housed in corrugated metal canisters. Toshi raised the lid to show Partridge how industriously a particular group of larvae were stripping the greasy flesh of a small mixed-breed dog. Clean white bone peeked through coagulated muscle fibers and patches of coarse, blond fur.

Partridge managed to stagger the fifteen or so feet and vomit into a plastic sink. Toshi shut the lid and nodded wisely. "Some fresh air, then."

Toshi conducted a perfunctory tour, complete with a wheezing narrative regarding matters coleopteran and teuthological, the latter being one of his comrade Howard Campbell's manifold specialties. Campbell had held since the early seventies that One Day Soon the snail cone or some species of jellyfish was going to revolutionize neurology. Partridge nodded politely and dwelt on his erupting misery. His stomach felt as if a brawler had used it for a speed bag. He trembled and dripped with cold sweats.

Then, as they ambled along a fence holding back the wasteland beyond the barn, he spotted a cluster of three satellite dishes. The dishes' antennas were angled downward at a sizable oblong depression like aardvark snouts poised to siphon musty earth. These were lightweight models, each no more than four meters across and positioned as to be hidden from casual view from the main house. Their trapezoidal shapes didn't jibe with photos Partridge had seen of similar devices. These objects gleamed the yellow-gray gleam of rotting teeth. His skin crawled as he studied them and the area of crushed soil. The depression was over a foot deep and shaped not unlike a kiddy wading pool. This presence in the field was incongruous and somehow sinister. He immediately regretted discarding his trusty Canon. He stopped and pointed. "What are those?"

"Radio telescopes, obviously."

"Yeah, what kind of metal is that? Don't they work better if you point them at the sky?"

"The sky. Ah, well, perhaps later. You note the unique design, eh? Campbell and I...invented them. Basically."

"Really? Interesting segue from entomological investigation, Doc."

"See what happens when you roll in the mud with NASA? The notion of first contact is so glamorous, it begins to rub off. Worse than drugs. I'm in recovery."

Partridge stared at the radio dishes. "UFOs and whatnot, huh. You stargazer, you. When did you get into that field?" It bemused him how Toshi Ryoko hopscotched from discipline to discipline with a breezy facility that unnerved even the mavericks among his colleagues.

"I most assuredly haven't migrated to that field – however, I will admit to grazing as the occasion warrants. The dishes are a link in the chain. We've got miles of conductive coil buried around here. All part of a comprehensive surveillance plexus. We monitor everything that crawls, swims, or flies. Howard and I have become enamored of astrobiology, cryptozoology, the occulted world. Do you recall when we closed shop in California? That was roughly concomitant with our lamentably over-publicized misadventures in New Guinea."

"Umm." Partridge had heard that Campbell and Toshi disappeared into the back country for three weeks after they lost a dozen porters and two graduate students in a river accident. Maybe alcohol and drugs were involved. There was an investigation and all charges were waived. The students' families had sued and sued, of course. Partridge knew he should have called to offer moral support. Unfortunately, associating with Toshi in that time of crisis might have been an unwise career move and he let it slide. *But nothing slides forever, does it?*

"New Guinea wasn't really a disaster. Indeed, it served to crystallize the focus of our research, to open new doors..."

Partridge was not thrilled to discuss New Guinea. "Intriguing. I'm glad you're going great guns. It's over my head, but I'm glad. Sincerely." Several crows described broad, looping circles near the unwholesome machines. Near, but not too near.

"Ah, but that's not important. I imagine I shall die before any of this work comes to fruition." Toshi smiled fondly and evasively. He gave Partridge an avuncular pat on the arm. "You're here for Nadine's grand farewell. She will leave the farm after the weekend. Everything is settled. You see now why I called."

Partridge was not convinced. Nadine seemed to resent his presence – she'd always been hot and cold when it came to him. What did Toshi want him to do? "Absolutely," he said.

They walked back to the house and sat on the porch in rocking chairs. Gertz brought them a pitcher of iced tea and frosted glasses on trays. Campbell emerged in his trademark double-breasted, steel-blue suit and horn-rim glasses. For the better part of three decades he had played the mild, urbane foil to Toshi's megalomaniacal iconoclast. In private, Campbell was easily the dominant of the pair. He leaned against a post and held out his hand until Toshi passed him a smoldering cigarette. "I'm glad you know," he said, fastening his murky eyes on Partridge. "I didn't have the nerve to tell you myself."

Partridge felt raw, exhausted, and bruised. He changed the subject. "So... those guys in the suits. Montague and Phillips. How do you know them? Financiers, I presume?"

"Patrons," Campbell said. "As you can see, we've scaled back the operation. It's difficult to run things off the cuff." Lolling against the post, a peculiar hybrid of William Burroughs and Walter Cronkite, he radiated folksy charm that mostly diluted underlying hints of decadence. This charm often won the hearts of flabby dilettante crones looking for a cause to champion. "Fortunately, there are always interested parties with deep pockets."

Partridge chuckled to cover his unease. His stomach was getting worse. "Toshi promised to get me up to speed on your latest and greatest contribution to the world of science. Or do I want to know?"

"You showed him the telescopes? Anything else?" Campbell glanced to Toshi and arched his brow.

Toshi's grin was equal portions condescension and mania. He rubbed his spindly hands together like a spider combing its pedipalps. "Howard...I haven't, he hasn't been to the site. He has visited with our pets, however. Mind your shoes if you fancy them, by the way."

"Toshi has developed a knack for beetles," Campbell said. "I don't know what he sees in them, frankly. Boring, boring. Pardon the pun – I'm stone knackered on Dewar's. My bloody joints are positively gigantic in this climate. Oh – have you seen reports of the impending Yellow Disaster? China will have the whole of Asia Minor deforested in the next decade. I imagine you haven't – you don't film horror movies, right? At least not reality horror." He laughed as if to say, *You realize I'm kidding, don't you, lad? We're all friends here.* "Mankind is definitely eating himself out of house and home. The beetles and cockroaches are in the direct line of succession."

"Scary," Partridge said. He waited doggedly for the punch line. Although, free association was another grace note of Campbell's and Toshi's. The punch line might not even exist. Give them thirty seconds and they would be nattering about engineering *E. coli* to perform microscopic stupid pet tricks or how much they missed those good old Bangkok whores.

Toshi lighted another cigarette and waved it carelessly. "The boy probably hasn't the foggiest notion as to the utility of our naturalistic endeavors. Look, after dinner, we'll give a demonstration. We'll hold a séance."

"Oh, horseshit, Toshi!" Campbell scowled fearsomely. This was always a remarkable transformation for those not accustomed to his moods. "Considering the circumstances, that's extremely tasteless."

"Not to mention premature," Partridge said through a grim smile. He rose, upsetting his drink in a clatter of softened ice cubes and limpid orange rinds and strode from the porch. He averted his face. He was not certain if Campbell called after him because of the blood beating in his ears. Toshi did clearly say, "Let him go, let him be, Howard... She'll talk to him..."

He stumbled to his room and crashed into his too-short bed and fell unconscious.

Partridge owed much of his success to Toshi. Even that debt might not have been sufficient to justify the New England odyssey. The real reason, the motive force under the hood of Partridge's lamentable midlife crisis, and the magnetic compulsion to heed that bizarre late-night call, was certainly his sense of unfinished business with Nadine. Arguably, he had Toshi to thank for that, too.

Toshi Ryoko immigrated to Britain, and later the U.S., from Okinawa in the latter sixties. This occurred a few years after he had begun to attract attention from the international scientific community for his brilliant work in behavioral ecology and prior to his stratospheric rise to popular fame due to daredevil eccentricities and an Academy Award-nominated documentary of his harrowing expedition into the depths of a Bengali wildlife preserve. The name of the preserve loosely translated into English as "The Forest that Eats Men." Partridge had been the twenty-three-year-old cinematographer brought aboard at the last possible moment to photograph the expedition. No more qualified person could be found on the ridiculously short notice that Toshi announced for departure. The director/producer was none other than Toshi himself. It was his first and last film. There were, of course, myriad subsequent independent features, newspaper and radio accounts – the major slicks covered Toshi's controversial exploits, but he lost interest in filmmaking after the initial hubbub and eventually faded from the public eye. Possibly his increasing affiliation with clandestine U.S. government projects was to blame. The cause was immaterial. Toshi's fascinations were mercurial and stardom proved incidental to his mission of untangling the enigmas of evolutionary origins and ultimate destination.

Partridge profited greatly from that tumultuous voyage into the watery hell of man-eating tigers and killer bees. He emerged from the crucible as a legend fully formed. His genesis was as Minerva's, that warrior-daughter sprung whole from Jupiter's aching skull. All the great directors wanted him. His name was gold – it was nothing but Beluga caviar and box seats at the Rose Bowl, a string of "where are they now" actresses on his arm, an executive membership in the Ferrari Club and posh homes in Malibu and Ireland. Someday they would hang his portrait in the American Society of Cinematography archives and blazon his star on Hollywood Boulevard.

There was just one glitch in his happily-ever-after: Nadine. Nadine Thompson was the whip-smart Stanford physiologist who had gone along for the ride to Bangladesh as Toshi's chief disciple. She was not Hollywood sultry, yet the camera found her to be eerily riveting in a way that was simultaneously erotic and repellant. The audience never saw a *scientist* when the camera tracked Nadine across the rancid deck of that river barge. They saw a woman-child – ripe, lithe and lethally carnal.

She was doomed. Jobs came and went. Some were comparative plums, yes. None of them led to prominence indicative of her formal education and nascent talent. None of them opened the way to the marquee projects, postings, or commissions. She eventually settled for a staff position at a museum in Buffalo. An eighty-seven-minute film shot on super-sixteen millimeter consigned her to professional purgatory. Maybe a touch of that taint had rubbed off on Partridge. Nadine was the youthful excess that Hollywood could not supply, despite its excess of youth, the one he still longed for during the long, blank Malibu nights. He carried a load of guilt about the whole affair as well.

Occasionally, in the strange, hollow years after the hoopla, the groundswell of acclaim and infamy, she would corner Partridge in a remote getaway bungalow, or a honeymoon seaside cottage, for a weekend of gin and bitters and savage lovemaking. In the languorous aftermath, she often confided how his magic Panaflex had destroyed her career. She would forever be "the woman in that movie." She was branded a real-life scream queen and the sexpot with the so-so face and magnificent ass.

Nadine was right, as usual. "The Forest that Eats Men" never let go once it sank its teeth.

He dreamed of poling a raft on a warm, muddy river. Mangroves hemmed them in corridors of convoluted blacks and greens. Creepers and vines strung the winding waterway. Pale sunlight sifted down through the screen of vegetation; a dim, smoky light full of shadows and shifting clouds of gnats and mosquitoes. Birds warbled and screeched. He crouched in the stern of the raft and stared at the person directly before him. That person's wooden mask with its dead eyes and wooden smile gaped at him, fitted as it was to the back of the man's head. The wooden mouth whispered, "You forgot your mask." Partridge reached back and found, with burgeoning horror, that his skull was indeed naked and defenseless.

"They're coming. They're coming." The mask grinned soullessly.

He inhaled to scream and jerked awake, twisted in the sheets and sweating. Red light poured through the thin curtains. Nadine sat in the shadows at the foot of his bed. Her hair was loose and her skin reflected the ruddy light. He thought of the goddess Kali shrunk to mortal dimensions.

"You don't sleep well either, huh," she said.

"Nope. Not since Bangladesh."

"That long. Huh."

He propped himself on his elbow and studied her. "I've been considering my options lately. I'm thinking it might be time to hang up my spurs. Go live in the Bahamas."

She said, "You're too young to go." That was her mocking tone.

"You too."

She didn't say anything for a while. Then, "Rich, you ever get the feeling you're being watched?"

"Like when you snuck in here while I was sleeping? Funny you should mention it..."

"Rich."

He saw that she was serious. "Sometimes, yeah."

"Well you are. Always. I want you to keep that in mind."

"Okay. Will it help?"

"Good question."

The room darkened, bit by bit. He said, "You think you would've made it back to the barge?" He couldn't distance himself from her cry as she flailed overboard and hit the water like a stone. There were crocodiles everywhere. No one moved.

The whole crew was frozen in that moment between disbelief and action. He had shoved the camera at, who? Beasley. He had done that and then gone in and gotten her. Blood warm water, brown with mud. He did not remember much of the rest. The camera caught it all.

"No," she said. "Not even close."

He climbed over the bed and hugged her. She was warm. He pressed his face into her hair. Her hair trapped the faint, cloying odor of sickness. "I'm so fucking sorry," he said.

She didn't say anything. She rubbed his shoulder.

That night was quiet at the Moorehead Estate. There was a subdued dinner and afterward some drinks. Everybody chatted about the good old days. The real ones and the imaginary ones too. Phillips and Montague disappeared early on and took their men-at-arms with them. Nadine sat aloof. She held onto a hardback – one of Toshi's long out-of-print treatises on insect behavior and ecological patterns. Partridge could tell she was only pretending to look at it.

Later, after lights out, Partridge roused from a dream of drowning in something that wasn't quite water. His name was whispered from the foot of the bed. He fumbled upright in the smothering dark. "Nadine?" He clicked on the lamp and saw he was alone.

It rained in the morning. Toshi was undeterred. He put on a slicker and took a drive in the Land Rover to move the radio telescopes and other equipment into more remote fields. A truckload of the burly, grim laborers followed. The technicians trudged about their daily routine, indifferent to the weather. Campbell disappeared with Phillips and Montague. Nadine remained in her room. Partridge spent the morning playing poker with Beasley and Gertz on the rear porch. They drank whiskey – coffee for Beasley – and watched water drip from the eaves and thunderheads roll across the horizon trailing occasional whip-cracks of lightning. Then it stopped raining and the sun transformed the landscape into a mass of illuminated rust and glass.

Partridge went for a long walk around the property to clear his head and savor the clean air. The sun was melting toward the horizon when Beasley found him dozing in the shade of an oak. It was a huge tree with yellowing leaves and exposed roots. The roots crawled with pill bugs. Between yawns Partridge observed the insects go about their tiny business.

"C'mon. You gotta see the ghost town before it gets dark," Beasley said. Partridge didn't bother to protest. Nadine waited in the Jeep. She wore tortoise shell sunglasses and a red scarf in her hair. He decided she looked better in a scarf than Toshi ever had, no question. Partridge opened his mouth and Beasley gave him a friendly shove into the front passenger seat.

"Sulk, sulk, sulk!" Nadine laughed at him. "In the garden, eating worms?"

"Close enough," Partridge said and hung on as Beasley gunned the Jeep through a break in the fence line and zoomed along an overgrown track that was invisible until they were right on top of it. The farm became a picture on a stamp and then they passed through a belt of paper birches and red maples. They crossed a ramshackle bridge that spanned an ebon stream and drove into a clearing. Beasley ground gears until they gained the crown of a long, tabletop hill. He killed the engine and coasted to a halt amid tangled grass and wildflowers and said, "Orren Towne. Died circa 1890s."

Below their vantage, remnants of a village occupied the banks of a shallow valley. If Orren Towne was dead its death was the living kind. A score of saltbox houses and the brooding hulk of a Second Empire church waited somberly. Petrified roofs were dappled by the shadows of moving clouds. Facades were brim with the ephemeral light of the magic hour. Beasley's walkie-talkie crackled and he stepped aside to answer the call.

Nadine walked part way down the slope and stretched her arms. Her muscles stood forth in cords of sinew and gristle. She looked over her shoulder at Partridge. Her smile was alien. "Don't you wish you'd brought your camera?"

The brain is a camera. What Partridge really wished was that he had gone to his room and slept. His emotions were on the verge of running amok. The animal fear from his daydreams had sneaked up again. He smelled the musk of his own adrenaline and sweat. *The brain is a camera and once it sees what it sees there's no taking it back.* He noticed another of Toshi's bizarre radio dishes perched on a bluff. The antenna was focused upon the deserted buildings. "I don't like this place," he said. But she kept walking and he trailed along. It was cooler among the houses. The earth was trampled into concrete and veined with minerals. Nothing organic grew and no birds sang. The subtly deformed structures were encased in a transparent resin that lent the town the aspect of a waxworks. He thought it might be shellac.

Shadows fell across Partridge's path. Open doorways and sugar-spun windows fronted darkness. These doors and windows were as unwelcoming as the throats of ancient wells, the mouths of caves. He breathed heavily. "How did Toshi do this? *Why* did he do this?"

Nadine laughed and took his hand playfully. Hers was dry and too-warm, like a leather wallet left in direct sunlight. "Toshi only discovered it. Do you seriously think he and Howard are capable of devising something this extraordinary?"

"No."

"Quite a few people spent their lives in this valley. Decent farming and hunting in these parts. The Mooreheads owned about everything. They owned a brewery and a mill down the road, near their estate. All those busy little worker bees going about their jobs, going to church on Sunday. I'm sure it was a classic Hallmark. Then it got cold. One of those long winters that never ends. Nothing wanted to grow and the game disappeared. The house burned. Sad for the Mooreheads. Sadder for the people who depended on them. The family circled its wagons to rebuild the mansion, but the community proper never fully recovered. Orren Towne was here today, gone tomorrow. At least that's the story we hear told by the old timers at the Mad Rooster over cribbage and a pint of stout." Nadine stood in the shade of the church, gazing up, up at the crucifix. "This is how it will all be someday. Empty buildings. Empty skies. The grass will come and eat everything we ever made. The waters will swallow it. It puts my situation into perspective, lemme tell you."

"These buildings should've fallen down. Somebody's gone through a lot of trouble to keep this like – "

"A museum. Yeah, somebody has. This isn't the only place it's been done, either."

"Places like this? Where?" Partridge said. He edged closer to the bright center of the village square.

"I don't know. They're all over if you know what to look for."

"Nadine, maybe...Jesus!" He jerked his head around to peer at a doorway. The darkness inside the house seemed fuller and more complete. "Are there people here?" His mind jumped to an image of the masks that the natives wore to ward off tigers. He swallowed hard.

"Just us chickens, love."

A stiff breeze rushed from the northwest and whipped the outlying grass. Early autumn leaves skated across the glassy rooftops and swirled in barren yards. Leaves fell dead and dry. Night was coming hard.

"I'm twitchy – jet lag, probably. What do those weird-looking rigs do?" He pointed at the dish on the hill. "Toshi said they're radio telescopes he invented."

"He said he invented them? Oh my. I dearly love that man, but sometimes he's such an asshole."

"Yeah. How do they work?"

Nadine shrugged. "They read frequencies on the electromagnetic spectrum."

"Radio signals from underground. Why does that sound totally backwards to me?"

"I didn't say anything about radio signals."

"Then what did you say?"

"When we get back, ask Toshi about the node."

"What are you talking about?" Partridge's attention was divided between her and the beautifully grotesque houses and the blackness inside them.

"You'll see. Get him to show you the node. That'll clear some of this stuff up, pronto."

Beasley called to them. He and the Jeep were a merged silhouette against the failing sky. He swung his arm overhead until Nadine yelled that they would start back in a minute. She removed her shades and met Partridge's eyes. "You okay, Rich?" She refused to relinquish her grip on his hand.

"You're asking *me?*"

She gave him another of her inscrutable looks. She reached up and pushed an unkempt lock from his forehead. "I'm not pissed, in case you're still wondering. I wanted you to see me off. Not like there're any more weekend rendezvous in the stars for us."

"That's no way to talk," he said.

"Just sayin'." She dropped his hand and walked away. In a moment he followed. By the time they made the summit, darkness had covered the valley. Beasley had to use the headlights to find the way home.

Gertz served prawns for dinner. They ate at the long mahogany table in the formal dining room. Jackson Phillips begged off due to an urgent matter in the city. Beasley packed him and one of the muscle-bound bodyguards into the helicopter and flew away. That left six: Toshi; Campbell; Nadine; Carrey Montague and the other bodyguard, and Partridge. The men wore suits and ties. Nadine wore a cream-colored silk chiffon evening gown. There were candles and elaborate floral arrangements and dusty bottles of wine from the Moorehead cellar and magnums of top-dollar French champagne from a Boston importer who catered to those with exclusive tastes and affiliations. Toshi proposed a toast and said a few words in Japanese and then the assembly began to eat and drink.

Somewhere in the middle of the third or fourth course, Partridge realized he was cataclysmically drunk. They kept setting them up and he kept knocking them down. Toshi or Campbell frequently clapped his back and clinked his glass and shouted "*Sic itur ad astra!*" and another round would magically appear. His head was swollen and empty as an echo chamber. The winking silverware and sloshing wineglasses, the bared teeth and hearty laughter came to him from a seashell. Nadine abruptly rose and fled, weeping.

Dinner blurred into a collage of sense and chaos, of light and dark, and he gripped his glass and blinked dumbly against the shattering flare of the low-slung chandelier and laughed uproariously. Without transition, dinner was concluded and the men had repaired to the den to relax over snifters of Hennessy. They lounged in wing-backed leather chairs and upon opulent leather divans. Partridge admired the vaulted ceiling, the library of towering lacquered oak bookcases, and the impressive collection of antique British rifles and British cavalry sabers cached in rearing cabinets of chocolate wood and softly warped glass. Everything was so huge and shiny and far away. When the cigar and pipe smoke hung thick and the men's cheeks were glazed and rosy as the cheeks of Russian dolls, he managed, "I'm supposed to ask you about the node."

Campbell smiled a broad and genial smile. "The node, yes. The node, of course, is the very reason Mr. Phillips and Mr. Montague have come to pay their respects. They hope to buy their way into Heaven."

"He's right, he's right," Mr. Carrey Montague said with an air of merry indulgence. "Jack had his shot. Didn't he though. Couldn't hack it and off he flew."

"I was getting to this," Toshi said. "In a roundabout fashion."

"Exceedingly so," Campbell said.

"Didn't want to frighten him. It's a delicate matter."

"Yes," Campbell said dryly. He puffed on his pipe and his eyes were red around the edges and in the center of his pupils.

"Shall I. Or do you want a go?" Toshi shrugged his indifference.

"The node is a communication device," Campbell said through a mouthful of smoke. "Crude, really. Danforth Moorehead, the Moorehead patriarch, developed the current model. Ahem, the schematic was delivered to him and he effected the necessary modifications, at any rate. Admittedly, it's superior to the primitive methods – scrying, séances, psychedelic drugs, that nonsense. Not to mention some of the more gruesome customs we've observed in the provincial regions. Compared to that, the node is state of the art. It is a reservoir that filters and translates frequency imaging captured by our clever, clever radio telescopes. It permits us to exchange information with our...neighbors."

Partridge dimly perceived that the others were watching him with something like fascination. Their eyes glittered through the haze. "With who? I don't – "

"Our neighbors," Campbell said.

"Oh, the things they show you." Carrey Montague sucked on his oxygen mask until he resembled a ghoul.

Partridge swung his head to look from face to face. The men were drunk. The men seethed with restrained glee. No one appeared to be joking. "Well, go on then," he said dreamily. His face was made of plaster. Black spots revolved before him like ashen snowflakes.

"I told you, Richard. Mankind can't go on like this."

"Like what?"

Toshi chuckled. "Assuming we don't obliterate ourselves, or that a meteorite doesn't smack us back to the Cambrian, if not the Cryptozoic, this planet will succumb to the exhaustion of Sol. First the mammals, then the reptiles, right down the line until all that's left of any complexity are the arthropods: beetles and cockroaches and their oceanic cousins, practically speaking. Evolution is a circle – we're sliding back to that endless sea of protoplasmic goop."

"I'm betting on the nuclear holocaust," Campbell said.

Partridge slopped more brandy into his mouth. He was far beyond tasting it. "Mmm hmm," he said intelligently and cast about for a place to inconspicuously ditch his glass.

"NASA and its holy grail – First Contact, the quest for intelligent life in the universe...all hogwash, all lies." Toshi gently took the snifter away and handed him a fresh drink in a ceramic mug. This was not brandy; it was rich and dark as honey in moonlight. "Private stock, my boy. Drink up!" Partridge drank and his eyes flooded and he choked a little. Toshi nodded in satisfaction. "We know now what we've always suspected. Man is completely and utterly alone in a sea of dust and smoke. Alone and inevitably slipping into extinction."

"Not quite alone," Campbell said. "There are an estimated five to eight million species of insects as of yet unknown and unclassified. Hell of a lot of insects, hmm? But why stop at bugs? Only a damned fool would suppose that was anything but the tip of the iceberg. When the time of Man comes to an end *their* time will begin. And be certain this is not an invasion or a hostile occupation. We'll be dead as Dodos a goodly period before they emerge to claim the surface. They won't rule forever. The planet will eventually become cold and inhospitable to any mortal organism. But trust that their rule will make the reign of the terrible lizards seem a flicker of an eyelash."

"You're talking about cockroaches," Partridge said in triumph. "Fucking cockroaches." That was too amusing and so he snorted on his pungent liquor and had a coughing fit.

"No, we are not," Campbell said.

"We aren't talking about spiders or beetles, either," Toshi said. He gave Partridge's knee an earnest squeeze. "To even compare them with the citizens of the *Great Kingdom*...I shudder. However, if I *were* to make that comparison, I'd say this intelligence is the Ur-progenitor of those insects scrabbling in the muck. The mother race of idiot stepchildren."

Campbell knelt before him so they were eye to eye. The older man's face was radiant and distant as the moon. "This is a momentous discovery. We've established contact. Not us, actually. It's been going on forever. We are the latest...emissaries, if you will. Trustees to the grandest secret of them all."

"Hoo boy. You guys. You fucking guys. Is Nadine in on this?"

"Best that you see first hand. Would you like that, Rich?"

"Uhmm-wha?" Partridge did not know what he wanted except that he wanted the carousel to stop.

Campbell and Toshi stood. They took his arms and the next thing he knew they were outside in the humid country night with darkness all around. He tried to walk, but his legs wouldn't cooperate much. They half dragged him to a dim metal door and there was a lamp bulb spinning in space and then steep, winding concrete stairs and cracked concrete walls ribbed with mold. They went down and down and a strong, earthy smell overcame Partridge's senses. People spoke to him in rumbling nonsense phrases. Someone ruffled his hair and laughed. His vision fractured. He glimpsed hands and feet, a piece of jaw illumed by a quivering fluorescent glow. When the hands stopped supporting him, he slid to his knees. He had the impression of kneeling in a cellar. Water dripped and a pale overhead lamp hummed like a wasp in a jar. From the corner of his eye he got the sense of table legs and cables and he smelled an acrid smell like cleaning solvents. He thought it might be a laboratory.

– Crawl forward just a bit.

It was strange whatever lay before him. Something curved, spiral-shaped, and darkly wet. A horn, a giant conch shell – it was impossible to be certain. There was an opening, as the *external os* of a cervix, large enough to accommodate him in all his lanky height. Inside it was moist and muffled and black.

– There's a lad. Curl up inside. Don't fight. There, there. That's my boy. Won't be long. Not long. Don't be afraid. This is only a window, not a doorway.

Then nothing and nothing and nothing; only his heart, his breathing, and a whispery static thrum that might've been the electromagnetic current tracing its circuit through his nerves.

Nothingness grew very dense.

Partridge tried to shriek when water, or something thicker than water flowed over his head and into his sinuses and throat. Low static built in his ears and the abject blackness was replaced by flashes of white imagery. He fell from an impossible height. He saw only high velocity jump-cuts of the world and each caromed from him and into the gulf almost instantly. Fire and blood and moving tides of unleashed water. Bones of men and women and cities. Dead, mummified cities gone so long without inhabitants they had become cold and brittle and smooth as mighty forests of stone. There loomed over everything a silence that held to its sterile bosom countless screams and the sibilant chafe of swirling dust. Nadine stood naked as ebony in the heart of a ruined square. She wore a white mask, but he knew her with the immediacy of a nightmare. She lifted her mask and looked at him. She smiled and raised her hand. Men and women emerged from the broken skyscrapers and collapsed bunkers. They were naked and pallid and smiling. In the distance the sun heaved up, slow and red. Its deathly light cascaded upon the lines and curves of cyclopean structures. These were colossal, inhuman edifices of fossil bone and obsidian and anthracite that glittered not unlike behemoth carapaces. He thrashed and fell and fell and drowned.

Nadine said in his ear, *Come down. We love you.*

The cellar floor was cool upon his cheek. He was paralyzed and choking. The men spoke to him in soothing voices. Someone pressed a damp cloth to his brow.

– Take it easy, son. The first ride or two is a bitch and a half. Get his head.

Partridge groaned as gravity crushed him into the moldy concrete.

Someone murmured to him.

– They are interested in preserving aspects of our culture. Thus Orren Towne and places, hidden places most white men will never tread. Of course, it's a multifaceted project. Preserving artifacts, buildings, that's hardly enough to satisfy such an advanced intellect...

Partridge tried to speak. His jaw worked spastically. No sound emerged. The concrete went soft and everyone fell silent at once.

Partridge stirred and sat up. He tried to piece together how he ended up on the back porch sprawled in a wooden folding chair. He was still in his suit and it was damp and clung to him the way clothes do after they have been slept in. The world teetered on the cusp of night. Parts of the sky were orange as fire and other parts were covered by purple-tinted rain clouds like a pall of cannon smoke. Partridge's hair stood in gummy spikes. His mouth was swollen and cottony. He had drooled in his long sleep. His body was stiff as an old plank.

Beasley came out of the house and handed him a glass of seltzer water. "Can't hold your liquor anymore?"

Partridge took the glass in both hands and drank greedily. "Oh you're back. Must've been a hell of a party," he said at last. He had slept for at least sixteen hours according to his watch. His memory was a smooth and frictionless void.

"Yeah," Beasley said. "You okay?"

Partridge was not sure. "Uh," he said. He rolled his head to survey the twilight vista. "Beasley."

"Yeah?"

"All this." Partridge swept his hand to encompass the swamped gardens and the decrepit outbuildings. "They're letting it fall down. Nobody left from the old days."

"You and me. And Nadine."

"And when we're gone?"

"We're all gonna be gone sooner or later. The docs...they just do what they can. There's nothing else, pal." Beasley gave him a searching look. He shook his shaggy head and chuckled. "Don't get morbid on me, Hollywood. Been a good run if you ask me. Hell, we may get a few more years before the plug gets pulled."

"Is Montague still here?"

"Why do you ask?"

"I heard someone yelling, cursing. Earlier, while I slept."

"Huh. Yeah, there was a little fight. The old fella didn't get his golden ticket. He wasn't wanted. Few are. He shipped out. Won't be coming back."

"I guess not. What was he after?"

"Same thing as everybody else, I suppose. People think Toshi is the Devil, that he can give them their heart's desire if they sign on the dotted line. It ain't so simple."

Partridge had a wry chuckle at that. "Damned right it's not simple, partner. I'm still selling my soul to Tinsel Town. No such luck as to unload the whole shebang at once." Partridge shook with a sudden chill. His memory shucked and jittered; it spun off the reel in his brain and he could not gather it fast enough to make sense of what he had seen in the disjointed frames. "Lord, I hate the country. Always have. I really should get out of here, soon."

"My advice – when you get on that bus, don't look back," Beasley said. "And keep your light on at night. You done with that?"

"Um-hmm." He could not summon the energy to say more right then. The strength and the will had run out of him. He put his hand over his eyes and tried to concentrate.

Beasley took the empty glass and went back into the house. Darkness came and the yard lamps sizzled to life. Moths fluttered near his face, battened at the windows and Partridge wondered why that panicked him, why his heart surged and his fingernails dug into the armrests. In the misty fields, the drone of night insects began.

He eventually heaved to his feet and went inside and walked the dim, ugly corridors for an interminable period. He stumbled aimlessly as if he were yet drunk. His thoughts buzzed and muttered and were incoherent. He found Toshi and Campbell in the den crouched like grave robbers over a stack of shrunken, musty ledgers with hand-sewn covers and other stacks of photographic plates like the kind shot from the air or a doctor's X ray machine. The den was tomb-dark except for a single flimsy desk lamp. He swayed in the doorway, clinging to the jam as if he were in a cabin on a ship. He said, "Where is Nadine?"

The old men glanced up from their documents and squinted at him. Toshi shook his head and sucked his teeth. Campbell pointed at the ceiling. "She's in her room. Packing. It's Sunday night," he said. "You should go see her."

"She has to leave," Toshi said.

Partridge turned and left. He made his way up the great central staircase and tried a number of doors that let into dusty rooms with painter's cloth draping the furniture. Light leaked from the jamb of one door and he went in without knocking.

"I've been waiting," Nadine said. Her room was smaller and more feminine than the Garden Room. She sat lotus on a poster bed. She wore a simple yellow sun dress and her hair in a knot. Her face was dented with exhaustion. "I got scared you might not come to say goodbye."

Partridge did not see any suitcases. A mostly empty bottle of pain medication sat on the night stand beside her wedding ring and a silver locket she had inherited from her great-grandmother. He picked up the locket and let it spill through his fingers, back and forth between his hands.

"It's very late," she said. Her voice was not tired like her face. Her voice was steady and full of conviction. "Take me for a walk."

"Where?" He said.

"In the fields. One more walk in the fields."

He was afraid as he had been afraid when the moths came over him and against the windows. He was afraid as he had been when he pulled her from the water all those years ago and then lay in his hammock bunk dreaming and dreaming of the crocodiles and the bottomless depths warm as the recesses of his own body and she had shuddered against him, entwined with him and inextricably linked with him. He did not wish to leave the house, not at night. He said, "Sure. If you want to."

She climbed from the bed and took his hand. They walked down the stairs and through the quiet house. They left the house and the spectral yard and walked through a gate into the field and then farther into heavier and heavier shadows.

Partridge let Nadine lead. He stepped gingerly. He was mostly night blind and his head ached. Wet grass rubbed his thighs. He was soaked right away. A chipped edge of the ivory moon bit through the moving clouds. There were a few stars. They came to a shallow depression where the grass had been trampled or had sunk beneath the surface. Something in his memory twitched and a terrible cold knot formed in his stomach. He whined in his throat, uncomprehendingly, like a dog.

She hesitated in the depression and pulled her pale dress over her head. She tossed the dress away and stood naked and half-hidden in the fog and darkness. He did not need to see her, he had memorized everything. She slipped into the circle of his arms and he embraced her without thinking. She leaned up and kissed him. Her mouth was dry and hot. "Come on," she muttered against his lips. "Come on." Her hands were sinewy as talons and very strong. She grasped his hair and drew him against her and they slowly folded into the moist earth. The soft earth was disfigured with their writhing and a deep, resonant vibration traveled through it and into them where it yammered through their blood and bones. She kissed him fiercely, viciously, and locked her thighs over his hips and squeezed until he gasped and kissed her back. She did not relinquish her fistful of his hair and she did not close her eyes. He stared into them and saw a ghost of a girl he knew and his own gaunt reflection which he did not know at all. They were sinking.

Nadine stopped sucking at him and turned her head against the black dirt and toward the high, shivering grass. There was no breeze and the night lay dead and still. The grass sighed and muffled an approaching sound that struck Partridge as the thrum of fluorescent lights or high-voltage current through a wire or, as it came swiftly closer, the clatter of pebbles rolling over slate. Nadine tightened her grip and looked at him with a sublime combination of glassy terror and exultation. She said, "Rich – "

The grass shook violently beneath a vast, invisible hand and a tide of chirring and burring and click-clacking blackness poured into the depression from far-flung expanses of lost pasture and haunted wilderness, from the moist abyssal womb that opens beneath everything, everywhere. The cacophony was a murderous tectonic snarl out of Pandemonium, Gehenna, and Hell; the slaughterhouse gnash and whicker and serrated wail of legion bloodthirsty drills and meat-hungry saw teeth. The ebony breaker crashed over them and buried them and swallowed their screams before their screams began.

After the blackness ebbed and receded and was finally gone, it became quiet. At last the frogs tentatively groaned and the crickets warmed by degrees to their songs of loneliness and sorrow. The moon slipped into the moat around the Earth.

He rose alone, black on black, from the muck and walked back in shambling steps to the house.

Partridge sat rigid and upright at the scarred table in the blue-gray gloom of the kitchen. Through the one grimy window above the sink, the predawn sky glowed the hue of gun metal. His eyes glistened and caught that feeble light and held it fast like the eyes of a carp in its market bed of ice. His black face dripped onto his white shirt which was also black. His black hands lay motionless on the table. He stank of copper and urine and shit. Water leaked in fat drops from the stainless steel gooseneck tap. A grandfather clock ticked and tocked from the hall and counted down the seconds of the revolutions of the Earth. The house settled and groaned fitfully, a guilty pensioner caught fast in dreams.

Toshi materialized in the crooked shadows near the stove. His face was masked by the shadows. He said in a low, hoarse voice that suggested a quantity of alcohol and tears, "Occasionally one of us, a volunteer, is permitted to cross over, to relinquish his or her flesh to the appetites of the colony and exist among them in a state of pure consciousness. That's how it's always been. These volunteers become the interpreters, the facilitators of communication between our species. They become undying repositories of our civilization...a civilization that shall become ancient history one day very soon."

Partridge said nothing.

Toshi said in his hoarse, mournful voice, "She'll never truly die. She'll be with them until this place is a frozen graveyard orbiting a cinder. It is an honor. Yet she waited. She wanted to say goodbye in person."

Partridge said nothing. The sun floated to the black rim of the horizon. The sun hung crimson and boiling and a shaft of bloody light passed through the window and bathed his hand.

"Oh!" Toshi said and his mouth was invisible, but his eyes were bright and wet in the gathering light. "Can you imagine gazing upon constellations a hundred million years from this dawn? Can you *imagine* the wonder of gazing upon those constellations from a hundred million eyes? Oh, imagine it, my boy..."

Partridge stood and went wordlessly, ponderously, to the window and lingered there a moment, his mud-caked face afire with the bloody radiance of a dying star. He drank in the slumbering fields, the distant fog-wreathed forests, as if he might never look upon any of it again. He reached up and pulled the shade down tight against the sill and it was dark.

The Great White Bed

Don Webb

Don Webb lives in Austin, Texas, where he once gave the editors of this book a really fine tour of the State Capitol Building, spiked with subversive and arcane anecdotes from Texas State history. He has published several novels, half a dozen collections of his short fiction, and a great many quirky short stories. As a former High Priest of the Temple of Set, he also has something of a reputation as a magician-philosopher and has published a number of nonfiction books in that vein. An unsung hero of the small press, Webb has a strong literary streak as is seen in his books from Black Ice and Fiction Collective and promises to do a breakthrough novel soon to complement his already 2000+ published pieces of short fiction.

"The Great White Bed," published in F&SF, is sort of the flip side of one of those "it was only a dream" stories. Or maybe it's another story about being absorbed by a book. Or maybe it's a be-careful-what-you-wish-for story. In any case, it's quite disturbing. And it reflects in its own distorted mirror the concerns of a number of the other stories in this book. A thirteen-year-old boy is staying with a grandfather who is growing increasingly senile. Grandpa asking if his grandson would ever like a book to read him.

I WANTED to write about the bed because I thought it would be therapeutic. For pretty obvious reasons I never got over that summer, and I know there's a mental part to go along with the physical part. I don't write about the book. And see, I'm already there. I can't make myself think about what I need to think about. The room. The bedroom. I can start with that. It smelled of geraniums. My grandmother had loved them and it had become my job to keep them alive after she died. She grew them in coffee cans, and when they got too root-bound she would put them in plastic buckets that she got working at the cleaners. Clay pots were an extravagance. There were five of the big light blue buckets on a special shelf built across the windows in the bedroom, so the bedroom always had a green smell.

It was hot too. There were two swamp coolers that cooled the house down. One in the living room at the front of the house, one in the den in the back. Neither supplied much cool air to the place where I slept. I remember the first thing that Grandpa had asked when I moved in with him that summer was if I wanted to sleep with him. I thought that was creepy and I said I'd sleep in the guest bedroom, where Granny did her sewing. It was so hot that I never turned down the big white thick bedspread on the bed and lay on the sheets. I just lay on top of it. I didn't want anything over my body. At home I slept on a twin bed; the king size bed seemed the biggest thing in the world to me.

I was thirteen. Next year would be junior high.

I helped Grandpa out. I cooked his meals, did his laundry, cut the grass. In retrospect it was a big job for someone my age, but I came from a family of workers. I didn't do a good job with the laundry and my food repertoire relied heavily on Spam baked in the oven covered with ketchup.

My friends were rich kids, mainly in camp or hanging out at the private swimming pool. These days I know they weren't rich, but they seemed rich to me. I amused myself with TV, watching old black and white comedies in syndication. I remember that summer had a good dose of *The Dick Van Dyke Show* mixed up with the strangeness. Cable TV was new to Doublesign that year. We got twenty-eight stations. Grandpa would get up early and wake me up. He had been a farmer, before they moved to town. Kids are not supposed to see the dawn in summer, no matter what anyone says. He liked cereal for breakfast. He really liked one called Team, I don't think they make it anymore. He would make coffee and I would pour the cereal. Afterward he would go off to read the paper and I would do the dishes. If I had any yard work to do I would do it in the mornings before it got too hot. I trimmed the hedge, cut the grass, weeded out the dandelions. Early on I had tried to keep a little garden going. I had planted some tomatoes and cucumbers. But one day Grandpa weeded them all out of the bed where I had planted them. His mind was going, but no one in the family would say so. When I tried to stop him he hit me with his cane and said I was stupid. Like I say, even without the weirdness, it was a big job.

Noon would come around and Mom would join us for lunch, which I had made. She worked downtown, a mysterious place full of much activity. She would eat my ketchup-covered Spam and canned green beans and visit with her dad. Sometimes he would ask her things like "How come I haven't seen you in a month?" even though she came every day. In the afternoons he would forget that we had eaten lunch and ask me when the hell I was going to fix it. He took a nap about three, and I know this will sound strange, but I started napping too. Summer was long and boring and it was easy to doze off. I would lay down in the green smell on the huge white bed and snooze.

School had been out about three weeks, when I woke one day to seeing Grandpa reading the book. I always took shorter naps than him so I was startled he was up. I went in the living room. He sat in his rocking chair and even though the light streaming in through the picture window lighted the room, he had Grandmother's prize lamp turned on. I loved that lamp. It had two globes, one above and one below. Someone had painted a rose on each globe. I wonder who has it now.

The book was small and thick – about the size of a Stephen King paperback.

It was bound in gold-colored leather, and had a green nine-angled design on its cover. I don't want to say more about it. I didn't mean to say that much.

Grandpa was totally absorbed, his lips moving slowly. I had only seen him with a few *Reader's Digests* over the years. His concentration had been slipping so much since Granny died I didn't know how he could be reading. I guessed he probably wasn't. Just distracting himself. I was always in favor of his distractions. He didn't get mad at me and I didn't have to think up things to talk about. It was a lot easier cutting his lawn than coming up with discussion topics.

I made macaroni and cheese plus canned yams for dinner. I didn't disturb him until I had food on his plate. He came in, we said our prayers, and afterward we watched the six o'clock news. We watched TV together every night. He would fall asleep about eight. I would get him up and tell him to undress about ten.

The next day I had a pleasant surprise. Sunlight woke me, not Grandpa. I got up, pulled on my clothes, and found him reading again.

"Hey, you ready for breakfast?" I asked.

"You bet," he said.

His eyes had the shine they used to have when I was a little kid. He got up out of his chair and told me, "You know, I think you're old enough to have coffee now."

He put a great deal of sugar and milk in my coffee. I loved it and I still do. We ate our cereal in our usual crunchy silence, until curiosity got the better of me.

"What's that book you're reading?"

He looked at me as though I had said something very strange, like, "Are we going to the moon this afternoon?" He said, "I'm not reading anything."

"Not now. I meant just before breakfast."

"I wasn't reading anything."

The light went out of his eyes just as though someone had hit the switch.

I did the dishes and went off to watch *I Married Joan*. The TV was in the den. After laughing at Joan Davis's antics for a quarter of an hour or so, I went to the front of the house and spied on Grandpa. He was reading. He seemed about halfway through the book. I cleared my throat. He didn't look up. "I'm going down to the park," I said. He didn't look up. I went back to watching TV. Maybe his senility had entered a new peaceful stage.

When Mom came that day, Grandpa was talkative and cheerful. He told Mom what a great job I did with the lawn, how much he liked my food, his opinion of the Mayor and otherwise talked like an adult human being. I didn't know what had happened, but I thought it was the greatest thing ever!

Mom gave me some money so that I could walk down to the Ice Palace and buy cones for Grandpa and myself later that day. I knew she was happy. She had been through so much grief watching her dad rot, and she thought that maybe, just maybe this time, God had listened to our prayers. I thought it was my cooking. Okay, I really didn't think that. I thought it was the book.

It was on the walk down to the Ice Palace that greed filled my soul. What if really and truly the book was making Grandpa well again? If it could fix up his tore-up mind, what might it do for mine? I mean, my mind was good; I made A's in math and English, and I could always outsmart people in game shows. I would get the book. Not take it from Grandpa, because I didn't want to stop his miracle, but read sometime when he was asleep and get my own benefit. I would begin junior high as a genius!

The first logical time would be afternoon nap. I watched the old Seth Thomas clock on the living room mantel with X-ray eyes. Grandpa read. It became three.

"Don't you want to take your nap?" I asked.

I had to repeat myself a couple of times before he looked up.

"I'm giving up naps in the afternoon," he said. "I think I've slept enough in my long life. But I bet you sure are sleepy."

The moment he said it, all I could think of was sleep. The great white bed filled my mind. Big and solid and soft. It seemed huge and inviting. The bed was in my head and I needed to be in the bed. I started to speak, but I just yawned. I got control of myself and said, "A nap does sound good."

I went to the bedroom and lay atop the thick white bedspread. Usually I had to lie still for a long while, staring at the round glass light fixture that Granny had put in. I would watch the center brass nut and focus on it while my thoughts drained away into the milky white glass around it. But today sleep came the moment I lay on the pillow. I slept until Grandpa woke me.

"Get up," he said. "I've made supper."

I couldn't figure out what had happened. My brain was all logy. I drifted into the kitchen, where the small brown dining table was. He had made dinner. Fish sticks and lima beans. He had poured milk for both of us. We prayed and ate.

"I thought it would be nice to make dinner for you. You're always making it for me."

"This is nice," I said. I hated lima beans. Still do.

"I've been thinking a lot about exchange lately. Too many things only go one way. You know what I mean?"

"I don't follow."

"Well it's like this. You do all this work for me and I don't do anything for you. That's supposed to be fair because I brought up your mother and her brothers. I bet that doesn't seem right sometimes, does it?"

I thought about being hit by the cane. I thought about not answering. But maybe this really was the time God was answering prayers.

"No sir, sometimes that does not seem fair."

"Or books. Do you ever think about books, Billy? We spend our whole lives reading them, but they never get a chance to read us. Would you like that, Billy, if a book read you sometime?"

"I don't know. I mean, I don't know what it would be like."

"Well you've heard the expression, 'He can read a man's character.' Haven't you?"

"Yes, but I don't really know what it means."

"Well, Billy, being read by a book is about the finest experience there is. Not everyone has it when they grow up, but maybe you will."

God wasn't answering prayers. He was crazy, but in a new way. I cleaned the table after dinner and we went to watch *The Carol Burnett Show*.

Sleep hit me hard again that night. I woke up to sounds from the living room. I don't know how long Grandpa had been talking. He was arguing. I couldn't make out the words, but it scared me. I didn't know what I was supposed to do if Grandpa went crazy by himself in the middle of the night. Finally I heard one statement clearly:

"No, I won't do it. It's not a fair exchange."

I got out of bed. I was wearing just my underwear, so I got dressed. I didn't want to confront Grandpa partially dressed. As I put my clothes on I heard him get up out of his rocker and make his way toward his bedroom. I lay back down on the bed. Even though Grandpa was pretty deaf, I didn't even dare breathe.

I would have bet a million bucks that I was not going to go back to sleep that night, but sure enough sleep hit me like a ton of bricks.

I felt the bed below me melt. I was sinking into half-melted vanilla ice cream, although it wasn't cold. As it passed my eyes, the scene lit up with a terrible whiteness. There was nothing but white, a great white blindness, a great white dark. I could feel myself pulled lower and lower. I couldn't struggle, couldn't swim. For a moment I wished I were one of my rich friends who was hanging out at the pool this summer. They would know what to do. They didn't have to take care of their goddamn grandfathers. The down-drift took forever, and it gave me time for a lot of thoughts and none of them were very good. Maybe I was in a children's story where bad thoughts made you sink.

Then suddenly it stopped. Although the non-landscape hadn't changed and all I could see was the thick whiteness; I felt something looking at me. Something big. I tried to analyze what it felt like. I mean, I had watched *Star Trek* and *Night Gallery*. But I couldn't get any feelings for old or young, human or alien, alive or undead. All of those charts were two-dimensional schoolbook ideas and this was floating above the white page of the book about nine inches. I felt it wasn't going to get bored staring at me, and that scared me. It could look at me forever and not blink. For a brief while I wanted to see it, but then I was glad I couldn't.

Slowly I felt something congeal under me. I wasn't floating anymore. Then a tiny speck formed a few feet above my head. It turned out to be the brass nut in the center of the light fixture. I was staring at the white glass of the fixture. The sun was up. I could hear Grandpa making coffee. The bed was dank with sweat. My nightmare had soaked the thick bedspread. I was already dressed, so I went on into the kitchen.

"Good morning," I said to Grandpa.

He just looked at me with hatred. The light and life had gone out of his eyes. We didn't talk during breakfast. I mowed the lawn afterward even though it didn't need it. I just didn't want to be around him. I don't know if he read his book. Or if the book read him.

Lunch was worse. He was still not talking, and Mom was so upset to see him regress she actually broke down in tears. After lunch she went out to her car and just sat in it and cried.

I went out to comfort her. I was thirteen and it was the manly thing to do. She rolled down her window to talk to me.

"Mom, are you okay?" I asked. I know it was a dumb question.

"What happened, Billy? Did you do something to him?"

I couldn't believe her response. I knew she was upset, but I wasn't some kind of miracle worker, some kind of jinni that could make Grandpa better or worse by blinking my eyes. I got really mad, so I turned away from her car and began running to the park. I knew she was late to work and didn't have time to follow me. She managed an office and everything depended on her. There were some cedar bushes in the park, about six feet tall. Underneath the green, make-out artists had hallowed and hollowed a space over the years. I dove into the cool dry dark to cry. I knew no one would be making out at twelve-thirty in the heat of the summer. I cried a long time. I messed up my clothes. Great – now I had laundry to do as well as the additional job of hating my mom and feeling guilty. I didn't give a damn about Grandpa at this moment.

I headed back to his house. This was going to end today. I would tell my mom and my uncle that I couldn't do this anymore. That I wanted some regular summer job like sweeping out a barber shop, which my friend Jerry had. I was going to tell things I had never told before, like the cane. I didn't think I would tell them about the book. That was probably Grandpa's craziness.

Sure enough, when I got back to his little brick house he was reading his book. He was almost to the end. I had been gone for nearly two hours. I hadn't cried that much since my grandmother died two years ago. I thought crying was supposed to purge you, make you feel better, but I felt all raw and sticky like parts of my soul had been through a blender and were hanging outside of my body. I didn't talk to the old man. I just went to bed.

To my initial relief the same magic that had brought sleep the last two times worked again. I was out like a light.

However, the world changed from a fabulous formless darkness to a great white thickness. I knew I was sinking into the world of the great white bed. The down-drift made me sick this time like a too-long downward ride in an elevator. Of course in those days growing up in Doublesign I had never even seen an elevator, but you can't enter a memory without carrying later memories in with you. Down, down, down.

It was an abrupt and unpleasant stop. I could hear my Grandpa saying something. It was a precise but muffled voice. The kind of voice you use giving a phone number. I began moving sideways. Slowly at first and then at a pretty good clip. Then the movement stopped again and I was lying next to someone.

I could move my head a little. It was Granny. She was dead and very, very white. I knew the great Whatever had been watching her for a couple of years, and had never got bored.

Then I felt the little knives.

Something was slicing through my feet. I couldn't raise my head enough to see it, but I could hear it and of course it hurt like hell. About an inch was being cut off. I didn't think I could stand it. Why didn't I wake up? Why didn't I black out?

Then after that section had been cut clean another cut started about an inch higher. I figured loss of blood or shock would get me. I kept telling myself it was just a nightmare, but that doesn't really help with that much pain.

Then another cut.

Then another.

And so slowly forth until my knees had been reached. All I was at this point was tears and pain.

Then a dark rope dropped down from above. I can't tell you what a relief it was to see something black in that great white space. It hit my face, snaking over my eyes and mouth, finally it touched my ears.

"Billy. Billy can you hear me?"

It was my uncle's voice. I woke up on the great white bed and then passed out from blood loss.

The rest of the summer and the fall and the winter and spring were physical therapy.

I had lost both of my legs up to my knees. This is not a euphemism. There was nothing there. There were no traces of my feet and lower legs anywhere in Grandpa's house.

But there were a set of feet and lower legs on his bed in his room. They were cold and embalmed and a couple of years old. They belonged to my grandmother.

I didn't find that out until just before my mother's death last year. It had been decided not to tell me everything, as though knowledge could make it any worse. There was no trace that my grandmother's grave had been disturbed in any way. They had dug up her coffin and put the legs in, burying it as well as any gossip with her. They put Grandpa in a mental ward afterward. Mom never went to see him again as long as he lived, but that turned out to be only three months anyway. When Mom got cancer she decided to tell me everything.

My uncle had dropped by that day because Mom had called him. She felt bad about what she had said to me. She couldn't leave her office, but her brother got off early. Mom told me that she felt guilty about what had happened to me every day of her life.

I live in a special home for people with mental and physical disabilities. When she was alive, Mom would come see me every day at noon. We always ate together just like she used to eat with her father. About two months before she died she got too sick to come, but they took me to see her in the hospital a couple of times, that was when she told about Granny's legs and so on.

I read and watch TV a lot. It hasn't gotten better in the last forty years, I can tell you that. I am kept here because I can't give an explanation of what happened to me that makes sense to anyone. I didn't get to finish school and I regret that. So I hobble around on my two fake legs. I even keep a little garden. Just flowers, no tomatoes this time. I never learned that Internet thing either; they don't like us looking things up. The only thing that some people would find odd about me is that I won't sleep on white sheets or have a white blanket or a white bedspread.

Mom told me that she searched every inch of Grandpa's house for the book. She told me that she never believed my story fully, but knew it had to have some truth. She didn't find the book. Maybe Grandpa found it at the park or bought it in a garage sale. I tried researching occult matters once, but the people running the home thought it was a bad idea for me. One time I had a dream, about ten years ago, of Grandpa lifting the thick white bedspread and looking under the bed for something and just finding the book. That still doesn't answer the question of where it came from.

Sometimes in my dreams I smell geraniums and find myself in the great white space. I can't scream in my dreams and I've never woken up my roommate with any odd sounds. I don't tell my doctor about it, as it seems to upset her. But the dreams are rare. I think they're really not dreams at all, I think it's just how things are. I think the great Whatever is always watching us.

And It's never bored.

Dance of Shadows

Fred Chappell

Fred Chappell lives in Greensboro, North Carolina. In 1997, he was appointed North Carolina's Poet Laureate by North Carolina Governor Jim Hunt. He taught from 1964–2004 at UNC-Greenville. He is a distinguished contemporary Southern fiction writer and poet (seventeen volumes to date). He also has deep roots in science fiction: He began writing science fiction in the eighth grade and is a member of Seventh Fandom, the generation of science fiction fans that produced Robert Silverberg and Harlan Ellison. His Lovecraftian novel, *Dagon* (1987), won the best foreign book award from the Academie Française. He has won the World Fantasy Award for short fiction twice.

"Dance of Shadows," published in F&SF, explores a fantasy world with a trade in shadows, difficult and expensive to acquire, in densely poetic prose. In the tradition of Clark Ashton Smith and Jack Vance, this is the finely detailed tale of Falco, a bit of a con man, who has become the assistant of the master shadow collector, Astolfo, who is hired to track down the person who once cast a sublimely beautiful shadow.

ASTOLFO, sometimes grudgingly admired as preeminent master of the shadow trade, is avidly sought out by collectors. His attraction is his genius, for he is not physically prepossessing. He will say to me, "Falco, must you loom your bulk over me so lubbardly?" Yet I am but half a head taller than the plumpish, sparse-haired, nimble man and my weight, at about fifteen stone, cannot be much greater than his. It is my office to take all such comments, including the many others more acerbic, in good part, for after all, it was my own conceit to apprentice to him. Four long seasons I had been trying to learn the skill, craft, and finally the art of shadows and if I were to advance in my ambition, Astolfo must be the one to teach me. I felt now almost as muddled as at first, when I broke into his mansion to prostrate myself before his tolerance and be taken into his service.

He once spoke a little in general about the vice of collecting. He seemed to be talking at idle random, but I found out early that he never spoke desultorily. "For it is a vice, you know," he said and looked at me with that gray-eyed gaze that so rarely gave away the cast of his humor. "I have known many a man to waste his substance upon trifles. He may bestow a fortune upon a trove of essence-bottle stoppers, upon elegant sword-hilt pommels, upon coins of fabled nations in fabled ages past. Then these connoisseurs expire in mortal fashion and their impoverished descendants scatter those spurious treasures to the round of the compass for a fraction of the true worth. This collecting, Falco, is a costly vanity."

"I take it that you make an exception for the collectors of shadows."

"Shadow collectors may be the worst of the lot," he replied. "For not only do the objects themselves extort fat prices, but a discriminating taste for them is difficult and expensive to acquire. And then there are the further costs of proper care and storage and restoration when that is necessary and possible."

"Yet you derive some large part of your income from collectors."

"Ah." He sighed and blinked. "I lead a superfluous existence. And I cannot fathom why you feel attracted to such an inutile way of life."

I might have talked at length of the fascination that the business of shadows held for me, why it stood in my mind as the subtlest, cleverest, most demanding method of maintaining oneself. But I also knew better than to give my sharp-tongued mentor reason to ply me with sarcasm. I only inquired what he thought he might occupy himself with otherwise.

"Why, I should retire entirely from commerce," said he, "and devote myself to the close study of the ancient mages. I would strive to achieve equanimity of mind and equability of temper. I would exercise to be always cheerful in this world of futile strife."

"Most who know you would say that you have already arrived at the goals you aim at. You are hardly a melancholy man."

"A long face discourages custom," he declared. "If my clients see me downcast, they may suspect I fret over an unsound business and carry their trade elsewhere."

"So then, your talk is not pure philosophical disquisition. We have a venture in hand, do we?"

"We do." He had not objected to the plural pronoun.

"And it has to do with the pursuit of shadow collecting?"

"As soon as you have made your appearance presentable to polished company, we shall go to the house of Ser Plermio Rutilius," Astolfo said. "I shall tell you about him as we travel."

"Will Mutano accompany us?" I asked. If Astolfo felt the need of his mute, large manservant so fierce in combat, we might be entering a situation of some danger.

"No," he replied. "If our host saw the three of us together he might doubt of my capacities. You shall answer well enough as a diverting companion and no more than that. He will see that you are harmless; Mutano does not readily present that aspect."

I bowed acquiescence, hoping he would note that my ironic grimace expressed disagreement.

*

Our travel was accomplished in handsome style, for Ser Rutilius had sent a well-appointed coach-and-two to Astolfo's mansion to fetch us the two leagues to his chateau. As we rolled smoothly through the green springtime countryside, Astolfo informed me that our host was the scion of an ancient race of warriors who hired out to duchies, principalities, and kingdoms to protect them from marauders, enemies and friends alike. Since our province of Tlemia had blundered into peaceful times, there had been naught to occupy the hereditary skills and services of Rutilius. And so, as a young man, he had entertained himself with dissipation, gathering from cellars their sumptuous wines, from tailors their most costly and elaborate cloaks and doublets, and from noble families their comeliest, most complaisant females.

"In short," said Astolfo, "he led such a life as you have dreamed of leading, Falco – idle pleasures following upon one another like raindrops in a sweet shower. And do you not dream of it still?"

I did not respond.

"But Rutilius is an intelligent young noble and in due season found these devices to pall. He educated himself in the sciences and the arts. He raised the farming practices of his estates to extraordinary levels; he has renewed and refined his martial skills; he has become a knowledgeable connoisseur of painting and tapestry, statuary and architecture. His senses and apprehensions having become so acute, it was perhaps inevitable that he should come to pursue shadow collecting, for no other cultivated attainment is so difficult to achieve. But, as it is the most expensive of such follies, so is it the most rewarding, for, as you have discovered, it is infinite in interest and delight."

I would assent to this latter assertion while envying the fact that one in Rutilius's station could become an adept of shadows without enduring the physical discomforts the discipline was inflicting upon me.

Astolfo seemed to have overheard my thought. "You must not think him some soft-handed, sweet-scented dilettante. He is an expert swordsman, an avid huntsman, a canny and alert man of business, and a fearless pugilist. Of his prowess with women I have heard nothing. Perhaps one of your town wenches has whispered to you whereof."

I shook my head.

"Well then, we understand that whatever commission he may propose to us must be a tangled one because the man himself is so very able and has such deep resources to command."

"Yes," I said, "and from these resources he can well afford whatever toplofty fee you may ask."

"It is for that reason we have come," Astolfo said, "for I am well past the age when mere difficulty itself is an attraction.... And so, here are we."

The carriage rolled to a stop, the driver opened the door and assisted us down the gilt steps he had deployed, and we stood in a pleasant greensward before the great oaken doors of the chateau.

We were brought to the presence of Rutilius in a foyer almost immediately inside the doors. The foyer spread large, with a high, arched ceiling of cedarwood, and enclosed a circular area three steps below the main floor. This sunken space contained a small pool lined with blue tile in which red and silver carp wafted long, filmy tails. Flowers and trailing vines spilled from the mouths of sand-cast urns. From an adjoining room a lute not visible to us was being played with gentle and pensive hand.

I had thought that the mansion of Astolfo, where it stood with its gardens and lawn and stable near the center of the port city of Tardocco, must be close to the apex of luxury. Now I knew that however large the fortune Astolfo had amassed, it was to the fortune of Rutilius as a ploughman's handful of seed is to a granary.

But Rutilius showed himself, however, as no pompous or overbearing sort. A slender, sandy-haired man in his mid-thirties with a manner easy and open, he seemed sincerely pleased to acquaint himself with us, though I noticed that he did not offer his hand. Yet his ease in his station was so confident that this oversight bore no hint of arrogance. He did offer the customary welcoming glass of wine, as fine as any I have tasted since.

The preliminary conversation consisted of our host and Master Astolfo trading reminiscences and guarded confidences about mutual friends and acquaintances. Ser Rutilius was sounding out Astolfo for his society connections, inquiring about the health of Princess A and the new foal in the stable of Count Z. The shadow master bantered his way through this testing, showing familiarity with the persons and affairs of one and all, but without giving impression he gossiped.

Rutilius broke off these preliminaries sharply. "Have you some inkling why I desired to meet you?"

"I have supposed you wished to acquire my services."

"Do you know in what regard? You must answer this question truthfully."

"I have no slightest notion," Astolfo replied mildly.

An expression of relief passed over the face of the baron. "I am pleased to hear you say so. I have feared that my comportment of late has given me away. There are those who observe me closely for any sign of weakness."

"Ah then," said Astolfo, "now I shall suppose it is some affair of the affections. I must tell you straightway, Ser Rutilius, that I am no mender of broken hearts. Nor, come to that, am I a broker of mended hearts."

"In neither case could I use your skills," Rutilius said. "But come along with me to another room. Let me fill your glasses once more and you shall fetch them with you."

"Thank you. It is an inspiriting vintage," Astolfo said.

Having regenerated our drink, Rutilius led us from the foyer down a long, tapestry-hung gallery and brought us into a small salon. Intricate carpets smothered large areas of the parquetry floor, ensuring a sleepy degree of quiet. Large windows admitted southern light and gave an impression of openness to the room. But it was the walls that we had come to see. Paintings and drawings covered them in close profusion. Some paintings were life-size portraits; some drawings were not much larger than Astolfo's leopard's-head belt buckle.

I marveled at them. The portraiture of shadows is the most demanding and delicate of the pictorial arts and the most skillful of artists might labor an arduous season to produce even a mediocre rendering. Here every example was a masterpiece. One or two I recognized from engraved reproductions in books, but all the others were new to my eyes and this first impression of them all together made the hairs stand up on my wrists.

Astolfo, whose constant watchword was *nil mirari*, gave over to rapt admiration, going from one frame to another, stepping forward and back, cocking his head to one side, shading his eyes with his left hand. I had never before seen him so avidly engaged and wondered if this display might be partly a show of manners, a way of complimenting Rutilius on his taste.

I also noted that the baron observed Astolfo attentively and seemed gratified when the shadow master kept returning to one drawing. Among the other, more imposing pictures, this one at first looked none so remarkable. It was no larger than a sheet of foolscap, a rendering of the shadow of a female in graphite and chalk. But the more I looked at it, the more it unfolded not only its artistic beauties but also an ineffable, closely personal charm that must have derived from its subject.

In spite of all the instruction Astolfo has set me to, the examination of scores of paintings and drawings in the collections of his clients, the volumes of prints and engravings, the crabbed treatises on the pictorial art, I have not sufficient knowledge to speak with any wisdom. I believe anyhow that pictures speak for themselves and much that is said in their presence by ink-smeared daubers and chalky schoolmasters is so much vain bleating. I would rather hear a goat fart than to listen to doddering know-alls speak of composition, impasto, contrapposto, and the other drivel.

From Astolfo's scattered remarks, however, I learned some good, practical sense, especially in regard to the picturing of shadows. First, he told me, your shadow artist must learn how to show *volume*, the dimensions of bodies in space. It is a childish error to see shadows flat, as unlit two-dimensional strips pasted to surfaces. The first task is to see that for all their seeming insubstantiality shadows have volume and extend round in three dimensions, to which – unlike solid bodies such as stones and trees – they add another surface borrowed from the ultramundane source to which they are allied. At the time, I could not see what he was asking me to see, but to this simple-seeming drawing his words fitly applied. The contours of the figure seemed to rise from the sheet on which they were limned. The shadow was modeled on paper as if it were a study for a sculpture in bronze or glass.

Astolfo spoke to Rutilius in a voice even milder than usual. "I take it that these works represent properties in your possession."

"All but a few are renderings of shadows I have gathered," Rutilius replied. "There are one or two works I acquired for their excellence as art. Some of those are quite old."

"Indeed," Astolfo said, "for I see that some were signed by the artists. There is a Manoni by the door and in the painting next to it the little salamander scrawled into the corner of the canvas is the sign of the celebrated Proximo. But the newer ones are unsigned."

"Shadow artists discovered that noising their names abroad was unsafe practice," Rutilius said.

"Yet there are some so skilled, so deep-thoughted, so individual that their work speaks their names. For instance, that drawing of the young female's shadow must have come from the hand of Petrinius. He is our contemporary genius of shadows and his touch is unmistakable."

"You are correct."

"I see too that this drawing is fresh. You must have come by it recently."

"He completed it only a sennight past."

"And the shadow itself is in your possession?"

"It is."

"I congratulate you. That shadow is a treasure to make any collector proud."

"Proud, perhaps. But not entirely happy."

"The reason?"

"I have a great, an overweening, desire to know what woman cast this shadow and where she is."

"Did not your purveyor tell you these things?"

"He did not know, for the one he got it from did not. It is possible that it passed through many hands before it came into mine."

Astolfo stepped forward and leaned for a closer view of the drawing. "Perhaps.

It is difficult to tell from a drawing. If I were to see the original – "

Rutilius said, "Before I chance showing the property I shall need to know if you accept my commission and what your terms may be."

"You wish me to find out about the person who cast the shadow?"

"I want you to find her, the woman herself, and tell me who and what and where she is."

"I can accept your tender only provisionally," Astolfo said, "because I cannot foresee what may be involved. A tedious, long search might be necessary and might prove fruitless."

"True enough. Yet you are the most experienced hound in the kennel to set upon the trace. Your renown must have been well earned. And you should be fitly rewarded."

"Provisionally, then – yes. Let us see the original. Then I may say more."

In this other smaller salon that opened off the collection room, I could discern that Astolfo admired the way in which Rutilius tended his shadows. Some collectors and dealers believe that shadows should be put away in secret recesses – closets, armoires, cellars – so that the surrounding darkness might keep them fresh. But darkness drains them of vitality, gradually absorbing a little of their natural vigor. A dim light is best, light that is not a steady glow but a fluctuating or flickering convergence of beams. These varying conditions keep the shades exercised, furnish them tone, and lend them suppleness. Their odors keep cleaner in a light like unto that of an overcast day and their edges are less likely to lose definition than if they are stored away in some dank hole.

For his most dearly prized shadow Ser Rutilius had ordered the construction of a special cabinet. It was a hand taller than myself and its glass sides enclosed an array of lightly smoked and unsmoked mirrors where the shadow floated among them in an ever-changing, vague light. These mirrors revolved slowly by means of a clockwork mechanism attached to the side of the cabinet. The shadow hung amid their surfaces like those carp wafting in the tiled pool in the foyer.

Astolfo walked three times round this cabinet, leaning this way and that to see the different angles. I could tell that he was considering how he might construct such a machine himself. I noted too that his gaze often left the glass box and its shadow to take in Ser Rutilius.

The baron must have looked upon this sight some thousand times and more, yet now he stood transfixed, again devouring it with his eyes. He had hooked his thumbs into his brocaded linen sash and his fingers played restlessly, hungrily, upon the band of cloth.

Well, it drifted there in ineffable beauty. There was about it such refinement and grace, such a lilting freedom, that it lightened the heart. Astolfo has described some of the most beautiful of shadows as being music, and, to speak in that vein, this one was a cool, clear soprano aria of purest tone. I was not so deeply enamored of it as our host; my taste is for the darker shade, the more satin-like texture, the deeper fabric. But for those who prefer the shadow that verges on the edge of disappearance, an image that is but the whisper-echo of an image, this shade was paragon. And it required some time well after Astolfo had finished his examination before our host was able to tear himself away.

"Any collector," Astolfo began, "of the greatest wealth or noblest blood, would consider this shadow his crown jewel."

"And so for me it is – and more than that," Rutilius replied.

"Your love for the object has persuaded me," Astolfo said. "I will accept the commission, as long as I am not bound to guarantee favorable result."

"And your fee?"

"I cannot tell that yet, but it will not discommode you."

In the coach as we rode back to our manse, Astolfo said, "This is to be a delicate business. We must tread gently. We shall have to require from Ser Rutilius a bond for our safety from his hand."

"Why should he wish to harm us?" I asked.

"Because lovers are madmen and may do violence in a passion. Did you not see how he looked upon the thing? He is in love."

"With a shadow?"

"In his mind he sees beyond the shadow."

"How so?"

"He has imagined the woman who spilled upon the air so graceful, so lissome, so lyrical a shade and this picture he has imagined has fastened upon his heart like a kestrel taking a minnow."

"You make him out a blushing virgin," I said, "but someone of his position – "

"A man who has had his fill of women in the flesh, who has tired of their jangle in his ear, their depletion of his purse, their weight upon his loins, may perhaps seek a different and higher experience with a shadow-woman."

"The caster is no shadow. She is flesh and bone like the rest of us."

"Flesh and bone, yes – but not like you and me."

"How do you mean?"

"What sort of person will cast so delicate a shadow?"

I pondered. "Some saintly lass, maybe. An ascetic student or a devoted temple maiden."

Astolfo nodded, but his expression was dubious. "A prophetess – except that those figures rarely attain to gracefulness and when they do, their grace is in a strongly individual, eccentric mode. The movements of this shadow have a high degree of finesse unavailable to the temperament of the hermit."

"You speak as if you have formed conclusions as to the identity of this female."

"A thin conjecture, no more. Let us try to lure the artist who drew the shadow to our dinner table for tomorrow eve."

"Petrinius? He will not come. He is said to disdain all company but his own."

"And even with that he is none too pleased. Yet I think he might make an exception for our invitation. At any rate, we shall send it round."

The silent, broad-shouldered Mutano ushered Petrinius into the large library where Astolfo and I stood by the great fireplace awaiting his arrival. It was too warm an evening for fire so Astolfo had ordered the hearth-space cleared and had installed small marble genius-of-flame statuettes within. From various rooms and corners of the mansion he had brought all his best works of art – paintings, drawings, tapestry screens, ceramic fooleries, ornately bound books – and distributed them around the room. He evidently thought it worth trying to impress our distinguished artist guest.

He even began, after the usual greetings, to make a witty speech of welcome, but Petrinius cut him short. "I came to eat your meat and drink your wine and to hear what sort of business you have with me, Astolfo. Let us not waste the hour with rhetorizing."

He was unperturbed and held Petrinius in one of the mildest of his mild gazes, unruffled by the artist's calculated gaucherie, a commodity he seemed to possess in abundant store. Petrinius was a short, almost dwarfish man whose gestures were swift and jerky. I could imagine him as a marionette whose strings were manipulated by a palsied puppeteer. He abounded with nervous energy; it crackled from him as from amber rubbed with lynx fur. His fingers twitched, his feet stuttered on the worn carpet. When he spoke, the words flew like darts and when he was silent his face betrayed his every thought and impulse in a succession of grimaces. One of the popular sobriquets bestowed upon him was "Candleflame," and he did indeed flicker with a fiery spirit, every motion animated.

"I am pleased that you have come to drink my wine," Astolfo said. He poured from a dragon-spout flagon a draught of aromatic inky wine for each of us.

Petrinius tossed his down his gullet and at once held forth his glass to be filled again.

"I feel no urgency to broach my question," Astolfo said as he poured the proffered glass to the brim, "for I believe you already know what I wish to ask."

Again, Petrinius drained the draught with one noisy swallow and again put forward the silver-enchased goblet. "This will be in the matter of the drawing commissioned by Ser Plermio Rutilius. Am I correct?"

"You are correct," Astolfo said. He smiled gently as again he filled the glass.

"I do not think we can content each other. I have no real knowledge of the shadow to impart and the little I do know must come at a cost to you. I believe you already divine what that would be."

"A certain shadow," Astolfo said, "or, more accurately, a portion of it."

"Yes."

"It must be that you are still designing your great mural. What is the title you have given this long-planned masterwork?"

"At present it is called *The Dead Who March to Shame the State*. Tomorrow it may take a different name. What do you offer me for the bit I can tell?"

"Of the shadow of Malaspino a cutting two fingers'-length in breadth. More, if your replies answer to my desire."

"What, then?"

"Do you think Ser Rutilius says true that he knows nothing of the provenance of that shadow you so brilliantly sketched?"

"Do not spend your breath upon flattery. I am aware of my capacities. It is in the interest of Rutilius to tell the truth. Why should he deceive you, his hireling, in the matter?"

Even the mean term, *hireling*, did not discompose Astolfo. "The way of shadow-dealing is as crooked as the shaft of the Great Wain. Did you form any surmises about where it came from?"

"Let us forego catechism," Petrinius said brusquely. "These things I know from observing the object itself: It passed through few hands before it came to Rutilius; it is fresh and without wear or soilure; its character is distinct. I would think the thief entrusted it to a middleman with Rutilius in mind as the sole buyer."

"The one who took the shadow was no thief by vocation or the middleman would have gained the name of the caster from him as a means of protecting himself."

"Of course, of course." Petrinius waved an impatient hand. "It implies too that the price the middleman obtained and the shadow he kept for himself were of secondary importance to the taker. He wanted chiefly to be rid of the thing."

"Yet not from fear, for the shadow is that of a young woman who could offer little harm."

"Unless she had lover, brother, or some other protector who would pursue the taker."

Astolfo nodded. "And yet – "

"And yet sufficient time has passed and no one has appeared. And I have some conceit that the lass might be an outcast or orphan."

"A slave girl, mayhap?"

"She is no clumsy bumpkin like your man here," Petrinius said, with a quick contemptuous gesture in my direction. "She has a grace not entirely inherent. She has been cultivated after some fashion."

"As I thought also."

"You have thought already all the things I have said. Did you call me here merely to annoy me? Lead me to the table. I will eat my fill and depart." He held out his goblet again.

Astolfo complied, saying, "We shall dine on trout and sorrel, lamb and flageolets shortly. The cook must set his own time to bring us to table. I promise you will not regret his tediousness in the matter."

"Even the most savory of meals is but fuel for the body's brazier," Petrinius said. Then he looked directly into my face and I saw for the first time that his eyes were of different colors, the left an opaque, steely gray, the right a brilliant ice-blue. "Has this briar-muncher learned the difference between mutton stew and oat straw? He would seem to be ill fitted for your machinations, Astolfo."

"Oh, Falco does well enough. He only requires a bit of polish."

"As does mule flop, but polish never alters its value."

"At what weight would you estimate the shadow's caster?"

"No more than eight stone. She will be right-handed, though in walking she will favor her left side. The bones of her arms and especially of her feet will be prominent, her instep a high arch. She is capable of swift movement and also of holding a set pose for a long while. The carriage of her shoulders is almost military in its steadiness and serves to emphasize a long, graceful neck. Her hands are puzzling to me; sometimes I think them too small for her body, sometimes too large."

"How was the shadow stolen from her? Forcefully, with a sudden violence? Or slowly and carefully, when she was unaware?"

"Not by violence. And yet not gradually either. The edges are not abrupt, yet neither are they vague in boundary."

"I will give over three finger-breadths of the shadow of Malaspino. And now we have done with this subject and you may speak at length of the plan of your mural."

"It is to be dark, gloomy dark, in its center. Only the shadow of an evil man taken from him as he stood upon the gallows will supply the necessary blackness. You were on the scaffold with Malaspino, were you not? I have heard the rumors."

"Since all excepting myself now are dead, I can affirm them. I bribed one of the hangmen to keep at home. I wore his robe and the filthy hood he lent. It was his duty to bind the feet of Malaspino just before the trap was sprung and when I knelt to the bonds, I slipped the shadow away at his bootsoles. I have never seen so black a shadow. The doomful poet Edgardo has been using minute parts of it as an admixture to his inkwell for some time now and his lines grow ever more ominous and sardonic."

"You allude to his poem, 'Chance,' of course. 'Bow down before the daemon of the world – This monstrous god, half idiot and half ape.... '"

"And to other poems he judges too bitter for auditors of our generation."

"Methinks he too much prides himself," Petrinius said. "Let him bring them at will, I shall swill his strongest alcohols."

"Since your appetite is so keen, let us go in to dinner," said Astolfo. "My nose tells me the dishes are in readiness. We must speak more of your great mural."

He was not loathe to do so. Between bold goblets of wine and weighty forkfuls of meat, Petrinius spun out at length his scheme for his beloved project. The name of it kept changing as he warmed to the subject. Sometimes he called it *The Triumphal March of Justice Upon the Contemptible Species*; another time it was *The Furies Well Deserved*, or *Look Upon Us for What We Are*. It was to be his revenge upon history as he knew it, upon life, regarded more as a crime than an affliction. "There shall appear upon my wall figures who will recognize their shames and wail in anger."

"'Twill be a most passionate masterpiece."

"Passion, yes, passion!" Petrinius sputtered fragments of lamb. "I shall put into it all my brimstone heart and all the skills of hand and eye."

"Will not the images you thus produce work ill upon the actual subjects?" Astolfo asked. "For I have heard it told of Manoni his art was so powerful that when he drew in ill will a person's likeness, that one fell sick. Some, they say, came near death."

"Pah." Petrinius took a generous swallow of wine. "Those are legends merely. Old superstitions. And I am not certain that Manoni deserves all his musty repute. I can show you clumsy passages in his best work."

"So then, it is not true that an artist's portrayal may alter the condition of his subject? I had always heard otherwise."

"It is not true, though many of the brotherhood promote the falsity. But of shadows, however, it is a truth. It can come about that the portrait of a shadow can affect the appearance of that shade, for good or for ill."

"I see. Is it the passion of the artist which effects this result?"

"That is one of the things, but now I perceive you work to worm secrets from me. Yet I am no longer thirsty or hungry and so will depart."

"Mayn't we tempt you with one thing more? A sweet wine of the Sunshine Isles? A fresh melon?"

"Useless to squander fine manners on me, Astolfo. I bid you good night."

After Petrinius had taken his brusque and slightly tipsy leave, brandishing happily above his head a moleskin packet containing his patch from the shadow of Malaspino, Astolfo proposed that we go into the small library for a last glass to invite slumber. Mutano was already there and sat at his ease by the writing table. A decanter of sherry and three small glasses stood ready.

At first Astolfo and Mutano conferred in one of their finger dialects with which I was unfamiliar and I wondered what their discussion concerned. Astolfo poured and we sipped in a momentary, contemplative silence. Then he turned to me: "What did we discover this evening?"

"That this Petrinius is eager to have his ears boxed," I said. "His artistry, however estimable on paper and canvas, does not extend to courtesy."

"Yes, he too referred to you as a cowherd chaff-brain. You are recognized in every place."

"Under your tutelage I shall become an urbane scholar, a polished wit and silken murmurer of vain compliment," I said. "You shall yet be proud of your creation."

My little sally must have caught him unawares, for he paused to consider. "There might be something in this wide apprehension to your advantage. It is rarely a mistake to appear less able than you are. The more willing others are to think you a fool, the more you should strive to appear so."

I nodded. His words strengthened my hope that our association might yet continue for a while.

Astolfo went on: "What physical attributes did you observe that would contribute to his power as an artist?"

"I am surprised at his comportment. He is a creature of jerks and starts, wriggles and itchings. He contorts his body as continually and absurdly as his facial expressions, yet his drawing is easy and gossamer; it seems to have been breathed upon the page."

"We cannot suppose that the man who swills grape and wolfs dripping at table is the same as he who stands before the easel. Once he engages the discipline of his craft, his demeanor and personality will change. The priest who expounds a pious and arcane theology in the morning is not the same as the identical priest you encounter that evening in the drunken brothel."

"He coils and uncoils like an adder in embers."

"To aid his way of seeing. Did you not take notice of his eyes?"

"They are of different colors."

"The clear blue is quick and precise. The left eye, colored like the iron of a dagger-blade, was shattered blind in a street brawl. He has to move his head continuously to see things in the round. The loss of sight in one eye has given him an advantage in depicting shadows."

"He has, then, acquired a valuable infirmity."

"He has made it valuable. His infirmities and eccentricities are avidly cultivated. His aloofness of manner and careless speech signal an independent spirit free of sycophancy and this bravura elevates the fees he commands. Where another might eat toads to gain favor, Petrinius spits venom and is the more prized. His great mural when finished will stand as one of the most powerful of misanthropic statements. Many in this city shall be furious to recognize themselves therein. If he includes representations of their shadows, those will suffer sad decline. The scrap of shadow from the felon Malaspino has lent him more power. Some high-placed persons will be savagely drawn in."

"'Tis risky," I said. "Some there are of the nobility would have him taken off the planet if he set them crossgrain."

"He depends upon his genius to protect him. Did you note what he said about how the shade was thieved in the first place?"

"He did not know. He said it was neither taken by force nor eased away quietly and subtly."

"You know the first two ways in which shadows are taken?"

"By stealth," I said, "and that is called *severance*. By violence, and that is called *sundering*. The third I do not know, as you have not yet informed me."

"Yet you might easily think it out for yourself. How do you acquire a possession of another and leave no trace of theft?"

I was momentarily perplexed. "Well, I suppose, if someone gave the thing to me – "

"If you voluntarily allow someone to take your shadow, it leaves no trace of theft or even of the act of taking. This act is called the *surrendering*."

"People do not lightly give up their shadows," I replied. "Under what circumstance would anyone do so?"

"That is the question I shall put to myself as I sleep. If my pillow is as informative as I hope it shall be, perhaps the three of us may need to wander about the city tomorrow," Astolfo said. He and Mutano began their silent colloquy again, their fingers flashing like a flock of sparrows in a mulberry.

I left them at it, retired to my solitary, almost barren room, undressed, bedded myself, and slept like a sentry relieved from a six-sandglass watch.

On the next morning, after my customary lone and frugal breakfast, I was standing in the east garden. My eyes were closed as I turned round and round, judging the placement of the shadows there. It is an error to suppose, as I had done before entering apprenticeship, that comprehension of shadows is exclusively a matter of the eye. All the senses are engaged. I listened to the breezes as they mingled darker and lighter tints together; I smelled the differences between those plants that were in the shade of wall or tree and those that stood in full sun; I tasted the perfumes of the air with the tip of my tongue; I felt on my face the dapple that fell upon me through the newly leaved plane tree. I heard with special pleasure birdsong, how when it pours from the interior darkness of a thick bush, it lightens and rises minutely in pitch as it trills out of the foliage into the bright day.

I thought that I was aware of all around me, but this illusion was rudely dispelled by a sudden, solid, but not vicious kick to my arse. Mutano, comrade and bear-sized manservant, he who looked as if he would lumber when he walked, could move as silently as any midnight wraith. Astolfo had appointed him my drillmaster and he was forever disciplining me to keener attention, with wooden swords, boxing bouts, equestrian exercises, and so forth. I was grateful to him for his boot up my backside. In another, similar situation an actual opponent could have buried a dagger in my spine.

He beckoned me to follow him into the small library where Astolfo sat in a worn leather armchair. He seemed half asleep when we entered and spoke in a lazy, almost slovenly drawl. This was his mode of speech when his mind was occupied with a problem. "My search has not been fruitless," he said, "but its results are uncertain. We shall go within the hour to the workplace of the ballet master Maxinnio. Before we leave, you must drink the pot of tea which has been prepared for you. That will give you excuse and opportunity to examine his establishment. Mutano shall serve as our protector, if need be, and also as observer, for, to say truly, I do not know entirely what to expect of this visit. My instinct of the matter may be correct or it may err. At any rate, you and I shall go unarmed, but Mutano will bear his short sword.... And so, prepare."

As I was bidden, I went to my room, performed brief ablutions, put on a clean doublet, and downed in hasty gulps the pot of tea that had been set out. Then I joined Astolfo and Mutano in the front of the great hall and we departed. Astolfo, I noted, had changed attire and was dressed in the customary gold-and-green trunks and doublet of a spice merchant. If he hoped to disguise himself, this clothing would not suffice. Master-of-shadows Astolfo was recognized by everyone in the city of Tardocco.

The door to Maxinnio's establishment was a shabby, unvarnished affair of oak boards with a small square cutout to see through. It was opened by a girl of ten or twelve years or so in a gray scullery smock; she was unremarkable except for the great, dark, almond-shaped eyes set in her young, impassive face. The eyes seemed older than the smudged face, a feature apart. Silently she showed us up the stairs to the studio salon.

Here were a half-dozen young girls stretching legs and torsos, clothed in the traditional white tights and frilly short skirts. Ranging in age from perhaps twelve to sixteen years, they leapt and pirouetted under the cold eye of a gray-haired chorus mistress. Maxinnio sat upon a campaign stool, looking without much interest upon the girls. The bored lutenist in his spare, wooden chair did not so much as glance at them.

Nor did Astolfo, as he hurried over to bow to Maxinnio and to press his unenthusiastic hand. Mutano and I gave each of the girls close and furtive examination, as we had been instructed to do. For me, such instruction was superfluous. These were remarkably pretty girls, in the very dawning of their beauty. I tried to ignore distraction, to concentrate on what I was looking out for.

"Strange colors for a shadow-thief to wear, Astolfo," Maxinnio said. "Why such a gaudy getup so early in the day?"

"Is it not jolly? I am happy that my thieving days, if ever there had been any, should lie behind me so that I can sport such livery as this. Today my green-and-gold signifies that I am just now in the service of another, a wealthy spice merchant who does not care to have his identity bruited about."

"What have I to do with spice merchants, whatever motley they require you to wear?"

"He is wealthy and that datum must interest you."

"How so?"

"Because he is considering whether he may wish to invest funds in your company of dancers."

"Did you bring this mass of gold with you, Astolfo, so that you require two ruffians to guard the treasure you bear? Your dumb manservant I have seen before, this Mutton, or whatever he is called."

"Mutano," Astolfo said. "He is the most discreet of persons."

"Let him keep so. But who is this clay-foot ox-goader by his side? He looks as if grasshoppers might spring from his codpiece."

"He enjoys to be called Falco and I perceive he is in a state of discomfort. I think he may have been swilling ale even at this early hour and, if so, shall not be in my service by this afternoon. Perhaps there is a place here where he may relieve himself."

"Out the door and down the long hall to the end he will find a pissing room. If some girl has engaged it, he must hold his water until she leaves," he said, and added: "I do not like the look of this Falco."

"I plan to improve his appearance," Astolfo said, and waved me away.

Mutano's bitter tea had worked its way with me so that I fairly trotted down the gloomy hall to an open door within which stood a row of four stoneware pissing jars. No female was in the room, so I closed the door and went about my business, making sure, according to instruction, that my urination would be audible even through the walls. Anyone set to watch me would be satisfied with the legitimacy of my need.

Afterward, I stood listening for a moment, then stole to the door and opened it gradually. The hall was deserted and I went into it, going along slowly and silently, stopping by each of the doors to listen for any sound within.

At the end of the hall was a stairway and I fancied that music sounded from the floor above. I mounted quietly to the door that closed off the stairs at the top. Here I heard distinctly the soft strains of harp music. When I tried to ease the door open, I found it locked and was gratified. To pry back this lock with a short strap of stiff leather was the work of brief moments and anyone inside would be unlikely to guard closely a locked door.

When I inched it ajar and peeped through I could see clearly because a panel of the roof was drawn back and daylight poured down upon a lank, abstracted youth with curly locks who sat playing his harp as if rapt by the music he produced. A girl dressed all in white tights to her neck danced in the sunlight. She did not wear the usual pleated dancer's skirt.

She could not be above sixteen years and so slender within the white sheath she wore that she looked like a spiral curl of silver as she made a slow turn with her hands held aloft. On her toes she barely touched the floor and so weightless-seeming were her motions that a puff of air might have carried her up and away like the downy dandelion seed. She looked upward, following the line of her arms to her small, long-fingered hands, and her blonde hair hung long and free down her back. She would be the principal dancer of Maxinnio's troupe and she danced in the shaft of light as the spirit of loneliness, as if she were the only being in a separate world. I felt that in looking upon her I looked upon my own spirit as I sometimes conceived it in melancholy humor – alone and uncompanioned in a moment of halted time, in a place that could not be reached from ordinary space. If every human soul is an orphan, as Astolfo once averred, this young girl embodied the soul of that soul.

I watched her, transfixed for long moments, before I recognized one of the things that caused her to emit such an atmosphere of solitude. Although she danced within a wide beam of full daylight, she cast no shadow on the polished maple floor. Shadowless, she seemed to burn in her space, a cool, silver flame as pure as starlight frozen in ice. The absence of a shadow attached her more closely to the music; she seemed a part of the music, as if when the harpist gently rippled his strings, he was caressing her body with his fingertips, bringing from her, and not his instrument, the strains and measures that fell upon my ears.

With difficulty I brought myself away down the stairs and returned to the salon where Maxinnio and Astolfo held conference among the other dancers. All the way back through the dim, grimy hallway the sight of the silver dancer floated before me. When I came into the room with the harsher light and the different music and the prancing girls, the sensation was disagreeable. Everything, and especially the dancers, seemed tawdry and dull and clumsy. Aforetime I had found the room pleasant enough, but now it was immediately stale, flat, and tiresome.

Astolfo greeted me. "Well, Falco, you have been gone a good long space. I must congratulate you on your bladder capacity. Perhaps we shall engage for you in a pissing tournament."

"It was tea and not ale that I had drunk," I said. "My innards are not so avid to entertain mere tea."

"Must we spend more time hearing how your oaf makes water?" asked Maxinnio. "I hold the subject but a shallow one."

"Perhaps we have overstrained your hospitality," said Astolfo. "Now that I have learned from you that you have no desire and no need to open your company to the investment of my client, we may decide our business is concluded."

"It is concluded, Astolfo," Maxinnio declared. "I do not know why you have come knocking upon my door, with unsavory fellows at your heel, blathering some suppositious story about a spice merchant. Whatever underhand affair you have underway, I am to be left out. And there's an end on't."

"I am sure you know best," Astolfo said. He bowed and then Mutano and I bowed and the gray-smocked, great-eyed girl showed us down the stairs to the street. The lute music grew louder behind us.

When I told Astolfo about the dancer I had spied upon, we sat in his large kitchen. He enjoyed this room with its enormous oven, its walls glowing with copper pans and kettles, its smells of breads and spices. He liked to leap up backward and perch on the huge butcher block in the center and dangle his feet. This he did now as we drank new ale from clay tankards and chewed on black bread and sour goat cheese.

When I finished my account, he closed his eyes and nodded. "The dancing master must have been asked to prepare an important entertainment for the municipality and has designed a particularly gratifying dance. You glimpsed her in rehearsal, Falco, and were transported. The full spectacle shall surely glow famously."

"It is a sight worth living to see," I avowed.

"Maxinnio will not be eager to give over this paragon of dance to Ser Rutilius."

"He will not give her over," I said. "Nor would you once you had set eyes upon her."

"You are certain it is her shadow in the Ser's cage of glass?"

"It can be no other."

"Then we must find out our choices. What would Rutilius do if we delayed awhile and then reported to him that we could not trace the caster of his shadow?"

"He would pay others to discover her."

"How might they do so?"

I thought. "He would tell these others that we had failed. Then they would follow in our footsteps, seeking any sort of intelligence. By that time our visit to Maxinnio's dancers would be known and they would find the silver dancer and inform Rutilius."

"When once Rutilius knew that we had seen her, he would consider that – "

" – That we had betrayed him, having designs of our own. He would not be pleased."

"What of the girl, once he knows where and what she is?"

"He will abduct her, despite all that Maxinnio can do."

"And then?"

I shrugged. "I cannot say. He shall have attained his desire. He shall possess the girl."

"The consequence of this possession?"

"I cannot say."

"There can be but one consequence. Did you gain any impression of her? Not of the dancer, but of the girl apart from the dance?"

I waited, but nothing came to mind. "I think there is no girl apart from the dance."

He blinked his eyes and nodded once, gravely. "Because she casts no shadow. Like the music itself, she casts no shadow. She has been changed like those boys lopped of their *coillons* to become soprano singers, pure vessels of the art. Apart from her dance, she hardly exists. Petrinius understood this matter. His drawing of the shadow has more vital spirit, more spark of the soul, than does the shadow itself. And the shadow has more substance of spirit than the girl who cast it."

"How does this fact serve Rutilius? I see advantage in it only for Maxinnio and the spectacle he is planning."

"'Twould serve him ill," he said, "and ourselves also. We must look for some other avenue of success or of escape."

"How so?"

He shrugged. "I am a-weary of pondering and drawing up schemes. My wits are not so nimble as formerly. Why do you not tickle the ribs of your ingenuity and produce a plan for us to follow?"

"I shall attempt," I said. I sounded my words out light and eager, trying to disguise my unconfident apprehension.

"We will await with indrawn breath your masterpiece of machination," Astolfo said. "You shall deliver it mid-morning tomorrow."

Well, I would have to prepare some scheme or other for the morrow, that was certain. Certain too was the fact that it would be dismissed by the shadow master as harebrained, lackwitted, and impossible of execution. So I did not trouble myself deeply about the matter and took his words to imply that this evening was mine to consume in whatever way I desired.

And so I launched out across Tardocco to The Heart of Agate, these days my favored tavern in which to recreate body and mind. It was there, between bouts of tankards and of bed-thumping, during one of those floating moments when I began to doubt the value of such dissipation, that a glimmer of a notion entered my head and I abruptly and unsteadily betook me homeward. It was no thunderbolt conception, but even so I did not want to drown it in ale-engendered forgetfulness.

I rose late, only just before the appointed hour, composed my corpus as best I could, and went out of doors to greet Astolfo where he sat in the springtime splendor under the great chestnut in the east garden. He eyed me with humorous disdain, shook his head, but said nothing. Mutano, standing by a small rustic table, poured a foaming beaker of ale from a pitcher with a cracked spout. I tried to turn from the sight and smell of it, but he thrust it upon me and I drank and began to feel a little better. He had infused it with some sort of spice that so inflamed the palate I had to fumble for speech when Astolfo put his question.

"You cannot gauge with what eager anticipation we have waited your proposal," he said gaily. "Speak at once and dispel our anxiety."

It hurt to swallow, but after I had done so, I said, "Did not you tell me that Ser Rutilius spent much of his youth in headstrong dissipations and carefree frivolities?"

He made no answer, so I plunged on. "He must have sown wild seed during this time. Perhaps he has fathered one or two that he knows nothing of. Perhaps he could be persuaded that the dancer is one of these, his own daughter."

"What then?"

"Then he can have no use for her as bedmate and will leave her stay as is."

"Yet he already adores her shadow to distraction. Will he not be proud to acknowledge the work of his flesh, seeing what dear loveliness it hath brought forth? Will he not be more avid than ever to have her within his house?"

"As his daughter – that is, as his supposed daughter – she may prevail upon him to accede to her wishes."

"And will not a young girl of no fortune, apprenticed to a stiff-willed tyrant of the ballet, be pleased to find a wealthy and doting father and enter into a life of luxurious ease and well-being?"

"Not if she be wedded to her dance and its music," I replied. "And that is what I saw when I watched her. It is difficult to imagine that she would give up the art willingly."

"Willingly she gave up her shadow."

Now I began to falter. "But that – that is different...."

He spoke as if from the depths of lassitude, saying the very phrase I had foreknown. "This will not serve. The risks are too threatening." But then he surprised me. "And yet, there is something in't to ponder on. Let us befriend our thoughts a while longer. You can be meditating upon it while Mutano instructs you in the brave art of the whip. The whip is a way of taking shadows you may not yet have considered."

Three days passed in which Astolfo seemed to neglect all this affair, the commission of Ser Rutilius, Maxinnio, and the shadowless dancer. I kept busy, of course; my training seemed never to abate for two hours together. Now the emphasis was on drawing. I had been put for a space of time last twelvemonth to draw the shapes of shadows splayed across irregular surfaces: the shadow of Mutano as he stood at the corner of the clay-walled springhouse in the back garden so that it appeared halved on both walls, the shadow of the black cat Creeper where he crouched by the rough stones of the outer wall, the shadow of my own left hand as it fell upon a clot of harebells.

It was discovered that I possessed no handy talent as a draughtsman, but Astolfo explained that the case was of small moment. This exercise was to train my discernment of the shapes surfaces might make of umbrae; it was a study in recognitions.

But this new regimen of drawing was less a geometry exercise and more in the vein of art. I sat with a sheaf of paper, trying to render likenesses not of shadows but of their casters: garden urns, hyacinths, quince bush, the sleeping form of Creeper, the huge hands of Mutano. Now and again Astolfo would stop by, leaf through a handful of my drawings, and with a finely pointed length of graphite make swift corrections. Each of his strokes was a revelation and, though I learned much in a short time, it was clear that I was destined to be no Manoni or

Petrinius and I felt, as I often had before, that hours were misspent.

I was pleased, therefore, when Astolfo informed me we were to pay another call upon Maxinnio and that I should prepare to answer certain questions that might be put to me. "I do not foresee that he will query you," Astolfo said, "but it is ever best to prepare. You are to recall each detail about the dancer you saw who has no shadow. If you are asked, you must answer truthfully."

"He will not be glad to find we know of her," I said. "If he offer to fight, shall I combat him?"

"I do not think you would fare brilliantly in swordplay with a dancing master. We must soon lesson you in dancing to lessen your pudding-footed lubbardness."

"But if he offer fight?"

"He will not," Astolfo said. "Go ready yourself. We leave within the hour."

Yet when we set out again Astolfo had buckled on that sword he called Deliverer. This time he did not bedeck himself in the cut and colors of a spice merchant, all green and gold, but wore his ordinary habit of russet doublet and trunks, and soft boots whose floppy tops concealed ingenious pockets. He carried now a rolled case of pliable leather, the sort used to transport largish maps.

We walked at leisurely pace into this seedy square of town with its sleepy shops of tailors and shoemakers, tinkers and tapsters. When we knocked at the street door of Maxinnio's establishment, it was opened again by the young girl who had attended us before. This time, at Astolfo's suggestion, I observed her more closely, but she was only as I remembered: a thin little thing of medium stature, with the jet hair and the great dark eyes that shone like wet obsidian. Of her figure in the dingy, gray scullery smock I could tell little.

When she led us into the rehearsal salon, the scene was as before, with the severe ballet mistress yapping crossly at her charges, the bored lutenist fingering along in rote fashion, and the lanky Maxinnio on his leather campaign stool, rapping the floor rhythmically with a short silver-headed cane.

He did not weep with joy at our appearance. "Here are you again, Astolfo," he snapped. "It seems you feel bound by some compulsion I cannot fathom to honor me with your presence and with the company of your overgrown henchmen."

"I bid you good morrow," Astolfo said in his mild voice.

"Have you auctioned off all your store of spices? I see you fitted today in a more customary livery."

"Today I come in my own interest and not in that of the merchant."

"That merchant who did not exist in the first place."

"That is true," Astolfo said. "But you must not complain of being deceived.

You did not credit my tale from the beginning. I had not really thought to deceive someone so perspicacious as Maxinnio."

"Now I sniff arrant trickery," he replied. "I warn you that if I grow impatient with your pitiable ruses, I shall have my troupe of young girls pitch you through the window onto the cobblestones. They will likewise defenestrate these two footpads that hang to you like baubles on earlobes."

"Cry you mercy," said Astolfo. "The day is too shiny new; a shame if violence should mar it. I came only to acquaint you with some intelligence that may not yet be in your possession."

"You came to monger gossip? I think you will not expect to be paid for this intelligence, as you call it."

"Only look upon these drawings I have brought. I am curious to know your judgment of these works." He untied the laces of the leather case and began to unroll it.

"The only artworks in which I am now interested are the designs for my new ballet," Maxinnio said. "The preparatory sketches are useless and we must begin them anew."

"But only glance at this bit of handiwork." Astolfo unrolled a drawing on fine-wove paper and held it up before the dance master.

When Maxinnio blinked his eyes wide and gave a start that shook his whole body, I edged around to see what image must produce such reaction. I judged it would be in our interest for me to give but a lackadaisical, cool look at the drawing, but when I saw the figure there I too was surprised and intook my breath audibly. Maxinnio did not notice, staring fixedly, oblivious to all else.

Here was the dancer without a shadow, the girl I had spied through the cracked door on the floor above. This was her face uplifted, her figure weightless and elongated, her arms raised above her flowing hair, her slender hands thrusting into the light of day. My late exercises in art, clumsy as they had been, gave me to appreciate, to savor, the achievement that lay on the sheet Astolfo upheld.

When Maxinnio turned his eyes from the drawing to the shadow master, his face was full of rage, every feature contorted. He looked for all the world like one of those small statues of demons that are set out to fend away evil spirits from temple gardens. When he spoke, his voice was low, choking with fury. "I would have your life for this."

"My henchmen, as you name them, will answer for my safety," Astolfo said. "Anyway, why do you threaten? I have brought this exquisite picture as a gift for you."

"This dancer is my secret. She is the guarantee of my success with the new entertainment. I do not understand how you come by her likeness. She has not been seen abroad. I keep her close. No one is to see her until the ballet of The Sylphs of Light is presented in the new season."

"She will not appear in your dance of sylphs. She will never dance in public."

"She must. All is settled and cast as in stone."

"You have rescued from a meager and grudging life many a young girl," Astolfo said. "You have made the pliable ones into dancers and found employment for some of the others. But your interest in them reaches only so far as the boundary of your professional purposes. You know little of where they come from or who they are or may have been."

"I maintain neither orphanage nor almshouse," Maxinnio said. "The girls learn to be not persons but only dancers. They learn to live solely for dance, as I do live."

"And that is why you do not know even the true name of this girl. That is how you could with impunity strip her of her shadow, sell it away so she could not retrieve it, and present her onstage in perfect purity."

"I could easily rid them all of their shadows. But only this one embodies the ideal I search for. It is not shadow-lack that composes her perfection."

"But I have found that she is the natural daughter of a great and powerful noble who does not care to have her prance before the garlicky, mutton-gorging rabble. You are to hand her over to me to deliver to him and thus spare your own life and the lives of those in your employ, saving too the razement of this place to smoking embers."

"Who is this giant terror you threaten me with?"

"You shall not know that."

"How do I know that he exists?"

"Because I tell you so and have the picture of her.... Here, look you upon this other likeness. What do you observe?" Astolfo rolled up the drawing of the dancer and gave it to Mutano who secured it with a black satin ribbon. Then he unfurled another drawing and held it up as before.

Maxinnio gave this new image a puzzled glance, then leaned forward in his little chair and peered closely. "I think I know this shadow," he said, "but I cannot say how."

"It is the shadow of your silver dancer, the shade you bartered away."

He shook his head. "No. Her shadow is a thing of unparalleled grace. There is something askew about the drawing of this one. It is impaired. It looks as if some wasting disease has befallen it, some distemper that wracks its shape."

"That is the condition it has acquired since it left your hands. This drawing depicts how it now looks at this moment and I shall deliver it to the girl's father. From this picture of her shadow he will draw conclusions about how she is being treated here. When his anger is at its flaming peak, I shall tell him your name and show him where to seek you out."

"You would play me false and destroy me and my work...for what purpose? There has been no enmity between us. I hold you in perfect indifference. If you go to ruin me, it will be only in order to fatten your purse."

"The father will reward me when his daughter is restored to him. There may be payment also for you."

"I care not." Maxinnio clenched and unclenched his hand, rapped the floor with his ebony cane. "Heap your coin till it drown you. My concern is with my Sylphs of Light. If I could spare my silver dancer, she should go to her father on wings of wind. But the entertainment cannot afford her absence."

Astolfo gave the picture of the shadow to Mutano who rolled it up and secured it with a red ribbon. "And now, if you will examine this third rendering." He unscrolled before Maxinnio a last drawing, a likeness of another young dancer. The pose was the same as in the picture of the silver girl, but this girl had black hair instead of blonde and the eyes that gazed sunward were of shining onyx. Though not so tall as the other girl, she was equally graceful, a creature of calm and guileless movement, with the ease of brook water.

Maxinnio looked at it with grave care. "This is an interesting fantasy of what a dancer might aspire to. No one but Petrinius could have drawn it so, but it is not a study from life. If 'twere, I would find the girl and put her to use."

"The drawing is not taken from life, but the girl is real enough. You may be acquainted with her. She is called Leneela."

"I think not," Maxinnio said. "The one Leneela I know is but a little servant girl in our household. She has been sweeping stones and scrubbing floors and pots for three years now since her mother died."

"This is she."

"If it be she, how could I not recognize her in this guise?"

"She is so customary to your eyes that she became invisible."

"She is no dancer, only a scullery maid."

"She can be trained."

"In time, perhaps, if she have ability. But time is short."

"You speak as if you had choice in the matter. The father will claim his silvery daughter. I have but offered you another to take her place. There is no cost to you except a delay in presenting your Sylphs. You can bargain a deferment."

"That will not be simple and will incur further expense."

"Expenses will be compensated. Again, I tell you that you have no choice. A carriage will call for the girl at first twilight. You will ascertain that she is in the best of condition and will hand her into the carriage yourself. To join a child with its parent – that is a handsome thing to do."

"Handsome or foul-featured, it shall be done. Yet I will not forget this tiresome japery you have turned upon me."

"I have secured your life," Astolfo said.

It was early evening before the three of us came together again, sitting at a table laid out in the kitchen, dividing an enormous beef and kidney pie Astolfo had besought from the cooks. A cask of aged cider stood ready to ease down the meat. The shadow master had traveled earlier in the day to the chateau of Rutilius and arranged how the girl was to come into his household.

"I hope this will prove a fortunate event for the lass," I said. "'Tis a sorrow, her loss to the art of the dance."

He nodded gaily and said he was obliged to me for a happy thought.

"How so?"

"I have told Ser Rutilius that I believe her to be his natural daughter and pointed out several similarities of feature and physique. You suggested some such thing. We may well have preserved the both of them from destruction."

"Destruction?"

"One who falls in love with a shadow loves an image of the ideal. No woman can approach to the perfection of such a fond delusion. When disappointment and disillusion set in, a rank distaste for the fleshly person follows, for she will be seen as a betrayer of the ideal, a spoiler of the perfection that once gloriously existed. In a passionate man, revenge will come to seem a necessity. The blade, the noose, the poison goblet stand forth in the mind, palpable and inescapable. There is none so desperate, none so dangerous, as one whose ideals have crumbled."

"It is well to deceive him then, in the matter of blood ties," I said.

"If indeed we have deceived. It is yet plausible that she is his own."

"Will he not go now to seek the mother and verify your story?"

"Alas!" Astolfo cried. "In my vivid account, the mother was strangled by a jealous lover and thrown into the harbor. The sea laves her sorrowful bones ceaselessly."

"And this lover? Shall not Ser Rutilius look for his track?"

"Alack! He has repented himself and lives in exile in the Fog Islands, leading a solitary, miserable existence lamenting the excesses of his former life."

"A pretty fable. But there are yet matters I do not comprehend. How was it possible for Petrinius to make the three drawings? He had seen neither of the girls and he had no way to observe how the shadow had deteriorated."

"I knew that he would have made a copy for his own collection of the drawing he made for Rutilius. I asked him to make another, only altering it as if the shadow had started to deteriorate."

"And the girls? I do not comprehend how he could have seen either of them without his presence at Maxinnio's establishment being remarked."

"Petrinius did not see either girl."

"How then did he make their likenesses?"

"He made none." Astolfo swallowed heartily from his mug of cider, set it down, and wiped his mouth with his wrist. "But there are others in this land who can draw besides that vain and impertinent artist. In fact, I have been known to dash off a sketch now and then, sometimes in the manner of Manoni, or the Anonymous Citadel Master, or even in the style of Petrinius himself."

"You produced those fine drawings? But you did not see the silver dancer. You were in the salon below, distracting Maxinnio from my prying."

"I made attentive note of your description of her," he said. "And then, of course, there was Petrinius's rendering of her shadow. Look you, Falco, if a person may cast a shadow, why may not a shadow cast a person?"

"A shadow may cast – "

" – Can cast the *image* of a girl, at least. Think upon your own lustful and lurid fancies. Do they not result in some kind of physical manifestation? But please do not tell us of it. I am a modest man and easily embarrassed."

Have you ever wondered how a mute person laughs? In Mutano's case, laughter takes the form of a gruesomely huge grin, a thunderous pounding of tabletop and thighs, and plenteous tears streaming from the corners of the eyes.

Grander than the Sea

T.A. Pratt

Tim Pratt aka T. A. Pratt (*sff.net/people/timpratt*) lives in Oakland, California, with his writer wife, Heather Shaw. They co-edit the zine *Flytrap*, and publish the occasional chapbook through their tiny micropublisher, Tropism Press. His fiction and poetry have appeared in publications such as *The Best American Short Stories: 2005*, *Year's Best Fantasy*, *Asimov's*, and *Lady Churchill's Rosebud Wristlet*, and he won his first Hugo Award for short fiction in 2007. His first novel, *The Strange Adventures of Rangergirl*, was published in 2005; his first collection was *Little Gods* (2003); his second, *Hart & Boot & Other Stories* (2007).

"Grander than the Sea" is another piece from *The Solaris Book of New Fantasy*. Pratt says it is "set in the same world as my Marla Mason urban fantasy series from Bantam Spectra." The first book, *Blood Engines*, was published in 2007. *Poison Sleep* and *Dead Reign* are out in 2008, and book four (as yet untitled) in 2009.

This is a fantasy detective story set in an insane asylum for mad sorcerers.

"DR. HUSCH IS HERE," Rondeau said, stepping into Marla Mason's cluttered office, where she sat poring over an eye-watering pile of expense reports from her spies abroad.

"Who's Elmer Mulligan, and why did our agent Brandywine spend $400 buying him lap dances at a strip bar in Canada?" she said, brandishing a piece of paper.

"I think Mulligan is the one who did that thing for us in Newfoundland," Rondeau said, shutting the door behind him and knocking over a pile of true-crime paperbacks with the covers ripped off. "You know, with that guy who had the ice palace?"

"Right," Marla said, rubbing her eyes. "I guess a lap dance is a small price to pay. Grizzly-polar bear hybrids are weird enough without some lunatic uplifting them to human intelligence. And did you see *this?*" She held up a flattened piece of seaweed, scrawled over with luminous green ink. It dripped briny water on the carpet. "It's from the Bay Witch. I can't even read it. Get somebody to go talk to her, will you?"

"Sure," Rondeau said. "Like I said, Dr. Husch is here, from the Blackwing Institute. She says it's urgent. But, ah, if you want me to keep her entertained for a while, I don't mind – "

Marla wrinkled her nose. "Rondeau, she must be a hundred and fifty years old."

He shrugged. "She only looks about thirty. Don't be ageist. And I've heard, when she was younger, she used to be quite the party girl."

"Yeah, I've heard that, too." Rondeau didn't know a fraction of the weirdness and debauchery in Husch's past, but Marla did, because the Felport archives went back a long time. "Is she here to beg for money?"

Rondeau shrugged. His attention was already wandering, and he riffled through a pile of back issues of *The Instigator*, which Marla still needed to comb for secret messages in the personals. On days like this she wondered why she'd ever agreed to become chief sorcerer. She was made for creeping around in shadows and kicking her enemies in the knees, not shuffling paperwork. Maybe she should hire an assistant. Rondeau was useful for many things, but alphabetizing wasn't one of them.

"Send her in," Marla said, wishing, not for the first time, that she had a better office for meeting people. When she had advance warning, she used her consigliere Hamil's office, all sleekness and modernity. But her working office, above Rondeau's nightclub, was an explosion of unfinished business, furnished with shelves, desks, and chairs scrounged from curbsides.

Rondeau went out, and Dr. Husch entered. "Leda," Marla said, leaning over her desk and extending a hand to shake. "Always a pleasure, assuming you aren't here to pester me for more funding."

Dr. Husch was only five and a half feet tall, rather shorter than Marla, but her presence was considerable. She had the body and face of a classical nymph, which she tried to de-emphasize, her curves restrained by a dark tailored suit jacket and skirt, her platinum-blonde hair pulled back in a severe bun. Her heels, though, were so high Marla felt unbalanced just looking at them. "The institute could always use more money," Husch said. "Since we *are* the only thing preventing the destruction of the world. But, no, that's not why I'm here. One of our inmates would like to see you."

Marla raised an eyebrow. "I'm not in the habit of visiting criminally insane sorcerers, Leda."

"It's Roger Vaughn, and he's quite insistent. I take him seriously."

Marla shook her head. "Vaughn? The name doesn't mean anything to me."

"He's the one who sank the ferry in the bay a hundred years ago, killing everyone aboard."

"Ah." That was one of the big disasters in Felport's history, though the details escaped her memory. "He must be getting on in years."

"Some of us do not age as rapidly as others," Husch said, without apparent irony. "More importantly, Vaughn has been in total seclusion since the disaster, without any contact with the outside world. I am curious to discover how he knows you *exist.*"

"Maybe one of the orderlies mentioned my name?"

Husch gave a sniff, contemptuous enough to make Marla blush in embarrassment, which pissed her off. "Sorry, I forgot your staff was all wind-up toys," she snapped.

The doctor waved her hand. "Mr. Annemann's creations are tireless and loyal, and I couldn't afford to hire human staff with the pittance you provide me anyway. No, Roger Vaughn must be acting on other information. He is quite lucid – his delusions only extend to certain, ah, fundamental aspects of world-view – and you would be in no danger. I think you should see him. He says the fate of the city is at stake."

If Felport was in danger, Marla had to go. Protecting the city was her one and only responsibility. "Crap," she said. "Okay, fine. I assume you want me to go *now?*"

Dr. Husch only smiled.

"You could've called first," Marla grumbled, rising from her creaking chair.

"One of our inmates discorporated and attempted to escape into the world via the phone lines last month, prevention of which required ripping out all the wires. I submitted a request for repair to you a week ago – in the meantime, we have no phone service." Dr. Husch reached down and plucked a sheet of pale green paper, with the raven logo of the Blackwing Institute at the top, from a heap on Marla's desk. "See?"

Marla groaned. "Fine, I'll have Hamil write you a check. Why don't you get a cell phone?"

"Because they're vulgar," Dr. Husch said, and Marla didn't have an answer for that.

"*Must* he come?" Husch said as Rondeau approached.

Marla drummed her fingers on the roof of Husch's silver Rolls Royce. "Yep, he must. You wouldn't believe the trouble he gets into if I leave him behind. You know, you could sell this car and get a nice chunk of change to buy extra blankets and Thorazine."

"The car is not mine to sell. It belongs to Mr. Annemann, and if he ever recovers, he will doubtless wish to have it. He graciously allows me to use it in the meantime."

"I thought Annemann got half his head blown off. I doubt he'll be driving anytime soon."

"His brain is not like that of other men. It has been regenerating steadily for the past several decades, and I expect it will be whole again someday."

You sound pretty cheerful about that, Marla thought, *considering you're the reason he got his skull broken apart in the first place.* She'd read about *that* in the archives, too.

Rondeau arrived, carrying a plastic bag. "I brought a bunch of leftover Halloween candy for the patients, Doc," he said. "Hope that's okay. I know they don't get many treats or visitors."

Husch's aspect softened, and she nodded. "Very thoughtful. Many of them will appreciate the kindness." She gestured, and Marla and Rondeau climbed into the cavernous back seat. Husch got into the passenger side. One of Annemann's creations – which seemed human, if you didn't look closely enough to notice the lack of pores and breathing – was in the front seat, dressed as a chauffeur. It probably wouldn't even know how to drive if you took off its hat and driving gloves. All Annemann's creations (with one notable exception) were fundamentally mindless, but acted like whatever you dressed them as.

"What do these guys eat, anyway?" Marla said, leaning forward to poke the chauffeur in the shoulder.

"Lavender seeds and earthworms," Husch said.

"That's messed up," Marla said.

"De gustibus or whatever," Rondeau said.

"It is the traditional meal," Husch said. "As you might imagine, it is quite expensive to feed twoscore homunculi a sufficient quantity of lavender seeds and earthworms. Even with the worm farm in the basement and our extensive gardens."

"I can tell this is going to be a fun drive," Marla said, sinking back into the leather seat. "You know I'd give you more money if I could, right? But, I mean, it's not like the mayor can tax ordinary citizens to pay for this stuff, considering most of them have no idea people like us even exist."

"And it drives Marla nuts," Rondeau said. "Because nobody ever thanks her for protecting the city from ravaging bands of wendigos or rat people from another star or things like that."

"I don't want *thanks*," Marla said. "Just...a little help. The mayor knows about us, but he's an ordinary, and he doesn't *like* us. He can't decide if I'm a mob boss or a vigilante or a superhero. He knows without me the city would have been destroyed a few times, though. Anyway, for something like the Blackwing Institute, I have to tax the other sorcerers...and no offense, Leda, but nobody wants to give money to the place where crazy sorcerers get locked up. It *worries* them."

Dr. Husch just sniffed.

The Blackwing Institute was an hour outside the city, and an hour outside Marla's comfort zone. She resisted the urge to turn around and press her face against the back window, to watch Felport diminish as they passed into the suburbs and then the fields and sleepy little towns beyond. Felport could be a pain in the ass, but it was *her* pain in the ass. She wasn't comfortable anywhere else.

Especially places that had cows and trees and shit like that. Fludd Park in the city was enough nature for anybody. It even had a creek and a duck pond and a botanical garden.

"My buddy Paul taught me this road trip game where you take the letters from license plates and make dirty words out of them," Rondeau said. "Anybody want to play?"

Marla groaned and tried to go to sleep.

"You want me to wear a *dress?*" Marla said, stepping back to put a chair between Dr. Husch and herself.

Husch held a ghastly long white dress embroidered at the neck and sleeves with lace flowers. "It will save a lot of trouble if you do."

"I like trouble better than dresses."

"Don't be stupid," Dr. Husch said. "Just put it on. Mr. Vaughn is from a different era. Do you really want to listen to him go on about the evils of women in pants for an hour?"

"I don't think I've ever seen you in a dress," Rondeau said. "Hmm..."

"Stop imagining it," she snapped, then sighed. "Yes, fine, all right. But I'm not wearing any of the petticoats or whatever. I wouldn't know where to begin."

"You've battled psychopomps and snake gods, but wearing a dress daunts you?" Husch said.

"It doesn't daunt me. I don't daunt. It's just unpleasant. Picking up a big handful of dog crap doesn't *daunt* me, but that doesn't mean I want to do it." Marla hadn't worn a dress in almost ten years. Her old mentor, Artie Mann, had made her dress up for a party once, when she'd first met the city's other sorcerers, but that was the last time. And at least that dress had been short enough to make kicking people easy, when it became necessary.

Dr. Husch and Rondeau left the room, and Marla shed her loose cotton pants and shirt for the dress. It was tight in the waist and bigger on top than she needed, and she wondered if it had been one of Dr. Husch's – it seemed more suited to her curves. Marla tugged the fabric fruitlessly away from her belly. "All right!" she shouted. "Let's go see the wizard!"

Husch reappeared with a heavy iron key-ring and beckoned. Rondeau tried not to stare at Marla, without much success, and she tried to ignore him, with similar results. "Seeing you like this just isn't natural," Rondeau said. "It's like putting a dress on – "

"You'd better stop right there," Marla said. "What have I told you about rehearsing what you're going to say silently in your head first?"

Rondeau looked upward, moved his lips briefly, then squeezed his mouth shut. He nodded once, then kept his eyes on his feet.

Husch unlocked a large iron door, incongruous in the wall of a formal sitting room. A wide white hospital corridor waited beyond. "This door divides my apartments from the Institute proper. This whole building used to be a private residence, of course."

"Mr. Annemann's mansion," Marla said.

"Yes," Husch said.

"Wow, so it wasn't always a hospital?" Rondeau said. "Huh. Wild. So, before we go into the dark corridors filled with madness and all that, I was wondering, how do you keep sorcerers *in* here? I mean, are there some kind of magical barriers that prevent them from using their powers, or what?"

Marla snorted. "Magical barriers? Right. Those *always* work. Nah, the doc just makes sure they don't get any books or chalk or skulls or bells or potions or whatever they liked to use for making magic when they were sane. A necromancer isn't much good without corpses to animate, and a pyromancer's not dangerous if you keep her in a chilled concrete room. It's like how you'd stop an ax murderer. You just lock them up someplace and make sure they never, ever get their hands on another ax."

"But sorcerers carry their axes with them inside their heads," Dr. Husch said, lingering by the door. "And while many of them do depend on props and tools and rituals, some are quite capable of working dangerous magics with only their hands and voices. Those are kept restrained and gagged, as necessary, for their own protection."

"What about the ones who can just, like, *look* at you and make you burst into flame?" Rondeau said, glancing at Marla. "The really powerful ones?" Marla wasn't sure whether to be flattered or offended. She wasn't sure she *could* do something like that – not without preparation, at least – but it was nice to know Rondeau thought she could.

"Ah," Dr. Husch said. "For those rare few, we keep a great many drugs on hand." She gestured, and they went past the iron door, which Husch carefully locked behind them. "But the house actually is well protected. The land here is magically neutral."

"Really?" Marla said. She hadn't realized that. "No ley-lines? No ancient Indian burial grounds? No restless ghosts of past atrocities? No psychic residue left over from epic battles or blood vendettas fought on this spot?"

"No monsters in caverns below ground, no eerie petroglyphs drawn by prehuman civilizations, no local spirits still clinging to sentience," Dr. Husch confirmed. "Mr. Annemann chose the location very carefully. He didn't want outside magical influences to affect his experiments. There's not much inherent magical energy in this area for our patients to draw upon."

Marla opened up her mind, and it was true, there weren't that many deep vibrations here. That *was* rare. Most places had *something* occultish about them. But... "Of course, now a dozen crazy sorcerers live here, and a couple have died in their rooms."

Dr. Husch sighed. "Yes. It's true. In another hundred years, this will be a *very* magically potent location. But for now, the effects haven't soaked into the earth."

"Only a dozen patients, huh?" Rondeau said. "In this big old place?"

"Not counting Mr. Annemann. We try to give each of them as much space as possible."

"Anybody famous locked up here?" Rondeau said.

"Once Mr. Vaughn was famous, or rather, infamous," Dr. Husch said. "One of our newest inmates is our escape artist, the one who tried to get out via the phone lines, Elsie Jarrow. Perhaps you've heard of her."

"I don't – " Rondeau said.

"Marrowbones," Marla said, shuddering. "That's what they called her. They still told stories about her, when I first came to Felport. How she'd suck all the fluids out of your body with a kiss."

"Hyperbole," Dr. Husch said. "But only just. We have others. Gustavus Lupo, the skinchanger, who lost track of his flesh one day and built a new body of the angry dead. A powerful psychic named Genevieve with a mind broken by trauma. Norma Nilson, who did not so much kill her enemies as crush them with despair until they begged permission to take their own lives. Others." She shrugged. "They all have special needs. I serve them as well as I can."

"Charming," Marla said. "Let's meet Mr. Vaughn. What's his mental malfunction, anyway?"

"He wants to raise a dark god from the sea and destroy all human life," Dr. Husch said. "Come along, his rooms are just down here."

Vaughn's room was crammed with bookshelves made of driftwood, and dried starfish dangled on strings from the ceiling. Despite the nautical theme, the room smelled of dust, not ocean. "Mr. Vaughn!" Dr. Husch called, and a small old man bustled in from another room. He wore an elegant gray suit, and his eyes were the darkest blue Marla had ever seen. Hands clasped behind his back, he bowed, and said "Thank you for coming to see me, Miss Mason. We have much to discuss." He nodded curtly to Dr. Husch and took no notice whatever of Rondeau. "Thank you for bringing her, Doctor. Hail Xorgotthua, and good day."

"Come, Rondeau," Dr. Husch said. "We'll take the candy you brought to some of the other patients."

Rondeau looked a question at Marla, and she nodded. Little old men who hailed Xorgotthua – whoever or whatever that was – weren't necessarily harmless, but if he were too dangerous for Marla to handle, Rondeau wouldn't be much help anyway. They left, and the door shut behind them. Vaughn gestured to an armchair, and Marla sat down, remembering to keep her legs demurely together. Stupid dress. Marla rubbed her hand on the arm of the chair and said, "Is this sharkskin?"

"Oh, yes," Vaughn said, sitting in an identical chair of his own. "Sharks are Xorgotthua's handmaidens, of course."

"Right. Why did you want to see me, Mr. Vaughn?"

"I need you to stop me," he said. "Kill me, probably. Well. Not *this* me. The other me."

"You're going to have to clarify that."

"Yes, I see." Vaughn took a handkerchief from his pocket and dabbed at sweat on his forehead, though it was cool in the room. "I assume you know of the sacrifice I made to the great god Xorgotthua a century ago? The ferry I sank, so that the screams of the dying might nourish the lord of all depths?"

Marla suppressed a shiver. So he was a religious fundamentalist. They always creeped her out. "Yeah, I know about that." Details were slowly coming back to her. "You were trying to conduct some ritual and raise some ancient god from the sea, right? But it didn't work?"

"Oh, it worked." Vaughn fingered a silver chain around his neck. "But it was only the first part of the ritual, you see. To raise Xorgotthua, I made a sacrifice to the waters, to wake the god. Then, a hundred years later, there must be another sacrifice, as large as the first, to entice the god to the surface, and onto the land. It is a long time to wait, but the attention spans of gods are not like those of men, and a hundred years is but a moment to Xorgotthua. The time for the second sacrifice is only a few days away."

"And you want me to...stop you from making the sacrifice?" Marla said. "Shouldn't be a problem, with you locked up here."

"Ah, well, no, not exactly. I want you to stop the *other* me. My reincarnation." He looked at her expectantly.

"Ah. So do I ring a bell or something to get Dr. Husch back here?" Marla said.

Vaughn sighed. "I know what you're thinking. Death is generally a prerequisite to reincarnation."

"Yeah. That's part of what I was thinking."

"I use the word as a convenience. It is not true reincarnation. You know the technique of putting your soul in a stone, to be retrieved later?"

"Sure. It tends to turn the soulless sorcerer into a pretty unsympathetic bastard with no sense of proportion, but it's a way to preserve your life." Marla was wary of the word "soul," but she knew a technomancer who talked about uploading personalities into computers and making backups of your mind, and he said the principle was the same.

"I did...something similar. But then I made a perfect copy of the stone where I kept my soul, through a certain alchemical process. I restored my original soul to this body, and left the copy in a safe place near the docks in Felport, with instructions to activate a few months prior to the centennial of my first sacrifice. It was a backup plan, you see. If I died or became incapacitated, my backup soul would be there to complete the ritual and raise Xorgotthua."

Marla frowned. "What do you mean 'activate'? Souls floating around loose aren't good for much. They need bodies."

"Oh, well, of course, the soul had instructions to seize control of the nearest suitable vessel."

"Vessel. You mean a *person.*" Marla gripped the arms of the chair. "You made a backup of your soul with instructions for it to *possess* some random passer-by?"

Mr. Vaughn nodded. "Yes, exactly! Such an honor for the vessel, too, being given the opportunity to help raise Xorgotthua."

Marla closed her eyes, counted to ten, and opened them again. The urge to strangle Vaughn had not passed, but it was under control. "So this person is wandering around Felport now?"

"Not *wandering,*" he said, offended. "He is *me* – or me, as I was a hundred years ago – and he has been learning all he can about the city. That's how I found out you were the, ah, person in charge."

"You're in communication with this double of yours?"

"I see and hear and smell and taste what he does." Vaughn frowned. "It is a side effect I had not expected, though I admit, it is good to smell the sea again. But I do not think this communication goes both ways. I've had no indication he sees what I see."

"Good. Where can I find him?"

Vaughn wagged his finger. "No, no. I will not help you stop him unless you help *me.*"

"What, do you want to go on a field trip? Deep-sea fishing or something? I can talk to the doc."

"No. What I want is for you to stop my reincarnation, so that I can be the one to raise great Xorgotthua. It should have been me. I cannot bear the thought of this *copy* of myself raising the god while I languish here, to die with everyone else when the waves cover the land. My copy was meant as a last resort, if I was dead or in a coma, but I am aware, and here, and quite capable of completing the ritual on my own."

"Uh huh," Marla said, standing. "So you want me to stop your copy from killing lots of innocent people, and help *you* kill lots of innocent people instead, and either way the result is a risen god who wants to destroy all human life? Sorry, doesn't sound like something I want to pursue."

"If you help me, I will intercede on your behalf with Xorgotthua. I can make sure you and your city are spared. My copy will show no such mercy, I assure you. But if you let me be the one who wakes the god, I will use my influence to convince it to spare your home." Vaughn rose to his feet and stood facing Marla. He extended his hand. "Do we have a deal?"

Marla contemplated. If a great dark god really *was* rising from the sea, such bargains might be necessary, but she wasn't ready to concede defeat yet. "No, thanks. I think I'll look for your copy on my own."

Vaughn closed his hands into fists. "Listen, *woman.* I brought you here to make an arrangement. You'll never find him without me. If you don't help me, the death of your city is a foregone conclusion. I offer your only hope. Take it, or face the consequences."

"Yeah, let me get back to you on that," she said, opening her cell phone and calling Rondeau. When he picked up, she said, "Hey, tell the doc I'm done here."

"You can't 'get back to me,'" Vaughn said, his face getting red. "You will make this bargain *now* or – "

Marla snorted. "Please. Like you won't jump at the chance if I come back in two days and tell you it's a deal. What, you're going to turn up your nose and refuse to help me because I snubbed you today? As if."

Vaughn sat down. He glowered at her. "You will regret the way you've treated me. When you return to beg for my assistance in a day or two days, I will know I have the power and will drive a much harder bargain."

"I look forward to negotiating with you," Marla said. "But don't expect me to wear a dress again." The door opened, and Marla slipped out.

"You didn't tell me he was the priest of a dark god," Marla said, hurrying down the hallway, with the shorter Husch striding quickly to keep up. "You might've mentioned."

"He's not," Husch said. "I told you, his fundamental worldview is delusional. He believes in the great god Xorgotthua, but no such god exists."

Marla stopped walking. "Are you sure about that?"

"Quite. There is no record of such a creature in any oral or written tradition I have consulted. Vaughn claims the god has inspired countless followers through the ages and has been worshipped by many societies, but it's just not true. Vaughn began talking about Xorgotthua after he nearly drowned in the mid-1800s, and his delusion intensified over time, becoming ever more baroque and sophisticated. It was considered a harmless eccentricity, until he arranged the ferry disaster. Then Felport's elite sorcerers realized he was a danger and had him put away here."

"Huh," Marla said, resuming her walk back to Husch's apartments. "That's reassuring. You wouldn't believe the stuff he told me."

Husch unlocked the door. Rondeau was on the other side, sitting on a couch, watching a television screen. "We heard it all," Husch said. "The guest rooms are under surveillance, of course."

"That dude is batshit," Rondeau said. "Now he's walking in circles and talking to himself and, I shit you not, *cackling*."

"So you brought me here to listen to a crazy guy's pointless babble?" Marla said.

"No. He did know your name and your position among Felport's sorcerers, and other details of daily life in the city he should not be privy to. I think he is probably telling the truth about this double of his, and his plans to conduct a sacrifice in a few days."

"So there's no giant sea god to worry about," Rondeau said. "Just the issue of a bunch of innocent people getting killed."

"Huh," Marla said. "How many people died in that ferry disaster?"

"Over a hundred, most bound for a family reunion on Bramble Island," Husch said. "And it sounds like Vaughn wants just as many people to die this time."

"Crap," Marla said.

"Indeed," Husch replied.

"Good morning, Bay Witch," Marla said, sitting on a bench on the boardwalk with a view of the bay's gray expanse.

The Bay Witch – who'd once been named Zufi, back when she was a surfer girl, before she became a student of the hidden arts – sat at the other end of the bench. She was blonde and dressed in a black wetsuit, a puddle of seawater spreading all around her.

"Nice of you to visit," the Bay Witch said. "You got my note?"

"I got an incomprehensible smear of goo on seaweed. But I needed to talk to you anyway. What's up?"

"Bay's getting more polluted every year. I've sent reports. You don't answer me."

Marla nodded. "I've been busy, but I'm taking bids to deal with the pollution. Unfortunately the best bid is from Ernesto, who wants to gather all the pollutants to create a filth elemental to smite his enemies. I'm thinking of accepting it, but I need to find out who his enemies are first."

"Fair enough," the Bay Witch said. "There's another thing. Probably nothing, but there's – "

"Let me guess. There's a crazy guy hanging around, talking about raising a dark sea god named Xorgotthua?"

The Bay Witch laughed. "They told me you have tentacles everywhere. Yeah, that's him."

"Where might I find this crazy guy?"

She shrugged. "He's been a regular in some of the bars these past few months, bothering people, but he hasn't been around lately. He was pretty irritated when nobody wanted to join his cult. He promised they'd all die if they didn't join him, the usual. Nobody took him seriously. He's just a kid, can't be more than seventeen. I felt kind of bad for him, but he was creepy, too."

Marla nodded. "I've got sort of a weird question. Let's say I needed to get a giant squid in a few days. Just out in the bay, you know. Waving tentacles around, the whole deal. Think you could hook that up?"

"I'm not Aquaman," she said. "I'm not friends with all the creatures of the sea."

"Yeah, but I bet you've got methods."

"A giant squid?" She frowned. "They do like cold water, but they're not exactly common, and they prefer deep water. If it's doable – *if* – I'd need some serious payback. I'd have to burn a lot of power and influence over something like this, and I'm guessing you don't even want to tell me why."

"True," Marla said. "Do it, and you'll be taken care of."

"I'd need the *bay* to be taken care of. You're the chief sorcerer of Felport, and the way you feel about the city? That's how I feel about the bay."

"We'll work it out," Marla said. "You know I'm good for it."

"Okay," the Bay Witch said. She shook her head. "I'll see what I can do. Meet me back here tomorrow." She walked to the edge of the boardwalk, climbed over the rail, and leapt gracefully into the sea.

Marla spent the afternoon talking to her various friends and informants by the boardwalk, the docks, and the boat harbor, but no one had seen the crazy guy lately. If Marla was going to find him, she'd have to get more creative.

"One giant squid, coming up," the Bay Witch said, looking pleased with herself. They sat at an outdoor café a block from the water, enjoying the mild spring air, though the Bay Witch was dripping water, as always. It was an occupational malady. "The thing's the size of a school bus. Where do you want it?"

"A few hundred yards from shore, two days from now, midnight, waving its tentacles around, splashing a lot, making a spectacle. Can you handle that?"

"I can hijack its brain for a little while," the Bay Witch said. "Squid are too big, and their anatomy is too weird, for me to control easily, but if all you want is flailing, I can manage that. What, are you trying to scare away a sperm whale or something?"

"Not quite," Marla said. "I need your help with something else. Where can I get a lot of seashells and other ocean crap like that?"

"You look like a kitschy seafood restaurant exploded all over you," Rondeau said.

Marla examined herself in one of the long mirrors in the dressing room of Rondeau's nightclub. It had been a strip club, once upon a time, and still had all the backstage facilities, though these days the only performers were DJs. She adjusted the bit of fishing net she wore as a cloak and tugged the cascade of shell necklaces around so they didn't drag quite so heavily on her neck. "That's the look I'm going for," she said. "You have to admit, the sword made from narwhal horn is pretty cool." It was useless as a weapon, but the long, spiraling horn on a hilt hanging from her belt was a nice bit of flash.

"I still don't see why I have to go," Dr. Husch said, emerging from the bathroom. Even dressed in sailcloth, net, and shells, she managed to look regal. She had a wicked whip hanging from her belt, a scourge with ends tipped by fishhooks.

"I might need backup," Marla said, "and the homunculus orderlies don't listen to anyone but you." She picked up two half-masks made of horseshoe crab shells, which, along with some drawn-on abstract tattoos, would serve to disguise their faces. Better if the original Mr. Vaughn didn't recognize them while looking through his copy's eyes.

Dr. Husch ran her finger along the top of a vanity, wrinkling her nose at the dust. "I don't think this place has been cleaned since last time I was here."

"You've been here before?" Rondeau said.

"When it was a burlesque house," Husch said. "Once upon a time, Mr. Annemann owned this place. I...worked for him."

Marla didn't say anything. Husch *had* worked for him. Sort of.

"Wow, you were a dancer?" Rondeau said.

"It was a long time ago," Husch said.

"I think we look suitably crazy and ocean-themed," Marla said. "Let's hit the bars."

"Why do you think he'll come here?" Husch said. They were in the back of an empty dive bar near the docks, sipping drinks and trying to ignore the smell of old beer and fish. Marla felt a little self-conscious in her sea-witch getup, and the mask cut her peripheral vision down more than she liked. The bartender clearly thought they were nuts, too, but image was important in situations like this.

"I started spreading the word that a priestess of Xorgotthua was in the area, planning the ritual that would raise the god, here to replace poor Mr. Vaughn." She shrugged. "I said this was her hangout. If Vaughn's copy is paying attention, he'll hear word. And if he does come in, well, we're kind of hard to miss." Marla grinned. "In the meantime, girl talk. You know Rondeau likes you."

Husch pursed her lips. "You don't mean to tell me I should be flattered? I doubt he's very discriminating in his tastes."

"Rondeau usually likes body-pierced college girls with flexible attitudes toward morality," Marla said. "You're not his usual type, so sure, be flattered."

"It's been a long time since I've been interested in what men thought of me, Marla," she said, looking at her levelly. "Given your position, I assume you know the...details of my origin. You can understand why I might be wary of men?"

Marla nodded. "Sure. Just making conversation. But Rondeau *doesn't* know your origins – I promise – so you don't have to worry so much about his expectations."

"I'll take that under advisement."

"Speaking of men," Marla said.

A young man in a T-shirt and swimming trunks came through the door, sunlight streaming in around him. He saw them in the back of the bar and started coming their way.

The bartender shouted at him. "Hold on, kid, I told you, you're under age, you can't come in here!" The kid gestured at the bartender and muttered a guttural incantation, and the bartender fell, eyes rolling back in his head.

"Well, well," Marla said. "Reckless and unnecessary use of magic. This must be our zealot."

"You!" he said, striding toward them. "You claim to worship Xorgotthua?" His hair was wet, and he had a large pimple on the side of his nose.

Marla sipped her beer before answering. "I claim nothing. I am the priestess of Xorgotthua, yes. And who are you, child?"

"I am no child. I am the reincarnation of Roger Vaughn himself!"

"Madness," Marla said. "Vaughn has not been seen in a century. I have come, with my followers, to complete the work he began so long ago." She gestured at him lazily. "Away with you. Enjoy your last days of life before the waters swallow you."

He crouched by the table. "You don't understand. I *am* Vaughn. I have pledged my life to Xorgotthua! How have I never heard of you and your followers?"

"We have lived in seclusion on an island," Marla said. "Waiting for the stars to come right. That time is now. The sacrifices are prepared, and the god will rise tomorrow night."

He frowned. "I've arranged a sacrifice. There are bombs, on a ferry bound for Bramble Island, and tomorrow – "

Marla snorted. "The bombs were discovered, you fool, and removed. Did you think the secret ruler of this city would fail to check the ferries, so close to the centennial of Vaughn's first sacrifice?"

The kid grimaced. "Marla Mason. Yes. I did not realize...I had heard she was effective. I should have been more careful. But surely I can still be of service – "

Marla waved her hands. "It's all arranged. The orphans have already been prepared."

Dr. Husch's eyes went wide, and she made a snorting noise, and after a moment Marla realized she was trying not to laugh. Dr. Husch, laughing – that would be something to see.

"Orphans?" the kid said.

Marla nodded. "Yes. Xorgotthua enjoys the taste of orphans. Something *Vaughn* would know very well."

"Of course I know," he said quickly. "I just...where did you get orphans?"

Marla turned her most withering glare on him, hoping the half-mask didn't dim its power. "They're *orphans*. The essential fact of orphans is that no one much misses them. Now, please, be gone. We are discussing preparations for the ceremony."

Vaughn stood up. "I...please, Xorgotthua is my life...how can I serve?"

Marla sighed theatrically. "Very well. Vaughn, if that is your name. Come to the boardwalk tomorrow, before midnight. You may watch the great god rise with the rest of my followers. Perhaps Xorgotthua will choose to spare your life."

"Thank you," Vaughn's copy said, and left the bar, looking punch-drunk and dazed.

"You'd better go check on the bartender, Doc, and make sure the kid didn't kill him." Marla cracked her knuckles. "We're on for tomorrow."

"Why didn't you just have me summon the orderlies?" Husch said. "They could have seized him, and he would have been safely housed in the Blackwing Institute before nightfall!"

Marla shook her head. "Then him and the *other* Vaughn would just keep plotting and planning and probably causing me more trouble in ten or twenty or fifty or a hundred years, gods forbid I'm still around then. No, we need to put an end to this, or at least build in a long delay." She opened her cell phone and called Rondeau. "Hey," she said. "Send some of our pet policemen to check the Bramble Island ferries for bombs. Yes, I know, I don't know why I didn't think to check there. I guess I expected Vaughn's copy to be more original. Make sure our people keep an eye on the copy, too, in case he decides to cover his bets by throwing firebombs at a yacht or something." She closed the phone. "When they find the bombs, we can say it was terrorists and get some of that sweet Homeland Security money. The mayor would totally owe me for that."

"How nice for you. So what happens now?"

"Squid happens," Marla said.

"Are the orderlies in place, Rondeau?" Marla spoke into her phone.

"Yep."

"And you talked to the Bay Witch?"

"Zufi says we're good to go," Rondeau replied.

"Good." She hung up. Dr. Husch and a handful of Annemann's homunculi – dressed in their own seashell-and-face-tattoo cultist disguises – stood on the boardwalk, by the railing, looking at the moonlit water. The air was cool, the tang of salt strong in the air. A good night for a ritual.

"The bay is really very pretty," Dr. Husch said.

"It's a good deep-water port," Marla said, with her usual civic pride.

"I hope we aren't mistaken about Mr. Vaughn and the accuracy of his ideas," Husch said. She swung her fishhook-tipped scourge idly over the railing. "I'd be very upset if a great sea god did rise tonight."

"Eh," Marla said. "The bombs were disabled, and I didn't *actually* sacrifice any orphans. I wouldn't worry about it. Even if Xorgotthua does exist, which he doesn't, he'll just slumber on." She glanced at her cell phone. Five minutes to midnight. "I hope he shows."

"I am here, priestess."

Marla and Dr. Husch turned and saw Vaughn's copy. He wore his own cape of net, woven with seaweed, and a ridiculous profusion of shell necklaces. His face had markings just like Marla's...only his were real tattoos. Marla winced under her mask. Damn. That must have hurt. She felt bad for the kid who'd been possessed. He'd probably never get his body back, and if he did, he'd have to walk around with that stuff on his face.

"Good," Marla said. "Then observe the water, where Xorgotthua will rise."

They all bellied up to the rail. Nothing much happened; moonlight, wind, waves. Then, slowly, the sea began to bubble and roil, and after a moment something vast broke the surface out in the water, and great flailing tentacles, each over fifteen feet long, whipped into the air, flinging water. The "cultists" dropped to their knees, and after a moment's hesitation, so did Vaughn's copy.

"Great Xorgotthua!" Marla shouted, still standing, raising her arms overhead. "We come to welcome you!"

The squid rolled, revealing an eye the size of a dinner plate for a moment before slipping back under the water.

"Yes!" Marla shouted. "I understand, great one! We live to serve you!"

The squid sank beneath the waves, and the cultists rose.

"My people," Marla said, her voice appropriately bleak. "Great Xorgotthua thanks us for the sacrifice, but says it is not yet time to rise. Xorgotthua wishes to wait until the ice caps have melted and the seas have risen to swallow the coastal lands. We are not to disturb its slumber until that time. We must keep the god's sacraments and teach the next generation of followers." She shook her head. "Our time will come. It only seems long to our pitiful human minds. Another few centuries are but moments to great Xorgotthua."

Vaughn's copy remained kneeling when the others rose. He looked up at Marla, stricken. "I can wait," he said. "I have no choice. I will wait. That glimpse of the god will sustain me through the centuries."

Show 'em a few tentacles and they see a squamous god of the outer darkness, Marla thought. "I have discovered something," she said, placing a hand on the copy's shoulder. "It seems Roger Vaughn did not die, as we all assumed. He is resting in a hospital, where all his needs are looked after. Would you like to meet him?"

"He – I – he lives? When I woke, I thought he must have died, but..." The copy stood up. "Yes. I'd like to see him very much. I wish to know what happened to my life in the past hundred years."

"Perhaps you and the older Mr. Vaughn can await the return of Xorgotthua together," Marla said. She nodded to Dr. Husch, who summoned her orderlies to lead Vaughn's copy to the car.

"They bicker like an old couple," Rondeau said, watching Vaughn – both Vaughns – on Dr. Husch's closed-circuit television. The two mad sorcerers shared a new, larger suite of rooms in the Blackwing Institute, and spent most of their time arguing over fine points of Xorgotthuan theology. They might have had the same mind, once, but you can't put one soul in two bodies without a little divergence.

"I'm just glad they're locked up," Marla said.

Rondeau nodded. "It was nice of you to bring all this stuff," he said. Marla had loaded a truck with blankets, drugs, and food, donations from the sorcerers of the city. Marla had told the other sorcerers that Dr. Husch was the one who saved the city from destruction by a great ocean-dwelling deity inimical to human life, and had encouraged them to show their appreciation with material goods. They had. No one liked to contemplate the coming of great indifferent gods, and Marla hadn't bothered to tell the sorcerers that Xorgotthua was imaginary.

"Where is Leda, anyway?" Marla said. "I thought she was coming back to the city with us."

"Yep. I'm taking her to see one of those homemade robot demolition derbies," Rondeau said. "It's going to be awesome. She said she had to take care of something before we go, though."

Marla rolled her eyes. She'd done her part to encourage Dr. Husch, but she doubted Rondeau would make it past one date with her.

Rondeau went back to watching the screen, snorting laughter as the two Vaughns argued about whose turn it was to clean the toilet. Marla went looking for Dr. Husch and found her in a room at the end of a short hallway, sitting beside a hospital bed.

Marla stood in the doorway for a moment, then said, "I don't understand why you still tend him."

Dr. Husch adjusted Mr. Annemann's catheter. He was hooked up to a number of machines, his head wrapped almost entirely in a thick padding of bandages.

Marla cleared her throat. "I mean, when you consider..."

"The fact that he created me?" Dr. Husch said. "You might expect me to be grateful for that."

Marla shifted uncomfortably. "But he created you to be his, well, his concubine, right?"

"I was created as his living sexual fantasy," she said, covering Mr. Annemann with a blanket. "Yes. And he used me as such. I was the most sophisticated of his many homunculi, the only one capable of independent thought. At first, I appreciated his attention. Even when he sold me to the highest bidder as a courtesan, and later, when he had me dance in a burlesque house and sold me more prosaically in the alley behind the club, I felt he deserved to treat me any way he wished. But as time passed, I began to resent him and to wish for my own life. The worst part was, I still loved him. He could be very kind, you know, and he loved discovery and knowledge more than anything, something I respected very much. And then one day, I began to wonder if perhaps Mr. Annemann *made* me love him. What if loving him was not a choice, but merely a spell he'd cast on me?" She stroked Annemann's hand.

"That's why you shot him?" Marla said. "Because you thought he'd cast a love spell on you?" The Felport archives had reports about the shooting, but not about the motives.

Dr. Husch bowed her head. "Yes. I thought he must be a monster, to cast such a spell. I thought I would kill him and free myself. He did not die, but his brain was... severely harmed. Any spell he cast on me would have failed, then, after the damage I inflicted." She looked up. "But I didn't stop loving him. I realized the love was not the result of a spell at all, but a true feeling. And so I have been caring for him ever since. Someday, he will wake, and I will tell him I'm sorry.

Perhaps then he will realize I am more than his creation, and he will see me as a woman, and his equal."

Wishful thinking, Marla thought. "I'm not saying it was right to shoot him. But you probably never would have had your own life otherwise."

"No one's life is solely their own," Dr. Husch said. "We are all bound by our devotions. Mr. Vaughn would understand that. I'm sure you do, too."

Marla thought of her own tangled allegiances, the web of obligations that made protecting the city possible... but that was the point, wasn't it? To protect Felport. She had devotions of her own and couldn't fault Dr. Husch for hers, however misguided they might be in Marla's eyes.

"Thanks for all your help, Leda."

"You can thank me by doubling my annual budget."

Marla laughed. "I'll see what I can do."

Princess Lucinda and the Hound of the Moon

Theodora Goss

Theodora Goss (*theodoragoss.com*) lives in Brighton, Massachusetts, with her husband Kendrick, a scientist and artist, and their daughter, Ophelia. She was born in Hungary, and lived in Italy and Belgium before coming to the United States. She began publishing her stories in 2002. She is associated with the Interstitial Arts movement: with Delia Sherman, she edited *Interfictions: An Anthology of Interstitial Writing* (2007). A collection of her short fiction, *In the Forest of Forgetting*, was published in 2006. Of fiction writing, she remarks, "The problem with being a writer is that reality is less real to you than the products of your imagination. To be a writer is to live among ghosts."

"Princess Lucinda and the Hound of the Moon" was published in *Realms of Fantasy*. It's a gonzo fairy-tale princess coming-of-age story in which the princess skips marrying the prince and instead gets a better deal. For after all, isn't that what a really smart young princess needs in these days of mediocre princes?

WHEN THE QUEEN learned that she could not have a child, she cried for three days. She cried in the clinic in Switzerland, on the shoulder of the doctor, an expert on women's complaints, leaving tear stains on his white coat. She cried on the train through Austria, while the Alps slipped past the window of her compartment, their white peaks covered with snow. She cried when the children from the Primary School met her at the station, bringing her bouquets of snowdrops, the first of the season. And after the French teacher presented her with the bouquets, and the children sang the Sylvanian national anthem, their breaths forming a mist on the cold air – she cried especially then.

"It doesn't matter, Margarethe," said King Karel. "My nephew Radomir will make a fine king. Look at how well he's doing at the Primary School. Look at how much he likes building bridges, and if any country needs bridges, it's Sylvania." For the Danube and its tributaries ran through the country, so that wherever you went in Sylvania was over a river, or perhaps two.

And then Queen Margarethe stopped crying, because it was time to greet the French ambassador, and she was after all the youngest daughter of the King of Greece. She had been trained to restrain her emotions, at least at state functions. And the blue satin of her dress would stain.

But that night, when the French ambassador was discussing business with the bankers of Sylvania, and her other guests were discussing French innovations in art (for although Sylvania was a small country, it had a fashionable court) or losing at cards in a cloud of cigarette smoke, the Queen walked out to the terrace.

It was a cold night, and she pulled the blue satin wrap more closely about her shoulders. The full moon above her was wearing a wrap of gray clouds. In its light, she walked down the steps of the terrace, between the topiaries designed by Radomir IV, boxwood swans swimming in a pool of grass, a boxwood stag running from overgrown boxwood hounds. She shivered because her wrap was not particularly warm, but walked on through the rose garden, which was a tangle of canes. She did not want to go back to the castle, or face her guests.

She reached the croquet lawn, beyond which began the forest that surrounded Karelstad, where croquet balls were routinely lost during tournaments between the ministers and the ladies-in-waiting. Suddenly, she heard laughter. She looked around, frightened, and said, "Is anyone there?"

No one answered. But under a chestnut tree that would be covered with white flowers in spring, she saw a basket. She knelt beside it, although the frost on the grass would stain her dress more certainly than tears, and saw a child. It was so young that the laugh she had heard might have been its first, and it waved its fist, either at the moon above or at the Queen, whose face looked like a second moon in the darkness.

She lifted the child from its basket. Surely it must be cold, left out on a night like this, when winter still covered Sylvania. Surely whoever had left it here did not deserve a child. She picked it up, with the blanket it was wrapped in, and carried it over the croquet lawn, through the rose garden, between the boxwood swans and the boxwood stag, up the terrace steps, to the castle.

"Surely she has a mother," said the King. "I know this has been difficult for you, Margarethe, but we can't just keep her."

"If you could send the Chamberlain out for diapers," said the Queen. "And tell Countess Agata to warm a bottle."

"We'll have to advertise in the *Karelstad Gazette*. And when her mother replies, we'll have to return her."

"Look," said the Queen, holding the child up to the window, for the cook had scattered cake crumbs on the terrace, and pigeons were battling over them. "Look, embroidered on the corner of her blanket. It must be her name: Lucinda."

No one answered the advertisement, although it ran for four weeks, with a description of the child and where she had been found. And when the King himself went to look beneath the chestnut tree, even the basket was gone.

Princess Lucinda was an ordinary child. She liked to read books, not the sort that princesses were supposed to like, but books about airplanes, and mountain climbing, and birds. She liked to play with her dolls, so long as she could make parachutes for them and toss them down from the branches of the chestnut tree. The Queen was afraid that someday Lucinda would fall, but she could not stop her from climbing trees, or putting breadcrumbs on her windowsill for the pigeons, or dropping various objects, including the King's scepter, out of the palace window, to see if they would fly.

Lucinda also liked the gardener's daughter, Bertila, who could climb trees, although not so well as the Princess. She did not like receptions, or formal dresses, or narrow shoes, and she particularly disliked Jaromila, her lady-in-waiting and Countess Agata's daughter.

But there were two unusual things about Princess Lucinda. Although her hair was brown, it had a silver sheen, and in summer it became so pale that it seemed purely silver. And the Princess walked in her sleep. When the doctor noticed that it happened only on moonlit nights, the Queen ordered shutters to be placed on Lucinda's windows, and moonlight was never allowed into her room.

For the Princess' sixteenth birthday, the Queen planned a party. Of course she did not know when the Princess had been born, so she chose a day in summer, when the roses would be at their best and her guests could smoke on the terrace.

Everyone of importance in Sylvania was invited, from the Prime Minister to the French teacher at the Primary School. (Education was considered important in Sylvania, and King Karel had said on several occasions that education would determine Sylvania's success in the new century.) The Queen hired an orchestra that had been the fashion that winter in Prague, although she confessed to the Chamberlain that she could not understand modern music. And Prince Radomir came home from Oxford.

"They ought to be engaged," said the Queen at breakfast. "Look at what an attractive couple they make, and what good friends they are already." Princess Lucinda and Prince Radomir were walking below the morning room windows, along the terrace. The Queen might have been less optimistic if she had known that they were discussing airplane engines. "And then she would be Queen."

She looked steadily at the King, and raised her eyebrows.

"But I can't help it, Margarethe," said King Karel, moving his scrambled eggs nervously around on his plate with a fork. "When the first King Karel was crowned by the Pope himself, he decreed that the throne must always pass to a male heir."

"Then it's about time that women got the vote," said the Queen, and drank her coffee. Which was usually how she left it. King Karel imagined suffragettes crashing through the castle windows and writing "Votes for Women" on the portraits of Radomir IV and his queen, Olga.

"How can you not like him?" asked Bertila later, as she and Lucinda sat on the grass, beneath the chestnut tree.

"Oh, I like him well enough," said Lucinda. "But I don't want to marry him. And I'd make a terrible queen. You should have seen me yesterday, during all those speeches. My shoes were hurting so badly that I kept shifting from foot to foot, and Mother kept raising her eyebrows at me. You don't know how frightening it is, when she raises her eyebrows. It makes me feel like going to live in the dungeon. But I don't want to stand for hours shaking hands with ambassadors, or listen to speeches, even if they are in my honor. I want – "

What did she want? That was the problem, really. She did not know.

"But he's so handsome, with those long eyelashes, and you know he's smart." Bertila lay back on the grass and stared at the chestnut leaves.

"Then you should marry him yourself. Honestly, I don't know what's gotten into you lately. You used to be so sensible, and now you're worse than Jaromila."

"Beast. As though a prince could marry a gardener's daughter." Bertila threw a chestnut, rejected by a squirrel the previous autumn because a worm had eaten through its center, at the Princess.

"Ouch. Stop it, or I'll start throwing them back at you. And not only do I have more chestnuts, I have much better aim. But seriously, Bertie, you'd make a better queen than I would. You're so beautifully patient and polite. And since you're already in love with his eyelashes..."

"There you are," said Jaromila. "Lying in the dirt as usual, and talking with servants." She tapped one shoe, as pointed and uncomfortable as fashion demanded, on the grass.

"You're not wanted here," said Lucinda.

"But you're wanted at the reception, half an hour ago."

"You see?" said Lucinda to Bertila, in dismay. "You'd make a much better queen than I would!"

"And she'd be just as entitled to it," said Jaromila. She had also seen Lucinda walking with Radomir on the terrace, but she had reacted quite differently than the Queen. She could not tell you the length of Radomir's eyelashes, but she knew that one day he would be king.

"What do you mean?" asked Lucinda.

"Yes, what *do* you mean?" asked Bertila. She was usually patient, just as Lucinda had said, but today she would have liked to pull Jaromila's hair.

"Well, it's time someone told you," said Jaromila, shifting her feet, because it was difficult to stand on the grass, and because she was nervous. "But you can't tell anyone it was me." From the day the Princess had been found, Queen Margarethe had implied that Lucinda was her own child, born in Switzerland. No one at court had dared to question the Queen, and the Chamberlain and Countess Agata liked their positions too well to contradict her. But Jaromila had heard them discussing it one night, over glasses of sherry. If anyone found out that Jaromila had told the Princess, she would be sent to her grandmother's house in Dobromir, which had no electric lights or telephone, not even a phonograph.

"Told what?" asked Lucinda. "You'd better tell me quickly. I have a whole pile of chestnuts, and you can't run in those shoes."

"That you're not a princess at all. You were found in a basket under this chestnut tree, like a peasant's child."

That afternoon, the Queen had to tell Lucinda three times not to fidget in front of the French ambassador.

As soon as the reception was over, Lucinda ran up to her room and lay on her bed, staring up at the ceiling. Who was she, if she was not the Princess Lucinda? After a while, she got up and took off the dress she had worn to the reception, which had been itching all afternoon. She put on her pajamas. But she could not sleep. For the first time in her life, she opened the shutters on her bedroom windows and looked out. There was the moon, as full as a silver krone, casting the shadows of boxwood swans and hounds on the lawn.

In her slippers, she crept down the stairs and out the French doors to the terrace. She walked between the topiaries and the rose bushes, over the croquet lawn, to the edge of the forest. There, she lay on the grass and stared up at the moon, through the branches of the chestnut tree. "Who am I?" she asked. It seemed to smile at her, but gave no answer.

Lucinda woke shivering, with dew on her pajamas. She had to sneak back into the castle without being seen by the footmen, who were already preparing for the party.

Jaromila had forgotten to set out the dress she was supposed to wear, a white dress the Queen had chosen, with a train she would probably trip over on the stairs. With a sigh, Lucinda opened the door of her dressing room and started looking through the dresses that hung there, all the dresses she had worn since her christening, for although Lucinda did not care about dresses, Queen Margarethe cared a great deal.

That was why she missed the excitement.

Jaromila had been afraid to go to the Princess' room that morning. Lucinda would certainly tell the Queen what she had said, and when the Queen found out – Jaromila remembered Dobromir. So she stayed in the ballroom, where Queen Margarethe was preparing for the party by changing her mind several times about who should sit where. Countess Agata was writing place cards, and the footmen were setting out the glasses for champagne.

King Karel, still in his slippers, wandered into the ballroom and said, "Margarethe, have you seen my crown? I thought I left it next to my bureau – "

That was when the shaking started. The ballroom shook as though the earth were opening beneath it. Jaromila, who was standing by the French doors, clutched at the curtains to stay upright. The Queen fell on Countess Agata's lap, which made a relatively comfortable cushion. The King, less fortunate, stumbled into the footmen, who toppled like dominoes. Most of the champagne glasses crashed to the floor.

A voice resounded through the ballroom. "Bring me the Princess Lucinda!"

The King, recovering his breath, said, "Whatever was that?"

Prince Radomir ran into the room and said, "Was it an earthquake?"

One of the footmen, who had fallen by the French doors, said, "By Saint Benedek, that's the biggest dog I've ever seen."

The King went to the French doors, leaving Prince Radomir to pick up the Queen and the Countess. There, on the terrace, stood a hound, as white as milk and as large as a pony.

"Bring me the Princess Lucinda!" he said again, in a voice like thunder. Then he shook himself, and the ballroom shook with him, so the King had to hold on to a curtain, like Jaromila, to stay upright. The remaining champagne glasses crashed to the floor, and the footmen fell down again in a heap.

Nothing in King Karel's training had prepared him for an enormous hound on his terrace, a hound who evidently had the ability to shake his castle to its foundations (his training having focused on international diplomacy and the Viennese waltz). But he was a practical man. So he said, from behind the curtain, "Who are you, and what do you want with the Princess?"

"I am the Hound of the Moon. If you don't bring me the Princess Lucinda, I will bite the head off the statue of King Karel in front of the cathedral, and the steeple off the cathedral itself, and the turrets off the castle. And if I'm still hungry, I'll bite the roofs off all the houses in Karelstad – "

"Here she is, here is the Princess Lucinda!" said the Queen, pushing Jaromila out the French doors. Jaromila, surprised and frightened, screamed. The Countess, who was leaning on Radomir, also screamed and fainted.

But the hound grabbed Jaromila by the sash around her waist, leaped from the terrace and landed among the topiaries, then leaped through the rose garden and over the forest, into the clouds.

Lucinda never noticed. When the castle had shaken, all the dresses on the shelves of the dressing room had fallen on top of her, along with most of the shoes, and when she had crawled out from beneath them, she imagined that she had somehow shaken them down herself. And still the dress for the ball was nowhere to be found.

The hound dropped Jaromila on the floor of a cave whose walls were covered with crystals.

The first thing she said when she had regained her breath was, "I'm not the Princess Lucinda."

"We shall see," said the hound. "Get up, whoever you are, and take a seat."

At the center of the cave, arranged around a table, Jaromila saw three chairs. The first was an obvious example of Opulentism, which had been introduced at the Exposition Universelle in Paris. Its arms were carved to resemble griffins, with garnets for eyes, and it was elaborately gilded. The second was a chair any Sylvanian farmer could have carved on a winter night as he sat by his fireside. The third was simply a stool of white wood.

Surely he didn't expect her to sit on *that*. And as for the second chair, she wasn't a peasant. Jaromila sat in the first chair, on its cushion of crimson velvet, and put her arms on the griffins.

"Can I offer you something to drink?" asked the hound.

On the table, she saw three cups. The first was certainly gold, and probably Lalique. The others were unimportant, a silver cup like those common in Dobromir, which had a silver mine, and a cup of horn that a shepherd might have drunk from. Of course she would drink from the first. She took a careful sip. The wine it contained, as red as the griffins' eyes, gave her courage.

"I'm not the Princess Lucinda. You will take me home at once!"

"As you wish," said the hound. "But the journey might be cold. Can I offer you a coat?"

In his mouth he held three coats. The first was a crimson brocade embroidered with gold thread, which she had seen just that week in a catalog from Worth's. That was the coat she would wear, not the plain green wool, or the dingy white thing that the hound must have drooled on.

But as soon as she reached to take it, the hound opened his mouth, dropped the coats, and once again grabbed her sash. And then they were off, over the forests of Sylvania, over Karelstad and the croquet lawn, to the castle terrace.

The King was still trying to soothe the Queen, who was crying, "What have I done?" Prince Radomir was waving smelling salts under the Countess' nose. The footmen were trying to sweep up the shattered glasses.

Upstairs, Lucinda had finally found her dress. It was in the Queen's own dressing room, behind an ermine cape. She sighed with relief. Now at last she could go to the party.

Just as the hound landed, Jaromila's sash ripped, and she dropped to the terrace.

"Bring me the Princess Lucinda!" said the hound. "If you don't bring me the Princess, I will drink up the fountain in front of King Karel's statue, and the pond by the Secondary School that the children skate on, and the river Morek, whose waters run through all the faucets of Karelstad. And if I'm still thirsty,

I'll drink up the Danube itself– "

"I am the Princess Lucinda," said a voice from the garden. Bertila walked up the terrace steps. She had woken early to see the preparations for the party, and had been watching all this time from behind the topiary stag.

"Isn't that the gardener's daughter?" asked Prince Radomir. But at that moment the Queen screamed (it seemed her turn), and nobody heard him.

Under ordinary circumstances, no one would have mistaken Bertila for a princess. Her dresses were often patched, and because her mother had died when she was born, she sewed on the patches herself, so they were usually crooked. But today all the servants not needed for the party had been given a holiday, and she was wearing an old dress of Lucinda's. Lucinda had been allowed to give it away because it had torn on a tree branch. Bertila had mended it (with the wrong color thread), but the rip was toward the back, so she hoped it would not be noticed.

"Climb on my back then," said the hound, and climb she did. She twisted her fingers into the hair at his neck, and held on as well as she could when he leaped from the terrace over the forests of Sylvania.

"Mama!" cried Jaromila, at which the Countess revived. But the Queen went into hysterics. And that was when Lucinda finally came down the stairs, holding her train, and stared about her, at the footmen sweeping the floor and the sobbing Queen.

"What in the world is going on?" she asked. King Karel tried to tell her, as did the Queen in broken sobs, and even the Countess, who clutched Prince Radomir's arm so hard that he could not answer. Jaromila tried to powder her nose in the mirror, because after all Prince Radomir was present.

"Radomir?" said Lucinda. And then Radomir explained about the hound and Bertila's deception.

"Well," said Lucinda, when the explanation was over. She turned to the King and Queen. "I think it's time you told me everything."

Bertila looked about the cave.

"Will you take a seat?" asked the hound.

"Thank you," said Bertila. Which chair should she choose? Or rather, which chair would Lucinda choose, since she must convince the hound? She had read Lucinda's copy of the Brothers Grimm, which Lucinda had left on the croquet lawn. This was surely a test. Her hands were shaking, and she could scarcely believe that she had spoken in the garden. But here she was, and the deception must continue. Whatever danger Lucinda was in, she must try to save her friend.

Surely Lucinda would never choose a chair so gaudy as the gold one. And a stool did not seem appropriate for a princess. But the wooden chair looked like the one her father had carved for her mother. Lucinda had sat in it often, when she came to the gardener's cottage. The wood had been sanded smooth by a careful hand, and ivy leaves had been painted over the arms and back. That was a chair fit for a princess of Sylvania. She sat down.

"Would you care for something to drink?" asked the hound.

"Thank you," said Bertila. "I really am thirsty."

Lucinda would make fun of the gold cup, and the cup of white horn was like the stool, too plain. But the silver cup, with the snowdrops in enamel, might have been made by the silversmiths of Dobromir, who were the finest in Sylvania. It was a cup fit for the Pope himself. She paused before taking a sip, but surely the hound would not hurt her. He had treated her well so far. The cup was filled with a delicate cider, which smelled like peaches.

"Thank you," she said. "And now I think I'm ready." Although she did not know what she was ready for.

"Very well," said the hound. "You must choose a coat for the journey."

Lucinda would never wear the crimson brocade. But the coat of green wool, with its silver buttons and tasseled hood, looked warm and regal enough for a princess. There was another coat beneath, but it looked tattered and worn.

"I'll wear this one," said Bertila.

"You're not the Princess Lucinda," said the hound.

Bertila stood silently, twisting the coat in her hands. "No" she said finally. "I'm sorry. I hope you don't blame me."

"It was brave of you," said the hound. "But you must return to the castle."

When he landed on the terrace with Bertila, Lucinda was waiting.

"You don't have to threaten anyone this time, or break any glasses," she said. "I'm Princess Lucinda, and I'm ready to go with you."

The Queen was sent to bed with a dose of laudanum. The King cancelled the invitations for the party. Countess Agata had a lunch of poached eggs with the Chamberlain and asked what the monarchy was coming to. Jaromila tried to find Prince Radomir. But he was sitting under the chestnut tree with Bertila, asking if she was all right, and if she was sure. Bertila was blushing and admiring his eyelashes.

"Will you take a seat?" asked the hound.

"What a strange stool," said Lucinda. She had never read the Brothers Grimm, although Bertila had handed her the book with a reproachful glance. "The wood seems to glow. I wonder where it comes from?"

"From the mountains of the moon," said the hound. "Down the slopes of those mountains flow rivers, and on the banks of those rivers grow willow trees, with leaves as white as paper. When the wind blows, they whisper secrets about what is past and what is to come. This stool is made from the wood of those willow trees."

"This is where I'll sit," said Lucinda.

"Can I offer you something to drink?" asked the hound.

"What a curious cup," said Lucinda, picking up the cup of horn. "It's so delicate that the light shines right through it."

"On the slopes of the mountains of the moon," said the hound, "wander herds of sheep, whose wool is as soft and white as thistledown. This cup is carved from the horn of a ram who roamed those mountains for a hundred years."

Lucinda drank from the cup. The water in it was cold, and tasted of snow.

"And now," said the hound, "you must choose a coat for our journey."

"Where are we going?" asked Lucinda. "Oh, how lovely!" She held up a coat that had been lying beneath the coats of crimson brocade and green wool. "Why, it's covered with feathers!"

"The rivers of the moon flow into lakes," said the hound, "and on those lakes live flocks of herons. They build their nests beneath the willow branches, and line them with feathers. There, they lay their eggs and raise their children through the summer. When winter comes, they return to Africa, leaving their nests behind. This coat is made from the feathers of those herons. As for your question, Princess – to meet your mother."

"My mother?" said Lucinda, sitting abruptly back down on the stool. "Oh, I don't know. I mean, until yesterday I thought Queen Margarethe – What is my mother like? Do you think she'll like me?"

The hound seemed to smile, or at least showed his teeth. "She's my mother also. I'm your brother, Lucinda, although we have different fathers. Mine was Sirius, the Dog Star. Yours was a science teacher at the Secondary School."

"And my mother – our mother?" asked Lucinda.

"Our mother is the Moon, and she's the one who sent me for you. Put on your coat, Lucinda. Its feathers will warm you in the darkness we must pass through. Now climb on my back. Mother is eager to see you, and we have waited long enough."

As though in a dream, for nothing in her life, not even the books on airplanes and mountain climbing, had prepared her for such an event, Lucinda put on the coat of white feathers and climbed on the back of the hound. He leaped to the edge of the cave, and then into the sky itself. She was surrounded at first by clouds, and then by stars. All the stars were visible to her, and the Pleiades waved to her as she flew past, calling out, "She's been waiting for you, Lucinda!" Sirius barked and wagged his tail, and the hound barked back. Then they were landing in a valley covered with grass as white as a handkerchief, by a lake whose waters shone like silver.

"Lucinda! Is that really you?"

The woman standing by the side of the lake had silver hair so long that it swept the grasses at her feet, but her face looked not much older than Lucinda's. She seemed at once very young and very old, and at the moment very anxious.

"It is," said the hound. "Go on," he said to Lucinda, nudging her with his nose. "Don't you want to meet her?"

Lucinda walked forward, awkwardly. "It's nice to meet you..."

"Oh, my dear," said the Moon, laughing and taking Lucinda in her arms, "I'm so happy to have found you at last!"

The Moon lived in a stone house surrounded by a garden of white roses. A white cat sat on the windowsill, watching Lucinda with eyes like silver kroners.

"The soup will be ready in a moment," said the Moon. "I find that the journey between the Earth and my home always makes me hungry."

"Do you travel to the Earth?" asked Lucinda.

The Moon laughed again. Her laughter sounded like a silver bell, clear and sweet. "You would not have been born, otherwise! In a shed at the back of the house live my bats. Whenever I want to travel to the Earth, I harness them and they pull me through the darkness. Perhaps later you'll help me feed them. They like the nectar of my roses. Here, blow on this if you think it's too hot."

She put a bowl of soup in front of Lucinda. It was the color of milk but smelled like chicken, and Lucinda suddenly realized that she had forgotten to eat breakfast.

"Tell me about that," said Lucinda. "I mean, how I was born. If you don't mind," she added. There was so much she wanted to know. How did one ask a mother one had just met?

"Well," said the Moon, sitting down at the table and clasping her hands. "Your father's name was Havel Kronborg. When he was a child, he would lie at night in his father's fields, in Dobromir, and look at the stars. But even then, I think, he loved me better than any of them. How glad I was when he received a scholarship to study astronomy in Berlin! And how proud when his first paper was published in a scientific journal. It was about me, of course, about my mountains and lakes. But when his father died, the farm had to be sold to pay the mortgage, so he worked as a science teacher at the Secondary School. Each night he wandered on the slopes of the mountains about Karelstad, observing the stars. And one night, I met him in the forest.

"How well I remember those months. I could only visit him when the moon was dark – even for love, I could not neglect my work. But each month that we met, our child – that was you, Lucinda – was closer to being born, and his book, *Observations on the Topography of the Moon*, closer to being completed.

"When you were born, I wrapped you in a blanket I had woven from the wool of my sheep, and laid you in a basket of willow branches. Your brother slept beside you and guarded you, and all the stars sang you lullabies."

"Was it this blanket?" asked Lucinda. Out of her pocket she pulled a blanket as fine as silk, which the King had given her in the course of his explanation. Her name was embroidered on one corner. She had been carrying it with her since, but had almost forgotten it. How far away Karelstad seemed, and the Queen, and her life as a princess.

The Moon reached out to touch it, and her eyes filled with silver tears. "Your father asked me to leave you with him for a month. How could I refuse? But I told him to set you in the moonlight every night, so I could see you. One night, while he was gathering mushrooms in the forest for a botany lesson, he placed your basket beneath a tree. I watched you lying there, laughing up at me. But suddenly a cloud came between us, and when it had passed, you were gone.

"You can't imagine his grief. He searched all that night through the forest around the castle. When the gardener found him in the morning, he was coughing, and could not speak. The doctor told him he had caught pneumonia. He died a week later. I found the basket by his bedside. It's the only thing I've had of yours, all these years."

Silver tears trickled down her cheeks. She wiped them away with the blanket.

Lucinda reached out her hand, not knowing what to say. The Moon took it in her own, and smiled through her tears. "But now we've found each other. How like him you look, so practical and solemn. I searched the world for years, but never saw you until last night, lying beneath the tree where he had left you. I knew who you were at once, although you've grown so tall. Will you walk with me, Lucinda? I want to show you the country where you were born."

The strangest thing about being on the moon was how familiar it seemed. Lucinda learned to feed the bats, gathering white roses from the garden, tying them together in bundles, and hanging them upside down from the rafters where the bats slept through the night, while the moon was shining. She learned to call the sheep that roamed the mountains, and to comb their fleece. The Moon spun the long hairs caught in the comb on a spinning wheel that sang as it whirled. She learned to gather branches from the willow trees and weave them into baskets, like the one the Moon had shown her, saying, "This is where you slept, as a child."

Sometimes, after the night's work was done, she would sit with the Moon beside the lake, watching the herons teach their children to fly. They would talk about Lucinda's childhood in Karelstad, or the Moon's childhood, long ago, and the things she had seen, when elephants roamed through Sylvania, and the Romans built their roads through its forests, and Morek drove out the Romans, claiming its fertile valleys for his tribe, and Karel I raised an army of farmers and merchants, and drove out the Turks. Then they would lie on the grass and look at the stars dancing above them.

"Their dances were ancient before I was born," said the Moon. "Look at Alcyone! She always wears diamonds in her hair. And Sirius capering among them. We were in love, when I was young. But we each had our work to do, and it could not last. Ah, here is your brother."

The white hound lay next to Lucinda. She put her arm around him, and the three of them watched the stars in their ancient dances.

One day, the Moon showed Lucinda her observatory, on a slope above the lake. "This is where I watch what happens on the Earth," she said.

Lucinda put her eye to the telescope. "I can see the castle at Karelstad."

"That was where I last looked," said the Moon. "Since you've been here, I've had no wish to look at the Earth. It reminds me of the years before I found you."

"There's Bertila, walking in the garden with Radomir. I can see Jaromila. She's looking in her mirror. And King Karel is talking to the French ambassador. Why do they look so sad? Well, except Jaromila. And there's the Queen. Why, she seems to be crying. And I've never seen her wearing a black dress. Oh!" said Lucinda. "Is it me? Do they think I'm dead?"

The Moon looked at her sadly.

"I'm so sorry," said Lucinda. "It's just – I grew up with them all. And Queen Margarethe was my mother. I mean, I thought she was."

"She was, my dear," said the Moon. "She was the best mother she could be, and so I forgive her, although she has caused me much grief. I knew that eventually you'd want to return to the Earth. It's where your father belonged, and you belong there also. But you will come to visit me, won't you?"

"Of course I will, Mother," said Lucinda.

That night, while the moon was shining, they harnessed the bats. Lucinda put on her coat of heron feathers, and took the reins.

"Before you go," said the Moon, "I have something to give you. This is the book your father wrote. I've kept it for many years, but I would like you to have it. After all, I have my memories of him." For a moment, she held Lucinda, then said to the bats, "Fly swiftly!"

The bats lifted Lucinda above the white roses in the garden, and above the stone house. The Moon called, "Goodbye, my dear," and then she was flying over the mountains of the moon and toward the Earth, which lay wrapped in darkness.

She landed on the castle terrace, just as the sun was rising over the forest around Karelstad. Lucinda released the reins, then ran into the castle and up the stairs, to the Queen's bedroom.

Queen Margarethe was sitting by the window. She had not slept all night, and her eyes were red with weeping. She thought she must be dreaming when she saw Lucinda enter the room and say, "Good morning, Mother."

Lucinda's sixteenth birthday party took place a month late, but was perhaps all the merrier. The orchestra from Prague played, the champagne flowed freely, and the footmen danced with each other in the hall. Under a glittering chandelier, the French ambassador asked Jaromila to marry him, and on the terrace, beneath a full moon, Radomir asked Bertila the same question.

When Lucinda went to her room that night, her head spinning from champagne and her feet aching from the narrow shoes, she found a white stool on which sat a white cup. In the cup was a silver necklace. From it hung a moonstone, which glowed like the moon itself, and next to the cup was a card on which was written, in silver ink, "Happy Birthday, my dear."

The next morning, Lucinda went to the graveyard behind the cathedral. There, by the grave of a forgotten science teacher, she laid a bouquet of white roses.

Observations on the Topography of the Moon received an enthusiastic reception among astronomers in London, Paris, and New York, and was widely quoted in the scientific journals. It was eventually included in the Secondary School curriculum, and the author's portrait appeared on the two-zlata stamp.

After her husband's death, Jaromila opened a couture house in Paris and became famous as the inventor of the stiletto heel. When Radomir finished his degree in engineering, King Karel retired. He and Queen Margarethe lived to a contented old age in the country. King Radomir and Queen Bertila guided Sylvania through two world wars. Karelstad eventually became a center of international banking, where even the streets were said to be paved with kroner. They sat together, listening to the radio, on the night Lucinda won the Nobel prize for her theories on astrophysics.

But no one, except the white hound that was occasionally seen wandering around the garden of her house in Dobromir, ever found out that she had been the first person on the moon.